He was a hardy rogue.
What did he want with her?

"Am I to be your hostage?" She thought of the chest full of money.

"No," said Jakob.

"Then why do you want me?" she asked, bewildered.

"I don't want you," he replied curtly.

Desire caught her breath. His sharp response cut straight through her defenses, hurting her where she was most vulnerable. She knew full well that her most attractive feature was her inheritance—but it was a long time since she'd been reminded of that quite so brutally. It didn't matter that Jakob was a brigand who'd just escaped from prison. He was still a handsome man who had no doubt enjoyed many beautiful women.

Shamed and humiliated, she turned her face into her shoulder in an instinctive effort to hide her scarred check from her abductor.

It was only when Jakob realized she was trying to conceal her scars that he guessed why his brief comment had wounded her so severely. He muttered a soft curse.

* * *

The Abducted Heiress
Harlequin® Historical #834—January 2007

CLAIRE THORNTON

THE ABDUCTED HEIRESS

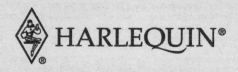

HARLEQUIN®

TORONTO • NEW YORK • LONDON
AMSTERDAM • PARIS • SYDNEY • HAMBURG
STOCKHOLM • ATHENS • TOKYO • MILAN • MADRID
PRAGUE • WARSAW • BUDAPEST • AUCKLAND

ISBN-13: 978-0-373-29434-3
ISBN-10: 0-373-29434-4

THE ABDUCTED HEIRESS

Author Note

The stories in the City of Flames trilogy take place in Europe during the reign of Charles II. This was an era of great color, drama and variety. The king scandalized some of his subjects with his many mistresses, but his reign also saw the emergence of modern banking among the London goldsmiths. Actresses appeared for the first time in London theaters, while members of the Royal Society met every week to witness scientific experiments.

Athena Fairchild, Colonel Jakob Balston and the Duke of Kilverdale are cousins, but they've led very different lives. Athena grew up in England, Jakob in Sweden, and Kilverdale spent his childhood exiled in France as a result of the war between Charles I and Parliament.

The cousins' romances take place in various locations, but London is at the heart of the **City of Flames** trilogy. The cousins all meet the one they love in the city—although Athena's happiness is destroyed almost before it begins.

Athena's story, *The Defiant Mistress,* begins in May 1666 in Venice and the events span the rest of the summer. Jakob's story, *The Abducted Heiress,* and Kilverdale's story, *The Vagabond Duchess,* both begin in London at the start of September 1666. In the early hours of the morning of September 2 a fire in Pudding Lane will burn out of control….

While I was writing these books I fell in love with the characters and their world. I hope you enjoy reading their stories as much as I enjoyed writing them.

Look for the Duke of Kilverdale's story in
***The Vagabond Duchess*—coming from**
Harlequin® Historical in April 2007!

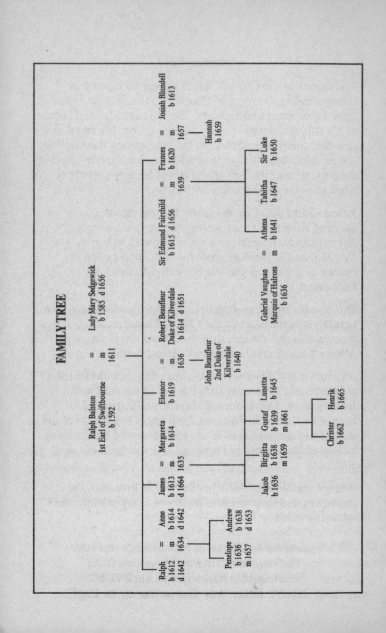

FAMILY TREE

Ralph Balston = Lady Mary Sedgewick
1st Earl of Swiftbourne m b 1585 d 1656
b 1592 1611

Ralph | Anne = | James | Margareta = | Eleanor = | Robert Beaufleur | Sir Edmund Fairchild | Frances = | Josiah Blundell
b 1612 | b 1614 m | b 1613 | b 1614 m | b 1619 m | Duke of Kilverdale | b 1615 d 1656 | b 1620 m | b 1613
d 1642 | d 1642 1634 | d 1664 | 1635 | 1636 | b 1614 d 1651 | | 1639 | 1657

John Beaufleur
2nd Duke of Kilverdale
b 1640

Hannah
b 1659

Penelope | Andrew
b 1636 | b 1638
m 1657 | d 1653

Jakob | Birgitta | Gustaf | Lunetta
b 1636 | b 1638 | b 1639 | b 1645
| m 1659 | m 1661 |

Gabriel Vaughan = Athena | Tabitha | Sir Luke
Marquis of Halross m b 1641 | b 1647 | b 1650
b 1636

Christer | Henrik
b 1662 | b 1665

Prologue

Stockholm, Sweden, 1653

'What's wrong, Father? Is it bad news?' Jakob asked.

Instead of replying, James Balston continued to stare at the letter in his hand.

Jakob's sense of unease grew stronger. His mother also noticed her husband's unusual reaction to the letter. Margareta lowered her embroidery to her lap and waited for James to speak, a crease of worry between her eyes.

'Andrew is dead,' said James. It was a measure of his shock that he spoke in English.

'*Förlåt?*' Margareta looked at Jakob in confusion. Despite the fact that she and James had been married for eighteen years, she still spoke very little English. '*Vad sade han?*'

'*Andrew är död,*' Jakob automatically repeated his father's words in Swedish.

'*Åh nej!*' The colour drained from his mother's face.

The depth of her distress momentarily surprised Jakob. None of them had ever met his cousin Andrew—

Jakob's wits suddenly caught up with him. Now that Andrew was dead, Jakob's father was first in line to an English viscountcy. They would all have to go to England. No wonder his mother was so upset.

'Must we leave at once?' he asked.

'*No!*' Margareta took a deep breath and visibly calmed herself. 'We will do as you think best,' she said to her husband.

'There's no immediate rush,' said James, his tone reassuring. 'By all accounts my father is in excellent health. But we must make some preparations. *Gustaf!*' He raised his voice. 'Gustaf! Birgitta, tell your brother I want him!'

Jakob's brother and sister were playing chess at a small table on the other side of the room. Birgitta had lifted her head at the sound of her father's voice, but Gustaf was still absorbed in studying the chess board. Birgitta gave his shoulder a shove.

'Father wants you,' she told him, when he looked up in surprise.

'I'm sorry, sir,' Gustaf apologised. 'I was engrossed in the game.'

'I understand,' said James, a slight smile briefly lightening his expression, 'but now it is time for you to become engrossed in work.'

Jakob saw a spark of excitement in his brother's eyes. 'Am I to join you and Jakob in the counting house?' Gustaf demanded.

'Yes.' James laid aside the letter and divided a thoughtful look between his two sons. 'Your cousin Andrew is dead,' he told Gustaf, 'which means that one day I will have to return to England and so will Jakob. I had hoped that the two of you would be equal partners in the business you will one day inherit from me here in Sweden. But now circumstances have changed,' he paused, pressing his lips together as he considered the implications of those changes.

Jakob listened with interest and some excitement at the prospect of the adventure that lay ahead of them. He knew his mother was dismayed at the idea of living in a strange country, but surely with the comfort of her family around her she would not find it too difficult. Jakob himself was eager to face the challenge.

'One day Jakob will inherit the title and estates in England,' James continued. 'If he is to do his duty by his inheritance, he will have to make his permanent home in England. He will not be able to take an active part in the merchant business I have established here in Sweden.'

Disappointment suddenly dampened Jakob's enthusiasm for his new life. He enjoyed working alongside his father, trying to prove he could be just as successful and shrewd a merchant as James. He would be sorry to leave that part of his life behind.

'You will start working with me tomorrow,' James said to Gustaf. 'We must waste no time in teaching you everything you need to know. As for you, Jakob—' he looked at his older son, a curious mixture of pride and resignation in his eyes '—we will have to make other plans for you. You would have made an excellent merchant—but it seems that is not to be your destiny.'

Chapter One

The Strand, Saturday 1 September 1666

Lady Desire Godwin stood in the middle of her rooftop garden, looking around at the results of her afternoon's labour. This small Eden above London was her domain and her sole creation. Servants kept the water cistern filled for her. Soon she would have her porters carry the orange trees down into the stove house to protect them from the first frosts. But she did all the other work in the elevated garden herself.

The early evening air was heavy with the sultry heat of late summer. Desire pulled off her broad-brimmed straw hat and brushed an earth-stained hand across her damp forehead. When she was finally satisfied that her sanctuary was in order, she lifted her gaze to look beyond the parapet.

The sun was setting, painting the western sky in glowing shades of gold and crimson. The earthenware-tiled roofs and church spires of London stretched away towards the east, deceptively peaceful beneath the honeyed evening light.

Desire tried to conjure an image of people hurrying or loitering through the streets and alleyways. She had little experience to draw upon. She had never been part of the jostling crowds. She rarely left the safety of Godwin House. The last time had been five years ago, when she'd watched the King's coronation procession from the window of an upper room on Cheapside.

From the corner of her eye she saw a sparrow swoop down to bathe in a shallow dish of water she provided for the birds. She turned her head to watch it, smiling at the pretty sight. The heady scent of stocks drifted on the warm air. A bee buzzed lazily among the flower heads. The sparrow ducked its head beneath the water, tossing a myriad glistening droplets over its back and half-opened wings.

A scraping sound from the other side of the wall disturbed the tranquillity of her haven. She frowned in puzzlement and took a step towards the unfamiliar noise, startling the sparrow into flight.

A man's head appeared over the top of the parapet. Desire swayed back in shock. An instant later the man's shoulders came into view. Desire stared in disbelief as a stranger vaulted on to her roof, landing neatly on his feet a short distance away from her.

She gazed at the intruder in frank astonishment, her heart thudding with surprise. She was too startled to be frightened— or even to hide her face.

It was years since she'd last met a stranger. And she'd never before laid eyes on a man who looked like *this*. An angel who had taken mortal form.

His eyes were the infinite blue of a summer sky. His face the most beautiful Desire had ever seen. His features were finely carved, yet full of masculine strength. He wore his blond hair long, according to the fashion of the times. The setting sun gilded his flowing locks, transforming them into a cascade of liquid gold about his shoulders.

He looked just like the archangel Desire had seen once in a stained-glass window. All the colours in the picture had been given heavenly radiance by the sunlight streaming through the glass. This man reminded her of that shining, golden image. He was too perfect to be made of human flesh and blood.

His flesh was smooth and firm, his skin bronzed like Apollo's by the rays of the sinking sun. He possessed the perfection of youth, but it was coupled with the strength and virile power of full maturity.

He wore only a white linen shirt and dark breeches. Beneath the shirt Desire could see the contours of lean, hard muscles. The shirt was open at the neck and the soft fabric revealed the uncompromising breadth of his shoulders. Desire's gaze travelled downwards, taking account of his flat stomach and narrow hips, and the long, powerful length of his legs.

Her eyes returned briefly to his perfect face…

And then she gasped with shock. Finally remembering what she so rarely completely forgot.

The man standing before her was perfect.

But she was not.

Shame and distress thundered through her. She half-raised her hands to cover her face, then turned her back on him instead. Now, belatedly, she trembled with shock at his abrupt intrusion. Confused questions raced through her mind, but she didn't yet trust her voice to challenge his trespass into her private domain.

Jakob was contending with some surprises of his own. He had been told that Lady Desire Godwin lived a reclusive life in her grand mansion on the Strand. He'd assumed her reticence was the result of sensible prudence, since apparently she had neither father or guardian to protect her. He had also been told that Lady Desire was usually to be found in her rooftop garden. He had therefore imagined her reclining gracefully in a shady bower, attired in silks and satin.

Instead he'd surprised a work-dishevelled woman wearing simple, unfashionable garments. Her skirt had obviously been torn and mended several times in the past. To Jakob's pleasure, the soft fabric of her bodice revealed the natural contours of her slim, shapely body. It seemed the lady had chosen not to endure the discomfort of heavy boning while she worked. Jakob admired her good sense, even as he wondered whether she could possibly be the woman he sought.

Her hands were stained with earth. Her face was beaded with perspiration, and there was a streak of dirt across her forehead. He had been told that Lady Desire was thirty years of age, but this woman appeared to be several years younger. Her chestnut hair was pinned haphazardly on top of her head in a style that owed more to convenience than fashion. The low sunlight burnished her errant curls to a rich red. A few tendrils, which had escaped the pins, were darkened with perspiration and stuck to her damp face.

Far more startling than her clothes were the scars on her face. They were blemishes that had no place on a woman so young, shapely and obviously full of healthy energy. The pale scars ridged one cheek, puckering skin that should have been smooth and youthful. The fairness of her other cheek revealed the beauty that should have been her birthright. The comparison between what her appearance could have been, and what it was, was cruel in its simple starkness.

Confusion held Jakob silent for several long seconds. How had she come to be so badly injured? Smallpox scars were not unusual among all sections of the population, but these scars looked more like the wounds a soldier might receive in battle. He felt a surge of pity for her, even as the analytical part of his mind strove to make sense of what he'd discovered. Was this the heiress he sought? Were the scars the reason for her seclusion? Or was this simply a maidservant toiling in the lady's garden?

The lady stared at him in equal confusion, for which he could hardly blame her. But there was an expression of wonder, almost awe, in her warm, velvet brown eyes he didn't understand at all. By rights she should have been haranguing him for his trespass or calling her servants to throw him out.

Instead she gazed at him as if he were a mirage, or some kind of ghostly vision. Jakob wondered briefly if the accident that had marred her body had also robbed her of her wits.

At that very instant, her expression changed. From wonder to horror. A variety of shifting emotions flickered in her eyes. Distress, shame, anger.

Her hands half-lifted towards her face. Then she turned her back on him.

The soldier in him was profoundly shocked that she chose a response which left her so defenceless. The man in him noticed the graceful line of her slim neck, exposed by her upswept hair. The skin of her nape was pale and soft, emphasising her vulnerability. Jakob cursed himself as his body tightened with unexpected desire for hers—even as he felt an equally strong, conflicting compulsion to comfort her.

He kept his hands resolutely by his sides and cleared his mind of everything but the reason he had scaled the wall of Godwin House. He was running out of time. He needed to make sure of the lady's identity. He cleared his throat.

'Do I have the honour of addressing Lady Desire Godwin?' he asked.

Desire's head jerked up. The stranger had spoken to her. There was an exotic quality to his words, as if English wasn't his first language. Perhaps he really was an angel of the Lord.

It had been so long since Desire had had contact with the outside world that the notion of an angel coming to call on her hardly seemed more unlikely than the sudden appearance of a strange man in her personal Eden.

But, if he was an angel, she thought chaotically, he ought to have descended *down* on to her roof from the heavens—not climbed *up* to it from the ground. Maybe he was a *fallen* angel...

'Lady Desire?' he repeated, with soft urgency.

She took a deep breath. It was time to regain control of events. This was *her* roof. Angel or no, she was entitled to an explanation for this intrusion. She turned around slowly, clutching her hat before her in both hands like a shield. But she held her head resolutely high, making no effort to conceal her face. It was too late to hide. She'd already gaped in amazement at the stranger for so long he'd had time to trace each of her ugly scars.

'Who are you?' she demanded.

As she spoke, she forced herself to look up and meet his eyes, expecting to see revulsion or pity in his gaze. When she'd momentarily forgotten her own appearance, it had been easy to gaze at his male beauty—now it was hard to look into his face.

But she saw nothing in his clear blue eyes except puzzlement and a certain amount of impatience.

The sun had fallen below the horizon and he no longer glowed with angelic radiance. He looked entirely like a mortal man. A very tall, powerful, athletic man who had scaled her wall like a brigand.

'Who *are* you?' Fear sharpened her voice. 'What do you want?'

'Jakob Smith,' he replied. 'My lady—'

'You aren't English,' she said, suspicious that a man of such exotic appearance truly owned such a commonplace name.

She saw another flicker of impatience, or possibly exasperation, flash in his beautiful eyes.

'My mother is Swedish, my father was English,' he replied crisply. '*My* pedigree, however, has no relevance to the current circumstances.'

'Are you suggesting mine *has*?' Desire demanded, astounded by his effrontery.

Despite the bizarre nature of their encounter, she no longer felt overawed by him. She was well aware of the hazards of fortune hunters. Her steward, Walter Arscott, had impressed upon her the need for caution. Only a few months ago Arscott had told her about Lord Rochester's recent attempt to abduct an heiress from her carriage as she travelled through Charing Cross. Lord Rochester had botched the abduction and been put in the Tower for his pains, but he was not the only fortune hunter in England. The stranger on her roof, handsome though he appeared, was probably just a more enterprising example of the breed. It was time to exert her authority

'Did you invade my garden to—?' she began.

'Are you Lady Desire?' Jakob Smith snapped, startling her with his urgency. As he spoke he threw a quick glance over her shoulder.

Desire automatically followed his gaze, feeling a flutter of uneasiness as his impatience communicated itself to her. To her relief, there was no one else on the roof, but it gave her an idea.

'My servants will be here soon—to carry down the orange trees,' she improvised. 'Stout fellows. They have to be to lift such burdens. You should escape before they get here.'

Jakob Smith grinned briefly, a dazzling expression on his already handsome features. 'If that were true, you wouldn't warn me,' he pointed out. 'You'd keep me here so they could seize me.'

'I would?' Desire rubbed her temple with gritty fingers, then realised she'd probably put a dirty mark on her face. She snatched her hand away and glared at him. 'You haven't answered my question,' she reminded him. 'What are you doing—'

'But you've answered mine,' he replied, smiling faintly. 'Your servants, your orange trees, my lady,' he added by way of explanation. 'And we don't have much time.' He glanced beyond her again and swore softly.

Desire threw a quick look over her shoulder—and this time her cold shiver of apprehension was justified. There were two more strangers walking towards her across the roof. Unlike Jakob Smith, they bore no resemblance to angels.

The leader was dressed in a green doublet and breeches. He wore a sword at his side and—Desire's apprehension turned to fear as she focussed on his right hand—he carried a pistol.

The other man carried neither sword nor pistol, only a short, brutal cudgel and a man's doublet.

'Don't be afraid,' said Smith in a hasty under-voice as the men approached. 'I won't let any harm come to you.'

'You *serpent*!' Desire whirled away from him.

As the two men came closer the second man threw the doublet in Smith's direction.

'Next time look after your own gear,' he said roughly.

'I told you to seize the lady—not dally with a serving wench,' said the man with the pistol to Jakob Smith. 'Where's your mistress, doxy?' For the first time he gave his full attention to Desire.

She saw the moment he noticed her scars. Surprise, then contempt appeared in his eyes as he waited impatiently for her answer.

Red-hot rage erupted within her. She was so angry she forgot to be frightened.

'Get off my roof!' She pointed one emphatic hand in the direction they had to take. 'Get off *now*!'

The man with the pistol stared at her—then he laughed. '*Your* roof?' he jeered. 'You're too ugly to be so pert. Where's your lady?' His tone abruptly became much more menacing as he waved the pistol in her direction.

Desire's racing heart skipped a beat. She was still angry—but now she had been reminded she was also in grave danger. She glanced quickly between the three men. All her senses seemed sharper than normal. Her confusion when Jakob Smith had first appeared was now replaced with intense alertness.

The lout with the cudgel appeared bored. Jakob Smith stood relaxed but vigilant. Unlike the other two men, he carried no obvious weapon—but he didn't need one. He'd already demonstrated his strength and agility when he climbed on to the roof. If he decided to manhandle her, Desire knew she'd stand no chance against him. It was a terrifying thought.

'Where's Lady Desire?' The man in the green doublet threatened her again with his pistol.

'There's no need to abuse the wench,' Jakob Smith said curtly, moving between them.

'Keep your mouth shut! You're paid to obey orders, not give them!' Green Doublet snarled. 'Stand away from her and watch we're not interrupted.' For a second he pointed his pistol at Jakob, not Desire, to reinforce his command.

Jakob stepped quietly aside, though his large body remained poised for action.

Desire took advantage of their momentary distraction to retreat a couple of places. For a few seconds her knees had weakened with shock, but now strength flowed back into her legs. Wit, not brute force, must be her salvation. If they fell into an argument, she might have a chance to escape.

'Stand still!' Green Doublet pointed his pistol at her. 'Where's your mistress?'

'I'll—I'll get her for you,' she offered, remembering too late that Jakob Smith already knew her identity.

Her gaze whipped to his face. She expected any moment to hear him denounce her. He was frowning—but she saw he was looking at the man with the pistol, not at her.

'I'm not a fool, you doxy!' Green Doublet sneered.

Another surge of fear spiked through her. She stared at him, afraid he'd guessed who she was—but he just laughed scornfully. 'You won't *get* her—you'll *warn* her! Tell me where she is?'

'Oh.' Desire's relief was so great she could hardly speak. She was ashamed of hiding in the guise of a servant, but she didn't know what else to do. She had no weapon and no way of raising the alarm without putting herself in immediate jeopardy. But she was afraid for the safety of her household. She couldn't let these criminals rampage through the house threatening her staff.

'Why do you want her…Lady Desire?' she demanded, playing for time. 'What's she to you?'

'A bride, you doxy! Now—' he lunged forward and seized her upper arm '—*tell me where she is!*'

Desire pitched towards him. Then instinctively dug in her heels and pulled away from him, appalled at his words.

His bride?

Her foot scraped against the oak boards surrounding a raised flowerbed. She nearly fell. Her heart pounded with panic. She managed to save herself, then changed direction so that the corner of the bed was between her and her attacker.

An outraged shout from the other end of the rooftop startled them both, interrupting their desperate tug-of-war. A musket shot roared in Desire's ears and the man pitched forwards into the plants. He still had a grip on her arm and he dragged her down with him. The scent of bruised lavender filled her lungs.

Horrified, she wrenched her arm out of his dying grasp. She flailed her hands through the lavender, desperate to gain solid purchase to stand. One hand touched his unfired pistol. She jerked away, then changed her mind. There had been three villains on the roof and only one shot fired. She could already hear the sounds of a grim struggle a few feet away. She picked up the pistol, thrust herself on to her knees, and then to her feet, glancing wildly around.

Twenty feet away, her steward, Walter Arscott, struggled with the cudgel-carrying lout.

A scream rose in Desire's throat.

Jakob Smith was nearly upon her, like a lion closing on his prey. In the dusk his golden hair had become a tawny mane, flowing around his broad shoulders. She saw the glint in his eyes, the intense expression of a predator on his handsome face. If he got close enough to touch her the pistol would offer no protection.

Desire jerked her hands up, pointing the weapon squarely at his chest.

He stopped instantly. Held his arms away from his body, palms towards her, in a gesture as easy to interpret as her levelled pistol.

Desire took a shaky breath, her gaze locked on his face, as she tried to read his intentions. The pistol felt unbelievably heavy. Only by an intense effort of will did she stop her arms from trembling. She *had* to stay in command of the situation. She didn't dare take her eyes off Jakob, even for a moment, to check on Arscott. But she could hear that the fight still continued.

'Tell him....' She swallowed and steadied her voice. 'Tell him I'll shoot you if he doesn't leave Arscott alone,' she rasped.

Jakob's brows snapped together. He looked away from her to frown at the two fighting men. 'Arscott?'

'My steward. Tell your…your *friend* to leave Arscott alone or I'll shoot you!'

Jakob's lips twisted into an ironic smile. 'Your man's won,' he said.

'He has?' Desire was so relieved she instinctively looked to see. Jakob was right. It was Arscott rising to his feet. The lout who'd carried the cudgel was lying across the path, his head twisted at an unnatural angle. A wave of nausea rose in Desire as she realised the man was almost certainly dead. Two dead men on her roof—

Fear punched in her stomach. She jerked her gaze back to Jakob, her finger tightening on the trigger. She'd just given him all the opportunity he needed to seize her.

He hadn't moved. He was watching Arscott with narrowed eyes. Fury burned through her.

'You'll hang for this,' she said harshly.

'Will he?' Jakob looked past her, an unreadable expression on his face as he looked at the man in the green doublet sprawled in the lavender.

'What?'

'Is he dead?'

'I don't know. I think…I think so.' Desire's voice faltered.

Jakob pressed his lips together. She sensed strong emotions ruthlessly concealed beneath his calm manner. For all his current passivity, she was sure he was still deadly dangerous.

'My lady! My lady!' The roof suddenly filled with her servants. A young porter ran past Arscott. He seized Jakob's arms in a cruel hold, twisting them up behind Jakob's back and forcing him on to his knees. The porter was joined by other members of her household. There were shouts for lights and ropes. Desire stared at Jakob as her servants surrounded him. She was afraid he might resist and there would be more injuries, but he let them bind him without protest.

'Hang him from the parapet! Fetch another rope for the noose, Tanner!'

'No!' Desire cried, horrified at the idea of her servants meting out such rough justice. She was sickened that two men had already died, but Arscott had discovered them armed and in the very act of attacking her. He had done what he believed necessary to protect her. The third was already tied up and no longer an immediate threat to anyone.

'My lady, he's nothing but gutter scum,' the head porter protested, visibly shaking with outrage at the violation of the house.

'He must go before the courts,' Desire insisted forcefully. 'There will be no lynchings from my roof. Take him to Newgate.'

The men muttered with dissatisfaction, but she knew they would not disobey her direct command.

'He must be held prisoner until he comes to trial,' she said, steel in her voice.

'Then he'll hang,' said the head porter. 'Waste of time and trouble—' He caught Desire's eye and ceased his audible disapproval of her command.

Jakob turned his head towards her. He looked straight into Desire's eyes. He was on his knees, her prisoner, but he had not been defeated. His raw, virile power might have been temporarily contained, but it hadn't been destroyed. She saw pride in his fierce gaze as their eyes locked.

The impact shook her to her core. She felt as if he had branded her with that burning glance. For several seconds, she was unable to move or even to look away.

'My lady? Are you injured?' Arscott asked.

Jakob shifted his attention from her to the steward, but Desire still felt the impact of his searing blue gaze. Had he been promising he would one day have his revenge on her for this defeat and humiliation?

'My lady, are you hurt?' Arscott said more urgently.

Desire gave a start and looked at him. The steward was of slight build and average height. At first sight he didn't appear much of a fighting man, but as a youth he had been a fearsome sharpshooter during the war between King and Parliament. It seemed his marksmanship was as accurate at the age of thirty-nine as it had been when he was seventeen. Now he was watching her with a worried frown.

'No,' Desire whispered, still shaken by the glance she'd exchanged with Jakob. She was only half-aware of Arscott taking the pistol from her. 'You saved me!' she exclaimed suddenly. 'Arscott, you saved me!'

He bowed slightly in acknowledgement of her words. 'I'm here to serve you,' he said, though there was a hint of anger in his well-controlled voice.

'I…I…thank you.' Desire's legs turned to water. She turned her head away and locked her hands in her skirts so that no one would see how badly they trembled.

As she did so, she noticed a surreptitious muttering among her household. Jakob was on his feet again. The head porter had put another rope around his neck and was using it to lead him towards the stairs. She was sure her servants would obey her direct orders within the confines of Godwin House—but she had a sudden premonition that a fatal accident might happen to Jakob Smith before he ever reached gaol.

'*Stop!*' The order ripped from her throat.

Everyone turned to look at her. Even in the half-light she saw the sardonic expression on Jakob's face. He knew as well as she did what the men planned for him.

Desire kept her arms by her sides and her shoulders square, but she gripped her skirts convulsively as she scanned the faces before her. Surely not every man was riven with the need to avenge the violation of the house? But to her dismay, even the usually level-tempered Arscott seemed to be suppressing simmering hostility.

Then she saw Benjamin Finch, her Gentleman of the Horse, who had only just arrived on the roof. Like most of her senior household, he had served her father before her. He was older than Arscott, and somewhat out of breath from running up the stairs, but he was always good at moderating disputes and he commanded respect among the other men.

'Benjamin!'

'My lady, are you hurt?' His voice was sharp with anxiety as he looked first at her, then at the disorder around her.

'No. Benjamin, this man is my prisoner.' She pointed at Jakob, letting her hand fall quickly before anyone could see it was shaking. 'It is my will and command that he be delivered safely to Newgate. He must stand trial for his crimes here today. I want you to make sure that he is delivered unharmed to gaol,' she concluded in ringing tones.

At the end of her speech Jakob gave a small, ironic bow in her direction. Several servants looked mutinous but, to Desire's relief, Benjamin immediately accepted the charge she laid upon him. In a quiet, but firm, voice he gave the necessary orders for Jakob to be taken under guard to the gaol.

Now the worst was over, Desire wanted to burst into tears. Two dead men were being carried from her roof. Only by a hair's breadth had she managed to avoid a lynching, and the angel who'd invaded her garden at sunset had turned into a devil at twilight.

Desire had been a child during the first Civil War. Her father, the Earl of Larksmere, had been a Parliamentarian. For five weeks in 1644 Larksmere House had been besieged by Royalists. For those five weeks Desire had lived in the heart of violence. She'd even suffered the consequences of it—she unthinkingly touched her scarred cheek—but that had been more than twenty years ago. Her life had been peaceful for a long time. The nightmares of the past were no more than distant memories, but she felt as if she'd once more become the frightened, helpless child who'd watched in confusion while adults fought around her.

'It would be best if you sit down, my lady.' Arscott guided her to a stone bench. 'It was an unpleasant incident, but soon everything will be back to normal.'

Desire looked around and saw that he was right. The roof was now deserted except for her and the steward.

'An unpleasant incident?' she repeated disbelievingly, amazed that Arscott could so lightly discount what had happened.

'My apologies,' he said stiffly. 'I did not mean to belittle what happened. But it is better not to distress yourself over such things. It is over now.'

'Yes.' Desire took a deep breath, determined to maintain her composure in the face of Arscott's stiff-backed demeanour.

Her family and his had been connected for several generations. Desire's grandfather had considerably enlarged Godwin House during Elizabeth's reign, and Arscott's grandfather had been the master stonemason who'd worked on the new wings. Arscott's father had also been a mason, but Arscott had chosen to serve the Godwin family more directly. He had begun as a footman and risen to be steward of Godwin House. The death of Desire's father, followed very soon after by the death of the man Lord Larksmere had appointed as her guardian, could have caused great upheaval in her life, but Arscott's competence and loyalty had protected her from many potential hazards. She was enduringly grateful to him, though she did not find him a particularly congenial companion.

'You are right,' she said, straightening her shoulders. 'We must not dwell on what just happened. But we must take steps to prevent it happening again. You have often mentioned the possible risk if I go out, but I never thought I would be attacked in my own home.'

'No, my lady. But you are a rich prize, as we've discussed before,' Arscott replied sombrely.

He spoke in his usual, measured tones, but Desire thought she saw a flicker of annoyance in his eyes. It occurred to her that he might have interpreted her comment as a veiled criticism. That hadn't been her intention but, now she thought of it, how had the villains gained access to the house?

'There are many men who wouldn't baulk at marrying you by force if they had the chance,' he said grimly.

'I know that. But I thought I was at least safe here. How did they get in?'

Arscott's expression blanked. 'I have done everything in my power to keep you safe,' he said, 'but there are gaps in even the best defences. They got in because they bribed one of the new porters. I thought he was acting oddly. When I questioned him, I discovered the villains were already on the roof. I came at once!'

'Thank you.' Desire looked around her darkness-shrouded garden. For years she had seen it as her sanctuary. Now it no longer seemed quite so safe. She shivered with fear as she remembered how the man with the pistol had claimed her as his bride.

'They didn't all come through the door,' she said. 'One climbed the wall.'

'He did?' Arscott muttered a curse, then quickly apologised. 'I'm sorry, my lady.'

He hesitated, then took one of her hands in a comforting grasp. Desire was startled at the unprecedented familiarity of his gesture. She had known Arscott all her life, but he very rarely touched her. She was disconcerted by his attempt to reassure her, and withdrew her hand from his as tactfully as she could.

'My lady, you know that I will always do everything in my power to protect you,' he said. 'But until you are married you will always be at risk from those who seek your fortune.'

'I know,' Desire said wearily. 'But how am I to find a husband? By all accounts the nobility is full of rapacious villains. I'd hate to fall prey to a man such as Lord Rochester. How am I to avoid such a fate?'

'By choosing a man you know to be honest and loyal,' Arscott replied.

'But I don't *know* any—' Desire began, her voice rising in exasperation.

'My lady, my family has served yours for three generations,' Arscott interrupted. 'Your father himself selected me to be his steward. I have always been honoured by the trust he placed in me and the high esteem in which he held me. Under any other circumstances I would never put myself forward in this manner. But your plight is desperate. Until you marry you will always be at risk of further attempts to take you by force. And the years are passing. Soon—'

'*I know!*' Desire longed to hold her own babe in her arms. She didn't want to be reminded that her chances of doing so diminished with every year she remained unwed.

'Forgive me.' Arscott bowed his head. 'I did not meant to cause you distress. But my lady, there is a way you can safeguard yourself from fortune hunters *and* have the children you long for.' He dropped suddenly on one knee beside the bench.

Desire stared at him in disbelief, too startled to notice when he took her hand in his once more.

'If you had a more worthy suitor I would never put myself forward,' he said. 'But as your husband I would continue to protect and serve you as loyally as I have done as your steward.'

'You want to marry me!' she exclaimed, dumbfounded by his proposal. The possibility of marrying the steward had never before occurred to her.

'I will make you a good and faithful husband,' he assured her, his grip on her hand tightening. 'You may be sure I will never expose you to hurt or insult.'

'I'm sure…' Desire swallowed, hoping Arscott hadn't sensed her instinctive dismay at the prospect of marrying him. She was grateful for the dim light, which prevented him from seeing her clearly.

What he suggested would no doubt provoke outrage in many sections of society. There was a vast gulf between their social rank and fortunes. But at that moment Desire did not recall that Arscott was the son of a stonemason. It was the thought of sharing his bed that chilled her heart.

She knew that such an objection was foolish and impractical. Most brides had little choice in who they wed. But when she imagined lying beside Arscott in the dark, every fibre of her being cried out against such intimacy. She respected the steward. Admired him even. And God knows she was grateful for his loyalty through all the years of his service. But she didn't want to marry him.

'I do thank you for your kind offer,' she said. She was too soft-hearted to reject him immediately, but she tried to prepare him for her ultimate answer. 'I will consider it very carefully. Perhaps we can discuss it again when we have all had a chance to recover from what happened earlier. I confess, I'm still a little shaken now.'

'Of course, my lady.' Arscott released Desire's hand and stood up. 'Perhaps I shouldn't have spoken so hastily. But until you are safely wed you will remain in danger. It will be best if you don't consider too long.'

Desire suppressed a shiver of apprehension. 'Perhaps not,' she said. 'Anyone else who might have been planning to abduct me will surely think twice now. Now they know they are more likely to end up dead than married.' The words emerged more harshly than she'd intended. She was still shaken by Arscott's ruthlessness on her behalf.

'I had no choice,' said Arscott. She could hear the thread of anger beneath the rigid deference in his voice. 'There were three of them. And my pistol misfired.'

'I *heard* it—!' Desire began.

'I fired the musket,' said Arscott, 'but the pistol misfired. I could not threaten the two remaining men with it. Only fight hand-to-hand to save you.'

'I will always be grateful,' Desire said. The last thing she wanted was ill feeling between her and her steward. 'It's dark. Let's go inside now.'

Chapter Two

Newgate, Tuesday 4 September 1666

'*Fire! Fire! Fire!*'

'The Papists have fired London!'

'Nay! The flames of hell are purging the corrupt city!'

'It's the French to blame. Throwing fireballs into the houses…'

''Tis God's punishment for the sins of the Court…'

'The Dutch are taking vengeance for our recent victory…'

'St Paul's burns…'

'*We'll all burn!*'

Jakob listened grimly to the uproar around and below him. He was in Newgate, awaiting the next gaol delivery to the Old Bailey. At the best of times the prison wasn't silent, but now the cries of his fellow captives had risen to a frenzied cacophony of panic.

Newgate was not only a gaol, it was also one of the seven ancient gateways into London. Its two massive stone towers straddled Newgate Street. Every day people crowded through the iron gates and beneath the portcullis on their journey into, or out of, the City. But for two days there had been no normal traffic through the gate. The sounds of London descending into chaos had filtered through the thick stone walls and iron bars of the gaol.

News of a fire in the east of the City had first reached the gaol on Sunday morning, but fires among the old wooden buildings of London were so common that initially only a few doom-mongers were alarmed.

All the same, speculation about the extent and cause of the conflagration quickly circulated among the prisoners. By Monday it was claimed that the fire extended from London Bridge in the south to Lombard Street in the north. That it covered the whole of the waterfront for almost the entire length of Thames Street. Rumours abounded. Many people believed absolutely that the fire had been started deliberately by a Dutch baker. Others that the French had ignited it by throwing fireballs into houses. England was at war with both countries. On Monday night the fire destroyed Cornhill and advanced inexorably on Cheapside.

By Tuesday morning, St Paul's Cathedral and Newgate were both under immediate threat. It no longer mattered to anyone trapped inside the prison how the fire started. Their only concern was to escape. Even in their confinement the prisoners could hear the terrified screams of those who fled through the gate in search of safety. They could also hear the thunderous roar of the fire raging towards the towers. The stench of burning was stronger than the usually overpowering stench of the gaol. The air was foul with smoke.

Jakob stood at a barred window, his throat raw from the polluted air. He took shallow breathes to avoid pulling the smoke too deeply into his lungs. He was in a better position than many prisoners. They were incarcerated in squalid quarters below ground. Fortunately Jakob had not come penniless to gaol. He'd bribed the Keeper of Newgate to house him in the more comfortable conditions of the Master's Side at the top of the prison.

He'd also taken the first opportunity to send out a message to his cousin, the Duke of Kilverdale. The Keeper had been impressed by Jakob's high-ranking connections and since then had treated him with careful respect.

But so far Kilverdale had neither returned the message nor appeared in person. On Monday morning, after two nights in Newgate, Jakob had reluctantly sent out another message. This time to his grandfather, who had a house in St Martin's Lane. Under other circumstances Jakob would have waited considerably longer for Kilverdale to respond before asking for Lord Swiftbourne's help, but he believed Lady Desire was still in imminent danger. There had been no reply to his second message either.

Jakob tested one of the bars at the window, while he wondered with some annoyance where Kilverdale had gone. His cousin seemed to be constitutionally incapable of staying in one place for more than five minutes.

The roar of the fire was louder, closer. Smoke curled through the bars. Burning embers swirled past the window, a terrifying portent of what was to come. Jakob's muscles tensed with horror at the thought of being caught like a rat in a trap before the flames.

He shook off the ghastly image and went to hammer on the locked door.

'*Hey!* Are you going to leave us to roast?' he shouted.

It wasn't the first time he'd demanded information about the fire. Since he had the money for bribes, the gaolers kept him reasonably well informed. This time no one replied. He waited by the door an instant longer, then returned to the window. He'd checked all possible escape routes when he'd first arrived, and he'd quickly discovered that the mortar holding the bars was in poor condition. Though the prison was a formidable building, it was old and in disrepair.

Jakob had spent much of his time over the past two days chiselling away at the soft mortar with a large iron nail he'd purloined during his transfer into the cell. The fire had been his ally in his escape preparations. Anyone who noticed how much time he spent at the window would assume he was trying to follow the progress of the flames.

Now he braced one hand against the wall and wrapped his other hand around the first iron bar. He focussed all his strength and dragged the bar free. It grated loudly against the crumbling brick, but there was no need for silence. If anyone heard him and came to prevent his escape, they'd open the door.

An open door was all Jakob needed.

He was about to drop the bar on to the floor when, beneath the ever-present roar of the fire, he heard the scrape of a key in the lock. In the few seconds before the door swung inwards he thrust the bar beneath his doublet.

'What took you so long?' he demanded, striding towards the terrified gaoler.

'Hurry! We're going to the Clink.' The gaoler coughed and gestured frantically towards Jakob with his left hand. In his right he held a musket.

'To hell, more like.' Jakob strode through the door, helped on his way by a shove between the shoulder blades.

All around him he could hear frightened, angry shouts. The gaolers were trying to march their prisoners away to the alternative confinement of the Clink Prison in Southwark. But the gaolers were disorganised and as terrified as the prisoners. Once they reached the street it was easy for Jakob to escape in the confusion.

As soon as he was alone in a debris-filled alley, he paused to get his bearings. Inside the prison he'd become almost used to the roaring approach of the fire. Outside in the street the noise was a physical assault on his whole body, pounding his ears and disorientating all his senses. Stones exploded in the high temperatures. It sounded as if a battle was being fought within the flames.

He turned to take his first real look at the fire—and shock

briefly held him completely immobile. The fierce gale that had been blowing since Sunday had whipped the sulphurous flames into a savage inferno. It towered high above the tallest buildings, dwarfing everything in its path. The sky above was black with smoke.

A shower of crimson fire droplets rained down upon him, covering his doublet with tiny, blackened pinpricks. The intense heat scalded his eyes and seared his face. Acrid smoke gusted suddenly around him. Choking him. Nearly blinding him. His lungs burned. The flames seemed almost alive in their malevolent intent to devour everything in their path.

He shook off his momentary horror and turned to run through the thick layer of ash that swirled in the streets.

By now his temporary lodgings in the City would surely have burned. There was no point in going to the house in St Martin's Lane because the message he'd sent there had been left unanswered. Besides, he wasn't keen to present himself to his grandfather in the guise of an escaped convict. Now Jakob was free, he regretted the necessity that had forced him to send that message.

He paused to check his location and a fit of coughing tore his lungs.

He remembered the moment her ladyship's steward had levelled his pistol at him. Jakob had dived flat behind the meagre protection of a bed of herbs. The steward had pulled the trigger, but the pistol had misfired. Jakob had no doubt the man had intended him to die on the roof of Godwin House.

He'd survived the débâcle because of a misfired pistol and Lady Desire's absolute determination he would live to stand trial. He recalled the way she'd held him at bay with the pistol she'd taken from her attacker. There was no doubting the lady's courage, but the fire would not respect her dignity or her privacy—and it was not the only threat to her safety. No doubt she'd already fled from her grand mansion in the Strand, but Jakob wanted to know where she'd gone.

He was covered in soot and ash. Just another desperate man escaping from the fire. As long as he avoided members of Lady Desire's household, he was unlikely to be recognised. Perhaps he could find someone to tell him what he needed to know. He owed the lady his life. He meant to repay the debt.

Desire stood in her roof-garden, the key to the river-gate clutched in her hand. She stared, transfixed, at the burning city. With the exception of a couple of watchmen left to guard the property from looters, she was alone in Godwin House. She wondered vaguely whether Arscott or Benjamin Finch had realised yet that they'd left her behind.

She hadn't intended to stay, but in the end she hadn't been able to leave. Godwin House was her home—this garden her sanctuary. She had a superstitious fear that if she deserted it she might never see it again.

The arrangements they'd made to convey the contents of the house to safety had made it easy for no one to notice her absence. The most valuable items had been taken away either by carriage or in the river barge. Arscott had gone with the barge, intent on protecting the locked chest that contained all of Desire's monetary wealth. There was more than nine thousand pounds in the heavy chest, the revenues from all the Godwin estates scattered throughout the country. Arscott had taken the head porter and several of the strongest menservants with him to guard the chest.

Benjamin had been in charge of the three coaches that had hauled away other chattels as well as most of the staff, including Lucy, Desire's personal maid. There had been some discussion about whether Desire would be more comfortable in the overcrowded barge or a coach. No clear decision had been made. In the confusion it had been easy for both men to assume that their mistress was safely in the care of the other.

Despite her fear that she might lose her home, Desire had not consciously intended to stay behind. Somehow she simply hadn't left. She wondered if she was living up to some deep-rooted family tradition of not running away in the face of danger. Twenty-two years earlier, her mother had lived—and Desire had nearly died—by that creed. In the absence of the Earl, the Countess had taken charge of their Devonshire estate. She had held the fortified house for Parliament against besieging royalists for five weeks of fierce fighting. Even the injuries to her daughter had not compelled the Countess to yield. Only the arrival of Parliamentarian forces, led by Desire's father, had brought an end to the siege.

The thunderous roar of the fire destroying London was horrifyingly reminiscent for Desire of the noise of the royalists' bombardment of Larksmere House because, trapped behind the defences of the house, there had been no peace and no escape from the fighting. Desire touched her cheek. Her scars were an ever-present reminder of that frightening period of her life.

The strong easterly winds whipped her skirts around her legs. Her dishevelled hair felt gritty with the ash swirling through the air. Her garden was full of flying debris. A charred piece of paper briefly caught against the side of a raised bed. It gusted up into Desire's face before spinning heavenwards once more.

All the previous night she had watched the fire light up the sky. She'd seen the crimson, snake-tipped flames dance obscenely over the rooftops and curl wickedly around the church spires and towers. She'd seldom visited the crowded streets of the City, but she'd imagined walking along them. She had always enjoyed knowing there was so much enterprising human life close by. She even enjoyed listening to the harsh, vulgar curses of the Thames boatmen as they plied their trade on the river adjoining her property.

Now London was being destroyed before her eyes. And the fierce wind was driving the flames dangerously close to Godwin House. She was almost sure that Fleet Street was already on fire. She pressed the shank of the river-gate key against her lips. She had prayed all night for the gale to cease and the flames to be quenched. But now it seemed inevitable that the fire would reach the Strand. It was finally time to leave. She would seek out her watchmen and take to the safety of the river.

She turned to leave the roof—and screamed in terror.

Jakob Smith stood three feet from her. A huge, wild-eyed, soot-grimed monster. She was sure he'd come for his revenge. Shock momentarily paralysed her.

His lips draw back in a snarl of fury as he made a gesture towards her.

She threw herself away from him, falling backwards into a bed of herbs.

He lunged after her.

She rolled frantically away, fetching up against the parapet wall. The impact knocked the air out of her lungs and she gasped for breath. Heard him curse.

'What the hell are you doing here?' he shouted, looming over her.

Desire didn't answer. She struggled to sit up, keeping a tight grip on the key. It wasn't much, but it was the only weapon she had. Even a monster like Jakob could not be entirely invulnerable. If she could only find his weakness…

Abruptly he moved away from her. Out of her reach. An expression of grim wariness in his red-rimmed eyes. Wild speculations raced through her mind. She wondered if he'd guessed her intent. The demon had a lot more experience of reading a foe's intentions than she had. She resolved to keep her expression impassive.

'Where are your men?' he shouted at her.

'What?' His question startled a response from her.

Too late she realised he wanted to assure himself that no one would interrupt his planned revenge on her.

'För bövelen!' he exclaimed, in apparent exasperation. 'At least on Saturday you had a small army to protect you—some of them even seemed loyal. Today I find you alone and defenceless, like a peach waiting to be—'

'Not by you!' Desire shouted back, too angry to be afraid. 'I'll die…*you'll* die first!'

She tried to dig her heels into the ground, to give herself purchase to scramble backwards along the wall. Instead her foot caught in her petticoats. Before she could untangle herself a large clump of fiery debris cartwheeled down from the smoke-filled sky. The wind bowled the tattered ball of flames across the roof until it was trapped between the parapet and Desire's tangled skirts.

The fire hissed and crackled as it found new food to feed on. Desire screamed, terror consuming her as flames seemed to engulf her legs.

In her panic she barely noticed Jakob seize her in his arms. A few seconds later he plunged her into the water cistern. Shock knocked the air out of her lungs and an instant later Jakob thrust her billowing skirts beneath the ash-covered surface of the water. The flames hissed and died. Desire panted for breath.

It took several long moments for her wits to return sufficiently to comprehend what had happened. She was sitting in the large cistern, water almost up to her neck, though a fair amount had washed out when Jakob had dumped her into the trough. Bits of soot and ash floated around on top of the dirty water in front of her. Jakob knelt beside her. One of his strong hands gripped her shoulder. The other covered the hand in which, to her somewhat detached amazement, she discovered she was still clutching the key.

She stared at Jakob, drained of all emotion.

He stroked a matted strand of hair gently behind her shoulder and smiled at her. He had a very attractive smile for a fiend—even though his face was black with soot and his eyes were red. His hair had lost its angelic lustre. It was stringy with sweat and grime.

Images of the long-ago siege of Larksmere House receded from Desire's mind. She focussed on the immediate past instead. She'd thought about Jakob often since Saturday. Confused by the conflicting emotions he aroused in her. She'd been a little captivated by him when he'd first appeared on her roof—and then he'd destroyed all her ridiculous illusions. She'd allowed herself to be deceived by his comely appearance. The fire-grime that now covered him gave a much clearer indication of his true character. Except, of course, that he'd just saved her from being roasted alive.

'What does the key open?' he asked, his voice soft, almost teasing. 'Your jewellery case?'

'The river-gate!' she exclaimed indignantly.

The iron key was large and ugly. It opened the gate in the wall that separated the edge of her property from the Thames. Even the keys to the sturdy locks on her treasure chest were more elegant. Besides, did he really think she was so vain and foolish that she would put jewels before her own safety?

'Good girl.' He smiled and slipped the key out of her fingers before she'd realised his intent, and stood up.

'*You scurvy, double-dealing—*'

'Language, my lady,' he chided her, laughing gently. 'No, don't get up,' he added, as she seized the edges of the cistern. 'We aren't leaving just yet.'

'We?' She stared at him warily, still clutching the sides of the water cistern.

'I didn't expect you to be here,' he informed her, shrugging out of his doublet. 'Not once I'd discovered the house was deserted. I only came on to the roof to get a better look at the fire. To see how far it extends. Lucky for you I did.'

'Why?' Desire asked warily. 'The house isn't deserted,' she added. 'There are porters guarding the gate—aren't there?'

Jakob grinned. 'Easily evaded, my lady,' he said, and stripped off his shirt.

Desire's eyes widened at the breadth of muscled chest and lean, hard-ridged stomach his actions revealed. Then, as the likely motive for his disrobing dawned on her, she tried to surge out of the water.

'Sit.' He put his hand on her shoulder and easily shoved her back under the surface. 'You're safer there till we get off this damned fire-trap.'

'Why are you—?'

'Not for the reason you think,' he retorted, casting a quick glance towards the advancing flames.

The sky above them was thick with roiling smoke. Desire's throat was raw. She could tell from the hoarseness in Jakob's voice that he was also suffering the effects of the smoke. Amidst the noise of the fire and the wind she heard something that sounded like an explosion.

'They're using gunpowder in Fleet Street,' Jakob explained. 'Blowing up houses to make a fire break. But unless the wind drops…'

He gripped his shirt tightly and jerked his hands apart. The fine linen ripped and. Desire watched in bewilderment as he tore his shirt into several pieces.

'Why are you doing that?' she asked.

'Just a precaution, my lady,' he replied, smiling in a way that she only belatedly realised was deeply suspicious.

In one smooth movement, he seized her wrists and efficiently tied them together with a piece of ragged linen.

Desire struggled valiantly. Water splashed everywhere but, but in the confines of the cistern, she had little chance to evade him.

She cursed him freely, anger temporarily displacing the underlying fear she continued to feel in his presence.

'You mangy, flea-ridden, thieving, ill-begotten cur!' she raged, just before he pushed one of the rags in her mouth.

He tied the strip of linen securely behind her head. Then he smiled at her.

She blinked water out of her eyes and glared at him over the gag.

'Time to go,' he said, and hauled her out of the cistern.

Instantly she swung up her bound hands in an attempt to hit him in the face.

He barely managed to dodge the blow as her hands rasped across the stubble on his chin. He swore briefly and concisely, and threw her over his naked shoulder.

Desire kicked viciously and tried to pound her fists against any part of his anatomy that she could reach. His grip on her tightened until it was painful as he went across the roof and down the stairs that led to a side entrance. From there he had only to run through the gardens behind the house to reach the river-gate.

Desire stopped struggling. He marginally relaxed his grip, but he didn't slow down. Instead of trying to hit him, Desire concentrated on getting rid of the gag. If she could only attract the attention of her watchmen…

But it wasn't easy when Jakob was jolting her along upside-down through the neatly clipped box hedges. By the time they'd reached the boathouse she'd only just managed to free her mouth, painfully pulling out several strands of her hair that had been caught in the knot as she did so.

Jakob laid her on the ground and began to drag up her charred, water-soaked skirts. Desire fought desperately, flailing at him with her clubbed fists, whimpering with terror. She had no breath to scream for help.

He threw himself over her, finally containing her struggles with the weight of his large body.

'Stop fighting, you vixen,' he said, through gritted teeth. 'I'm only trying to find out if your legs are burnt.'

'You *lecher*!'

'I should have left you to roast!'

'Hell-spawn.'

'Hell-cat.'

For a few moments they both lay still, breathing heavily. Reason slowly replaced the terrifying images of rape that had filled Desire's mind. She didn't trust Jakob, but so far he hadn't actually hurt her.

'My legs aren't burnt,' she said frigidly

She shoved ineffectually at the solid bulk of his torso. The weight of his hard body pinning her to the ground was profoundly disturbing. She wasn't used to intimate physical contact with any human being—much less with a large, powerful man naked to the waist. She felt trapped and frightened—and furious at her sense of helplessness.

'You're too upset to know if they are,' he retorted, easing himself cautiously away from her.

'I'm not stupid!' she snapped. 'I'd know if my own legs were burnt.'

'I've seen men wounded in battle who didn't even know their legs had been cut *off*!' Jakob countered.

'Battle…? Are you claiming to be a soldier?' Desire jabbed her knuckles against the ridges of his stomach, ineffectually trying to increase the distance between them.

Jakob winced. 'Until lately I was an officer in the Swedish army,' he growled.

'An *officer*?' she scoffed. 'A cowardly deserter more like. Or a camp-following scavenger who steals from wounded me—'

He clamped one large hand over her mouth.

'*Var tyst!* We'd have been on our way by now if you weren't such a wildcat.'

'Way? Where?' Desire demanded, as soon as he took his hand away.

Jakob didn't reply. Instead he moved so suddenly she was left gasping with shock. One minute he was lying half on top of her, the next he was straddling her hips, his back towards her head as he doggedly pulled up her skirts.

Outraged, Desire hammered his broad shoulders with her bound fists. His naked flesh was hard and unyielding. Only his occasional grunt indicated he wasn't entirely immune to her assault. Desire kicked wildly, trying to clout him in the face with her knees.

With a muttered curse he finally managed to contain her struggles. Half-blinded by her hair, panting with her exertions, Desire endured the insufferable indignity of having her captor satisfy himself that her lower limbs were only minimally scorched.

'All this material must have protected you,' he announced at last, 'your chemise isn't even singed. I don't think you're much damaged.'

'*That's what I said!*' Desire was beside herself with rage. 'How *dare* you...'

He jumped off her, springing aside just in time to avoid a well-aimed blow to his groin as she scythed her hands upwards.

He grabbed her joined fists, pulling her to her feet in one smoothly continuous movement.

'I should have trussed you tighter!' he declared in exasperation.

'You oaf! I'm a *lady!*' Desire was incensed at his impertinent suggestion.

'Not like any I ever met before.' He dragged her along behind him. 'You'd have made this a lot easier on both of us if you'd had the good sense to swoon when you first saw me.'

'I *never* swoon.'

'More's the pity.'

Jakob found some rope in the boathouse and tied it around Desire's knees, over her blackened, dirty wet skirts.

'You'll hang,' she taunted him, from her undignified position on the ground. 'At Tyburn, you'll hang for this.'

Jakob merely grunted. Now that he was no longer hampered by Desire's stubborn resistance he made short work of getting the small rowing boat on to the Thames and Desire into the boat. He even locked the gate, thoughtfully safeguarding the house from river-borne looters. He dropped the key on Desire's lap, pushed the boat away from the river stairs and began to row upstream.

Desire stared at him in baffled fury, then twisted around to look at the burning city behind her. The boat rocked precariously in the waves stirred up by the wind and the other crafts that thronged the river. Desire was stunned by the scenes of devastation all around her.

The Thames was full of people escaping the inferno. Boats

were piled high with belongings. She could hear a woman sobbing, children screaming...

She abandoned her half-formed plan to shout for help. Amidst this chaos her cries would either go completely unnoticed or would be ignored in the general pandemonium.

She strained to see one last glimpse of her home as Jakob rowed steadily upriver. When they were well beyond the outskirts of London she turned to face him, noticing at once the familiarity with which he handled the oars. His naked torso glistened from his exertions. There was a light dusting of golden curls on his hard-muscled chest, but Desire was sure that beneath the sooty grime that covered him his skin was smooth and blemish free.

For the first time since he'd appeared on her roof she had an opportunity to reflect on her situation. It wasn't good. She was bound hand and foot in the power of a man who should have been languishing in Newgate, awaiting his trial. Not only that, none of her household even knew she was missing. There would be no hue and cry for her until it was far too late. She bit her lip, wishing she'd had the good sense to leave with Arscott in the barge that morning. But it was too late to repine over her decision now.

Her gaze narrowed on Jakob. He was a hardy rogue. What did he want with her, now that the man he'd served was dead?

'Are you to be my bridegroom now?' she demanded.

'No.'

She stared at him, confounded by his brief reply. 'Arscott shot the other one,' she reminded him.

Jakob grinned briefly, but there was no amusement in his eyes.

'As you say,' he agreed. 'I value my continued good health too much to risk a similar fate. Is that—' he timed the rhythm of his words to fit easily into that of the oars '—how you've managed to remain unwed so long? Your steward shoots all your hopeful suitors?'

'What? No, of course not!' Desire frowned at him. 'What do you want then? Ransom? Am I to be your hostage?'

She thought of the chest full of money Arscott had taken away with him.

'No,' said Jakob.

'Then why do you want me?' she asked, bewildered.

'I don't want you,' he replied curtly.

Desire caught her breath. His sharp response cut straight through her defences, hurting her where she was most vulnerable. She knew full well that her most attractive feature was her inheritance—but it was a long time since she'd been reminded of that quite so brutally. It didn't matter that Jakob was a brigand who'd just escaped from prison. He was still a handsome man who had no doubt enjoyed many beautiful women. His sharp rejection was deeply wounding.

Shamed and humiliated, she bent her head to gaze hazily at her bound hands. For the first time since her ordeal began she felt tears pricking her eyes. She was determined not to cry. She turned her face into her shoulder in an instinctive effort to hide her scarred cheek from her abductor.

Jakob saw the moment the fight left Desire. It baffled him. One minute she was matching him point for point, the next she hunched her shoulders and turned her head away from him.

It was only when he realised she was trying to conceal her scars that he guessed why his brief comment had wounded her so severely. He muttered a soft curse. It hadn't occurred to him she'd interpret his barely considered words as a rejection. If anything, he'd intended them to be comforting—a reassurance that he had no intention of raping her.

He'd been surprised by her scars the first time he'd seen her, but now he barely noticed them. From the moment she'd held the pistol on him, her beautiful brown eyes blazing with anger, he'd been far more impressed by her fiery personality. Even after such a brief acquaintance he knew her to be brave and resolute. He didn't understand why she'd been alone on the roof of

Godwin House—but he suspected it had been by her own choice. She'd already demonstrated she wasn't the kind of person who fled in panic from danger.

He was sorry he'd inadvertently hurt her, but he was irritated with her for being ashamed of her scars. She ought to hold her head up proudly and damn him for his impudence—not cringe from him like a mistreated puppy. Somewhat to his surprise, he realised he was also angry with whoever had taught her to feel that shame.

He gritted his teeth with annoyance and pain. Desire had escaped lightly from the fire in her petticoats, but both of Jakob's hands were blistered and sore from his efforts to quench the flames. Now every pull on the oars caused him intense discomfort. He wasn't in the mood to ease Desire's distress with gentle words.

'So why did your murderous rabble of a household desert you?' he asked, and waited with interest to see how she would respond to his wantonly insulting question.

Chapter Three

It took a few seconds for the full import of Jakob's words to dawn on Desire. As soon as it did her head reared up, her eyes hot with indignation.

'They didn't desert me!' she declared fiercely. 'And they aren't a murderous rabble—'

'They were going to lynch me!'

'Only because they were shocked and frightened by what happened.' Desire pushed a strand of wet hair out of her face with her bound hands and glared at him. 'Abducting helpless females might be all in a day's work for you, but *they* were horrified. They're all better men than you'll ever be. Any one of them would make three of you!'

'I didn't notice they were *that* fat,' Jakob retorted, pleased with the success of his ruse. Desire had completely forgotten to hide her scarred cheek.

'I wasn't referring to your great hulking bulk!' she shot back. 'I was talking about character…courage…integrity. None of *them* would mistreat a lady.'

'Because, in their dotage, they can't remember what a woman is for!' Jakob had noticed that, with the exception of the steward and a couple of young porters, nearly all the men who'd rushed to Desire's rescue on the roof had been well over fifty.

'Because they are honourable!' Desire snapped.

'So where are these honourable, creaking gallants in your hour of need?' Jakob winced slightly and shifted his grip on the oars.

To his relief the tide was finally on the turn. Until now, if he'd stopped rowing, the current would inexorably have carried the small boat back down the Thames towards the burning city.

'Taking the contents of the house to safety!' Desire retorted.

Jakob grinned, despite his discomfort. 'You mean they were more interested in rescuing the virginals than the virgin herself?' he countered.

Desire gasped with offended dignity at his inflammatory question. Despite the fact that her feet and hands were still tied up, she tried to kick Jakob. Without her hands to stabilise her, she lost her balance on the wooden seat. She fell sideways, then slid ignominiously into the bottom of the boat. The key to the river-gate fell onto the boards beside her.

The little craft rocked alarmingly for several seconds before Jakob managed to restore equilibrium.

'*För bövelen,* woman! Are you trying to drown us both!' he shouted, exasperated.

'I hope *you* drown,' she shouted back, undaunted, from where she was huddled in the shallow puddle of dirty water that slopped over the boards.

'For God's sake!' He reached down to help her up. As soon as he touched her she jerked away, once more rocking the boat. 'I'll leave you there if you do that again,' he warned her.

'If you untie me, I could get up by myself,' she said mutinously.

'If I untie you, you'll no doubt take a lump out of my skull with an oar,' he said through gritted teeth.

She sniffed inelegantly, but otherwise didn't deign to reply.

Jakob sighed, wondering how the devil he'd managed to get himself into such an absurd situation. His plan to provoke her out of her sad mood had worked only too well.

'If I untie you, will you give me your parole?' he asked.

'No.'

'Stubborn wench.' He rested for a minute. There were dark bloodstains on the oars, and the palms of his hands were exquisitely painful. 'Why did your men leave you behind?' he asked.

'They didn't know they did.' Desire lifted her head clear of the dirty wet planks. She couldn't remember the last time she'd been so uncomfortable, but she was determined not to beg.

'How did they manage to miss you? Did you hide behind the potted orange trees?' Jakob asked.

Desire was pleased to note that, in addition to his obvious exasperation, he also sounded somewhat harried. She found that minor revelation very gratifying. It made the impossibly handsome, physically overwhelming vagabond a little less intimidating.

'Arscott took the barge, Benjamin was in charge of the coaches,' she explained. 'They both thought I was with the other one.'

'Why didn't you leave when you could?'

'I don't know,' she admitted. 'It's my home. Do you think—?' She broke off. 'Do you think it burned?' she asked, hating the quiver in her voice, and the humiliating awareness that she was asking her abductor for reassurance.

'I don't know, my lady,' he replied, his tone gentler than usual. 'The wind has started to drop. Without the wind to drive it on, the fire may not have spread as far as the Strand.'

This time, when he reached towards her, she let him lift her back on to the seat. As he did so she saw the state of his hands.

She gasped with shock at the painful mess.

'What happened to them?'

'It's not important.' He took up the oars again. She saw the slight flinch in his eyes, but otherwise his face remained impassive as he continued to row smoothly upriver.

'You halfwit!' Desire wasn't impressed by his stoicism.

She stared at him in confusion for a few moments while she

tried to work out how he'd been hurt. At last a possibility suggested itself to her.

'Were you hurt when you saved me from burning…on the roof?' she demanded.

He nodded fractionally, his jaw set with determination.

She considered the situation in silence for a few more seconds. 'Untie me,' she ordered at last.

He raised one sceptical eyebrow, his expression clearly indicating he wasn't about to take such a foolhardy risk, and rowed steadily onwards.

'Numskull! If you untie me, we can wrap the linen round your hands,' she pointed out. 'It will protect them from the oars.'

Jakob rested again, apparently considering her suggestion. Now that the tide had fully turned the boat continued to drift upstream, even without his efforts to propel it.

'You were hurt saving my life,' Desire said stiffly. 'I won't give you my parole, but you can trust me not to…attack you…while we're in the boat. Where are we going?' she added, with belated curiosity.

He smiled faintly as he began to unravel the knots at her wrists. 'Putney,' he replied.

'Oh.' Desire smoothed out the creased linen as she absorbed that information. 'Give me your hand,' she instructed Jakob.

He did so, and she wrapped the strip of material carefully around his palm and fingers. She bit her lip as she saw how sore his hands were. She didn't think the flames had scorched him very badly. But he'd had a few blisters from the fire and rowing had rubbed them raw. He must have been in considerable pain ever since they'd left Godwin House, but he'd never complained—or blamed her because he'd been hurt saving her.

'No, wait,' she said, when he moved to pick up the oars again. 'We can use this to wrap the other one.' She untied the gag still hanging around her neck and used it to bandage his other hand, touching his sore fingers gently.

'Thank you,' he said.

She looked up—straight into his eyes. She'd leant towards him to tend his hands. Their faces were only a few inches apart. His blue eyes were startlingly vivid in his soot-grimed face. His quiet gaze was steady, and unexpectedly gentle.

He didn't look like a monster. He looked like a pain-weary man who was doing what he had to do without fuss. She felt guilty that she'd taken so long to notice his discomfort. She should have tended to his hands sooner.

The direction of her thoughts disconcerted her. She swayed away from him, annoyed with herself. He had abducted her, very forcibly, from her home. He didn't deserve her sympathy.

'Why are we going to Putney?' she asked.

'Because it's convenient. Reasonably convenient,' he said as he plied the oars again. 'My hands feel much better,' he added.

Desire nodded an acknowledgement to his comment, her thoughts distracted. Now she knew their destination, she experienced a shiver of apprehension over what awaited her there.

'Are you going to…going to give me to someone else, when we get there?' she asked cautiously.

'No.' Jakob cast her a swift glance. 'I was planning to feed you,' he said.

'Feed me!' Desire was astounded.

'Aren't you hungry?' he demanded. 'I am. My plan is to obtain food. Clean water. And clothes,' he added as an obvious afterthought. 'For both of us. You may have to make do with the housekeeper's best. But since you normally dress like a washerwoman, I dare say you won't mind.'

'I *don't*…only when I'm gardening,' said Desire, defensively smoothing her disreputable skirt. The scorched outer layers had started to dry, but the material closest to her skin was still horribly wet and clammy.

'Or fire-watching,' said Jakob, casting a critical eye over her clothes.

'Is it your house?' Desire asked, uncomfortable with discussing her clothes.

She selected her gowns for their hard-wearing practicality. And with a very conscious awareness that vanity did not become her. She was determined never to make a fool of herself in the fancy silks, laces and brocades more suitable for a beautiful woman. But she had no intention of confiding that information to Jakob. When she was talking to him, more especially when she was arguing with him, she often forgot her appearance for minutes at a time—but she knew *he* would always be aware of it.

'No,' he said, breaking into her thoughts. 'It's not my house.'

'Is the owner expecting you?'

Jakob rolled his eyes. 'Of course he's expecting me to row half-naked up the Thames to have supper with him, in the company of an ill-tempered baggage—'

'I am *not* an ill-tempered baggage! And since I am bound not to hurt you while we are in the boat, you must not insult me,' she added haughtily. 'It is not honourable.'

He threw her a grin that contained a large portion of pure devilment. 'Very well, my lady,' he agreed.

Then his eyes narrowed slightly as he flexed his fingers around the oars.

'I think I should row now,' Desire announced, unable to suppress a wince in sympathy with his. She was sure his hands must feel as if they were on fire.

It annoyed her that she felt beholden to him, but there was no help for it. Since he'd been injured because of her, she was honour bound to take care of his wounds.

'Have you rowed a boat before?' he asked.

'No. But if you can do it, I'm sure I can,' she retorted. 'How hard can it be? We must swap places.' She started to stand up.

'Sit down!' he barked.

She did so, out of sheer surprise.

He heaved in an exasperated breath.

'Sit still, and be quiet,' he ordered her. 'How can one woman be so much trouble?' he asked the world in general.

'If you didn't want the trouble—you shouldn't have abducted me,' she returned, with spirit.

'I didn't abduct you, I rescued you,' he shot back.

'*Rescued me?* I don't recall any mention of St George tying his lady in knots when he rescued *her*!' Desire said energetically.

'If she was half as much trouble as you, I'll wager he did,' said Jakob. 'No doubt the chroniclers suppressed the information from the tale to protect the lady's reputation. Or…' another alternative occurred to him '…to avoid discouraging the chivalrous instincts of future generations of gentlemen.'

'You're not a gentleman!'

Jakob raised an insufferably arrogant eyebrow in response.

'You're a paid bravo who steals women for upstart fortune-hunters!' Desire accused him.

'I haven't made a career of it!' Jakob huffed out a breath of pure exasperation. 'If you had any sense, you'd be trying to ingratiate yourself with me—not insult me.'

'Ingratiate…? I've *never* tried to ingratiate myself with anyone! Ever! I wouldn't know how!'

Jakob smiled briefly. 'I can tell.'

Desire glared at him, her indignation fading as it occurred to her how good-tempered her abductor seemed to be. She'd undoubtedly caused him considerable inconvenience—and repeatedly provoked his exasperation—but he'd never responded with anger. She wasn't fool enough to believe she could have stopped him if he'd tried to hurt or violate her.

He was a puzzle to her.

'Whose house are we going to?' she asked.

'Kilverdale's,' he replied.

'Kilverdale?' Desire repeated blankly. 'The Duke?'

Jakob nodded.

Enlightenment crept over Desire in slow, sickening waves of understanding. She stared at Jakob in shock as every piece of the puzzle finally became clear to her.

On the roof, three days' ago, she'd believed the brute with the pistol had intended her for his own bride. Now she knew better. He'd been stealing her for another man—the Duke of Kilverdale. And when the original plan had failed, Jakob had returned at the first opportunity to complete the task.

What a fool she'd been. Insensibly she'd begun to trust Jakob's motives—now she knew better. He'd admitted he'd been a soldier. A mercenary, no doubt. He was still selling his loyalty to the highest bidder. She tasted the acid of bitter disappointment as she absorbed her new understanding. No wonder Jakob had saved her from burning and hadn't hurt her in any other way. He was being paid to deliver undamaged goods to the Duke.

'How much?' she croaked.

'What?' He looked at her blankly.

'How much is he paying you for me?' she demanded.

'Who?'

'Kilverdale! How much is he paying you?' her voice rose angrily.

'*Kilverdale?*' Jakob sounded dumbfounded by her question, but Desire was too upset to notice.

'I'll double it,' she promised him. 'If you take me to Arscott, I'll give you twice as much as the Duke is paying you. I swear I can.'

She lurched forward, sinking on to her knees in front of Jakob. The boat rocked as she seized one of his knees, gripping it urgently in her anxiety to make him attend her.

'I'll pay you,' she repeated, staring desperately into his eyes to see if her words were having any effect on him. 'From my chest. Arscott rescued it from the fire. Take me to him. You'll be rich. Don't give me to Kilverdale. Please! Don't give me to him!'

Her voice cracked on her last words. Panic threatened to overwhelm her.

'Don't give me to him,' she whispered, starting to tremble as the full horror of her situation finally came home to her.

Jakob released the oars, letting the boat drift as he gave all his attention to Desire. He was shaken by the sight of her begging on her knees before him, stunned by her obvious terror. Until now he'd only been aware of her courage, not her fear. Why did Kilverdale's name reduce her to panic? The Duke had a reputation for being something of a rake, but he wasn't cruel to his female conquests.

'I'm not giving you to anyone, *älskling*,' Jakob said gently.

She was so close to him, on her knees between his spread legs. He put his hands on her waist, feeling how she trembled. He stroked his bandaged hands reassuringly up and down her sides. Her bodice wasn't boned and he could feel the supple warmth of her body through the fabric. Her fingers clutched convulsively at his leg. Despite her obvious distress he couldn't help finding the situation arousing. He knew that wasn't her intention. He doubted if she was even aware that she was touching him.

Her face was white beneath the grime of the fire, her eyes wide with fear. She stared at him desperately for a few seconds longer, then abruptly closed her eyes and lowered her head. A deep shudder coursed through her body.

He pushed a strand of wet hair behind her ear with sore fingertips. The bandages she'd wrapped around his hands were already soiled and ragged.

'I'm not giving you to anyone, *älskling*,' he repeated softly. 'No one is going to hurt you. You saved my life on your roof. Now I'm doing my best to protect you from harm. And when you are safely restored to your home, I will be insulted if you open your treasure chest for me.'

Another shiver rippled through Desire. She kept her head resolutely bowed. He wasn't sure if she'd comprehended—or even heard—what he'd just said.

He gave in to temptation and slipped an arm around her shoulders, pulling her closer until she was cradled against his chest. Over her head he could see the thick, horrifying pall of smoke which shrouded the now distant London. He'd been watching it through all the twists and turns of the river since they'd left the

Strand. He wondered if any of the city was left. How had the fire started? Were any of the rumours he'd heard while he was trapped in Newgate true?

Desire still trembled against him, neither resisting nor yielding to him. He held her close, needing the comfort of her warm supple body in his arms as much as he suspected she needed his reassurance. Well, perhaps he wasn't her ideal comforter, he acknowledged, with a wry twist of his lips, but he was the best available.

'You're safe, milady,' he murmured against her tangled hair. 'No one will hurt you now.'

Desire kept her eyes tightly closed. She heard Jakob's reassurances, but she didn't know how to respond to them. She didn't know how she'd ended up in his arms. Her cheek was pressed against the firm plane of his upper chest. Her head nestled under his chin. She felt him stroke her back and a gentle touch against her hair.

One of her palms lay flat against his shoulder. As her panic subsided she became acutely aware of his hard, half-naked male body against hers, surrounding her with his virile strength. The sensation was unfamiliar. Disturbing, but not entirely unpleasant. Her pulse rate began to increase once more, not from blind terror this time, but from a peculiar mixture of excitement, shyness and illicit pleasure.

It was shocking to let Jakob hold her like this. She was shocked at herself that she could enjoy it even a little bit. But she did. She tried to tell herself it was just because it was so long since anyone had held her in a comforting embrace—but she knew it was more than that. Her fingers flexed against his skin. She wanted to slide her hand over his torso, explore all the firm planes and ridges of his muscles with her fingertips—not just her eyes.

'No one will hurt you,' he said softly, and she remembered Kilverdale.

She jerked against him in a silent protest at being reminded of the humiliation that lay ahead of her.

'*Älskling*, you have my word,' Jakob promised her. She felt his words vibrating deep in his chest. 'I did not take you for Kilverdale. I will not let him—or anyone else—harm you.'

'Not Kilverdale?' she whispered, not quite able to believe the reassurance.

'Not Kilverdale,' Jakob confirmed. 'He does not even know I've met you. He certainly isn't expecting you to arrive at his house. There's nothing to fear. But why are you so afraid of the Duke?'

'I'm not afraid of him.' Desire lifted her head indignantly. 'He is a hateful slug and I loathe him. But I am *not* afraid of him.'

'Hateful slug?' Jakob murmured disbelievingly. 'In silk brocade and lace?'

His face was very close to hers. His cheeks were grimed with soot, but she could see the small, pale smile creases around his eyes. After a moment she saw his gaze drop to focus on her mouth. She caught her lower lip between her teeth. Excitement fluttered behind her ribs. She found herself looking at *his* mouth. It was quite beautiful. His lips were well shaped, firm and sensual.

Unfamiliar tension wound through her belly. Of its own accord, her hand began to slide over his body. She heard his quick intake of breath, felt the crinkled hair on his chest tickle her fingers. Her breathing grew quick and shallow. She felt the rapid rise and fall of Jakob's broad chest beneath her hand. His blue eyes darkened until they were almost black.

In a breathtaking instant he took her captive. His powerful thighs closed, holding her hips still. He curved one possessive arm around her waist, while his other hand gripped the back of her head.

Then he kissed her.

His action stunned Desire. No one had ever kissed her on the mouth before. She was unprepared for the strength of her physical and emotional response. One moment she wanted to wrench herself out of Jakob's dominating embrace. The next second she wanted to press closer to him. Her thoughts were too chaotic to allow her to take rational action.

His lips were warm against her mouth, sometimes command-ing, at other times gently coaxing. His tongue stroked her lower lip, half-scandalising her, even as she experienced a new throb-bing deep in her belly. She gasped, stirring restlessly between his legs. His tongue immediately probed between her parted lips. She was overwhelmed with the virile taste and smell of him.

The deep, compelling needs that consumed her suddenly be-came too powerful. Too unfamiliar. Alarming in their wild inten-sity.

She jerked her head away from Jakob's. Turned her face aside as she panted for breath.

After a moment she felt his legs relax their grip on her hips. He still held her in his arms, but she was trembling so much she might have collapsed if he'd released her. She didn't look at him, but she could almost see the disturbing tension that pulsed be-tween their bodies.

Her hand was still pressed against his naked shoulder. She snatched it away, curling it into a fist she hugged protectively to her body. As her heartbeat slowed a little, no longer thundering in her ears, she realised Jakob's breathing was also ragged.

For several long moments they remained frozen in the same position, neither making any attempt to speak. At last Jakob cleared his throat.

'You were well named, my Lady Desire,' he said hoarsely, a hint of wry amusement in his voice.

'No!' Desire threw him a startled glance, then scrambled out of his reach to the relative safety of the wooden seat opposite him.

'My father desired a child. A child who would live,' she said vehemently. '"Hope deferred maketh the heart sick,"' she quoted furiously from the Bible. '"But when the desire cometh, it is a tree of life." None of his other children survived. It was in gratitude to God's mercy Father named me. Not…not…I am *not* wanton!'

'I never said so!' Jakob exclaimed. 'It is the desire you arouse in others—in me—that I meant.'

'*Desire?*' Desire stared at him, startled and disbelieving. '*You* desire…?'

Her eyes dropped. She had lived a sheltered life for many years, but she still retained a vivid recollection of her mother's account of a wife's duties in the marital bed. Her knowledge of what that might entail had been greatly enhanced when she had arrived unheralded in the stables one day and discovered one of the grooms in an intimate embrace with a maid.

It was the last occasion for a long time she'd ever visited any of the servants' quarters without making sure *everyone* knew about her plans in advance. But the incident had left her with a certain residual curiosity.

Was that…? Was there a greater bulge in Jakob's breeches than there had been before?

Disconcerted, uncertain how to react, she pressed her hand against her lips.

She heard Jakob's rough, disbelieving laugh and her eyes flew to his face.

'Yes,' he said.

'What?' Desire's blush was so intense she was sure it covered her entire body.

'My lady…' He dragged in a lungful of air, and exhaled in a long, disbelieving breath. 'You have discountenanced me,' he declared. 'What can I say?'

'Nothing.' Desire was burning up with mortification. 'You are to say nothing,' she ordered him in a strangled voice. 'Take me to Arscott!' She pointed an imperious finger in an entirely random direction.

'Why? Do you imagine he will satisfy your needs better than I can?' Jakob demanded, his voice suddenly harsh.

'He's my *steward*!' she denied energetically. But she flushed with embarrassment at the objectionable image Jakob's words called to mind. The growing threat of the fire had enabled her to delay giving Arscott a response to his proposal, but soon she would have to tell him she didn't want to marry him. She hoped it wouldn't create an awkwardness in their future relationship.

'You *do*!' Jakob's voice emerged as little more than a growl. 'Are you lovers?'

'No!'

'What then? Why did you flush when I—?'

'I'm…I'm going to marry him!' Desire interrupted, before Jakob could finish his dreadful accusation.

'*Marry* him? When did you decide that?'

'I…it seems a sensible solution.' Desire lifted her head. It was far better for Jakob to believe she'd blushed because she was Arscott's betrothed than that the steward was her lover. Besides, there might be some measure of protection in allowing Jakob to believe she was already promised to another man.

'I'm sure Arscott will be an excellent husband,' she said, putting as much conviction into her voice as she could.

'Have you tried him?'

'*No!*'

'Then how do you know? What if he fails to rise to your expectations after the knot has been tied?'

Desire gasped. 'You are crude and unmannerly. You should learn to control your tongue.'

'You should learn to control your eyes.'

Desire gripped her hands together and locked her gaze firmly on her lap. Not because she was following Jakob's advice. She'd temporarily run out of verbal ammunition.

'When is the wedding?' asked Jakob, with heavy politeness.

'It has not…no date has yet been fixed,' Desire replied stiffly.

'Why not? You're available. He's available—and living under the same roof. Why delay even a day? Or are you waiting for his ailing wife to die first?'

'He's not married!' Desire said indignantly. 'I would never consider marrying someone who already had a wife!'

'Hmm.' Jakob gazed at her thoughtfully. 'When did you first take a notion to marry Arscott?'

'That is none of your business!'

'Did he, by any chance, first mention it on Saturday evening, after I was dragged off to Newgate?'

Desire stared at him, startled by the accuracy of his guess. 'How…? I mean, that is none of your business!' she repeated, angry at finding herself discussing such a subject with her abductor.

'It wasn't my business until I was propositioned in a Dover inn,' Jakob muttered. 'If I'd known I was going to get thrown into gaol, nearly burned alive and abused by a hornet-tongued harridan for my pains, I'd have done more to suppress my chivalrous instincts.'

'Chivalrous!' Desire glared at him. 'Hornet-tongued! You're as gallant as…as a *toad*!'

'That may be so. But why would you choose to marry your steward? A man far below you in rank and wealth, when you could have anyone—'

'No, I couldn't,' Desire interrupted him, her voice raw with remembered pain. 'I'm a harridan. You just said so! I can have any man who wants to marry a *fortune*—as long as he's not already encumbered with a wife,' she added as a bitter afterthought. 'That's what you meant, isn't it? That I should buy a young, virile husband? Then pretend I don't notice when he scorns me for a beautiful whore? Or pay him for every night he condescends to lie in my bed?'

Jakob didn't immediately answer. The rowing boat had long since come to rest against the riverbank, and now they were attracting a crowd of curious observers. The sun had nearly set. Soon it would be dark and he knew they were vulnerable. He'd left the iron bar from the prison on Desire's roof. He had nothing to defend them with but the oars and Desire had all but announced she was a prize worth taking.

He manoeuvred the boat back into the middle of the Thames, determined to get them to the safety of Kilverdale House without delay.

He understood Desire better now. She was sitting bolt upright on the wooden seat opposite him, her shoulders braced with pride—but her head was averted. He was sure she regretted her heated, unwary words. He wasn't proud that he'd provoked her into humiliating herself. Despite her determination to stand up to him, it was obvious how little experience she had of the world. He remembered only too clearly how she'd turned her back on him when he'd first appeared on her roof. She'd never learnt how to guard her emotions behind a mask of sophistication. Everything she felt was written in her expressive eyes. Anger, fear, indignation, curiosity…

He had to suppress a disbelieving laugh as he recalled how her eyes had boldly sought for the tell-tale signs of his arousal. In another woman he might have interpreted such a blatant assessment of his condition as a saucy invitation to continue his seduction. Desire, he had no doubt, was simply too naïve to disguise her curiosity.

As she'd already discovered, she aroused more than his curiosity. He found her passionate nature fiercely attractive. She'd fought him with uninhibited vigour outside the boathouse. He'd been acutely aware of her terror. He'd done everything he could not to hurt her. But even then he'd been partially aroused by her unrestrained resistance.

He wanted her. He wanted to transform her resistance into desire. He wanted to feel her supple, passionate body beneath his as he roused her to a state of physical ecstasy. He wanted to grapple with her, feel her arms and legs convulsively gripping him, as he pushed her over the edge.

He tried to suppress the erotic images that crowded his mind. He needed to keep a clear head. He needed to remember that the woman sitting in frigid silence opposite him was more than a passionate, hot-blooded wench. She was also a very wealthy woman. And her fortune made her a target for the unscrupulous.

Chapter Four

Desire kept her back straight and her head up, though she couldn't bring herself to look in Jakob's direction. She was grateful for the gathering twilight. It hid her humiliation. She wished she could curl up into a protective ball like a hedgehog or, better yet, return to the safe familiarity of her garden at Godwin House. She had never felt so alone. So far adrift from all the accustomed securities of her life.

As the small boat cut through the dark waters of the Thames, her thoughts skittered from one subject to another. The probable, heart-wrenching loss of her home. Jakob's kiss. Her household's worry when they discovered she was missing. Jakob's kiss. Anxiety over what she would encounter at the end of this journey. Jakob's kiss...

He'd *kissed* her. She slid a nervous glance in his direction. Her lips still tingled from the amazing feel of his mouth on hers.

He had *wanted* her. Desire still wasn't quite able to credit the evidence of her own senses, but Jakob had bluntly admitted as much.

To her knowledge, no man had ever wanted her before—not like that, as a man wants a woman. So why did Jakob—so full of handsome male grace—want *her*? Desire was sure he could charm any woman he chose into his bed. Why did *she* arouse his lustful instincts?

It was confusing, disturbing—and a little exciting.

Desire threw another nervous glance at him. What would she do if he kissed her again? Or if he tried to do more than that?

She blushed with mortification at his scornful response when she'd claimed she was to marry Arscott. It was easy for Jakob to sneer. He did not understand the complications of her situation.

Even before the events of Saturday, Desire had known she needed a husband. At thirty she was well past the age of marriage. But it was hard to find an honourable husband when she had no one to negotiate on her behalf. Her father had not meant to leave her so unprotected. Unfortunately the man Lord Larksmere had appointed as Desire's guardian had died in an accident less than a year after the Earl's own death. By then Desire had already been over twenty-five and Arscott had been Lord Larksmere's trusted steward for years. Life had continued in Godwin House much as usual. The only problem was Desire's lack of a suitable husband.

If she'd had more knowledge of the world—or if she'd considered herself a more attractive bargain—she might have found it easier to tackle the difficulty herself. But she knew it was her wealth that possessed the greatest appeal and she lacked the experience to distinguish between a fortune-hunter and genuine suitor. If she made the wrong choice, the consequences would be devastating. Marriage to Arscott would be a practical solution to the problem, but she could not bring herself to take such a course.

So how was she to find a trustworthy husband, one who was not disgusted by her scars and who might even, as Jakob apparently did, find her in some limited way attractive? Perhaps a man who resembled Jakob in some other respects as well—she threw a swift glance at his broad shoulders as he plied the oars—but a man with a much more tractable nature. And definitely not a man who was both a mercenary and an escaped prisoner.

Despite her perilous situation, Jakob's kiss had inspired her with a small flicker of unfamiliar optimism for her future. For years she had been convinced that no young man could ever find her personally attractive. Yet from virtually the first moment he'd appeared on her roof, Jakob had paid little heed to her disfigurement. He had argued with her, fought with her and kissed her without any reference to her appearance. She had been so certain—and so afraid—that all young men would be of the same opinion as the Duke of Kilverdale and his fashionable friends. What if she'd been wrong? What if she could find a man who would—?

The boat bumped gently against a landing stage.

A flare of anxiety jolted Desire from her musings. In only a few short minutes she would be face to face with the Duke. She lingered in the boat as Jakob tied it up, taking the opportunity to grope for the river-gate key in the dirty water at her feet.

'Is there no one else you can call upon for assistance?' she asked, hating the unsteadiness of her voice. 'Does it have to be Kilverdale?'

'I know very few people who live near London,' Jakob replied. 'And Kilverdale is the only one who won't be disconcerted by our unconventional arrival. But he didn't reply to the message I sent him from Newgate, so he probably isn't here, and you won't have to face him at all.'

Kilverdale's failure to respond to Jakob's message fitted perfectly with Desire's opinion of the ramshackle Duke, but her mood marginally improved at discovering he might not be home.

'I don't suppose he'd be disconcerted if you turned up with a band of minstrels, a dancing bear, and half a dozen whores and declared you were going to have an orgy,' she said, allowing Jakob to help her out of the boat.

Then she became aware of his startled appraisal, and wished her impetuous words unsaid.

'I think he would,' Jakob said after a considered pause. 'I'm not generally known for travelling with musicians and dancing bears.'

He paused again, leaving Desire rather sick at the implications of what he *hadn't* denied.

'As to holding an orgy,' he added, a few heartbeats later, amusement in his voice, 'it would be damned inconvenient hauling half a dozen wenches with me everywhere I go. One is quite enough trouble!'

'Oh.' Desire flushed in the darkness. She wondered if *she* was the one who caused him trouble or…was he talking about another woman? Was he *married*? The idea had never occurred to her before. She faltered, then rallied. 'It wasn't *your* conduct I was commenting on!' she said pertly.

'I know.'

Before she realised what he was doing, Jakob slipped his arm around her waist and drew her closer to him.

'What did he do to you?' he murmured against her temple.

Desire was too shaken by his action to reply. She didn't understand Jakob, or what he wanted with her. It was foolish to find his gentle embrace and quiet question comforting. He was her *abductor*! An escaped prisoner who had forcibly removed her from her own house. So why did she have an almost irresistible urge to lean against his tall, powerful body? And why did she have the strangest feeling that, if she did so, he would support her? It was only a silly fantasy. With an effort she gathered her composure and stepped away from him.

'It's not important,' she said, her voice sounding spiky to her own ears.

'Very well.' Jakob took her hand and drew it through his arm. 'Then let us go and beard the lion in his den,' he said.

'It's you that's the lion,' Desire replied, with forced brightness. 'Your mane is real.'

Jakob laughed, and she sensed him shake his head in the darkness. 'My mane, like the rest of me, is in a disreputable state,' he declared. 'I need a bath.'

Their arrival at Kilverdale House caused consternation. The porter clearly didn't recognise Jakob. He was all for having the disreputable, soot-grimed—and, in Jakob's case, half-naked—visitors thrown off the property. Desire hovered behind Jakob's broad back, fearing at any moment to hear the Duke's arrogant voice. Instead it was the Duke's steward who appeared.

'Colonel Balston!' he exclaimed, after staring at Jakob for a few seconds. 'You're safe! I heard the commotion, I thought his Grace had returned. Stand aside, Dawson,' he added peremptorily to the porter. 'Come in, sir! Come in! His Grace has been looking for you all over.'

'Is he here?' Jakob asked.

'No, sir. He arrived earlier this afternoon—briefly. Demanding to know if you were here. Then he read a message that had been delivered in his absence. It was from you. His Grace expressed…er…agitation.' The steward cleared his throat. 'And left again.'

Desire took note of only one thing the steward said—the Duke was not present. Her relief was so profound her legs turned to water. She clung to Jakob's arm, only half listening as she regathered her composure.

'*För bövelen!* Why the hell can't he stay in one place for more than five minutes at a time?'

'His Grace was very anxious about your welfare,' said the steward, looking disapprovingly at Jakob's naked torso.

'He would have contributed far more to my comfort if he'd been at home on Sunday,' Jakob grumbled. 'Well, never mind. I dare say he'll turn up eventually. He usually does.'

'*Colonel Balston?*' said Desire suspiciously, finally catching up with the conversation.

'My lady?' Jakob swivelled on his heel to look at her. A flicker of concern replaced the impatient expression in his eyes.

'Henderson,' he addressed the steward. 'Send for the housekeeper at once. Her ladyship must be waited upon immediately.'

'Yes, sir!' Henderson sent a hurrying minion to perform the errand. 'I'm sorry, sir. My lady, please come this way.' He led them into a large room leading off the hallway. 'Your arrival took me by surprise. I apologise for my lack of hospitality. Please.' He gestured for Desire to sit in a high-backed chair, carved with Kilverdale's coat of arms. 'His Grace would wish you to have everything needful for your comfort.'

Desire hung back, disconcerted by the steward's effusiveness. Jakob had not introduced her by name—perhaps deliberately to protect her reputation. Her morale had already begun to lift when she'd discovered that the Duke wasn't at home, and improved even more when she hadn't recognised Henderson. It seemed likely that Kilverdale kept entirely separate staff in his houses in Putney and Sussex. As long as none of the other servants recognised her, and she managed to leave before the Duke returned, there was a good chance no one would ever need to know of her ignominious adventure. Especially since Jakob seemed willing to be discreet.

'Comfort,' she said suddenly, recalling the last thing Henderson had said. 'We must tend to your hands,' she told Jakob, deciding for the moment to set aside the peculiar matter of his changed name. 'Do you have any salves for burns?' She turned back to the steward. 'Are any of your household skilled in the care of wounds?'

'N-no, my lady,' Henderson stammered, obviously disconcerted at being addressed so briskly by his unknown and tattered guest.

'Then I need lights,' Desire announced, heading for the door. After all the upsets of the day it was reassuring to feel once more in control. 'At once, if you please,' she added, when the steward simply stared at her. 'There are a number of plants which can be beneficial to burns. I must see if any of them grow in the gardens here. I need light!' she repeated firmly, when Henderson still didn't respond.

'Light! Yes, my lady, of course.' He finally stirred into action, calling for the porters to provide illumination for her. 'I'm sorry, sir. I did not realise you had been hurt,' he apologised to Jakob.

'There's no need to make such a fuss,' Jakob growled. 'My hands will do very well without any plants.'

'It is you who will be making an unnecessary fuss if you do not let me tend to them,' Desire retorted. 'Are you afraid the salve will sting? I will be very gentle, sir.'

Jakob exchanged a speaking glance with the steward as they followed Desire into the hall. By now the housekeeper had appeared on the scene, but Desire made it clear she would do nothing to improve her own comfort until she had found the appropriate plants and made a salve for Jakob's hands.

Jakob had little option but to follow her into the garden, along with a small cavalcade of light-bearing servants. It was soon apparent that Desire was used to running her own household. Even covered in grime, with her hair hanging around her shoulders and her skirt in tatters, she inspired respectful—if somewhat bewildered—service from the Duke's servants.

When Desire had located the plant she needed she retired to the kitchens. She ground up the roots herself and mixed the paste with butter to make a salve for Jakob's burnt hands. She gave it to him, and only then allowed herself to be escorted to a more suitable chamber to seek her own comfort.

An hour later, Desire emerged from her guest chamber, dressed in the housekeeper's best clothes, to discover Kilverdale's steward hovering in the gallery.

'The Colonel is waiting for you in the Great Parlour,' he said. 'May I show you the way?'

'Yes.' Desire followed him, her nerves on edge. She wasn't sure if she was ready to face Jakob again so quickly, but she was hungry—and he had promised to feed her. She focussed on that mundane thought to keep the worst of her apprehension at bay.

Jakob stood as she entered the room. She took one look at him and her breath caught in her throat. He was magnificent. He wore a coat of black brocade which fell halfway down his thighs. A flamboyant knot of black satin ribbon at the top of his right sleeve emphasised the breadth of his shoulders. On his legs he wore black breeches trimmed with more ribbon and black silk hose. His coat sleeves were fashionably short to reveal an abundant fall of snowy lace to his wrists. At his throat folds of crisp white lace contrasted dramatically with the dark grandeur of his coat. There were silver buckles on his shoes and an impressive row of silver buttons on his coat. He wore his own hair, despite the current fashion for extravagantly long, curled wigs—but Desire could hardly blame him for that vanity. Many country maids who grew and sold their hair to the wigmakers would be jealous of Jakob's glorious locks. Even now, when his hair was still damp from the thorough washing he had given it, it fell around his shoulders in shimmering waves of gold.

He looked the very image of a rich nobleman. Only the red rims of his eyes—still suffering the effects of too much exposure to heat and smoke—suggested he hadn't spent the day lounging at his ease.

Desire stared at him, overwhelmed by his magnificent, aristocratic appearance. Despite his luxurious attire and handsome face, only the very unobservant would mistake him for a fop. He moved with the controlled power and virile grace of a male in the prime of his life. She swallowed, remembering all too easily the sleek, powerful muscles hidden beneath the lace and brocade.

He smiled a little quizzically and she realised, too late, that she'd been gawping at him like an awestruck serving wench.

She flushed and bent her head, instinctively turning her scarred cheek away from him. Her fingers locked nervously in her borrowed skirt. For once in her life she yearned to wear the silks and satins suitable to her rank. It was one thing to opt for comfort and practicality when she was working in her garden— but to present herself to the most handsome man she'd ever met in the over-large, dowdy clothes of the Duke's housekeeper was excruciating. The maid had laced the bodice as tightly as possible, but it was still far too large.

Jakob looked like a prince. She—as he had so aptly pointed out when they were still in the boat—looked like a badly dressed washerwoman. An ugly one to boot.

She heard the soft rustle of expensive fabric as he came to stand in front of her. She stared down at his row of silver buttons and those shiny oval buckles on his shoes, incidentally giving herself another good look at her ugly brown woollen skirt. She hated brown. Brown was so dingy. She wished the housekeeper had a taste for blue—or even red. Anything but this sad colour.

'Look at me,' said Jakob.

She started at his soft command. He was very close to her. Her embarrassment mingled with strange nervousness. She couldn't swallow. Her throat was too dry and tight.

'Desire, look at me,' he repeated compellingly.

She flinched at the sound of her name—and the echo of cruel words spoken years earlier. She still didn't raise her head.

'What is it?'

'Don't…' she whispered, swallowed and tried again. 'Don't call me that.' She finally lifted her chin, but only to stare at the lace of his cravat. She had not yet found the courage to meet his eyes.

'Desire? Does my impertinent use of your name offend you?' He sounded mildly amused. 'After all we've shared, your ladyship, such formality seems a little redundant.'

'No—' Desire broke off, unable to explain why it disturbed her when he used her given name.

'Or perhaps you're offended that a lowly soldier should gaze with desirous eyes upon a lady of quality,' he murmured provocatively.

Desire jerked away from him, but he seized her shoulders in his hands and turned her back to face him.

'You may curse me and kick me and try to browbeat me into obeying your orders—but don't turn your face from me in shame,' he said.

'I am *not* ashamed!' Desire cried, finally lifting her head to meet his eyes.

It was a shock to look into his face at such close proximity. He had shaved and washed away all the grime of the fire. Now he reminded her of the impossibly handsome man who'd first appeared on her roof.

'Then don't hide from me,' he growled. 'Damn me to hell for inconveniencing you—but don't hide!'

'*Inconveniencing* me?' Desire gasped. 'You *abducted* me!'

'I rescued you. A little gratitude would not go amiss.'

'Gratitude? You expect me to thank you for tying me up, manhandling me—'

Jakob kissed her.

His firm mouth stifled the rest of her indignant outburst. This time Desire hadn't seen it coming. She was startled into complete immobility. Before she'd had time to react he lifted his lips from hers.

'Half the household is probably listening at the keyhole,' he murmured, briefly resting his forehead against hers. 'I'm sure you don't want everyone to know I dragged your skirts up to your—'

Desire made a high-pitched, closed-mouth hum of protest in the back of her throat.

Jakob grinned and lifted his forehead away from hers.

She glared at him, and turned her head to give a pointed glance at one of his hands, still gripping her shoulder. Then she frowned. He grasped her firmly between his long, strong fingers and his thumb, but he held his palm clear of contact with the fabric of her bodice.

'Why are your hands not bandaged?' she demanded. 'Have you applied the salve?'

'Not yet. I thought you would prefer to tend to me yourself,' he replied. 'So that you could assure yourself it had been done properly,' he added blandly.

Desire grabbed one of his arms and turned his palm up towards her. He'd cleaned away the soot and dried blood, but it still looked raw. She was sure he was in considerable discomfort.

'You are a fool. Where is the salve?' she demanded, channelling the nervous excitement aroused by his unexpected kiss into her exasperation with his foolish behaviour.

'There.' He nodded in the direction of a small table. Desire saw the small pot of salve she had prepared as well as several strips of clean linen. She was slightly mollified by the sight. And a little flattered that he had waited for her to care for his hurts.

She pushed that sweetly insidious thought aside and dragged Jakob over to the table by her hold on his sleeve. When he was safely seated in a high-backed chair she fetched a stool and planted it on the floor in front of him.

'By rights, lady, you should have the chair and I the stool,' he observed.

'It's a little late to worry about protocol, don't you think?' she retorted. 'Give me your right hand.'

He held it out to her and she gently folded the lace ruffles out of the way.

'You should not have worn such fine lace,' she scolded him. 'I'm going to tie it back with a couple of bandages—otherwise the butter may spoil it.'

'You are thoughtfulness personified,' he said lightly. 'But it's not my lace—so I'm not much bothered by its fate.'

'Whose?' Desire looked up from tying a strip of linen round his forearm. 'The *Duke's*!' she gasped, realisation coming to her. 'You're wearing the Duke's clothes? Take them off at once! If he comes back and finds you in them—!'

Jakob laughed. 'Are you afraid he'll have me hanged for a thieving rogue?' he teased her.

Desire's initial panic subsided. She stared at Jakob through narrow, assessing eyes, once more reminded of how little real knowledge she had of her abductor and his dealings with the Duke of Kilverdale.

'What is your connection to the Duke?' she asked.

Jakob smiled, a little crookedly. 'Not one that will recommend me to you, I fear,' he said ruefully.

'What?'

'He's my cousin,' said Jakob.

'Cousin?' Desire stared at him blankly. 'How can that be? I never heard his Grace had such a cousin as you. How…?'

'His mother was sister to my father,' Jakob explained, watching Desire's face for her reaction.

'His mother…' Desire frowned, mentally recreating the Duke's family tree. There had been a time when she had been quite familiar with it. 'She was the daughter of Viscount Balston…*Balston*?' She stared at Jakob as she made the connection. 'The Viscount was created Earl of Swiftbourne for his part in King Charles's restoration to the throne,' she said slowly. 'But, as I recall, Swiftbourne's oldest son and *his* son both died during the wars, leaving the new Earl without heirs. Who are you, sir?'

'Your knowledge of my family is extensive.' Jakob sounded surprised. 'Not complete but…how come you to know so much about it?'

'I don't,' Desire denied quickly. 'It was Kilverdale's family I was interested in, not…well, never mind.' She bent her head over her task, carefully tying back the lace from Jakob's hands.

She reached for the salve and began to stroke it delicately over his sore palms. She heard his slight intake of breath and caught her lower lip between her teeth as she concentrated on touching him even more gently. At last the task was done and she wrapped the protective strips of linen around his hands and fingers.

She sat up straight and looked at Jakob. She saw he was watching her intently and instinctively lowered her eyes. Then she hastily looked up again in case he should accuse her of hiding.

He smiled briefly, but his gaze remained strangely intent.

'Swiftbourne had two sons,' he said quietly. 'The oldest re-

mained in England, but his second son—my father, James—
forged a career for himself in Sweden. Like Kilverdale, I am one
of Swiftbourne's grandsons.'

'One of them?' Desire said thoughtfully. 'Is your father still
alive?'

'No.'

'I am sorry to hear that,' she said, briefly but sincerely. 'Do
you have brothers?'

'One. He's younger than me,' Jakob replied, pre-empting her
next question.

'Ah.' Desire stared at him. 'If everything you have said is true,'
she said slowly, 'then it would appear you are not only a soldier,
an abductor, an escaped prisoner—and God knows what else!—
you will also be the next Earl of Swiftbourne.'

'If I outlive my grandfather,' Jakob agreed.

Chapter Five

Desire gazed at Jakob for several long, disbelieving moments. He smiled a little quizzically, but did not otherwise seem disturbed by her intense scrutiny.

At last she dragged in a deep, indignant breath.

'If you are who you say you are—and I have no proof of that!—then what did you mean by sneaking on to my roof like a common thief?' she demanded. 'And taking orders from that...that *dead* man?'

'He wasn't dead when I took his orders,' Jakob replied calmly.

'He was...' Desire tried to think of a suitable term of abuse for the man who'd died in her lavender.

'Yes, he was,' Jakob agreed quickly, obviously trying to forestall any further observations she might make about the dead man.

'Has your grandfather disowned you, that you've been obliged to stoop to such—'

Jakob put one of his bandaged hands over her mouth. He held her shoulder steady with his other hand. His action took Desire completely by surprise.

'Lady, I know you have little reason to think well of me,' he said softly, 'but it would be to your advantage to be a little more discreet.'

Desire seized his forearm and tried to drag his hand away from her mouth. He was far from hurting her, but she was outraged by his attempt to silence her. She felt the steely sinews beneath the fine lace. She knew she couldn't force him to move his arm. She strained her neck as far back as she could instead, in a determined attempt to free her mouth.

He released her, apparently amused by her obvious annoyance. But his posture became noticeably more wary.

'*Discreet?*' she exclaimed. 'You want *me* to be more discreet? You're the one who—'

Jakob threw up one bandaged hand. 'A truce, lady!' he exclaimed. 'I'm hungry, and you must be too. May we at least call a truce until after supper?'

Somewhat to Jakob's surprise, but definitely to his relief, Desire acquiesced to his proposed truce. Rescuing her was turning out to be more complicated than he'd anticipated. When he'd first hauled her off her roof he'd thought she would be safe in Putney. He'd also hoped he could leave her there while he dealt with the problem of who had *really* ordered her abduction. That clearly wasn't going to be possible. And his connection to Kilverdale added another layer of difficulty. Jakob didn't know exactly why Desire held his cousin in such abhorrence, but it might make it harder to convince her of the truth of his story. He wouldn't even attempt to explain his part in the attempt to abduct her until he'd won a little more of her trust.

In the meantime, he was pleased to see that she had a robust appetite. It partially compensated him for the annoyance he felt when she turned her face away from him. It also exasperated him to see her wearing the housekeeper's over-large clothes. He knew she had a trim waist—he'd had his hands on it more than once—but the stiff boning of the housekeeper's bodice held its shape so stubbornly Desire appeared to be with child.

He frowned, wondering where he could obtain more suitable garments for her. All his knowledge of women suggested they felt at a disadvantage if they were not dressed at their best. It might irritate him when Desire turned her face from him, but he understood why she was wary of showing her scars to others. There was nothing he could do about her face, but he hoped that if she didn't have to worry about looking pregnant every time she sat down she might feel a little more confident about meeting new people. Although Desire didn't know it yet, Jakob couldn't see any help for it—until this business was satisfactorily resolved she would be meeting a lot of new people.

'Why are you scowling?' she asked suddenly. 'Don't you eat mutton in Sweden?'

'We have to do something about your clothes!' he announced, following his own train of thought. 'Was that the best you could do?'

'The housekeeper isn't the same shape as me.' Desire looked down at her oddly protuberant stomach. She touched it experimentally, as if she didn't really think it was part of her—which it wasn't. Then, to Jakob's astonishment, she started to laugh. Her laughter made the false stomach wobble—and that made her laugh even harder.

Jakob glared at her, somewhat put out because he'd been feeling sorry for her and now he felt like a fool for his concern.

'Oh, don't…don't…' Desire gasped, between gusts of laughter. 'Don't look so disapproving. Just because you look like an angel…'

'I *what*?'

'You know you do.' Desire wiped her eyes, sounding far more relaxed than she had done earlier. 'If I must not hide my face from you, you cannot deny that truth either.'

'That I look like an *angel*?' Jakob demanded, strangely unsettled by her claim.

'You can't deny it,' Desire repeated, her composure regained.

'I'll not deny I'm not displeasing to the eye,' Jakob conceded warily.

'Not displeasing…?' she mocked gently. 'You are beautiful, and well you know it.'

'Pale hair is unusual in England—that's all,' Jakob countered edgily, increasingly uncomfortable with the subject. 'It isn't so in Sweden.'

'Then Sweden is a land full of mortal men who look like angels?' Desire queried, raising her eyebrows. 'I've never heard that before.'

'I do not look like an angel!' Jakob thumped his fist unwarily on the table, then winced. '*Heliga guds moder!* I am a soldier!'

'Did not Jacob spend an entire night wrestling with an angel?' Desire retorted, undisturbed by his anger. 'I see no contradiction in the fact that you have the face of an angel and the body of a warrior. No doubt you often take advantage of your…advantages.'

'My advantages?' Jakob repeated, seeing the faint blush creep up Desire's neck as she gave an inordinate amount of attention to a dish of roasted pigeons. 'In what way do you consider it to my advantage that I have the face of an angel and the body of a warrior?'

'It is obviously very necessary for a soldier to have the skills of a warrior,' Desire said, frowning severely.

'And my…er…angel face?' Jakob's lips twisted a little as he said the words out loud, but he was far too interested in Desire's reply to coddle his own sensibilities.

'Useful for deceiving the enemy,' she said energetically. 'As, in fact, you deceived me the first time I saw you. If I hadn't mistook you for an angel, I would never—'

'You *what*?' Jakob had received many compliments about his handsome face—and the occasional insult. But no one had ever before mistaken him, however briefly, for a real angel.

'You really thought I was an angel?' he said incredulously. It seemed to be out of keeping with Desire's usually down-to-earth personality.

She blushed and glanced away. 'It was the fault of the sun,' she mumbled, obviously embarrassed. 'It made you glow all over…all golden. Just like an angel. But as soon as the sun stopped shining on you, you looked like a mere man,' she added with spirit. 'And then you turned out to be *worse* than a mere man. In fact, you—'

'Yes, very well,' said Jakob hastily. 'Let's not discuss that now.'

He remembered how at the time he'd been surprised by Desire's initial reaction to his sudden appearance on her roof. She'd stared at him as if he were a ghost. He'd even wondered if she'd lost her wits. At least he now had an explanation for her strange behaviour.

And she thought his face and his warrior's body were advantages to him. He'd seen how her eyes had strayed time and again to his naked chest and arms as he rowed the boat. He pleased her. His chest inflated with masculine satisfaction at his certain awareness of that fact.

'You don't have to smile—so smugly proud of yourself!' Desire snapped. 'I'll not make the mistake of confusing you with an angel again.'

'I hope not,' Jakob retorted. 'If you treat me as a man, you will find our encounters much more to your satisfaction.'

Desire gasped at his blunt comment. Then her brown eyes blazed with hot indignation.

'Don't mock me!' she said. 'And don't think—because you are beautiful and I am not—that I am flattered to be the butt of such crudity. Other women may fawn over you—but *I* won't do so.'

She stood up and strode over to stand by the window, her back towards him.

Jakob had dismissed the servants once they'd had finished laying out the supper. He was not sure now whether to be glad or sorry for their absence. If they had been present, the conversation would not have got so out of hand, but he was more to blame for that than Desire. He disliked being forced into inactivity when there was so much chaos all around him, so many questions unanswered and so much to be done. He'd relieved his frustration by provoking Desire with outrageous comments; she had fired up so rewardingly, but he didn't want to hurt her.

He rose and followed her over to the window.

Desire stared at the window shutters. She crossed her arms over her chest, but she kept her head up. She felt like a fool. She should never have revealed she'd mistaken Jakob for an angel. Not even for an instant. Nor should she have told him about her intention to marry Arscott. Now he knew she'd been willing to contemplate marriage with her steward, he must believe she was desperate for a husband. No wonder he made fun of her— mocked her with a reference to his manly capacity to satisfy her.

She heard footsteps behind her, but she didn't turn round. He might accuse her of hiding, but she felt more exposed than she had for years. All the safety and certainty of her normal life had been stripped away. She still didn't even know why Jakob had abducted—or, as he put it, rescued—her from London that afternoon.

'You have told me how I appear in your eyes,' he said quietly. 'Some of the ways at least…abductor, lecher, angel…'

Desire jerked her shoulders in protest at the wry amusement in his voice.

'You don't know how you look to my eyes,' he continued. 'So I will tell you. When I first met you I noticed the scars. But from the moment you pointed that pistol at me…I never saw the scars again.'

'You were afraid I was going to kill you,' Desire whispered, blinking back tears. 'No one cares about looks at a time like that.'

'I cared a great deal about the look in your eyes,' Jakob responded. 'It was the only clue I had as to whether you were really going to shoot me.'

'I would have done, if you'd come one step closer.'

'I know. You are a very brave woman. Determined, resourceful—irritating as the devil on occasion.'

Desire sniffed. 'You can't expect the victim of an abduction to be sweet and amenable,' she said, but her defiance was only half-hearted at best. She was too tired and her spirit too bruised to endure another heated conversation.

'You have beautiful eyes, my lady,' said Jakob simply. 'Beautiful hair that tempts a man to touch. Beautiful lips that disrupt rational thought when a man comes too close to them. A shapely body that should be clothed in silk and satin, or, better yet, not clothed at all. This is what I see when I look at you.'

Desire gasped and covered her face with her hands. No one had ever before told her that any aspect of her person was beautiful. She had never expected to hear such words from Jakob. A sob rose in her throat. She felt his touch on her shoulder and pulled away from him, humiliated that she was about to cry in good earnest. She ran past him and out of the room, past several startled servants, heading for the sanctuary of her temporary bedchamber.

The house was dark and still when Desire tiptoed to her door. She hesitated a moment, building up her courage for what she was about to do. Until Jakob had forcibly taken her from Godwin House she had never left the shelter of her home without an escort. The thought of making her own way back to the Strand was a daunting one—but she did not see that she had any option.

She still had no idea why Jakob had abducted her, but discovery of his true rank—if he'd been telling the truth—did not necessarily make her situation any more secure. It was only eighteen months earlier that the Earl of Rochester's men had seized an heiress from her coach. It was true that Lord Rochester had been consigned to the Tower for a few weeks but, according to gossip Arscott had heard, the Earl had not lost the King's favour. Arscott had rather cynically suggested Rochester had not been punished for attempting the abduction—but for bungling it. The King had even made Lord Rochester a Gentleman of the Bedchamber a few months later.

Jakob, on the contrary, had not bungled his forced removal of Desire from her home and, from what she'd heard, his grandfather, the Earl of Swiftbourne, was high in the King's favour. Desire did not know exactly what Jakob had in mind for her, but she was sure it would be best for her to escape at the first opportunity. She didn't have either the skill or the strength to row against the current back to London, but she had been trying to mark the hours since the last change in the tide. If she left quickly, she would be able to take advantage of the ebb tide to carry her back to the Strand.

She had picked up the key to the river-gate from the bottom of the boat and hidden it in her pocket while Jakob was mooring the small vessel. Once she was safely back at Godwin House, she could wait for Arscott or other members of her household to find her. Even if the house itself had burned, she could hide in the gardens until they returned for her. She had no doubt Arscott would return to Godwin House as soon as he discovered she was missing.

She bit her lip, wondering if Jakob would accuse her of cowardice for running away like a thief in the night. He had told her she had beautiful eyes and lips that disrupted a man's thoughts…

Nobody…no *man*…had ever said anything like that to her before. Much less implied it would give him pleasure to see her without her clothes…

She would think about it later. It wasn't safe to think about it now.

She eased the door slowly open, listening intently for any sound of human activity. The gallery was dark and silent. She heard nothing and opened the door wide enough to walk through.

'Don't tread on me,' said Jakob, from the shadows at her feet.

She had been about to take a step forward and she was too startled to alter her intentions. She gave a muffled scream as she tripped over his legs and ended up in a heap on the floor beside him.

Jakob grunted as one flailing elbow struck him in the chest.

Desire's heart raced with surprise and alarm. Her legs were

all tangled up in her borrowed skirt. She couldn't get her arms free to push herself away from Jakob. It was too dark for her to see anything except his dark silhouette as he managed to subdue her struggles and roll half on top of her.

'*Get off!*' she panted.

'Only when you promise not to attack me again.' He sounded as winded as she felt.

'I didn't attack you, you numskull!' she flung at him. 'I fell over you—like a stupid great log in my way.'

'Unlike a lump of wood, I'm sensitive to clumsy feet and jabbing elbows!' he retorted. 'Lie still.'

Desire stopped struggling and breathed deeply for a few moments, trying to gain some kind of understanding of the bizarre situation in which she'd suddenly found herself. Both of her legs were pinned beneath one of Jakob's powerful thighs. His upper body rested half on hers and he'd managed to gain control of one of her wrists. It was too dark for her to see his face, but she could feel the rhythmic pressure of his broad chest against her body as he breathed in and out.

Something tickled her cheek and then her nose in a very irritating way. She wrinkled her nose, trying not to sneeze, then realised what was annoying her.

'Get your hair out of my face,' she ordered him. 'It's going to make me sneeze.'

'My angel hair, you mean.' He tossed his head back, presumably in an attempt to fulfil her wishes.

She heaved up against him, outraged by his teasing. He moved his body over hers, so she was more securely pinned, though he did not exert any undue pressure on her softer form, or hurt her in any way.

'What are you doing?' she asked nervously.

'Protecting myself from further injury,' he replied. 'You make a more comfortable resting place than the floorboards.'

'Why are you sleeping on the floor by my door?' Desire demanded.

She'd already guessed the answer to that question, but she was afraid to stop talking in case he—or she—gave too much thought to the unconventional circumstances of their conversation.

'To stop you escaping, of course.' He moved cautiously, managing to prop himself up squarely on his elbows, which were braced on either side of her body.

'You could have just locked me in.' She flexed her arms carefully, wondering if she now had enough room to slip them out of his grasp.

'True. But then you would probably have climbed out of the window. Given a choice of lying on floorboards outside your door, or gravel under your window, I decided in favour of the floorboards,' said Jakob, sounding annoyingly cheerful about the situation.

'I see.'

'There was always a chance you'd behave in a reasonable way—in which case you'd never have known,' he offered.

'*You* wouldn't be a reasonable prisoner,' Desire scoffed.

'On the contrary, I was an extremely reasonable prisoner—right up till the moment I escaped.'

'How…never mind.' Desire muttered.

She was very conscious of the warm, hard length of his body pressed against hers. He possessed a potent masculinity that she found both disturbing and exciting. It was only an hour or two ago he had told her flattering things about her lips and eyes. What if…?

His chest heaved in a great sigh. In an agile move he rolled clear of her, sprang to his feet and reached down to help her up. Bewildered by his sudden action, she allowed him to lead her back into the chamber and close the door behind them.

There was more light inside the room. She'd opened the shutters while she was waiting for the right moment to escape. Moonlight threw a cool, pale patch of brightness across part of the floor and the large, four-posted bed.

Jakob towed her inexorably towards that bed, then picked her up and dumped her on it before she had a chance to object. She bounced back up again, but he grabbed her wrists before she could do any more.

'I'm tired, you're tired—or you should be after such an exhausting day,' he said. 'At least let us have our next argument lying down in comfort. Maybe you'll fall asleep,' he added hopefully.

'Hah!' Desire allowed him to press her gently back on to the mattress. She held her body tense and wary as he stretched out his powerful form beside her. She was ready—but for what, she wasn't sure.

He was silent for several minutes. At last she rolled on to her side, impatient for him to say something. In the moonlight she saw that his eyes were closed, his chest rising and falling in a steady rhythm. He was asleep!

Desire watched him in fascination for a while. Now that she didn't have to worry about him noticing her look at him, she indulged her curiosity. He had a very nice mouth, she thought. And long, straight, powerful limbs that only a little while ago he had used to gently restrain her. He was an enigma to her. She could not remember being so curious about a man in all her life. But since he was asleep she could not waste this opportunity. She began to slide cautiously to the edge of the mattress.

His hand shot out and caught her wrist. Neither his minor injuries nor the bandages had done much to slow his reflexes.

Desire threw a startled glance at his face, but he hadn't even opened his eyes, though his far-too-arrogant mouth had quirked into an irritatingly superior smile.

'Where, precisely, are you planning to go?' he asked.

'How could you lie about on the floor in lace and brocade?' Desire asked, scandalised. 'They aren't even your clothes.'

His smile broadened into a grin. 'Would you have preferred me to lie on the floor naked?' he enquired. 'As I recall, you did order me to remove my clothes earlier. I will, if you will, my lady.'

Desire opened her mouth to make a hasty retort, then thought better of it. Her previous attempts to put Jakob in his place had all been noteworthy for their lack of success. She would give some thought to finding a more effective way of spiking his guns. In the meantime, she would not let him ruffle her temper with his teasing comments.

She relaxed back on to the bed. She was very tired and Jakob didn't seem inclined to do anything…inappropriate. Mainly he seemed inclined to sleep, although she couldn't be sure he actually was asleep—which was a tendency she found particularly frustrating in him.

'If you're planning to go to sleep, you could at least *go* to sleep,' she muttered rebelliously.

He grinned. 'To give you a better chance to escape?' he murmured, still with his eyes closed.

To Desire's annoyance he hadn't looked at her or even opened his eyes once since he'd laid down on the bed.

She huffed wordlessly and pulled her arm out of his grip so she could tuck both hands under her cheek as she lay on her side looking at him.

'At least you haven't taken off your bandages,' she said. 'You should be taking care of your hands—not going around seizing people with them.'

'You're the only person I've seized,' he replied, his voice drowsier than before. 'And apart from your sharp elbows, mostly you're quite soft. Pleasing to the touch—even for a man with sore hands. Though you'd feel much nicer without your clothes, I'm sure.'

Desire swallowed, not quite certain if Jakob was fully aware of what he was saying, or if these were the sleep-hazed musings of a very weary man. She held her breath, waiting to see if he would say anything else. She *liked* being told nice things about herself. It might be foolish, but she couldn't help it.

He sighed deeply, then he turned his head and looked directly at her. She couldn't see his expression in the moonlight, but she knew she had his full attention. She felt herself blushing, afraid he would guess what she had been thinking.

'*Älskling*, don't run from me,' he said softly. He rolled on to his side so he was lying face to face with her, only a few inches separating them. 'I don't know what dangers you may be running into—and I can't protect you if you're not close by.'

'*You're* the biggest danger,' she retorted, although she didn't entirely believe that.

In her mind the Duke of Kilverdale was a much greater threat to her safety. She doubted if *he* would content himself with sleeping in front of her door if he had her in his power.

'The man who hired Potticary is your biggest danger,' said Jakob, startling her.

'Potticary?'

'The man who died in your lavender,' he said.

'His name was Potticary?' Until that moment he had simply been a nameless villain who had invaded her house. 'Someone hired him?' she added, with a kick of anxiety.

On Saturday, Desire had assumed Potticary had been acting on his own behalf. When Jakob had revealed Potticary hadn't intended to marry her himself, her suspicions had focussed on Kilverdale. But now it seemed Jakob was suggesting someone *else* was behind the original attempt to abduct her.

'Who hired him?' she demanded. 'Kilverdale?' Despite Jakob's reassurances she couldn't quite let go of her prejudice against the Duke. 'What about *you*? Who hired *you*?'

'Potticary hired me,' Jakob replied. 'To assist in your abduction.'

'You admit it!' Desire bounced into a sitting position. 'You scurvy, double-dealing—'

'Yes, yes. You've said all that before,' Jakob interrupted impatiently. 'My motives for getting involved were entirely honourable. Though damned if I don't wish I'd left you to your fate. At least I'd be able to get a peaceful night's sleep.'

'Hmm.' Desire chewed her lip. She wasn't used to interrogating criminals. It was important she asked the right questions.

'And you're sure Kilverdale had nothing to do with it?' she said.

'Quite sure.'

'Then how did you get involved?' she demanded. 'Do you make a habit of consorting with thieves and scoundrels?'

'No. I had a unlucky encounter in a Dover tavern. Let us sleep now.' Jakob locked one hand around her wrist, rolled on to his back and closed his eyes.

Chapter Six

His action infuriated Desire.

'Open your eyes and talk to me.' She prodded him in the ribs with her free hand.

'*För bövelen!*' Jakob grabbed her other wrist. Now he held both her arms prisoner. 'What's the point in talking to you if you refuse to believe anything I say?'

'How do I know if I can believe you, if you won't tell me anything?' Desire started to pull away from him, then hesitated, unwilling to hurt his sore palms. 'Let me go. You ought to be taking better care of your hands.'

Jakob sighed in obvious exasperation. 'If you stopped flailing about and attacking me, I would be able to take better care of them. Besides, they are still safely bandaged.' Nevertheless he released her. He relaxed on to his side, propping up his head on his knuckles, so he could look at her.

Desire fidgeted under his scrutiny. She smoothed down her borrowed skirts, even though the gesture probably wasn't necessary in the dim light.

'Tell me about Potticary, and why you abducted me,' she said.

'If you mean this afternoon, I didn't abduct you, I rescued you,' Jakob corrected her. 'Potticary's attempt to take you on Saturday was thwarted by your steward.'

'Yes,' said Desire, glad that she and her household had at least one victory to their credit. 'Arscott was a match for him. And *I* was a match for *you*,' she remembered. '*I* captured you with Potticary's pistol.'

'Very heroic,' said Jakob. 'Do you want to hear my story or simply preen over your martial prowess?'

'I want to hear your story. And I was *not* preening.'

'Very well.' Jakob rolled on to his back and stared up at the bed canopy for a few moments. 'To start at the beginning,' he said, just as Desire was about to prompt him with another question, 'I'd just resigned my commission from the Swedish army and I was on my way to England when, quite by accident, I met Kilverdale at Ostend—'

'Kilverdale!' Desire exclaimed. 'You said—'

'Will you be quiet and listen! My meeting with Kilverdale was entirely accidental and I mention it only to prove that he was not in England when your abduction was first planned,' said Jakob. 'And to offer a witness to the truth of what I say. Or at least to the time at which I first arrived in England.'

'Go on.' Desire remained suspicious, but she wanted to hear the rest of the tale.

'Kilverdale and I crossed to England together in the packet boat, but he was in a great hurry to reach London on business of his own *that had nothing to do with you*,' Jakob continued, emphasising his last few words. 'He took the only horse at the posting inn, leaving me to follow. That's when I first met Potticary. While I was waiting for a horse at Dover.'

'Oh!' Desire was surprised. 'Didn't you know him before?'

'No. Our entire acquaintance lasted only a few days.'

'A few days? But I don't understand. You said he hired you. You don't *look* like a criminal—even if you act like one. How could he have hired you for such a villainous task if he didn't already know and trust you?'

'He was desperate,' said Jakob. 'You should know that neither Kilverdale nor I were travelling with much pomp. In fact, by the time we reached Dover, Kilverdale in particular appeared a most disreputable scoundrel. He'd spent several months chasing all over Europe, and by then he'd managed to lose every single one of his attending servants.'

'He travelled without servants?' Desire was amazed. Her recollections of the Duke had not given her any reason to suppose he could survive without the cushion of luxury provided by his lackeys.

'He started out with servants,' said Jakob. 'But by the time he'd sent one servant home because the man was worried about his pregnant wife, allowed his valet to visit his mother in France, and had to leave a third behind in Italy to recover after he broke his leg, Kilverdale ended up quite alone. He was delighted to see me at Ostend.'

'How…strange,' said Desire, disconcerted by this unexpected description of the Duke. 'I cannot imagine the Duke without his servants. How did he manage?'

'Well enough,' said Jakob drily. 'He took the only sound horse at the inn, stole my best suit of clothes and left me stranded in Dover.'

'Ah.' That sounded more like the Kilverdale of Desire's memory. 'He is thief and a scoundrel,' she said positively. 'Just like you. I suppose that's why Potticary didn't realise you are a…gentleman.' She hesitated over the last word.

'No, he mistook me for a mercenary soldier,' Jakob replied. 'I told him I'd fought with the Swedish army and he assumed I'd come to try my luck in England.'

'So he hired you to help him abduct me?' Desire couldn't believe her ears. 'How could he have made such a wicked bargain with a stranger? And why did you agree?'

'He did not state his business immediately,' Jakob replied. 'But he was desperate. He'd gone to Dover to enlist his brother's aid, only to find the brother was too ill to be of use. Potticary needed an accomplice and the very fact I was a stranger to England recommended me to him. We did not come to the bargain immediately, but approached by degrees as he tested to see if he could trust me.'

'But why did you even listen?'

'I had no horse and I was bored,' Jakob replied negligently. 'And Potticary amused me.'

'Amused you!' Desire remembered her terror on the roof when Potticary threatened her with his pistol and then grabbed hold of her arm.

'He had no conscience,' said Jakob, 'but his mode of conducting business aroused my curiosity. I played him on my line until he revealed what he wanted.'

'Me,' said Desire. She shivered at the thought of her fate being so callously discussed in a public tavern.

'He didn't, at first, reveal your identity,' said Jakob. 'Only that I was to help him take a lady from her home by force.'

'Why didn't you stop him?' Desire demanded, outraged.

'Because I didn't know which lady was to be abducted or who had hired Potticary to carry out the task,' Jakob replied. 'Stopping Potticary would have been easy enough. But discovering the names of the lady and the man who had hired Potticary to steal her was not so straightforward. I did not know until shortly before we arrived at your house that you were the intended victim.'

'But then you should have sent warning to me!' Desire exclaimed. 'It was only by good fortune that Arscott discovered your presence in time and sh—*stopped* Potticary.'

'Great good fortune,' said Jakob.

'If he'd had more warning, he would have prevented all entry into the house,' said Desire. 'That would have been a much better outcome. You are completely at fault. How could you have allowed the abduction to continue?'

'If you recall, I did try to warn you when I first appeared on the roof, but you were too busy quizzing me on my antecedents to listen.'

'You should never have *been* on my roof!' Desire retorted.

'There can have been no purpose to allowing the abduction to continue once you knew my name. You were going to let Potticary take me from the house unopposed. You are worse than a scoundrel. You are a wicked, wicked cockroach!'

'Hmm,' said Jakob. 'Does a wicked cockroach rank above or below a loathsome slug in your estimation?'

'This is not a matter for humour!' Desire was furious. 'Your actions were irresponsible and unkind. Did it amuse you to see Potticary terrify me? You and Kilverdale are well matched.'

'I had no chance to leave Potticary or even to send a message that would not have aroused his suspicions before we arrived at Godwin House,' said Jakob. 'And I wanted to learn the name of the man who hired Potticary.'

'Didn't he tell you?'

'No.' Jakob hesitated briefly. 'But he did tell me that someone in your household would connive at the attack on you. I knew he had an ally within your walls. So even if I had managed to send a warning message before our arrival, I could not have been sure it would not fall into the wrong hands.'

'The new porter,' said Desire, pressing her lips together unhappily. 'Arscott told me he'd been bribed to let you in.'

'Yes,' said Jakob.

'Do you mean we still don't know who hired Potticary to abduct me?' she demanded suddenly.

Jakob hesitated again. 'He never told me,' he said at last.

'Then I am still at risk of another such attempt.' The realisation shocked Desire. 'With a different set of villains. Whoever hired Potticary will just hire someone else instead.'

'Perhaps,' said Jakob. 'If your would-be bridegroom was willing to make one attempt to force you into marriage, I'm sure he's willing to make another.'

Desire swallowed back a wave of apprehension. 'I thought Potticary wanted me for himself,' she whispered. 'I thought it was all over when Arscott shot him and…and killed the other man. And you were taken to Newgate. Who was he?' she added. 'The man who fought with Arscott?'

'He said his name was Ditchly. An old friend of Potticary's we ran into in London,' Jakob replied. 'If Potticary had met him first, I doubt he would have hired me. That was good fortune for you, my lady.'

'Great good fortune,' Desire said tartly. 'But Arscott and I were equal to one attack. I'm sure Arscott will make sure any further attempts also fail.'

'You place a lot of confidence in your bridegroom,' said Jakob. His voice was devoid of expression, but Desire thought she detected a note of criticism.

'It was not Arscott's fault Potticary was able to bribe the porter,' she defended him.

'And he was ruthless in protecting you,' said Jakob. 'Do you find it exciting your bridegroom is so ready to kill for you?'

'*No!* And he's not—' Desire broke off. She was furious at Jakob's insulting suggestion—that she'd enjoyed seeing Arscott defend her so ruthlessly—but a mixture of personal pride and loyalty to her steward prevented her from admitting he wasn't her bridegroom.

'Not what?' Jakob asked.

'Nothing. Be quiet. You are not a gentleman.'

'I'm the man who saved your life this afternoon. Will you find me more stimulating if I kill—?'

'*Be quiet!*' Desire thumped his shoulder in her distress. 'I don't want anyone to die. Arscott was shocked to see the intruders on the roof. He had to do whatever he could to protect me. There were three of you and only one of him.'

'You wouldn't let them hang me from the parapet,' Jakob said.

'Of course not.' Desire drew in a deep, shaky breath as she remembered her household's clamour to take instant vengeance against Jakob. 'It was a horrible, horrible scene,' she said. 'It reminded me of the siege.'

'What siege?'

'Of Larksmere House, by the Royalists.' Desire was momentarily surprised that Jakob didn't know about it. Her mother's determined defence of the house had been quite famous at the time. 'Oh, I suppose you weren't in England during the wars,' she said.

'No. Tell me about it.'

'It was in 1644,' said Desire. 'The Royalists attacked Larksmere House. My father was away, but Mother led the defence for nearly five weeks before Father returned. Arscott was there. He was one of the youngest, but also the best, of the sharpshooters.'

'A sharpshooter!' Jakob exclaimed.

'Mother often said that Arscott was the best sharpshooter she had,' Desire said, with a hint of pride as she remembered how her mother had held firm throughout the long weeks of the seige. 'The Cavaliers barely dared show their faces in case Arscott hit them. And after dark he'd leave the house. He'd make trouble for the Royalists and bring back food for us.'

'A dangerous man,' said Jakob. 'Judging by the events on Saturday, I'd say his marksmanship is as good as ever.'

'He is only dangerous to those who try to hurt his friends,' said Desire, hearing the critical note in Jakob's voice. 'You're a soldier, and by your own account quite unprincipled in your methods. Arscott would *never* have allowed an attempt to abduct me to proceed simply so that he could learn more information.'

'He certainly has your loyalty,' said Jakob. 'And, if I'm any judge, your admiration. Are you looking forward to becoming his wife? Have you perhaps spent the past few years dreaming of the night he will hold you in his strong arms and—?'

'Be quiet!' Desire's face flamed with embarrassment. 'Do not speak of such things.'

'Does that mean your dream of being kissed by him is so precious to you that any mention of it is a violation of your love?'

Desire leapt off the bed and made a lunge for the door. She

was absolutely mortified by Jakob's suggestion. Not to mention appalled by the image his words created in her mind. She'd *never* dreamed of kissing Arscott.

Jakob's arms closed around her from behind. She tried to struggle, but he'd pinned her elbows to her sides. She was too agitated to be cunning in her resistance.

'Has he kissed you?' Jakob asked in her ear. 'Has he held you in his arms and whispered sweet words to you?'

'No! Of course not! How can you be so crude?'

'I'm not crude at all.'

Jakob picked her up and carried her back to the bed. 'I've kissed you,' he said, with satisfaction. 'You liked that. Will you dream of my kiss tonight, *älskling*?'

'You are an impudent, scurvy knave! What are you going to do with me?' Desire hammered his shoulders with outraged blows.

She felt him shake with silent laughter.

'That is a very provocative question.' He put her on the bed, following her gracefully down on to the mattress. 'What would you like me to do with you?'

Desire found herself lying on her back, with Jakob close against her right side. His hand rested on the bed on the opposite side of her. The cage of his arm prevented her from easily escaping the intimate contact.

'I don't want you to do anything to me!' she exploded. She struggled to free her arms, intent on striking him again. 'You are a vile, disgusting leech.'

'I think you mean lech,' he said helpfully.

'I mean a vile, bloodsucking creature found in the stinking mud of a corrupt pond!'

'Oh, that kind of leech,' said Jakob. 'A most medicinal and appropriate comparison, my lady. I believe it is not the leech that is vile, but the corruption it sucks from the diseased body. I have every intention of removing the corruption from—'

Desire jerked her knees upwards, aiming at his groin.

He'd clearly anticipated her infuriated response. Her movement was only half-formed when he rolled on top of her, pinning her legs to the mattress.

'You dolt! You *toad*! How dare you call me corrupt! You—'

'I did not call you corrupt! Have you ever considered using your feminine wiles to get what you want from a man—rather than simply beating him over the head with insults?' Jakob enquired, lifting himself away from her with deliberate caution.

'Of course not! I haven't got—' Desire flushed in the darkness. 'I would *never* demean myself by pandering to your vanity!' she spat at him.

'I think you underestimate your capacity, *älskling*,' he said softly.

'I…' Desire closed her mouth and swallowed. It had never before occurred to her that she might have any feminine wiles to use. Was Jakob mocking her? Or did he really mean…?

She pushed the question to the back of her mind, unwilling to reveal any further vulnerability on the subject.

'I meant—what are you going to do about restoring me to my household?' she said stiffly, turning on to her side so she could peer at him in the darkness. 'And how are we going to find the man who hired Potticary?'

'Hmm.' Jakob gazed into the shadows, apparently considering the problem.

'What does that mean—"hmm"?' Desire demanded impatiently. 'It is very important to me that we find out who wants to abduct and marry me. If you can't think of any way to find him, I'm sure Arscott—'

'I'd like to speak to Potticary's brother,' said Jakob. 'Though Potticary didn't confide the full story to me, he may have placed more trust in his relative.'

'Well, that does seem sensible,' Desire said, after a moment's reflection. 'You can take me to Kingston tomorrow, and then go on to find the brother.'

'Kingston?'

'I have a house there. Arscott and the others went there today.'

'Ah. But I do not intend to go directly to Dover,' said Jakob slowly. 'In the first instance I must return to London. But you will be safe enough here—'

'I will *never* stay here!'

'Then you'll have to come back to London with me,' he said. 'We'll take the Duke's barge tomorrow.'

'I can go back to Godwin House?' Desire said, suddenly hopeful that she could return home.

'Not to stay,' Jakob warned her. 'But we can look at it on the way.'

'Oh, God, maybe it's burnt,' Desire whispered, terrified of what they might find.

'Maybe It hasn't.'

Jakob leant forward, and she felt his lips brush against her forehead. She had been doing her best not to notice the interesting and, indeed, pleasurable sensations their close proximity aroused in her. Now all her awareness focussed on Jakob. Without being aware of doing so, she sighed.

'Don't fret, *älskling*,' Jakob said softly. 'You may have to put with a little more discomfort, but soon you'll be safely home— if not in the Strand, then at Kingston—and working in your garden again.'

'What does that mean—*älskling*?' she murmured. 'Is it Swedish?'

'Yes. It means "tiresome wench",' he replied, without skipping a beat.

'Tiresome wench?' She lifted her head indignantly.

She couldn't see his face clearly. Since he no longer had her arms pinioned by her sides, she laid her fingertips over his mouth. Just as she'd suspected, the devilish rogue was smiling. Her heart did a little flip at the certainty he was teasing her. She wondered what the word really meant.

'From now on, you must only insult me in a language I understand,' she told him firmly.

He kissed her fingers and she felt a responsive tingle run all the way up her arm.

'*Ach, ja, liebling,*' he murmured provocatively.

'I am not your German sweetheart either.' But her protest was half-hearted—was *that* what he'd just said to her in Swedish? Surely a language closer to his heart than soldier's German?

He laughed softly and rolled them both over. Desire found herself lying on her back, looking up at his shadowy outline as he held himself poised above her. The bed was much more comfortable than the floor had been. She felt nervous, excited—and very unsure of herself. They were not arguing now. Not exactly. Did he mean to kiss her again? Here in the darkness of the bedchamber?

She locked her fingers in the folds of his sleeve. Despite the angry heat with which she had earlier responded to him, it didn't occur to her to push him away. She moistened her lips uncertainly, breathless anticipation fluttering in her throat.

He lowered his head and she felt his breath caress her skin. His hair rippled down on either side of her face, then his lips brushed gently over her cheek. She gasped. In the darkness his mouth moved over her sensitive skin until he discovered her parted lips.

He gave a low hum of satisfaction at finding his goal. He kissed her, then stroked her lower lip with his tongue. Unaware that she did so, Desire uttered a soft whimper in reply. She moved her lips beneath his, in direct response to his caress. She liked the feel of his mouth on hers, and the weight of his upper body pressing her down into the mattress. He slipped his tongue deeper, stroking the inside of her lip. Her heart beat faster. One hand crept up behind his head. She buried her fingers in his thick, heavy hair.

His mouth became more urgent upon hers. Hot and demanding. His tongue probed deeper. Excitement spiralled through her. Her world narrowed until it contained only Jakob—yet her sensual awareness of her body expanded beyond all her previous experience. Her lips tingled with heightened sensitivity. Her heart beat faster. She was filled with hot, pulsing excitement.

She kissed him back, touching her tongue hesitantly, then more confidently, against his. She tried to lick his lip as he had licked hers and he growled deep in his chest. He moved over her more demandingly. His hard thigh pressed between her legs, though her voluminous skirts limited his access. He kissed her cheek, then her throat and neck. She tilted her head back, too involved in the experience to realise she uttered a soft moan of pleasure when Jakob sucked warmly at the sensitive skin beneath her ear, then kissed her throat.

Her entire body throbbed with eager arousal. She clung to him, her eyes open in the darkness, but with little thought except to experience more of the delight he was giving her. One of his bandaged hands slipped down her body, pressing her overlarge bodice close against her waist.

He went quite still. Desire was confused by the change in him. His body had been full of virile urgency—now it was rigidly unmoving. He was *forcing* himself to remain still. Before she had time to comprehend the difference in him, he groaned harshly and rolled away from her.

The abrupt loss of the weight of his body against hers was disorientating. Desire wanted to protest, even as the shocking reality of what had just happened slowly took shape in her mind.

He had kissed her without ceremony, and with more passion than she had imagined possible, even after her experience with him in the boat.

She was stunned. Breathless. Uncertain how to react. She couldn't chastise him. She'd been a willing participant. She trembled in the darkness and heard his quickened breathing as he lay beside her. She wanted to say something. Tell him that, even though she had behaved improperly on this occasion, he must not think he could take advantage of her in the future

But he had been the one to break off the kiss. He had *already* stopped behaving improperly. Perhaps he had no intention of kissing her again. Perhaps he'd been disgusted by the way she'd responded. Had she done something wrong?

Desperate for a little more distance between them, she rolled on to her side with her back towards him. She tucked her hands under her cheek and tried to breath slowly and evenly. She hoped he would think she'd fallen asleep, completely indifferent to his presence—but her eyes were wide open. She was acutely aware of unfamiliar sensations in her body. There was a swollen, un-fulfilled ache between her legs she'd never before experienced. Only with Jakob, in the boat, had she briefly felt something like this before. Was this lust? Was she as carnal in her needs as a man?

She stared into the darkness, confused and anxious, as she listened for the slightest sound Jakob might make.

Jakob lay on his back, cursing himself, Desire and the situation in general. He hadn't meant to kiss her again. He'd intended to explain to her how he'd become involved with Potticary's attempt to abduct her, in the hope that she would then stop trying to escape and they could both go to sleep.

But for all his sensible plans he'd kissed her because…

Simply because he'd wanted to. Because all the time he'd been lying next to her, talking to her, he'd been burning with the need to taste her lips again.

And she'd kissed him back. Inexpertly and somewhat tentatively, but with perfect willingness. His body was still taut with the need to haul her back into his arms and continue the seduction he'd started. He'd been right about her passionate nature. She didn't play coy or coquettish games. Her responses to him were honest and straightforward. When he angered her she told him so. When he pleased her—and he knew damn well his kisses had pleased her—she put her arms around him and kissed him back!

Just the thought of how she'd kissed him made him even hotter and harder, till the need to roll her on to her back, drag up her skirts and bury himself deep inside her was almost painful in its urgency. He imagined the feel of her naked legs wrapped around his hips and bit back a groan.

He didn't dare move for fear that he might act on his fantasies. He stared up at the shadows of the bed canopy, listening to Desire breathe, knowing with absolute certainty that she wasn't asleep and that she was as acutely conscious of him as he was of her.

Tension vibrated between them, so thick and strong the very air seemed saturated with their hot, sensual awareness of each other. He listened—and realised she was holding her breath in the darkness. He stifled a groan that would have been as loud as an explosion in the heated silence.

He could not think of a single jesting comment to lighten the mood between them. He wasn't even sure if he was capable of speech. This was torture of a kind he had never before experienced.

He closed his eyes and tried to compel his body to relax by sheer effort of will. He imagined plunging himself into the icy fiords of his youth. Mountains. Glaciers. Miserable cold marches through rain and mud. Who could have guessed he would one day try to lull himself to sleep with memories of mundane military discomfort?

Desire woke slowly. For a few moments she was suspended in a featureless void which contained no sense of time or place. Blank confusion flooded her when she remembered she wasn't at home. She opened her eyes and gazed at the unfamiliar wall in front of her. Slowly the events of the past few days fell into place in her mind.

She was lying on her side on the bed. The sun had risen. Cool morning light illuminated the chamber. She listened and could hear Jakob's steady breathing behind her. He hadn't left her, and somehow they had both managed to fall asleep.

Agitation fluttered in her stomach when she recalled the dangerously potent tension that had stretched between them in the darkness of the night. She had been acutely conscious of every breath Jakob had taken, every tiny movement he'd made. She hadn't dared to speak, for fear of what her words might precipitate.

In the darkness she'd been convinced he was as attuned to her movements as she was to his. In the grey light of dawn she found that idea much harder to credit. It might be the first time *she* had ever slept on a bed with a man, but it surely wasn't the first time Jakob had slept beside a woman. If he had been paying special attention to her, it was most likely only to make sure she didn't make another attempt to escape.

Having talked herself into that reassuringly pragmatic explanation for the unfamiliar undercurrents she'd sensed between them, she rolled cautiously on to her back. She felt very shy at the prospect of confronting Jakob this morning. She didn't want to wake him by unwarily bouncing the mattress. Fortunately, he didn't stir as she carefully repositioned herself. She rubbed a hand over her eyes and pushed her hair out of her face—then turned her head to look at him.

He was lying on his side, his back towards her. His shoulders were amazingly broad. His legs were so long. Everything about him was alien—different from her. Even his hair, in all its abundant glossiness, was different from hers. She remembered the sensation of heavy, rough silk between her fingers. By contrast, her own hair, though very thick, was much softer to the touch. She knew from observation—and more intimate experience— that his body was lean, hard and powerful. She remembered how his muscles had flexed as he'd rowed upriver. She wished she could look at him again without his coat or shirt.

She rolled on to her side towards him, resting her cheek on her hand as she studied him at her leisure. In the dawn light his hair was pale gold, but it still tempted her like a forbidden, delightful sin.

She was torn between her longing to touch and her fear that

he might wake up and catch her in the act. He still breathed with the unmistakable rhythm of sleep. She edged a little closer and lightly touched a burnished golden curl. Instantly she drew her hand back, watching intently to see if he would wake. He didn't. She moved a little closer. She wanted to slip her fingers through his hair and stroke him like a great cat. Instead she touched a single, enticing strand of gold.

'Don't tease me.' His voice rumbled in his chest.

She started back as if she'd been burned.

'If you mean to groom me, do it properly.' He rolled onto his back and she found herself gazing into his alert, sky blue eyes.

'I didn't...I don't...I thought you were asleep!' she stammered, utterly mortified at being caught indulging her curiosity.

He smiled slightly. 'Not once you'd moved. And I'd prefer to avoid Samson's fate,' he added, a wicked glint light in his eyes.

Desire latched on to his comment as a way of diverting attention from her embarrassing behaviour.

'Do you think your strength lies in your hair?' she asked, surreptitiously edging further away from him.

'No. Do you?'

'Well...I...no, of course not,' Desire replied, flustered. She hadn't expected him to bat the question straight back at her. 'Anyway, I had no intention of cutting off your hair—I haven't got anything to cut it with,' she added as an afterthought.

'I'm grateful for that!' Jakob said. 'Does it please you, my lady?' he added, smiling. He shook his head to make his hair ripple around his shoulders.

She frowned. His teasing made her feel awkward and defensive. 'Vanity is a sin, and you have more than your share of it,' she said severely.

'And you don't have enough,' he retorted immediately. 'Your hair is beautiful too. It would please me to see it loose around your shoulders.'

Desire blushed and looked away, disconcerted by his compliment. She seemed to be thoroughly at a disadvantage this morning.

'You saw it loose yesterday,' she mumbled.

'Wet and full of soot. This morning its natural lustre has been restored.' He reached towards her.

A little shiver of apprehensive excitement tingled through her. He was making her nervous. She didn't know how to deal with him. She had promised herself she would not allow him to play his seductive tricks on her any more—but he was so hard to resist…

The door crashed open and Desire gasped with shock. Jakob immediately twisted to face the intruder.

Chapter Seven

The door slammed against the wall and juddered on its hinges. Desire's whole body jerked with shock at the violent interruption. Her head snapped around to stare at the newcomer.

The Duke of Kilverdale stood in the doorway.

Her heart lurched with alarm, then began to pound sickeningly in her throat. She'd forgotten she was the Duke's uninvited guest.

Kilverdale was an inch or two shorter than Jakob, but his arrogant bearing and magnificent black periwig more than compensated for the slight difference in height. He scanned the room, his hawklike gaze sweeping impatiently over Desire before coming to rest on his cousin. His eyes narrowed as he looked Jakob up and down.

'*Diable!* Are you hurt?' he demanded.

His question surprised Desire. The Duke's voice was harsh and impatient, completely lacking in warmth, but she did not associate him with even this hard-edged concern for another's well-being.

'No,' said Jakob calmly.

For several long moments Kilverdale continued to stare at his cousin. Desire wasn't sure whether to be relieved or offended that he had barely registered her presence. Perhaps he hadn't recognised her. Could he have *forgotten* her? Their brief interaction had had a profound effect on her life. It was a double humiliation to realise how quickly he'd dismissed her from his memory.

Behind him she could see several members of his curious household, many of them craning to get a better view of her and Jakob on the bed.

Horror seized her at being caught in such a compromising situation. With more haste than dignity she scrambled to the edge of the bed and stood up. Her sudden movement attracted Kilverdale's attention. He turned his head to look at her and she felt like a panicked rabbit drawing the eyes of a hawk.

She lifted her chin, defiantly returning his penetrating gaze. She knew the housekeeper's ill-fitting clothes made her appear even more unsightly than usual—perhaps even ridiculous. What cruel words would Kilverdale have to say at finding her alone on the bed with his handsome cousin?

Her hands locked in the folds of her skirt so he wouldn't see them tremble. Would he accuse her of *bribing* Jakob to lie with her?

She saw the moment Kilverdale recognised her. He stared at her for a few moments in unmistakable shock, then glanced between her and Jakob as if he couldn't believe what he was seeing.

Desire's heart beat so rapidly she felt sick. She wanted to look at Jakob, but kept her head rigidly facing forward. She could not bear it if she saw Jakob exchange a glance of crude, hurtful male camaraderie with his cousin. She braced herself for the two men to joke at her expense.

'I was told you were sleeping outside the door,' Kilverdale began, addressing Jakob. Behind him there was a muffled titter from one of his watching household.

Without a backward glance, Kilverdale took another step into the room and slammed the door shut with a deceptively casual gesture. Desire heard a muffled groan from the other side of the heavy oak. She felt no consolation that at least one eavesdropper had received his or her just reward.

'I did,' said Jakob, his deep voice sounding quite unperturbed. 'But this morning her ladyship kindly agreed to examine my hands. There is more light in here than in the gallery.' As he spoke he swung his long legs off the bed and stood, placing himself slightly in front of Desire and between her and Kilverdale.

Desire took an instinctive step backwards so that she wasn't standing quite so close to Jakob. She was glad he was trying to pass off the situation in such a matter-of-fact way, but she was embarrassed by any proximity between them.

Kilverdale's gaze flicked to Jakob's bandaged hands. He frowned. 'What's wrong with them?' he demanded.

'They are a little sore.' Jakob shrugged dismissively. 'Inconvenient, but not significant.'

'He burnt them!' Desire burst out, her overwrought nerves finding outlet in irritation at Jakob's casual response.

'*Burnt* them?' Kilverdale's eyebrows flew up. 'I thought you had more sense than to put them in the fire,' he said, once again exclusively addressing his cousin.

'He *didn't* put his hands in the fire!' Desire exclaimed, indignant on Jakob's behalf. 'He burnt them putting out my skirts.'

'Your *skirts* were on fire?' said the Duke, for the first time speaking directly to Desire. Her heart sank as she saw a well-remembered glint replace the momentary confusion in his eyes.

'My dear coz…' he glanced at Jakob '…I had no idea you are such an incendiary lover. You must share—'

'*Var tyst!*'

'Be quiet?' Kilverdale repeated, anger suddenly throbbing in his voice. 'You want me to be quiet? I've just spent the past day and night searching for your ill-begotten hide through the dregs of London! How the hell did you end up in Newgate?'

'It's a long story,' said Jakob.

'*Diable!*' Kilverdale looked from Jakob to Desire and back again. 'I shouldn't have wasted my time. I'm going to have breakfast.' He walked out, the door slamming once more behind him.

'Worry can make a man bad-tempered,' said Jakob, in the intense silence created by Kilverdale's sudden absence.

'Worry!' Desire said disbelievingly.

'Henderson told us last night that Kilverdale only read the message I sent from Newgate yesterday. I expect he's been searching for me ever since,' Jakob said.

'Looking for you?' Desire stared at Jakob. 'Because he was *worried* about you?'

'How did he offend you?' Jakob asked.

Desire crossed her arms in front of her and turned her head away. The memory was hurtful and humiliating. She couldn't bear the idea of Jakob knowing what his cousin had said about her. When he'd heard Kilverdale's cruel words, would he look at her differently, see her through the same eyes as the Duke?

'Älskling?' Jakob moved towards her.

She stepped back and fetched up against the wall. Before she could duck away he braced his arms on either side of her, resting his knuckles rather than his palms against the wooden panel. He was far too close, confusing her emotions and her thoughts.

She glared at him. 'Stand away!' she ordered, doing her best not to let him see her agitation.

'In a minute.' He frowned down at her, as if trying to divine her secrets. 'Are you hungry?' he asked, after a few moments.

His question took her completely by surprise. She been expecting a more determined interrogation. She stared at him blankly, then realised what he was most likely suggesting.

'I'm not eating with *him*!' she exclaimed vehemently. The idea of sitting at table with Kilverdale was unthinkable. 'I want to leave. Now!'

'You may not be hungry, but I am,' Jakob said reasonably.

'Send a message to Arscott at once,' Desire commanded. She laid her hands on Jakob's chest and tried to shove him away from her. She might as well have been pushing at a block of granite. Jakob didn't budge.

'Arscott?' He frowned at her suggestion.

'At my house in Kingston. I don't know why I didn't think of it last night,' she said impatiently. 'He'll come and fetch me and you will not be troubled with me any more. *Move!*' She pushed against him more violently.

''Will you tend to my hands?' Jakob asked, allowing her to dislodge him from his position.

Desire put her hands on her hips. 'Have you heard a word I said?'

'Yes, my lady.' He smiled faintly, though his amusement didn't seem to reach his eyes. 'We have things to discuss before we leave here,' he said.

'I have nothing more to say to you.' She clamped her lips angrily together.

'No, but I have things to tell you.'

'About what?' Something in his voice caused her to feel a *frisson* of apprehension. For some reason she didn't think he was looking forward to the discussion he claimed he wanted.

He put his hand out to her and she stepped smartly out of his reach. He let his arm fall.

'I'm going to get something to eat,' he said. 'I'll have something sent up to you.'

'I don't want anything.'

'You'll feel better when you've eaten,' said Jakob, with irritating disregard for her stated preference. 'And then we'll talk.'

Jakob found Kilverdale in the small parlour, eating a plate of cold turkey pie. For his comfort the Duke had removed his periwig and sword. His own hair was less than half an inch long, though just as black as the wig he favoured. Without the abundant curls cascading around his shoulders, his lean face seemed even more hawklike.

The Duke looked up as the door opened. His gaze rested

briefly on Jakob, then roved past his cousin, as if he were looking for someone beyond.

'Where's her ladyship?' he asked, an uncharacteristic edge to his voice.

'Upstairs. I've ordered some food to be taken up to her.' Jakob strolled over to sit at the table with his cousin.

The rigid set of Kilverdale's shoulders eased. 'Good,' he said. 'Have some pie.'

'In a minute.' Jakob put the small pot of Desire's salve and some fresh strips of linen on the table, and then unwound the bandages from his hands.

Kilverdale leant across to look at the damage and grimaced. 'Messy.'

'Superficial.' Jakob applied some more ointment to his palms. 'They're already healing. Her ladyship's salve eased the sting.'

'She made it from the plants in my garden,' said Kilverdale, his tone unreadable. 'I've now had a full account of your arrival here half-naked and her ladyship in charred, burnt skirts.'

'You didn't take the time to hear all that *before* you burst in on us?' Jakob said, well aware of his cousin's impatient temper.

'Of course not!' Kilverdale watched as Jakob tried to manipulate a clean bandage with awkward fingers. '*Diable!* You are clumsy, I'll do that.'

Jakob surrendered the bandage without protest. His cousin looked tired. His touch was gentle as he wrapped Jakob's hands, but his eyes were stormy.

'Did you catch up with Athena?' Jakob asked. The last time he'd seen Kilverdale, the Duke had been in a hurry to find their mutual cousin. In April, Kilverdale had gone to escort Athena home from the English convent at Bruges, only to find she'd already left for Venice. He'd spent the summer chasing her all the way across Europe and back again. 'Is she safe?'

'She's to marry Halross,' said Kilverdale curtly. 'At the moment they're both guests of Swiftbourne. Halross blew up his house in Fleet Street with gunpowder to make a fire-break, so they have nowhere else to stay.'

'Do you know how the fire started?' Jakob asked. 'I've heard it blamed on everything from a Dutch baker to French fire-setters. Not to mention God's punishment for the decadence of the Court,' he added drily.

'It did start in a bakery, but the baker isn't Dutch,' said Kilverdale. 'It was an accident. A normal house-fire that burned out of control. Enough chatter!' He finished binding Jakob's hands and banged the pot of salve on the table. 'Why were you in Newgate?' he demanded. 'And what are you doing here with *her*?'

'We're here because this was the only safe place I could think to bring her,' said Jakob, 'that was in rowing distance of London.'

'You rowed with these hands?'

'That's what did most of the damage. I only had a few blisters from the fire.'

'You're a fool.' Kilverdale swore comprehensively in French.

'Not that much of a fool,' Jakob said drily. 'I didn't know when I set out that you and the lady are sworn enemies.'

'I'm not—' Kilverdale chopped off his hasty reply.

Jakob sat back and looked at his cousin. Kilverdale gave his full attention to cutting a slice of pie for Jakob. Jakob had already noted the absence of servants. A sure indication the Duke had not wanted witnesses to their conversation.

Jakob wanted to know what lay between Desire and Kilverdale, but it seemed the Duke was no more eager to enlighten him than Desire.

'It's your fault I was consigned to Newgate,' Jakob remarked.

'*What?*' Kilverdale's head jerked around.

'If you hadn't stolen my clothes and taken the only horse at the inn, I wouldn't have fallen into bad company,' Jakob said.

'It didn't take you long to make free with my wardrobe,' Kilverdale retorted, eyeing the splendid brocade coat Jakob wore.

'Lady Desire wanted me to remove my finery when she discovered it was yours,' said Jakob. 'She seems to regard you as the devil incarnate.'

He glanced sideways and saw a dull flush darken Kilverdale's lean cheeks.

'I just spent the night searching the Clink for you!' The Duke's temper exploded. 'What the hell happened to you?'

Jakob described his first meeting with Potticary at the Dover inn and how that had led to the attempt to abduct Desire on Saturday.

'Her steward killed Potticary and Ditchly,' he concluded, 'and I was sent to Newgate. There was some notion of lynching me from the roof parapet, but her ladyship would not permit it.'

'*Diable!* You are a bigger fool than I ever realised. If you are not in a hurry to answer Swiftbourne's summons—that I understand. But don't *die* to avoid him.'

'I didn't die,' said Jakob, remembering too late that Kilverdale's father had been hanged by Parliamentarians after the Royalists lost the Battle of Worcester. As far as Kilverdale was concerned, his father's death had been murder. An unlawful lynching. It wasn't surprising he reacted so strongly to the possibility of Jakob meeting the same fate.

'I shouldn't have left you at Dover!' Kilverdale thumped the side of his fist against the table. The crockery rattled and a knife jumped over the edge and clattered on to the floor. 'What the hell are you laughing at?' He glared at his cousin.

'The main reason Potticary thought I was the kind of shady character he might be able to hire was because of my association with the disreputable Jack Bow,' said Jakob mildly, referring to the alias under which Kilverdale had been known at the Dover inn. 'If you hadn't left in such a rush, he would probably have tried to hire *you*.'

'To abduct Lady Desire.'

'Yes. Though I didn't know our intended quarry until the day of the attempt.'

'*Diable!* How did you escape Newgate? And why in the name

of God did you then proceed to abduct the lady while the whole of London is in flames!' Kilverdale's voice rose. 'There was no need to prove your ability to succeed where Potticary failed.'

Jakob smiled briefly. 'Despite the determination of both you and the lady to think the worst of me, my intention was to rescue her, not harm her.'

'I *know* that!' Kilverdale shouted in exasperation. 'But does she?'

'We managed tolerably well together—at least until you arrived.'

'True.' Speculation suddenly gleamed in Kilverdale's eyes. 'I was told you were sleeping at her door—but the lady seemed most taken with your charms when I found you in bed together.'

'I *was* sleeping outside the door,' said Jakob. 'Until she trod on me in the darkness as she tried to escape.'

'So, not content with holding her against her will, you set out to seduce her?'

'No.' Jakob's flat denial cut across Kilverdale's angry French muttering. 'I did *not* seduce the lady. Her virtue and her honour are intact.' He held Kilverdale's gaze with his own.

Kilverdale's lips twisted. 'She is a very wealthy woman. Many men would be overjoyed to be caught in a compromising situation with her.'

'You do the lady a disservice,' said Jakob quietly. 'Her wealth is not her most appealing quality.'

Kilverdale's gaze dropped. 'We have still to discover who hired Potticary,' he said.

'We?' Jakob was used to his cousin's impulsive behaviour, but he sensed something more than a restless spirit lay behind Kilverdale's implied intention of helping Desire.

'Did he give you any indication at all?' Kilverdale asked, ignoring Jakob's quizzical expression.

'He didn't tell me directly, but he mentioned a name in my presence,' said Jakob. 'I didn't know who he referred to at the time.'

'Now you do?'

'Yes.' Jakob repeated the name and his suspicions.

'*Diable!*' Kilverdale stared at Jakob. 'Have you told her?'

'Not yet. My credit has been a little shaky with her ladyship. Especially when she found I was bringing her to *your* house. It took all my efforts to convince her it wasn't you who had hired Potticary.

'She thought *I*—' Kilverdale's shock was unmistakable. 'My God.' He rubbed a hand across his face. Jakob saw that his fingers weren't quite steady. 'How could she think that?'

'Why don't you tell me?' said Jakob.

'Tell you? She hasn't—'

'She refuses to discuss you.'

Kilverdale threw Jakob a quick glance, but looked away again before he spoke.

'It was the late autumn of 1660,' he said. 'The King had been back in England for five months. I'd returned from exile in France in June. I was taken out of England when I was three years old—I had almost no memories of this country.' He broke off, shaking his head. 'This is of no relevance.'

Jakob waited.

'Our estates—*my* estates—had been confiscated by the Roundheads,' Kilverdale continued. 'Given to a regicide high in Cromwell's favour. That was fortunate for me!' His hard crack of laughter held no humour. 'Not all Royalists loyal to the King regained their estates, but no amnesty was granted to regicides, so my trustees recovered my principal estates quite easily. Then Heyworth decided to arrange a marriage for me. I knew nothing of the matter till Heyworth informed me I was to play host to Lord Larksmere and his daughter.' Kilverdale's voice rose in remembered outrage. 'The damned Roundheads had murdered my father and stolen everything that was mine, but for the sake of expediency I was to marry the ageing daughter of one of my enemies—because she was an heiress!'

'Hardly ageing!' Jakob said, startled. 'This was six years ago!'

'She is four years older than me,' Kilverdale countered. 'I was twenty, she was—' He dragged in a deep breath and clenched his hands convulsively, then made an obvious effort to appear more composed. 'They visited us in Sussex.'

'I can see why you objected to Lord Heyworth's interference,' said Jakob, after Kilverdale had been silent a few seconds. The Duke's father had named Lord Heyworth as his son's guardian, but Kilverdale had spent all his youth in exile in France. Heyworth, on the other hand, had returned to England in the mid 1650s. For several years he'd had minimal influence on his young ward. Jakob suspected Heyworth's overzealous marriage plans for Kilverdale might have been prompted by guilt at his earlier lack of care.

'He was a meddling old fool.'

'So you rejected the lady?' said Jakob, and received another sidelong glance from his cousin. This was the part of the story Kilverdale clearly didn't relish telling.

'We could leave it at that,' said Kilverdale. He leapt to his feet and took a hasty turn around the room.

'I was half-drunk! I was playing billiards with Denby. Fortescue was there, and a couple of others. You recall how large the bow windows are in the long gallery? The billiard table stands in one of them. From where we were, we could not see Lady Desire and her father approaching us from the other end of the gallery. Denby and Fortescue were twitting me about my match to an aging Roundhead heiress, and I said—'

Kilverdale broke off, his lips twisting as if he'd bitten into something horrible. Jakob waited.

'Larksmere challenged me, right there by the billiard table,' Kilverdale continued. 'My friends laughed and said I couldn't fight an old man, it would be murder. The lady…she begged her father to come away. It was…an ugly scene. They left. There was no marriage.'

'What did you say?'

Kilverdale threw Jakob a fleeting, tension-filled glance.

'I said…' He paused and took a deep breath. 'I said she was

ill named, that she could not arose desire even in a satyr.' He in-
haled again, his nostrils flaring. 'I said that, if I had to take such
an old, ugly, scar-faced wench to wife, I'd need a beautiful whore
in the bed with us to stir my passion—or I'd never be able to rise
to my husbandly duty.'

'Heliga guds moder!' Jakob was appalled at Kilverdale's uncharacteristic cruelty. 'I'm surprised her father didn't run you
through immediately!'

'Feel free to assume his mantle.' In a few quick strides
Kilverdale crossed the room and seized his sword. He tossed
it to Jakob.

'You want me to skewer you to appease your guilty conscience?' Jakob caught the sword automatically. He knew his
cousin well enough to be sure that Kilverdale was bitterly ashamed
of what he'd said, but that wasn't of much value to Desire. She had
been deeply wounded by Kilverdale's words. Jakob was angry on
Desire's behalf, but she needed restitution, not revenge.

'Did you never think of simply *apologising*?' he said. 'Explaining it was not *her* who had offended you? She was as much
a victim of Heyworth's meddling as you were.'

'Would you forgive anyone who spoke so of Birgitta or
Lunetta?' Kilverdale demanded.

Jakob paused, considering his sisters. 'I would probably kill
him,' he admitted.

'Later, I—' Kilverdale began.

Henderson, the Duke's steward, suddenly burst through the
door. Jakob and Kilverdale swung round simultaneously at the
interruption.

'The lady's gone!' Henderson gasped.

'What?'

'She was standing outside the door. I thought she meant to
join you—but then she ran to the front door. She—'

'Overheard me!'

'The river!' said Jakob, cutting across Kilverdale's horrified
exclamation. Under any other circumstances the Duke's appalled

expression would have been comical, but Jakob didn't have the leisure to enjoy it.

He ran after Desire. Kilverdale called out to him. He lifted a hand to acknowledge his cousin's words, but didn't slow his pursuit of Desire. He caught up with her just in time to see her jump from the landing stage into the little rowing boat. The boat pitched and Desire waved her arms wildly, then virtually fell on to the wooden seat. She quickly regained her bearings and pulled in the rope. Jakob made it into the boat just as Desire pushed away from the shore.

'Get out!' She tried to whack him with the oar.

Jakob managed to grab it before she did him any serious damage.

'You don't want to hurt me,' he reminded her.

'I want to fry you in hot oil,' she said through gritted teeth. 'Let go!' She jerked at the oar.

'You've got another one,' he pointed out. 'An oar's almost as good as a pike in the right hands. Have you had much practice?'

'What?' She stared at him as if he'd gone mad. 'I don't want to fight you—I want to row!' She gave another tug at the oar.

'Oh, very well then.' He released his hold and Desire nearly overbalanced backwards.

She righted herself and angrily fitted the oars into the rowlocks. Then she settled herself squarely on the wooden seat, took the oars in a commanding grip, and began to row.

Jakob decided to keep quiet and wait out events. The tide was against them. Through a combination of poor technique and lack of strength, Desire was making very little progress. He assumed that, when her first rage had passed, she would surrender the oars to him.

He'd underestimated her. At first she dug the oars fiercely into the water as if she was vicariously battering the Duke with every stroke—but it didn't take her long to realise she wasn't getting very far. As Jakob watched, her mood changed from anger to determination. She frowned direfully as she struggled to make the boat go where she wanted.

'Don't bite your lip,' he said suddenly.

'What?' Her eyes focussed on him, almost as if she was surprised he was still there.

'You might bite through it.'

'Oh.' She took his advice and continued to wrestle with the oars.

'Don't dig the blades so deep,' he said, a few minutes later. 'You waste effort.'

Desire frowned and adjusted her stroke.

She was breathing heavily and her face was wet with perspiration when she abruptly stopped rowing.

'I shouldn't have run away!' she said vehemently. 'I should have forced that evil-tongued serpent to eat his words.'

'A very reasonable ambition,' Jakob agreed.

'Father tried.'

'I heard.'

'I was so frightened. I thought they would kill him! There were four of them—the Duke's friends!' She slapped her hand angrily against the oar handle. 'They sprawled about—insolent and disrespectful. Hateful long legs sprawling everywhere! They despised us because Father had fought for Parliament. And they were young and strong.'

'Very young.'

'When you were twenty, did you think it funny to belittle a man three times your age and ten times your worth?' Desire demanded fiercely. 'My father was sixty-seven years old when we were guests of the Duke. He was a brave, honourable man—and they treated him like a senile old fool! They had nothing to recommend them but their silk and lace and their cruel, clever little verses—but they despised us. *He* despised *me*.'

Jakob had no difficulty identifying who *he* was. He was sure Kilverdale's antipathy to Desire and her father had been far less personal than she believed, but he judged that now was not the time to say so.

'We knew the King favoured Kilverdale,' she continued more calmly. 'That's why Father considered the marriage. As soon as the King returned, Father bought the Letters Patent of Pardon— to absolve him of anything he might have done against the King during his Majesty's absence—but he still wanted to do everything he could to protect my future. He wanted me to have a *good* husband who would *protect* me.'

Jakob nodded. 'I will seek the same for my daughters— should I be granted any.'

Desire threw him a quick, almost suspicious glance.

'I thought…after that event, I thought that if the Duke and his friends represented the future of England, I wanted no part of it,' she said defiantly. 'Nothing I have heard about the Court over the past six years has made me change my mind.'

'Not all men are courtiers,' said Jakob.

'Some are rude abductors!'

'I rescued you.'

'You are a scurvy, dissembling rogue!' she told him angrily.

Jakob grinned. 'If you don't stop arguing and start rowing we'll soon come to grief,' he told her.

'What? Oh, no—'

A waterman cursed fluently and fended the little boat off with an unmannerly shove of his long oar just before it collided with his wherry.

'A fop and his strumpet quarrelling over command of their flagship!' the waterman mocked them.

'I am not a strumpet!' Desire was still far too angry to be self-conscious. In any case, the disrespectful and frequently foul-mouthed shouts of the Thames watermen had often drifted up to her on her rooftop. She had never before encountered such a fellow at water level, but she knew they often tried to intimidate their passengers. Desire wasn't in the mood to be intimidated, so she just switched from arguing with Jakob to bandying words with the wherryman.

'You don't deny he's a fop, then?' the waterman jeered, jerking his head towards Jakob. 'Soft hands all bandaged, relying on a woman to do the work. Do you use that sword to pare your nails, pretty boy?'

'Don't provoke him!' Desire ordered the waterman, alarmed.

She looked at Jakob, fearful his natural outrage at the waterman's insult might lead to immediate violence. But Jakob's expression was so placid she decided he must not have understood the waterman's thick London accent. Just to be on the safe side, she tried to grab the Duke's sword that, securely contained in its scabbard, Jakob held across his knees.

'Now what?' he demanded, refusing to yield it to her. 'If you want to brawl with the man use your oars—then you'll be evenly matched.'

'I don't want to brawl!' Desire was scandalised. 'I don't want you to stick that sword in him.'

'Why the devil would I want to do that?' Jakob sounded completely exasperated.

'He insulted you?'

'I've heard worse.'

'I thought you didn't understand.' Desire gazed at him in confusion.

'You've used up all your guts to decorate your fancy sleeves,' the waterman contributed, sneering at Jakob.

'I lived a straightforward and well-ordered life before I met you,' Jakob told Desire, ignoring the waterman.

'You *stole* me!'

'I should have left you to burn.'

'Oh, your hands!' Even in the midst of her bad temper, Desire had already realised she would never be able to row all the way back to London. 'We'll hire you,' she told the wherryman, making an instant decision. 'Give him your buttons,' she ordered Jakob. 'You can use the sword to cut them off. They're silver,' she added to the waterman.

'How do I know that?' he asked suspiciously. 'They could just be gilt.'

'Oh, I don't think—' Desire stopped. She'd been about to say she didn't think the Duke of Kilverdale would wear anything less than real silver, but it occurred to her that the boatman might then think the coat was stolen and refuse to accept the buttons in payment.

'Give him your coat,' she said to Jakob. 'That will more than pay our fare back to London.'

Jakob sighed. 'I admire your enterprise, lady, but if we are to hire the fellow I would much prefer to pay with coin.'

'You mean you have money?' Desire was quite astonished at the idea. 'On your person?'

'It's an idiosyncrasy of mine,' he replied. 'To carry a small amount of money when I venture out.'

The waterman laughed. 'I see you aren't as ill matched as I first thought,' he declared. 'Why don't you spend less money on your back and more on hers?' he asked Jakob. 'I've never seen a sadder gown on a wench. She'd do you more honour in a comely dress.'

'My clothes were burnt in the fire,' said Desire. 'It's not *his* fault I had to borrow someone else's.' She accepted the waterman's steadying hand to help her into the wherry. 'His hands were burned saving me,' she added. She wasn't feeling at all charitable towards Jakob, but it wasn't fair to let the waterman think he was nothing but an idle fop. 'And then he rowed me halfway to Putney last night before I found out he was hurt and bandaged his hands. He is a halfwit.'

The waterman grinned. 'It's a common failing of men—so says my wife.'

'She is a wise woman.'

Desire settled herself as comfortably as she could; then, for the first time since she'd run down to the river, she was at leisure to look towards London. While she'd been rowing, she'd done no more than throw quick glances over her shoulder.

There was still a thick pall of smoke over the City.

'It's still burning,' she whispered. 'Oh, Lord, it's still burning.'

She gripped her hands together on her lap and kept her eyes fixed on the column of smoke as the waterman and his apprentice propelled the wherry towards her home. Yesterday she'd had her back to London as Jakob rowed her to safety. Now she was facing the horror. She sat, straight-backed and silent, as the two pairs of long oars dipped in and out of the Thames in practised unison, taking her to a home which might be no more than a smouldering, blackened shell.

At last, after a couple of miles had been covered, she bent her head and put her face in her hands. Her world was in a state of total flux. London was burning. Kilverdale's cruel words rang in her ears over and over again. Jakob was sitting close to her, confusing her with his presence. He'd kissed her and taunted her until she did not understand what he wanted from her—or how to behave with him. She longed for the quiet sanctuary of her garden. A place where she could feel safe from the curious or hostile gaze of strangers. But her garden might have gone for ever.

Chapter Eight

As London grew closer, Desire leant forward in her seat, straining to see what lay ahead. The fierce winds of the previous day had thankfully dropped, but the smell of the fire grew stronger with every sweep of the oars. The surface of the Thames was scattered with fire debris. A thick layer of smoke blocked out the sky. London was still burning.

A gust of smoke at water level caught in Desire's throat. She coughed and the acrid taste of destruction filled her mouth. Deep foreboding filled her. Was Godwin House still standing?

For a moment she closed her eyes, unwilling to see the realisation of her worst fears, but after only a few seconds she opened them again. She *had* to see what had happened to her home.

But from water level, with the smoke hanging so heavily over the river-bank, she could see nothing except the wall that protected the grounds of Godwin House from access by the Thames. Her heart thudded with the effects of fear, smoke and frustration. She half-stood up, prompting an instant rebuke from the wherryman.

'Sit you down!' he ordered. 'Otherwise you'll be swimming the rest of the way.'

She sank back on to the seat, her hands tightly gripped in her lap. She felt sick from more than the smell of smoke. At last the wherry was in line with the watergate. She scrambled on to the first of the river-stairs without waiting for assistance. She didn't hear Jakob exchange a few words with the wherryman before he followed her up the slippery steps.

She grabbed the bars of the gate, peering through them, past the formal gardens to the house…

'It's still standing!' Her relief was so great her knees sagged. She clung to the gate, tears pouring down her cheeks. It was only as the crushing fear for Godwin House released its grip on her that she discovered just how deeply afraid she'd been of losing her home.

But the house still stood. As solid, reassuring and familiar as it had ever been. Laughing and crying at the same time, she fumbled in her pocket for the key to the gate.

'We can't go in now, my lady.' Jakob put his hand over hers, preventing her from lifting the key to the lock.

'Of course we can.' She tried to shake off his restraining grip, impatient to be back within familiar walls.

'Not now. We'll come back later.'

'I don't want to come back later. I'm going in now!' Desire tried to wrench her hand out of his clasp and banged her shoulder against the bars of the gate.

He muttered under his breath and pulled her towards him.

'Stop struggling, you'll hurt yourself,' he warned her. 'I know you want to go home.' His voice softened. 'I'm sorry I can't let you go in now. But if any of your household have returned while you've been gone, your welcoming party will most likely be the death of me.'

Desire was shocked to realise he was right. She had forgotten that he was an escaped prisoner. She stared at him, torn between conflicting impulses. She wanted to go home, but it wasn't safe for Jakob to go into Godwin House.

'You need not come in with me,' she said. As soon as the words left her mouth she felt her happy mood dim. If she left Jakob at the watergate, she would most likely never see him again. Arscott and the rest of her household would be able to protect her from any future attempts to abduct her.

She wished now that she'd behaved differently on the journey back to London. Ever since Kilverdale had crashed into the bedchamber, she'd been distracted by past hurts and injustices. But she should have spent the little time she had left with Jakob talking about more agreeable subjects, rather than ranting about the Duke. It wasn't Jakob's fault he had an arrogant, cruel-tongued cousin. Jakob was the only attractive, truly likeable young man she'd ever met. He'd kissed her and she didn't know why, and now she probably never would. It was very disheartening.

He'd released her once she stopped struggling. She transferred the key into her left hand and held out her right to him.

'Thank you for rescuing me from the roof,' she said, forcing herself to smile, trying to pretend she didn't care she'd never see him again. 'There's no need for you to come any further with me. I'll be quite safe now. As soon as possible I will withdraw my allegations against you. Although I believe you should also ask Lord Swiftbourne to make sure everything is sorted out satisfactorily,' she added. 'I'm not quite sure what will be involved.'

Jakob took the hand she offered. After a few seconds she tried to reclaim it, but he wouldn't release her. Her heartbeat quickened, even as she stared at him in confusion.

He glanced upwards into the smoke-filled sky, as if seeking patience, then grinned at her. 'Do you really believe I'd let you wander around unescorted at such a time?' he asked.

'What?' She tugged on her hand, but he didn't let go. It dawned on her that he *still* intended to drag her wherever he wanted, without the slightest regard for her expressed wishes. She suddenly felt a lot more cheerful, even though her opinion of him underwent a rapid transformation. He wasn't likeable and charming at all. His arrogance was intolerable.

'So where are you taking me now, little dunghill king?' she demanded, lifting her chin. 'I'm not going back to Putney.'

'I thought I'd introduce you to one or two more of my relatives,' Jakob said. 'My grandfather has a house in St Martin's Lane, not far from here.'

'Why didn't you take me there yesterday?' Desire let him lead her back down the steps to the waiting wherry.

'I didn't know if he would be there. Besides, I thought it was best to get as far away from the fire as possible.' Jakob steadied her as she climbed into the boat.

'Oh. That makes sense, I suppose.' Desire brushed her hands over her tearstained cheeks in the only preparation possible before her arrival at Lord Swiftbourne's house.

'Colonel Balston, you're safe!' Lord Swiftbourne's steward clasped his hands together almost as if he was praying with gratitude for Jakob's safe delivery from the fire. 'His lordship has been so worried about you.'

Desire glanced up at Jakob and saw an unmistakable gleam of scepticism in his eyes before he masked it behind a cheerful response to the steward's anxious enquiries.

'His lordship has gone to see the King. He isn't here, but Mrs Quenell and Lord Halross are in the small parlour,' the steward said. 'I'll take you to them. Mrs Quenell will be *so* pleased to see you.'

For the first few minutes the steward was too preoccupied with Jakob to pay much attention to Desire. The news of their arrival had sped quickly through the house and she became aware of curious eyes staring at her and Jakob from various discreet shadows around the hall.

Lord Swiftbourne's heir was naturally of interest to members of his household. One day Jakob would be master here. Desire resisted the urge to seek the protection of the shadows herself. Her natural instinct was always to manoeuvre so that the unblemished side of her face would be closest to any companion. She had done so walking into the house with Jakob, when she had kept her smooth cheek towards him, but now her action left her scars fully exposed to the gaze of strangers. It took all her self-control not to sidle around Jakob so that his large frame provided a shield from unkind watchers. She kept her hands by her sides and forced her expression to remain impassive, trying to pretend that she was listening with polite interest to the steward's conversation with Jakob.

But the steward quickly recovered his poise and turned towards her, casting a discreetly questioning glance at Jakob as he did so. It was almost a repeat of the moment when Kilverdale had belatedly remembered her presence, except that the steward had never met her before and her scars and ill-fitting clothes were the only reason his eyes widened in shock. Desire returned the steward's scrutiny with as much serenity as she could muster.

'Her ladyship has been put out of her home by the fire,' said Jakob.

In the midst of her discomfiture Desire realised that, once again, he had avoided identifying her.

'I was sure my grandfather would grant her temporary sanctuary,' Jakob continued.

'Oh, indeed, sir.' The steward redirected his gaze from Desire's scars to her eyes. 'I know his lordship would wish me to welcome you, my lady. Lord Halross has lost his home too.'

Desire was just about to say her home hadn't been lost when the steward said, 'He blew it up with gunpowder to make a fire-break. Such a noble, generous action. If only more people had been willing to make the same sacrifice days ago, perhaps we wouldn't be facing such a disaster.'

Desire closed her mouth again. It had never once occurred to her to destroy Godwin House to protect other people's houses. Whoever Lord Halross was, he'd already earned her respect.

'Mrs Quenell and Lord Halross are in the small parlour,' said the steward. 'I'll take you to them.'

A few moments later he opened the door for them. Desire was standing next to the steward and she heard his startled intake of breath. She glanced at him in surprise. He was gazing into the room, a slightly disconcerted expression on his face. Intrigued, Desire edged closer to see what had caught his attention.

There was a gentleman sitting in the window alcove with a lady on his lap. Neither of them had noticed the door open. The gentleman was kissing the lady with single-minded intensity—and the lady had her arms around the gentleman as she kissed him back just as passionately!

Desire's eyes widened with amazement. She instantly recalled the way Jakob had kissed her. Her body began to tingle at the memory. A moment later she was filled with embarrassment at unintentionally witnessing the couple's embrace. She averted her gaze and stepped back into the hall. The steward mumbled something incoherent and began to shut the door.

Jakob, however, didn't seem to suffer from their scruples. He put the steward aside with a firm, though courteous, hand and strolled into the parlour. Desire was scandalised at his indelicacy but, since he was the only person she knew in the house, she was unwilling to be separated from him. She followed him, keeping her gaze resolutely turned away from the couple in the window.

Jakob gave a cough which sounded suspiciously like a laugh. Desire heard a gasp of feminine surprise, followed by a glad exclamation. 'Jakob!'

She looked around in time to see the lady scramble off the gentleman's lap and run across the room towards them. Desire just had time to see her becomingly flushed face and her dishevelled blonde hair, before the lady flung her arms around Jakob. He received her warmly, returning her embrace with so much enthusiasm he lifted her off her feet.

Desire stared at them, unable to account for the strange pang she felt at seeing another woman in Jakob's arms. It was foolish to be so dismayed. She'd *always* known there must be other women in his life. He was far too handsome and virile to live like a monk. And this lady was as beautiful and fair as Jakob himself. Her hair was only a shade or too darker than his.

Desire finally managed to look away, one hand fussing aimlessly with the fold of her skirt. She suddenly remembered the gentleman the lady had previously been kissing. Her alarmed gaze flew in his direction. He'd risen from the window seat and now he was watching his lady greet Jakob with an odd, but not hostile, expression. When he noticed Desire looking at him he gave her a slightly crooked smile and strolled over to her.

'For the lack of a more formal introduction, allow me to present myself,' he said, with a glance of wry amusement towards Jakob and the blonde lady. 'Halross, at your service, madam.' He bowed gracefully.

Halross? Desire blinked, then remembered that the steward had said Lord Halross and Mrs Quenell were in the parlour.

'Lady Desire Godwin,' she identified herself, too disconcerted to emulate his easy address. 'I am, I mean,' she said, then flushed bright red at her gaucheness and dipped her head. She sank into a curtsy to cover her embarrassment. 'How do you do, my lord?'

'Very well, thank you. It is a pleasure to meet you, Lady Desire. I take it the golden giant my betrothed is petting is Swiftbourne's prodigal grandson?'

'Er, yes,' said Desire. 'That is, he is Colonel Jakob Balston. Your betrothed?' she couldn't help asking.

'Mrs Athena Quenell,' Halross said helpfully. 'Athena is another of Swiftbourne's grandchildren.'

'We thought you were in Newgate!' Athena exclaimed, stepping back from Jakob at last and looking him up and down.

'I was for a couple of days. Then it burnt down.'

'And you escaped!' Athena's blue eyes lit with excitement. 'I told you he was too clever to be imprisoned for long,' she said, turning to Halross.

'When you weren't fretting yourself sick with worry,' he said with affection. 'My dear, may I introduce you to Lady Desire Godwin.'

'I am so sorry.' Athena immediately turned to Desire. 'I didn't mean to be so rude. I was just so *pleased* to see Jakob. We've all been so worried about him.'

'Yes, I…yes, I can imagine,' said Desire, struggling to maintain her poise. She had been reluctant to come among strangers but, so far, though her scars had drawn curious glances, no one had said or done anything hurtful.

But Athena was the most beautiful woman Desire had ever seen. Her hair was a golden frame around a lovely face. It was clear she'd experienced some of the effects of the fire. Her eyes were slightly red-rimmed from smoke and there were a couple of grazes on her otherwise unblemished fair skin but, like Jakob, her glowing good looks were undimmed by the catastrophe around them.

Desire would have been daunted by the encounter at any time, but finding herself face to face with such feminine perfection when she was dressed in the housekeeper's too-large clothes she'd slept in all night was almost unendurable. She kept her face carefully blank and forced herself to meet Athena's eyes. She would never give the other woman the satisfaction of realising she was crying inside.

'How do you do, Mrs Quenell?' she said through stiff lips.

'Oh, you've been hurt!' Athena exclaimed, reaching towards Desire without hesitation.

Somehow Desire found her hand held in a warm clasp. 'So many buildings have fallen,' Athena said, touching a hand to a graze on her temple. 'Were you—oh, no, the scars have healed. You can't have been hurt in the fire?' She flushed brightly with obvious embarrassment and glanced away, biting her lip.

Desire tried to pull her hand away, but to her surprise Athena tightened her grip and wouldn't let her withdraw.

'I'm sorry, I did not mean to upset you,' said Athena. 'I was remembering when Gabriel's building blew up yesterday. I haven't been thinking very clearly recently. I am sorry.'

Desire was horribly aware that Lord Halross and Jakob were silently watching her encounter with Athena. She hated being the centre of everyone's attention. She wanted to jerk her hand away from Athena's, but pride wouldn't let her. She forced her cramped, stiff muscles to respond and lifted her head to look at Athena. To her surprise she saw a sheen of tears in the other woman's beautiful eyes. Desire tensed to resist pity, but she didn't see pity in Athena's expression. Desire stumbled to the conclusion that Athena was upset because she was afraid her tactlessness might have hurt Desire's feelings.

'It was in the war, during the siege,' she said, her voice sounding raspy as dry leaves in her ears. 'The siege of Larksmere House.'

'Larksmere? I remember,' said Halross. He moved behind Athena and put his hands on her shoulders. 'That must be more than twenty years ago now. I was a child—as you must have been, my lady—but I remember the stories of your mother's gallant defence.' He smiled, but his eyes were grave. 'The wars and their aftermath cast long shadows upon us all,' he said. 'Let us hope there will be no more such conflicts.'

'I hope not,' Desire whispered. She shivered at the memory of the long-ago bombardment of her house, and then noticed that Jakob had put his hand on her arm.

'Let us all sit down,' he said. 'And perhaps—we left Putney in such haste this morning there was barely time to draw breath—perhaps we could have something to eat?' He looked hopefully at Athena.

'Of course. I will give the order at once.' She went quickly to the door to relay the command. 'Putney?' she said, coming back. 'What were you doing in Putney?'

While they ate, Jakob gave a brief account of what had happened to him and Desire. His description of meeting Potticary in the Dover inn tallied exactly with the story he'd told Desire, but she noticed he touched only briefly on their visit to Kilverdale's house, simply mentioning they'd spent the night there and that he'd had a short conversation with the Duke before he'd escorted Desire back to London

'Lady Desire was anxious about the fate of her house,' he concluded. 'But as soon as we saw it was still standing we came here.'

'I'm glad you saw Kilverdale,' said Athena. 'He was so worried about you yesterday. My lady, I am sorry you've had such a frightening time. I have been thinking—I hope you will not consider the offer impertinent—that perhaps you might like to try on one of my gowns?' She smiled at Desire. 'We are much of a size. I'm sure it will fit you better than the housekeeper's clothes.'

'I…thank you, that is very kind of you,' Desire stammered. Athena's offer made her feel a bit uncomfortable, but she could see nothing but friendliness in the other woman's expression. 'Yes, I would like that,' she said more confidently.

'In a little while. I wish to speak to you first, my lady,' Jakob said, setting aside his plate.

'To speak to me?' Desire looked at him. There was an unusually serious expression in Jakob's eyes, and he had spoken in a far more formal tone than usual. Her breath skittered in her throat. What did he want to say to her than he hadn't already said?

'When you're ready, send a footman to find me,' said Athena.

Desire nodded and even managed to smile, but most of her attention was on Jakob as he waited for the others to leave the room. She had been alone with him more often than not in the course of the past twenty-four hours, but when Halross and Athena left she suddenly felt shy and self-conscious in his presence. Why did he want to speak to her now? Was it about the fact they'd spent the night together and Kilverdale had seen them?

She played nervously with the folds of her skirt. She couldn't bring herself to look at him. She knew the events of the last day and night had compromised her virtue. She'd always known that to be the case, but it was only as she heard Jakob carefully editing their story for Athena and Lord Halross that she realised how serious the situation was. Would Jakob feel obliged to salvage her reputation with an honourable proposal of marriage? Or did he see it as an opportunity to gain an heiress for his bride?

He did seem to like kissing her, which was more than she'd come to hope for in a husband, but was that enough on which to base a marriage?

If her father had arranged for her to marry Jakob six years ago, she would have been pleased at the choice of bridegroom. But now she was wary, unwilling to risk her happiness and independence on such a short acquaintance. Her horror of being tied to an unwilling bridegroom ran very deep, and she had lived apart from the world for so long that, even if the world did decide she was a fallen woman because she'd spent the night beside Jakob, she couldn't see how that would make any difference to her life.

Butterflies danced in her stomach as she tried to settle on a suitable reply to him. She decided she would not say either 'yes' or 'no', but would ask for more time so that they could get to know each other better. She would tell him that he was handsome and charming and she thought he would make a very good husband, but that she didn't want to make a hasty decision in the midst of such chaos. He surely couldn't take offence at such a flattering but practical response? Her decision made to her own satisfaction, she lifted her gaze to look at him as she awaited his proposal.

She discovered he was studying her thoughtfully, a small frown creasing his forehead. She considered the frown a rather uncomplimentary prelude to a marriage proposal. When his expression grew even more sombre a spurt of indignation brought her to her feet. If it was this much effort for him to make his proposal, she didn't want to hear it.

'Since you don't have anything important to say,' she began, 'I will—'

'Sit down!'

She was so surprised at his clipped order that she did. It was easy to imagine him speaking in just such a tone to his officers and men. But she was not a soldier and did not have to endure such treatment. She was just about to say so when he said:

'Tell me about your betrothal to Arscott.'

'What?' She had completely forgotten about her mythical engagement to the steward. She had no intention of marrying Arscott, but perhaps she could use the false betrothal to avert a proposal from Jakob. Despite her common-sense resolve to ask for more time, she wasn't sure she'd have the strength of will not to say 'yes' immediately if he put the question to her directly. He was kind, handsome, virile. She was sure he would give her beautiful babies—the thought made her blush. It was hard to be sensible when she knew this might be the only offer she would ever receive.

'*För bövelen!* You *are* besotted by the man. Just the thought of him makes you blush!'

'What?' Desire touched her hands to her hot cheeks. 'Oh, you are a halfwit!' she exclaimed, angry with him because it was his fault her mind was full of scandalous images.

She jumped up and walked over to the window, hoping she might feel cooler, if not calmer, next to the glass panes.

'Does that mean you are *not* besotted by him?' Jakob followed her. She was aware of his large form crowding close behind her back, overwhelming her senses with his forceful presence.

'I am not besotted by any man. You think too much of your-self!' She didn't dare turn to face him. She would find herself almost breast to breast with him, and that would certainly be a mistake. She tried to calm her racing pulse. It was ridiculous to allow Jakob to affect her so powerfully.

'*I* think too much of myself?' he repeated thoughtfully. She could almost hear the dawning male satisfaction in his voice as he considered her hasty words. 'Were you thinking of *me* a moment ago, *älskling*?' he asked. 'Is it the thought of *my* kiss that makes you blush?'

'Of course not!' Desire sat down on the window seat with a billow of brown wool. She turned her head and tried to look as if she was deeply interested in the view. Ash coated every-thing in sight. As she watched a fragment of charred paper, its edges black and curled, floated delicately down to earth. The small part of Desire's mind that was not filled with thoughts of Jakob prayed for rain to extinguish the fire still burning over London.

He sat down next to her, hooking one knee up on the seat so he could turn to face her directly. Now her knee nearly touched his ankle. He had an infuriating way of filling the space around him until she felt invaded by his person, even when he wasn't actually touching her.

And when he did touch her hand with his fingertips, she felt tingles of excited awareness in every fibre of her body. Despite her efforts to remain aloof, her gaze flew to his face.

'I'm sorry,' he said quietly. 'Now is not the moment to tease you. This is too important. Did you and Arscott ever discuss marriage before the attempt to take you from your roof on Saturday?'

The question disorientated Desire. She didn't understand why he was making such an issue of her supposed betrothal. Even if her betrothal to Arscott were genuine, surely the heir to an earldom had little to fear from the competition of a steward? Especially when Jakob was so arrogantly sure of his own appeal.

'Desire?' he persisted.

'No,' she said, since he seemed determined to get an answer from her. 'Though I cannot see what business it is of yours.'

He took her hand in his. She felt the warmth of his fingers even through the linen bandage that still encased them. Excitement fluttered in her stomach. Arscott had taken her hand in his just before he asked her to marry him. Was this how men usually went about proposing?

'Did Arscott use what had happened—the attack on you—as a reason why you should marry him?' Jakob asked.

'He said that under other circumstances he wouldn't have presumed, but it was the best way to keep me safe,' she said impatiently. 'Have we finished talking about Arscott now?'

'So then you agreed to marry him?' Jakob's voice was unreadable.

'No, I didn't!' said Desire, with a flare of annoyance. She

drew her hand away from Jakob's. Even Arscott hadn't prefaced his proposal with an interrogation. 'I said I'd think about it.'

'And you decided to say yes?'

'If you must know, I can't abide the notion of marrying Arscott!' she said, thoroughly provoked. 'But I didn't want to hurt his feelings, so I thought it best to refuse him by easy stages.'

'You can't abide the thought of marrying him!' Jakob exclaimed.

'It makes me shudder to think of it!' Desire glared at him. 'But he has served my family loyally all his life, and I didn't want to hurt his feelings.'

'You have a generous heart.' Jakob took her hand again.

Desire held her breath. Now that he'd got all the possible hindrances out of the way, was he *finally* going to ask her to marry him? Even Arscott had got to the point more swiftly.

'Well, get on with it,' she said, too nervous to even pretend to wait patiently for his next question.

'Get on with what?' Jakob looked startled.

'Whatever you want to say!'

'Did Arscott ever drop hints about marrying you *before* Saturday?' Jakob asked.

'Why on earth do you keeping talking about *Arscott*?' Desire exploded.

'Because I believe he is the man who ordered Potticary to abduct you.'

Jakob's words dropped like stones in the sudden silence that filled the parlour. Desire stared at him, struggling to make sense of what he'd just said. It was so far from what she was expecting to hear that for several moments she didn't understand.

He tightened his grip on her hand. His blue eyes were grave and compassionate as he waited for her to speak.

The compassion was too close to pity. For a few seconds that hurt Desire more than anything else. What a fool she was. Jakob hadn't been building up to a marriage proposal, but to make a ridiculous accusation against Arscott. He'd probably never even *considered* marrying her. Even Jakob could not be willing to make that sacrifice. To marry an ageing, ugly woman—she remembered Kilverdale's words of only a few hours ago—just to salvage her reputation.

She dragged her hand away from him and stood up. Her knees felt shaky, but she walked away with a fair pretense of composure.

'That's the silliest thing I've ever heard,' she said over her shoulder. Her voice sounded brittle. She hoped Jakob didn't notice. 'Arscott *defended* me from all of you.'

'Yes, he did,' said Jakob. 'But the attack gave you such a fright that he had a good reason to persuade you to marry him.'

'I didn't say yes.'

'But had you ever given him any reason to suppose you might refuse him?'

Desire folded her arms across her chest and stared at the floor.

'My lady?'

'How can I answer that? He's my steward. I never even considered marrying him before Saturday. It certainly didn't occur to me to drop hints his suit wouldn't be welcome!'

She spun round to face Jakob, just in time to catch him suppress a quick smile at her hasty words.

'Don't stand there smirking!' She was angry and hurt by his reaction. 'This is not a laughing matter.'

'I know.' His expression sobered. 'My lady, why have you stayed shut up in your house for the past six years?'

'I don't want to discuss it.' She turned away from him again, instinctively favouring her scarred cheek.

'What Kilverdale said was cruel,' Jakob said quietly. 'But he was not the only eligible man in England. Why didn't your father arrange another match?'

'That's none of your business.'

'My lady?' he persisted.

'I begged him not to, at least not at once,' she said, after a short silence. 'And then he fell ill. He died soon after and the guardian he appointed for me died a few months later.'

'But that would have been how long ago? Three years? Four years?'

'Five years since Father died,' she whispered.

'And you've remained behind the walls of your house ever since?'

'Arscott told me—' She broke off.

'What did he tell you?'

'He told me that I would be at constant risk from fortune hunters if I went out.' She paused, thinking about what she'd just said. She was still upset that she'd been so devastatingly wrong in what she'd expected Jakob to say to her, but she was finally able to focus on what he *had* said.

'Arscott told me about Lord Rochester's attempt to abduct an heiress,' she said slowly, for the first time wondering about the steward's motives in discouraging all her aspirations to venture out into the world. 'He said that would happen to me if I didn't do everything I could to avoid the notice of society.'

She heard Jakob release a long, slow breath and closed her eyes, as if by doing so she could also close her mind to the doubts that now stole into it.

'Did he also encourage you to believe that all people would be unkind about your scars?' Jakob asked gently.

Desire swallowed. She felt tears trying to seep from beneath her tightly closed eyes. Had Arscott done that? Or had it been her own fears that had kept her safely locked away from the world? She didn't know for sure.

'He said Kilverdale was typical of young men,' she said unsteadily.

'Not that typical,' said Jakob, a dry note in his voice. 'For both good and ill, Kilverdale is far from typical. I believe Arscott deliberately tried to keep you shut away from the world so you would become completely dependent upon him.'

'Perhaps.' Desire rubbed the back of her hand across her eyes.

She thought about her many conversations with Arscott. Comments he'd made that had once seemed quite innocent now took on a shocking new interpretation. On more than one occasion he'd talked about the merits of an older husband—he was nine years her senior. Sometimes he'd talked delicately, but unmistakably, about the loneliness of a woman who had no husband. He'd made certain small gestures—nothing as blatant as taking her hand, as he had done on Saturday—which might have been overtures of courtship. Had she, in her lack of experience and total lack of attraction to Arscott, missed the fact he was trying to win, or at least manipulate, her affections?

'Here.' Jakob offered her a snowy, lace-edged handkerchief. She noticed the elaborate K in the corner and almost defiantly blew her nose.

'I don't suppose anything you are wearing belongs to you,' she said.

'Only my money belt,' he replied cheerfully.

'But if Arscott hired Potticary to abduct me, why did he shoot him?'

'So there would be no witnesses to accuse him of the crime,' said Jakob. 'Arscott didn't want the abduction to succeed. He only wanted it to frighten you into his arms.'

Desire shuddered at the idea. A part of her thought: *he got frustrated because I didn't respond to his subtle courtship.* But then she rebelled against the dreadful suspicion.

'That's absurd. Unthinkable!' she said vehemently. 'No one would plot the coldblooded murder of two men just so he could marry me.'

Jakob didn't say anything.

'Not me, my fortune,' she whispered, after a moment. 'Men kill every day for a lot less than I am worth.'

'Do you believe Arscott could be capable of such a scheme?' Jakob asked.

'No,' she said, but she remembered occasions when she'd heard the older members of her household discussing Arscott's activities during the Larksmere siege. And it was only days ago since he had killed two men without apparent remorse.

'This is all nonsense,' she said. She couldn't bear the idea that she had been misled and betrayed by someone she'd trusted all her life. 'You have a suspicious imagination, but I am sure Arscott did not order my abduction.'

'The matter needs further investigation,' said Jakob. 'I know it has been a cruel shock to you. We can talk about what we do next when you've had a little time to think about it and—'

'Think?' Desire pressed her fingers to her temples. 'Wait! You haven't produced one piece of evidence that Arscott ordered my abduction. In fact, you told me last night you didn't know. What have you to say to *that*?' She stared at him challengingly. Had he thought she wouldn't notice the inconsistency?

'I said Potticary didn't tell me who hired him,' he reminded her. 'He did say a couple of things that gave me clues to the man's identity. Unfortunately they didn't mean anything until after Potticary was already dead. And yesterday you were declaring your intention to wed Arscott so fervently, and you were determined to escape me and run to him, that I didn't think it was wise to mention my suspicions.'

'Your suspicions based on your wounded pride because you were bested by Arscott on the roof,' she accused him.

'I was bested by you, not Arscott, and my pride is not wounded because I was too honourable to overpower you,' he retorted.

'I would have shot you!' Desire was incensed by his arrogance.

'You would have fired the pistol,' he agreed. 'Nevertheless, if I'd meant to seize you, I would have done so.'

'You are so cocksure!' But when she remembered how frightened she'd been, and the mistake she'd made when she'd taken her eyes off Jakob to look at Arscott, she knew he was probably right. If he'd wanted to seize her, perhaps hold her hostage to force her household to let him escape, he could have done so.

'Now you are trying to distract me,' she said. 'You still haven't offered any proof that Arscott is guilty.'

'Potticary didn't tell me who hired him,' Jakob said, 'but he did mention several times that we had allies within your household. On the way to Godwin House he said "Arscott says we'll find her on the roof." I didn't know who Arscott was then. On another, earlier, occasion, when he'd had a few mugs of wine, he said, "I'll be going up in the world soon. Walter won't forget his old friend." What's Arscott's Christian name, my lady?'

'Walter,' Desire whispered. 'Oh, my God.' She covered her face with her hands.

Her insidious doubts about Arscott suddenly grew to overwhelming proportions. She remembered the shot that had killed Potticary. The awful sight of the other man lying across her path with a broken neck. It had been only minutes later that Arscott had taken her hand in his hand. The hand with which he had just killed two men.

She shuddered. A wave of nausea swept over her and she pressed her fingers to her lips.

She was dimly aware of Jakob guiding her to sit in the nearest chair. She sank down on to it and took several deep breaths. After a few moments she opened her eyes to see Jakob on his knees beside her, watching her with unmistakable concern in his eyes.

'I'm sorry,' he said. '*Älskling*, if there had been a way to spare you the news of such betrayal, I would have taken it.'

'No,' she said. Her voice rasped hardly above a whisper.

Two men had now knelt before her in less than a week. And neither of them had said what she'd expected them to say. She'd never for a second anticipated Arscott would propose to her. She'd been halfway convinced that Jakob *was* about to do so, and now it was clear marriage couldn't be further from his mind.

She suppressed a bubble of slightly hysterical laughter, wishing she could impose some order on her thoughts.

'Arscott must be questioned,' she said, latching on to one certainty amid so many doubts. 'I will not permit him to be accused, without the chance to defend himself.'

God forgive her for suspecting her steward of anything so vile. Perhaps it was only the shattering events of the past few days that made it so easy to believe he could be guilty. She hoped it was so.

'Of course not,' said Jakob. 'There is a great deal to be done, and many decisions for you to make. But you don't need to make them at once. There isn't much we can do until Swiftbourne returns.'

'I wish I was at home,' she said, hardly noticing what Jakob said.

'It's not safe,' he replied. 'I'm sorry, *älskling*.'

'Don't call me that!' Desire didn't know exactly what the word meant, but she was sure it was something akin to 'sweetheart'. It seemed a terrible mockery of all her earlier jumbled fears and expectations that Jakob was on his knees, calling her sweetheart—while accusing one of her most trusted servants of dreadful crimes. She turned her head aside, avoiding his compassionate gaze.

'Get up,' she said. 'How long do you intend to keep me here for my own safety?' she asked grittily.

'You are not a prisoner,' Jakob said.

'You mean you'd let me walk out right now?' She made no effort to hide her scepticism.

'If you leave, I'll have to go with you,' he replied. 'But even the honest members of your household are more likely to shoot me than thank me for saving you from the fire. In their eyes I am an escaped prisoner.'

'Then what am I to do?' she asked, confused and frustrated by the situation.

'We'll wait until Lord Swiftbourne returns,' Jakob replied. 'He will be glad to see that his heir has escaped damage—' Jakob's lips twisted in a humourless smile '—and no doubt he will be able to help us deal with Arscott. He has resources not available to lesser men. In the meantime, shall I summon Athena? I'm sure you would be more comfortable in one of her gowns.'

Chapter Nine

The sound of voices in the hall forewarned Jakob of Lord Swiftbourne's arrival. He stood and turned to face the door. He felt his body tense and consciously relaxed his muscles. This was not a meeting he anticipated with pleasure.

Swiftbourne had managed to stay on the winning side for over thirty years. He had been an ambassador for Charles I during the 1630s, but at the outbreak of Civil War he had thrown in his lot with Parliament. He had become Cromwell's ambassador to various foreign countries, including Sweden and France. After Cromwell's death, and the collapse of the Commonwealth, he had changed allegiance for a third time. He had been one of the influential Parliamentarians who had invited Charles II to return to England. It was for that act of belated loyalty to the Stuarts— and perhaps for more clandestine services to the crown—he had been rewarded with the Earldom.

But though Swiftbourne had prospered, he had done little to protect his less politically adept relatives. At the same time that he had been acting as Parliament's foreign ambassador, Parliamentary forces had hanged Kilverdale's Royalist father after the Battle of Worcester.

Unlike Kilverdale, Jakob had never been even technically at war with their grandfather. But he had been Kilverdale's friend, as well as his cousin, ever since the Duke had first visited Sweden at the age of sixteen. As a matter of instinct as well as personal preference, Jakob's loyalty to his cousin was much stronger than his loyalty to the man whose title and estate he would one day inherit. He accepted that his destiny ultimately lay in England, but he did not intend to dance to Swiftbourne's tune. It galled him that he had to meet his grandfather in the guise of an escaped prisoner.

The door opened to admit the Earl. He paused briefly on the threshold, his gaze unerringly finding Jakob. His pale blue eyes raked his grandson up and down. After scrutinising Jakob for several piercing seconds, he closed the door and walked across the room to the unlit hearth. Though now in his seventies, Swiftbourne still possessed the lean, straight-backed frame of a much younger man. He was dressed in deep green velvet and gold lace. A periwig of light brown hair framed his predatory face.

Jakob waited, making no effort to break the silence. He'd met his grandfather on several occasions in the past, although only twice on English soil. The last time they'd spoken had been two years ago, before the unexpected death of Jakob's father. This was their first face-to-face encounter since Jakob had become Swiftbourne's direct heir.

The Earl looked uncharacteristically tired, and Jakob noticed deep lines of tension bracketing his thin lips. He wondered if his grandfather's greatest concern was for the fate of the city or for the inconvenience caused by nearly losing another heir. He was under no illusion that Swiftbourne felt personal affection for him.

The Earl pivoted to face his grandson with almost military precision. As he did so Jakob caught the smell of fresh smoke clinging to Swiftbourne's clothes. The fire in the city was an ever-present threat and tragedy.

After Swiftbourne had studied his grandson for several long seconds, the tension around his mouth eased. Cold fury suddenly blazed in his eyes.

'I summoned you to England seventeen months ago,' he said, his harsh voice serrated by anger.

'I had more pressing duties,' Jakob replied evenly.

'As my heir, your only duty is to me, here in England.'

Jakob controlled a surge of anger at Swiftbourne's callous dismissal of the people and responsibilities he'd left behind in Sweden.

'I owe nothing to you,' he said. 'To the Swiftbourne land and tenants one day, perhaps—but nothing to you.'

Swiftbourne's eyes narrowed. 'So you thumbed your nose at me by dallying in gaol?'

Jakob chose not to answer a question intended to provoke him into self-justification or defiance. The tense silence lengthened. A battle of wills between them.

'Why were you in Newgate?' said Swiftbourne abruptly.

'For the attempted abduction of an heiress.'

'What? Have you squandered your father's inheritance already?'

'No.' Although Jakob's brother had taken over their father's business, James Balston had left his oldest son some land in Sweden and considerable wealth. Since his father's avowed intention had always been that Jakob would receive the English inheritance and his younger brother the Swedish, Jakob had not anticipated such generosity. It meant a great deal to him on a personal level. On a practical level it meant Swiftbourne was unlikely to make the error of thinking he could control Jakob by controlling the purse strings.

'The heiress, I take it, was Lady Desire Godwin,' said Swiftbourne.

'Yes.' Jakob had done his best to be discreet when they'd arrived, but Desire had introduced herself to Lord Halross with her full name. There was no point in concealing her identity now.

'And she came here willingly?'

'She was reluctant to impose upon your hospitality,' said Jakob. 'But I assured her you would never turn away anyone in distress,' he added ironically.

Swiftbourne looked at Jakob. Then he sat down.

'I am too old to waste my energy sparring with stiff-necked grandsons. Simply tell me the story, I beg you.'

'You've just come from the King?' said Jakob, momentarily surprised by Swiftbourne's unexpected concession, but wanting some answers of his own. 'What is the news of the fire?'

'It is contained. There are rumours there will be a French or Dutch attack on London tonight,' said Swiftbourne.

The soldier in Jakob came to full alert. Desire's situation needed to be resolved as soon as possible, but she would be safe from Arscott in Swiftbourne's house and a threat to the city required immediate action.

'Do you have details of where they intend to strike?' he demanded. 'You must provide me with a letter of introduction to the commanding officer. I will—'

Swiftbourne raised a hand. 'Rumours, I said,' he interrupted. 'London is in a ferment of gossip, but my sources are much more reliable. I believe it is very unlikely there will be an assault on London—at least within the next few days.'

'Your sources?' said Jakob. 'Spies?'

'The King values my assessment of the situation,' Swiftbourne said obliquely. 'I have a great deal of diplomatic experience.'

'As you say, my lord,' Jakob replied drily. It didn't surprise him that his grandfather was actively involved in acquiring such information. 'And your reliable sources do not believe there will be an attack on London by the French or Dutch?'

'No. Precautions will be taken, but you do not need to concern yourself with them. Are you still an officer in the Swedish army?'

'No. I resigned my commission.'

'Good. Since you are now assured London is not in imminent danger of invasion, sit down and explain why you abducted an heiress and why that same heiress is now a guest in my house. Are you trying to make me an accessory to your crime?'

'No, my lord. Though I hope you will intercede to prevent me for hanging for mine,' said Jakob, willing to request Swiftbourne's aid now that his grandfather had unbent enough to ask for an explanation rather than hurling accusations at him.

'Of course.' Swiftbourne's lips stretched in a thin smile. 'Now explain why the need arises.'

'There now, my lady, I think we are done.' Athena nudged one last chestnut curl into place and stepped back to admire the hair-style she had created for Desire.

'Thank you.' Desire pushed aside her worries about Arscott and Jakob to smile at Athena. 'I'm sorry, I have been a poor companion,' she said. 'You're very kind to do my hair as well as lend me your dress. Thank you.'

Athena smiled and lifted her hand in a graceful gesture that both acknowledged Desire's gratitude, yet indicated there was no need for it. Desire wondered if she would ever be able to command such natural elegance.

She looked down at her new finery, stroking the folds of blue silk that covered her knees. The tightly-laced bodice pushed up her breasts, exposing more cleavage than she was used to. Beneath the bodice she wore a soft white chemise. The sleeves of the chemise were trimmed with an extravagant quantity of lace, which fell from her elbows almost to her wrists.

Impractical for gardening, she thought irrelevantly.

'It is a very beautiful gown,' she said aloud. 'I am so grateful. But are you sure it is quite suitable?' she couldn't help adding, touching her hand to the expanse of bare skin revealed by the low neckline.

'It feels strange, doesn't it?' said Athena, taking Desire by surprise. She couldn't imagine this lovely woman ever feeling ill at ease. 'After so many years living as a guest in the convent I found it odd to dress fashionably too. But it was my aunt, the Duchess of Kilverdale, who gave this gown to me. And I know she would never give me a dress that is improper.'

'Your aunt?' Desire said, her attention caught by the reference to the Duchess. 'I—' She broke off quickly. She didn't want to arouse Athena's curiosity by admitting she had once spent a few days as a house guest of Kilverdale's mother. It might lead to questions she didn't want to answer.

Desire conjured up an image of the Duchess as she had been six years ago. She remembered an elegant, fair-haired woman with a poise she'd envied. The Duchess had been a considerate hostess, doing her best to make Desire feel comfortable but, not surprisingly, most of her attention had been focussed on the home to which she had only just returned. The Duchess had spent seventeen years in exile in France. Her belated return to the home where she had lived for a few happy years with her husband, and where her son had been born, had filled Kilverdale's mother with bittersweet memories. Perhaps it wasn't surprising the Duchess hadn't been fully aware of the tension between her son and Desire.

Desire put the unsettling memories aside to focus on the present. She was sure Athena was right. The Duchess would not have given an improper gown to her niece.

Her anxieties partially relieved, Desire smiled uncertainly at Athena. 'It is not that I am afraid the *gown* is improper,' she said, 'only that it might not be…' She took a deep breath and tried again. 'A beautiful gown is obviously very suitable for you to wear but, in short, I usually dress more plainly.' Her stomach knotted with tension as she spoke, but she looked directly at Athena, refusing to hide her scars.

'It is not a gown made for comfort,' Athena agreed cheerfully. 'I do not wear it when I am working or resting. But it is very suitable for you to wear in formal company.' She hesitated a moment. 'I don't want to seem impertinent, but you have lovely shoulders and a trim waist, my lady, and the gown shows them to good advantage,' she said.

'It does?' The knots in Desire's stomach eased. There was no indication that Athena was mocking her. She stood up and put her hands on her waist, delighted by how well the bodice fitted her. It was true she'd been annoyed that the housekeeper's over-sized clothes concealed her figure. When she looked down, she could see the blue sweep of her skirts glowing softly in the muted light from the window. The lace at her elbows might be impractical, but it brushed against her forearms in a very pleasing way. She had never worn such a lovely dress. Her mother had always worn sober colours and insisted her daughter do likewise.

'You are a beautiful woman,' said Athena quietly. 'Your scars cannot hide that.'

'Oh.' Desire touched her fingers to the ridges on her cheek. She hadn't expected Athena to comment on them directly. It was a long time since she'd been exposed to the comments and questions of strangers. Athena's willingly offered friendship meant a great deal to her, but she'd had so little company over the past few years that she could not respond in the same easy manner.

'And gentlemen often find it difficult to keep their gaze focussed on a lady's face at the best of times,' said Athena, a thread of humour in her voice. 'There's no harm in discreetly drawing attention to the rest of your charms.'

She demonstrated what she meant by pushing the neckline of the Desire's borrowed bodice a little lower. Then she stepped back to consider the effect.

'That's shameless!' Desire gasped, instinctively pulling the neckline back up the bare quarter of an inch Athena had lowered it.

Athena blushed, but a mischievous light danced in her eyes. 'I would not advise this if you were in the unprotected company of strangers,' she said. 'Or among men you should not trust. In those cases, it is better *not* to draw attention to yourself. But Jakob is a very honourable, noble man.'

'Yes, I know. I—' Desire stopped and looked at Athena suspiciously.

'It is so lucky Kilverdale stole his clothes and left him behind in Dover,' said Athena blithely, as if she hadn't noticed anything in Desire's glance. 'Otherwise he would never have heard of the plot to abduct you and rescued you. I wonder who is behind it?'

'Jakob thinks it is my steward, Arscott,' said Desire. For a few brief minutes she had forgotten Jakob's shocking revelations. A wave of disbelief washed over her. She stepped back and sank on to the stool, wondering what on earth she was to do.

'Your *steward*?' Athena exclaimed. 'Why does he think that?'

'We need to speak to Gabriel!' At the end of Desire's explanation Athena jumped up and seized her hand. 'Come on.'

It was a long time since anyone had held Desire's hand with such unforced, friendly companionship. The simple gesture meant more to her than Athena could possibly realise. So, although she had no idea why Athena suddenly considered it essential to speak to Lord Halross, she didn't object at being led into his presence

That didn't prevent her from feeling a momentary *frisson* of nervousness when she saw the Marquis stand up to greet them. He was an imposing man, nowhere near as handsome as Jakob, and in repose his features looked somewhat austere.

But when he saw Athena his expression was transformed. As they entered the room his eyes went first to his betrothed. The look of undisguised love that dawned on his face was so intimate Desire looked away so she wouldn't intrude. Yet at the same time it filled her with an odd, sweet yearning. It must be wonderful to be loved like that.

The exchange of glances between the lovers only took a few seconds, and then Halross turned to Desire. She saw a brief flicker of undoubted surprise in his eyes, and then his gaze travelled quickly down her body before returning with well-bred courtesy to her face. There had not been even the faintest hint of lascivious interest in his eyes. He had paused only momentarily to take note of her changed appearance before he greeted her, but it was very definitely approval, not distaste that she detected in his expression.

'Athena's gown is much more to your style than the house-keeper's dress,' he said, setting chairs for the two women.

Athena threw Desire a quick, conspiratorial smile. 'Lady Desire needs your advice,' she told Halross.

'I *do*? I beg your pardon, my lord.' Desire continued hastily, realising her startled outburst wasn't very complimentary. 'I am sure your advice is excellent, but why…? I don't understand?' She looked questioningly at Athena. What advice could Lord Halross give her that Jakob couldn't?

'It is because you need a disinterested advocate,' Athena said. 'I mean someone who has *your* best interests at heart that do not conflict with his own interests.'

'Oh.' Did that mean Athena thought Jakob's advice *wouldn't* be in her best interests? 'I am sure Colonel Balston would never act dishonourably,' Desire said, a cool note unconsciously creeping into her voice.

'Of course he wouldn't!' said Athena indignantly. 'It is not *Jakob* you need to be protected from.' She paused, apparently to gather her thoughts.

Desire glanced at Lord Halross and saw he was watching Athena with a hint of amusement in his eyes, as if he understood perfectly what she was thinking.

'You haven't met Lord Swiftbourne yet, have you?' said Athena.

'No.' Desire wasn't looking forward to the meeting. Lord Swiftbourne sounded extremely formidable.

'He is a very clever, devious man,' said Athena. 'I don't believe he would ever do anything to harm you—apart from anything else, Jakob wouldn't let him. But nor do I think Swiftbourne would let an heiress slip through his fingers, either, without somehow taking advantage of the situation. And Jakob is a stranger to England, and an escaped prisoner into the bargain. That's why I think it's best if you have someone to speak on your behalf who is not only independent of my grandfather, but also has his own undeniable authority in England.' She paused for breath, and looked at Desire anxiously, as if she was afraid she might have offended her.

Desire didn't know whether to laugh or cry. She'd been worried about Lord Swiftbourne's possible plans for her when she'd tried to escape from Jakob the previous night, but she hadn't given the problem a thought since then. Perhaps she'd been right all along in her anxieties about falling into the clutches of Jakob and his powerful relatives?

'I know it probably seems presumptuous of me,' said Athena. 'Under any circumstances I would not thrust myself upon you, or even Gabriel. Though he has such a wide experience of the world and is so competent in all he undertakes that you could not seek a better adviser—'

'Hush, love,' Halross caught one of Athena's eloquently gesturing hands in his and kissed it lightly. 'You will make me blush. My lady, the situation is not as melodramatic as Athena makes it sound,' he said to Desire. 'And I am sure Jakob Balston is more than capable of providing all the protection you need. But I would be honoured to speak for you if you wish. You need have no anxiety about my motives. I am more than content with my existing bride, and I have no male relatives desperate to marry a fortune.'

Desire took a deep breath. Events were moving so quickly. So much had changed over the past twenty-four hours. There was a strong possibility a man she had trusted all her life had bitterly betrayed her. And now she was being offered the help and kindness of strangers. She could refuse out of pride and fear. Or she could trust the good faith of her new friends.

'Thank you. I will gladly hear your advice,' she said, smiling at her companions.

'My lady, I am sorry I was not here to welcome you to my house in person.' Lord Swiftbourne bowed over Desire's hand. 'I trust you have been made comfortable in my absence.'

'Oh. Yes, thank you, my lord. Everyone has been very kind.'

After her first moment of surprise, Desire managed to gather her wits sufficiently to frame a coherent reply. She had been worried about Lord Swiftbourne's reaction to her scars, it had never occurred to her that she might be disconcerted by her host's appearance. 'You look just like the Duke!' she exclaimed before she had time to censor her reaction. 'Except—'

'Except Kilverdale is dark and I am fair—and the small matter of nearly fifty years' difference in age,' Swiftbourne replied calmly. 'I hope my likeness to my grandson does me no disservice in your eyes, my lady.'

'No, indeed, my lord.' Desire cursed the blush she felt rising in her cheeks. 'It merely took me by surprise.'

She glanced instinctively at Jakob, and immediately forgot her embarrassment at her unruly tongue. Though he said nothing, she saw him take full notice of her trim figure revealed by the borrowed gown. She wasn't used to admiration. It was a heady moment when he smiled at her, his eyes full of masculine appreciation.

'And I understand that Colonel Balston has been of some assistance to you recently,' Swiftbourne said, his words breaking into her thoughts. 'I am glad he was able to help you.'

'He saved my life,' said Desire. She was disconcerted to realise she'd been staring at Jakob and said the first thing that came to mind to cover her confusion. 'I would have burned—'

'Burned?' Swiftbourne looked startled. He glanced from her to Jakob.

'On my roof,' she said. 'My skirts caught fire. Colonel Balston put me in the water cistern.'

'*That's* when you hurt your hands?' Swiftbourne raised a thin eyebrow in Jakob's direction. 'He told me he blistered them at the oars, my lady.'

'Rowing made them worse,' she said, feeling calmer now she'd diverted the Earl's attention away from her.

'We've just been discussing Lady Desire's situation,' said Lord Halross, when they'd all sat down.

His words drew Desire's attention back to her immediate problems. She looked at Jakob and saw him throw the Marquis a sharp glance. Was he offended by the fact she'd talked to Athena and Lord Halross? She folded her hands in her lap, trying to pretend a composure she didn't feel. She would have preferred an opportunity to talk to Jakob in private, before Halross took on his role as her spokesman, but there had been no chance for her to do so. Besides, she still felt confused about the nature of Jakob's interest in her. She didn't understand if he was only motivated by an honourable wish to protect her, or whether he also cared about her as…she stumbled on the thought…as a *woman*.

'Lady Desire would like to return to her own house as soon as practicable,' said Halross.

'I am very grateful for your hospitality,' Desire hastily assured Swiftbourne, 'but I don't like to inconvenience you, and I would like to go home.' She was careful not to look directly at Jakob as she spoke. She didn't want any of them—including Jakob— to believe her decisions were dependent on his approval. But she could see him from the corner of her eye, and she was glad that his expression seemed thoughtful rather than angry.

'That is hardly a safe or wise option in the circumstances,' Swiftbourne replied.

'Not without protection,' Halross agreed. 'However, I have a solution to that difficulty. As we all know, I blew up my London house yesterday. As you may not realise, Colonel—' he turned to address Jakob directly '—many members of my household are now crammed into the servants' quarters here. I kept the youngest and most able-bodied on hand yesterday to help with emptying and destroying my house. It was my plan to send them into the country in the next few days, but now Lady Desire and I may be of service to each other. My servants are in need of occupation and lodging, and she has need of trustworthy protection until this matter is resolved.'

'Arscott went to my house in Kingston,' said Desire. 'I would like—I *intend*—' she locked her fingers tightly together '—to go there to confront him.' She lifted her chin as she spoke, turning her head to meet Jakob's gaze boldly and a little defiantly.

He smiled faintly. 'Kilverdale's already there,' he said. 'He went this morning.'

'What?' She couldn't believe she'd heard correctly. 'Why?'

'To safeguard the wealth you sent out of London with Arscott,' Jakob said gently. 'Arscott wanted you, my lady, and all your fortune. But if he's afraid you've slipped through his fingers and decides to cut his losses…how much money is in that chest you sent away with him?'

Shock knocked the air from Desire's lungs. It hadn't even occurred to her that Arscott might steal from her. She had been too appalled at the deaths he'd caused and the thought of marriage to him.

She took a deep, unsteady breath, dimly aware of the rustle of skirts as Athena came to stand supportively beside her.

'Nearly…' Her voice cracked. She swallowed and started again. 'Nearly nine thousand pounds,' she said. 'It is the accumulation of several years' income. I am not…I do not have large personal expenses, so the unspent annual income has increased since father's death.' She exhaled carefully, gathering her composure, then looked at Jakob, ignoring everyone else. 'Why didn't you tell me this earlier?' she challenged him.

'The news that Arscott ordered the abduction attempt was hard enough for you to hear,' he said. 'This risk follows from that, but you didn't need to be confronted by it all at once.'

'It is *my* business. I have a right to hear what you suspect and what is being done in my name!' Desire's temper flared. 'You sent *Kilverdale* to Kingston?' She could hardly believe it.

'I didn't send him. He chose to go. It was obvious that someone needed to go there, and even before you decided to leave Putney in such haste I was bound to bring you back to London. You may depend upon Kilverdale to protect your property with utmost vigilance.' Jakob's voice was uncharacteristically stiff and he spoke more formally than usual, as if he anticipated Desire's displeasure.

She hardly noticed. She put her hands against her cheeks. A myriad of furious responses hovered on the tip of her tongue, but she did not want to argue with Jakob in front of the others.

'It would have been better if you'd told me,' she said. Despite herself, she couldn't entirely hide the anger throbbing in her voice. 'And *asked* me before—'

She was interrupted by a sudden commotion in the hall from raised voices loud enough to penetrate through the heavy oak door. She half-started to her feet as she thought she recognised one. Without warning the door burst open and several struggling men crashed through it.

'Benjamin?' she cried.

'My lady?' Benjamin Finch, her Gentleman of the Horse, fell on his knees, two of Swiftbourne's footmen still clutching at his arms. 'My lady, thank God I've found you.' His voice cracked on a sob of relief.

'Let him go!' Desire ran across the room.

At a nod from their master, Swiftbourne's servants stepped back, though they remained close to Benjamin's side.

Desire reached out to help him to his feet. Benjamin stared into her face, his eyes wild with worry. She had never seen him so distressed.

'Are you hurt?' he demanded, his grip on Desire's hands so tight it was painful.

'No! No, I am very well. What are you doing here?' Desire couldn't understand how Benjamin had found her.

'That devil said you'd be here, but I had to see you with my own eyes.'

'That devil?' She was confused.

'Kilverdale. The black-hearted villain. At this very instant he's lording it in the great parlour in Kingston.'

* * *

It took a while for Benjamin to regain his composure and assure himself that Desire had truly come to no harm.

'No one knew where you were,' he said, the anxiety of the past hours still carving deep grooves into his face. It was barely a day since Desire had last seen him, but he seemed to have aged years in the interval.

'I am so sorry.' Remorse filled her. 'I should never have stayed behind. I should have gone in the coaches with you.'

'Yes, you should.' Benjamin was clearly in no mood to pander to his mistress's whims. 'It was dangerous and foolish to remain behind. I thought you had more sense.'

'Her ladyship has come to no harm,' said Jakob, his calm voice a striking contrast to Benjamin's emphatic tones. 'You have my word of honour.'

'Your word?' Benjamin sat back and looked at Jakob through narrowed eyes. 'He said you'd be here.' Desire guessed *he* must be Kilverdale. 'Some rigmarole about your being an army officer and a gentleman, and only interested in protecting her ladyship. How did you get out of gaol?'

'I was a Colonel in the Swedish army until recently,' said Jakob. 'It is true that I only became involved in the plot to abduct Lady Desire so that I could protect her.'

Benjamin didn't say anything, but his opinion of Jakob's explanation was clearly visible in his eyes. Desire saw him glance from her to the door and realised he was estimating his chances of rescuing her from Swiftbourne's house, by force if necessary. The thought of more violence was too awful to contemplate.

'Where's Arscott?' she asked quickly, hoping to distract his attention.

'I don't know,' said Benjamin. 'He left Kingston to look for you this morning, before that de—before the Duke arrived. The Duke told me you'd either be at Godwin House or here, so I went there first.'

'Arscott wasn't there?'

'No. The porter told me Arscott had been back, found you

weren't there, and left again,' said Benjamin. 'I don't know where he went after that. Now what is going on? Why did the Duke of Kilverdale turn up at Kingston this morning with eight armed men and insist on mounting guard on your money chest?'

'Why did you let him in?' Desire demanded, somewhat affronted by Kilverdale's uninvited invasion of her property. Even if he had, apparently, done it in her best interests.

'The house was in an uproar with you missing,' said Benjamin. 'We were not prepared to repel such an assault,' he added sourly.

'He assaulted you?' Desire's temper kindled.

'No. Not physically. But he's high-handed as the devil. Insisted on checking for himself that the chest was still there and had not been tampered with, and then posted guards all over the house. It was damned insulting. If I hadn't been so worried about you, I'd have—' Benjamin stopped and rubbed his left hand up and down his right forearm. 'At least I had the pleasure of creasing his fine coat,' he muttered.

'How did you to that?' Desire asked worriedly. Benjamin had never been much of a warrior and Kilverdale was more than thirty years younger.

'I shook him by his fine brocade until he told me where you were!' Benjamin's voice rose to a near shout of anxiety, exasperation and frayed pride.

'*Benjamin!* Oh, I am so proud of you!' Desire exclaimed, thrilled at the notion of the Duke's odious arrogance being shaken out of him. 'He didn't retaliate, did he?' she added with belated concern.

'No, he told me to come here.' Benjamin sounded thoroughly disgruntled. 'Now, my lady, why are you here? And what the de—what on *earth* is going on?'

Chapter Ten

Desire picked up a piece of charred brocade. She paused briefly to wonder where the brittle, blackened fabric had come from. Had it once hung around a lady's bed, or been part of a gentleman's favourite coat? How strangely and unexpectedly the fire had interrupted everyone's lives. She dropped the burnt material into her sack and moved on to the next piece of detritus.

Night had long since fallen and the roof was illuminated by a combination of moonlight and several torches. In the east, sulphur-coloured flames still leapt high into the sky over London. The smell of burning filled the air, though smoke no longer blew in fierce gusts across the rooftop. The fires had been burning for four days now. Perhaps the destruction would only end when there was nothing left for the flames to consume. Desire shuddered at the thought. She stooped to pick up a piece of paper, which strangely did not seem burnt at all, and put that in her sack as well.

Her rooftop sanctuary was almost unrecognisable beneath the accumulated debris of the fire. Ash lay like a shroud over everything, its weight twisting familiar plants into strange and unfamiliar shapes, eerie as phantoms in the flickering torchlight. Desire crouched to brush the ash from the leaves of one of her favourite plants. A cloud of fine dust blew up into her face and she jerked her head backwards to avoid breathing it in. She could *taste* the destruction as well as smell and see it.

Restoring the garden to order would be a huge task. She'd already decided there was no way to clean the thin layer of gravel that covered the roof leads. It would have to be swept up and replaced. That was a job for later, and one Desire would quite willingly leave to the strong arms and backs of her porters.

She wasn't on the roof at nearly midnight because she had a compulsion to set the garden to rights immediately, but because this was where she always came when she sought peace of mind.

Jakob was sitting on a stone bench several feet away. He'd insisted on coming with her, for her own safety. Desire hadn't objected. Though her garden was still her emotional haven, she no longer took it for granted the high parapets protected her from intruders.

After explaining everything to Benjamin, and writing a note to her household in Kingston authorising Kilverdale's presence, she had returned to Godwin House. Benjamin, Jakob and several of Lord Halross's servants had accompanied her. There had been no point in going to Kingston to confront Arscott because he wasn't there, but Desire had half-expected to find him in the house on the Strand. By the time they'd arrived, her nerves had been wound tight in expectation of a traumatic meeting with Arscott. But there had been no sign of the steward. He'd hadn't returned since his fleeting visit that morning.

Desire's immediate reaction at Arscott's absence had been relief. She was dreading the moment when she must question him. But she was also anxious and frustrated. Where was he? When would he be found? The uncertainty played on her nerves. She almost believed Jakob's allegations, but she wanted to talk to Arscott herself. Hear his defence or confession. And then—she sighed heavily enough to create a small eddy of ash—she would have to make some painful decisions.

She stood up and moved on a couple of paces. A large piece of wood lay aslant a small bed of ash-encrusted herbs. The smell of the fire overpowered the scent of the herbs. Desire reached across and tried to lift the wood. She discovered she needed two hands to do so. She was amazed that such a heavy object had been whirled aloft by the fierce winds that had blown over London earlier in the week.

She lifted the wood clear of the plants and dropped it on the gravel. The impact kicked up a small billow of gritty ash that settled on the bottom of her skirt. The shabby work clothes she'd changed into earlier were filthy. Her thoughts jumped to her maid. She'd needed Lucy's help to unlace the beautiful blue gown. The maid had arrived at Godwin House at twilight, riding pillion behind one of the grooms. They had followed Benjamin from Kingston, but hadn't travelled at such breakneck speed. Lucy had burst into tears of relief on discovering her mistress safe and sound, but her attention had been very happily diverted into admiration for the blue silk gown.

'I knew you'd look good in silk, my lady. You must have some gowns made up just like this,' she said firmly.

'I believe I will,' said Desire, laughing at Lucy's eager expression. Some good had come of the catastrophe. She would please herself and her maid by extending her wardrobe.

Desire's disorganised thoughts returned abruptly to her immediate surroundings. She looked around and saw Jakob sitting at his ease on the bench. His dark clothes blended into the shadows. She could see the pale outline of his head, but not his expression. Even though he made no sound or movement to attract her attention, behind all the other thoughts buzzing randomly through her mind she was constantly aware of his presence.

He hadn't tried to dissuade her from coming on to the roof. Nor had he tried to talk to her. He just sat quietly and let her flit from one half-finished task—or thought—to the next. His patience was both comforting and disconcerting. She wondered what he was thinking. Had he spared a moment's consideration for the kiss they'd shared last night? Or was he wholly preoccupied by bringing Arscott to justice?

She abandoned the half-filled sack of rubbish and went to stand by the parapet overlooking London. She crossed her arms over her chest, trying to imagine the dreadful destruction she hadn't seen with her own eyes just as, a few days ago, she had tried to imagine the people hurrying along the lively streets. Most of those streets were gone now. Tears filled her eyes. She lifted her hand and realised it was encased in a heavy leather glove. She dragged off both gloves and laid them on the parapet. Despite the protection of the gloves, her fingers were still covered in a fine layer of dust and grit. She caught a tear on her knuckle and swallowed a sob that would betray her volatile emotions to Jakob.

'My lady?' he said softly, from just a few feet behind her.

She caught her breath in surprise. She hadn't realised he'd left the bench. 'You move as silently as a ghost!' She kept her head turned away from him and tried to insert a cheerful note into her voice.

'You were lost in your thoughts. It is a sad sight.'

'Yes.' Desire was very conscious of him standing behind her, looking over her shoulder towards the burning city. He didn't touch her, but she could sense his solid strength very close to her.

'It is so…foolish,' she said, suddenly driven to share her thoughts with him. 'I stood here on Saturday afternoon, wishing I could go into London, even thinking of ways I could—and now it is too late. London has gone. I'll never…I'll never see it.' Her voice wavered on a sob. Of its own volition her mouth turned down at the corners. She struggled to control her trembling lips, grateful for the darkness and the fact she wasn't looking at Jakob.

He put his arms around her. The comfort of his embrace almost destroyed her self-control. She squeezed her eyes tight shut, determined not to surrender to tears.

'It will be rebuilt,' he said against her hair.

She took several careful breaths, focussing her attention on the sensation of being held in his strong arms rather than her grief. The dawning quiver of excitement he aroused within her was a pleasant distraction from her regrets.

'It won't be the same,' she said, when she could trust her voice.

'It may be better.'

'I won't be able to make a true comparison. I hardly knew it at all, and now I never will. I never took the chance to see it while I could and now it's too late.'

Too late.

Such sad and final words. The distant flames blurred before Desire's eyes. She blinked them away. There was no one to blame but herself. When her father had still been alive it had been her duty to abide by his wishes. But since his death she had been responsible for herself. It was true she had suffered from the interference of other people, but the ultimate decision to hide from the world these past five years had been hers. She had been afraid. And while she waited for courage too many chances had passed her by. She stared at the burning city and resolved she would never leave it too late again. Her caution had resulted only in loneliness and, according to all the indications, made her vulnerable to an over-ambitious, murderous steward.

'Come and sit down,' said Jakob.

She let him guide her to the bench. Earlier she'd laid a large piece of sacking over it to protect his fine clothes. She sat down beside him, taking care not to let her ash-covered skirt brush against his black brocade coat. All her jumbled thoughts about the events of the day slid into the background. When she was this close to Jakob she could think of nothing but him. All her senses were attuned to his tiniest movement. She wondered what he'd been thinking of while he'd been sitting so patiently. She wanted to know his thoughts and feelings and intentions. Most important of all, she wanted to know how he felt about her.

'How are your hands?' she asked, taking refuge in common courtesy.

'Healing nicely, thank you.' He'd replaced the bandages with a pair of soft gloves given to him by Lord Halross.

'I'm glad.' She glanced at Jakob and saw he was watching her.

She quickly looked away, gripping her skirt nervously. Then she realised what she was doing and folded her hands in her lap, trying to give the appearance at least of serenity.

His long leg was stretched out lazily beside her. She remembered the feel of it lying across hers and her whole body flushed with self-conscious heat. She forgot about the anticipated reputation-saving marriage proposal he had not made earlier and remembered instead how he'd kissed her in the darkness last night. She tingled with embarrassing pleasure as she recalled the exhilarating weight of his body upon hers, pressing her into the mattress, filling her with tumultuous sensations.

Perhaps it was because they were alone beneath the moon that her thoughts were so wayward. Most of the torches had now burnt out and there was little chance they'd be interrupted. Benjamin had been exhausted from his hard ride and anxiety and had gone early to bed and no one else was likely to bother them.

Desire stole another glance at Jakob. Perhaps he would kiss her again. She caught her lower lip between her teeth, unconsciously sucking it as she considered the possibility. There was no denying she'd enjoyed the experience. No other man had ever shown any interest in kissing her. To be fair, she'd never felt any urge to kiss any other man. If Arscott was captured tomorrow and Jakob no longer felt any obligation to guard her, this might be her last opportunity. He'd apparently enjoyed kissing her before and, although it was probably very shocking of her, she didn't see how one more kiss would do any harm.

How did she indicate to him she wouldn't mind if he kissed her? Athena would surely know, but Desire had no idea. She glanced down at herself. The shabby old dress was suitable for delving in the dirty ash covering her garden, not enticing the interest of a handsome man. It covered her from throat to ankles. She recalled Athena's trick with the bodice of the blue gown, but it would be far too obvious and immodest to adjust her neckline in Jakob's presence.

Then she remembered that he'd kissed her last night after

she'd nearly stepped on him lying outside the door. Perhaps she should stand up and pretend to fall over his outstretched leg? She'd have to jump up fast before he had a chance to rise also as courtesy demanded. But he already believed she was a trifle clumsy, and if she accidentally fell on to his lap...

Jakob took her hand. Her heart gave a startled thump and then began to beat so fast and loudly she was sure he could hear it. But the last time he'd taken her hand it had been the prelude to bad news, not a kiss.

'Are you going to tell me some other bad thing?' she burst out.

'I hope not.' He sounded taken aback.

'Oh.' Desire flushed with embarrassment. If he'd been planning to kiss her, of course he wouldn't consider it bad. And if *he* now believed *she* thought it would be a bad thing, she might have put him off. How did other women manage in this kind of situation? Perhaps next time she saw Athena she should endure the embarrassment of asking for advice. In the meantime, she decided a *small* amount of encouragement to Jakob might be in order.

'You may if you wish,' she said, keeping her eyes studiously fixed on the corner of the water cistern because she was far too self-conscious to look at him.

''That is very gracious of you, my lady.' He'd sounded mildly perplexed before, but now there was not a shadow of doubt that he was amused.

Mortified and incensed, Desire leapt to her feet. 'It's late. I'll say goodnight to you, sir—'

He gave a deft tug on the hand he still held and she landed on his lap.

'How dare you!' she sputtered, startled by how he'd turned the tables on her. 'Unhand me!'

'I'm not handling you,' he pointed out. He demonstrated by holding both arms out on either side of her. 'You can dismount any time you wish.'

'I am not mounted!' She was half-scandalised by his turn of phrase. She supposed he was flirting with her—and the reality was even more overwhelming than the memory of his kisses.

She could feel his muscular thighs through the layers of her skirts. He rested one arm casually across her lap, but he didn't constrain her in any way. The weight of his arm across her legs was very…stimulating…in a rather subtle way. She was surrounded by his strength, but he wasn't using force to hold her captive.

This close she could see the teasing light in his eyes. His smile was a wickedly enticing dare, tempting her to come closer. Without realising what she was doing, she rested one hand on his shoulder as she waited to see what his next move would be. He just tilted his head back a little further. The look in his eyes said he was perfectly well aware of what she was thinking and what she expected of him—and somehow she just knew he was inviting *her* to kiss *him*

It wasn't what she'd expected. He was the one who was supposed to kiss her—wasn't he? She caught her lower lip between her teeth as she worried over the problem. But his hair was a temptation she couldn't resist. Almost without realising it, she began to stroke and play with the long golden strands. Even in the moonlight she saw how his eyes darkened at her actions.

Suddenly she snatched her hand back.

'I'm all ashy!' she gasped, belatedly remembering her hands were far from clean.

'I can stand a little ash,' he replied, his voice so deep it reverberated throughout Desire's body. 'Don't stop for that.'

'Oh.' She lifted her hand again, a little tentatively. For a moment she looked beyond Jakob and saw the distant fires and the stark black silhouettes of ruined buildings. Soon perhaps most of the city would be gone.

Too late. She was never going to leave it too late again.

With sudden resolution she lowered her head and gently touched her mouth to Jakob's lips. Her heart hammered with nervousness at her boldness. Her blood sang in her ears, drowning out any other sound. She was so overwhelmed by her own brazen behaviour that for several seconds she forgot to be excited by the feel of Jakob's mouth against hers.

She expected him to kiss her back. Instead she felt him smile against her lips.

She jerked her head away and tried to scramble off his lap.

For the first time he tightened his hold on her, easily preventing her half-hearted attempt to escape.

'You're laughing at me!' she accused him, hurt and indignant.

'No. Never.' His deep voice was soothing and seductive. 'Again,' he murmured, 'try again.'

Desire looked at him warily. He didn't *appear* to be laughing at her. She couldn't quite read his expression, but when he smiled and lifted his chin very slightly she could only interpret the gesture as a renewed invitation to kiss him. She would much have preferred him to kiss her, but she wasn't bold enough to say that.

She took a deep breath, her courage in both hands, and lightly brushed her lips across his a second time. He didn't smile this time, but nor did he kiss her into the state of delirious confusion she'd experienced the previous night.

'More,' he murmured against her mouth. 'More, *älskling.*'

'*More?*' Desire lifted her head once more to stare at him in suspicion and frustration.

'Kiss me the way I want to be kissed,' he said softly. 'Kiss me the way a man dreams of being kissed when—'

'You *are* making fun of me!'

'Do you have any idea of what torture it was to lie beside you all night and not touch you again?'

'I... Oh...*torture*?' Desire gazed at him, intrigued and pleased by what he'd just said. 'Really? You wanted to kiss me again?'

'And now you're torturing me,' he pointed out. 'Giving me such insipid little pecks when I know—'

'You are trying to provoke me into kissing you!' Desire exclaimed, thumping his shoulder. 'To make me prove I can do better than…than… You are devious and underhand! That is not gentlemanly!'

Jakob laughed softly. 'Such energy. Such passion. Show me, *älskling*.'

'You are a scoundrel,' she told him, a smile tugging at her lips despite herself.

'Mmm.' Jakob hummed in amused, wordless agreement with her assessment of his character. For the first time he put his hands on her waist.

She held her breath as he spanned her slim waist, then slid his hands up her back towards her shoulders, very gently urging her closer.

She let him pull her closer, but her hand on his shoulder kept a certain careful distance between them.

'You are trying to take advantage of my lack of worldly experience,' she said, far more confident than she had been a few minutes ago.

'Not with any great success,' he retorted. 'And at considerable expense to my manly pride.'

'You mean it normally only takes one glance from your fine blue eyes and women melt into a pool at your feet,' Desire said, exhilarated by their teasing conversation.

'Or thereabouts,' he agreed. 'You are the first wench ever to beat me black and blue, abuse me and scorn—'

'I did *not* beat you black and blue,' she interrupted indignantly. 'Did I really hurt you?' she asked, a little worriedly.

'Would you like to see the bruises?' Even in the lantern light she could see the wicked gleam in his eyes.

'No. Thank you.' She was determined not to seem flustered. 'I will make you a salve for them if you like.'

'A kiss would be much better medicine.'

'You didn't kiss me back!' Desire burst out, then became mortified at what she'd just said.

'You gave up too soon. Persistence is a virtue—and would have been rewarded.'

'Insufferable arrogance!' Desire was outraged. 'It is not *I* who should stoop to tempt you, but you who should—' She broke off as she felt Jakob shake with laughter. 'Humph.' She turned sideways on his lap and folded her arms across her chest.

It would be more dignified if she stood up and left the roof, but that seemed a rather extreme—not to say irreversible—step to take. She settled for not looking at him, but she felt both vulnerable and frustrated. He understood the rules of this game far better than she did.

He kissed her temple.

It was very pleasurable, but she refused to surrender immediately to his seductive caresses. He had made her feel foolish. She kept her face averted from him.

'Desire?' he murmured against her skin.

'Don't call me that.'

'Don't you think I do?' His kissed her temple again, brushed his lips over her cheek and kissed the corner of her mouth. She drew in a quick, responsive breath, then nervously moistened her lower lip with her tongue.

Jakob stroked the tender skin beneath her ear with light fingertips. A second later his mouth replaced his fingers. Desire sighed as his warm lips tantalised her sensitive flesh. She closed her eyes, surrendering to the intoxicating sensations he conjured within her.

His hand slid lower. For a moment he laid his palm flat on the upper plane of her breast. Even through her bodice she could feel the heat of his touch. On a surge of excitement she turned her head towards him. Instantly his mouth claimed hers.

The shock of possession was overwhelming. She felt rather than heard his deep, satisfied hum as he ravished her mouth. She twisted to face him more fully, instinctively pressing her breasts against his firm chest. Her hand slipped up around his neck. He filled her entire awareness. The tip of his tongue stroked inside her mouth and she shivered at the exotic, masculine taste of him. His tongue pressed more urgently past her lips in an erotic rhythm. She began to ache with a hot, unfulfilled need in a different place entirely. She wriggled in his lap.

He groaned against her mouth and his hand clamped on her hip, holding her more tightly against his lower body. Even through the layers of her skirts she became aware of a hard pressure against her hip. It partially distracted her from his hot kisses. She squirmed again, experimentally, eager to discover if what she thought she could feel was what she really could feel.

'Do that one more time and your skirts will be up around your waist and you'll be astride me,' Jakob warned her harshly.

She was shocked into abrupt stillness, hardly even daring to breathe. Her body was flushed and aching with arousal, her lips swollen and tingling from Jakob's kisses. But he had just spoken to her more harshly than ever before. She felt disorientated. Confused. She looked at him in bewilderment. His face was in shadows and she couldn't see his expression. Instead she heard his ragged intake of breath. The thigh muscles beneath her were solid with tension. He deliberately moved his arms away from her. His embrace had been warm and welcoming, now his whole body was rigid with silent rejection.

Desire found herself sitting on the lap of a man who clearly didn't want her there. It was one of the most humiliating experiences of her life. Even Kilverdale hadn't tempted her with kisses before slighting her.

A crashing tidal wave of anger came to her rescue. Fury at Jakob for playing games with her. Fury at herself for so naïvely allowing him to do so. It must have greatly amused him to tease her into kissing him. She had behaved like the most wanton alehouse wench and now he was treating her accordingly. It was intolerable.

She tried to stand up, desperate to put as much physical distance between them as possible.

Instantly his arms closed around her, preventing her from moving.

'Let me go!' She sat stiffly upright, refusing to sacrifice her dignity in a struggle.

'Desire—'

'I wish to go in now,' she said coldly, refusing to look at him. 'Kindly release me.'

He allowed her to slip off his lap and she stood up. Her legs felt like water, but she stiffened her knees and hoped he wouldn't notice how she trembled.

'Goodnight, sir,' she said, proud of her steady voice.

'Desire—'

Her step faltered briefly, then she walked away without looking back.

Jakob let her go. He wasn't sure what he would have said if she'd stayed. He was frustrated by the outcome of their tryst and angry with himself. He had meant to do no more than indulge them both in a little light-hearted flirtation. He should have known better. The need Desire created in him was far too powerful to be satisfied by a mere kiss. His hasty words had been provoked by the deeply conflicting emotions she aroused in him, but he'd regretted them as soon as they were out of his mouth. It had been unfair to speak so harshly to her. But it was easy to forget how inexperienced she was, and to mistake her genuine confusion or indignation for the provocative ploys of a more knowing woman.

He stretched out his arms and legs in an effort to release some of the tension cramping his muscles. When he'd set out for England, he hadn't expected his life to become so complicated so quickly. He'd lingered at Dover because he hadn't been in a hurry to present himself to his grandfather. But now his status as Lord Swiftbourne's heir was the least of his immediate problems. There was Arscott to bring to justice. Desire to keep safe. The continuing but reduced danger of the fire. Even the possibility of invasion by the French or Dutch—though he was inclined to trust Swiftbourne's sources that there was no imminent threat.

And in the midst of everything else was his powerful attraction to Desire. He'd been drawn to her from the first moment he saw her, flushed and contented in the middle of her garden. His admiration for her had grown during the failed abduction attempt. She had held him at bay so courageously with Potticary's pistol and then prevented her angry household from lynching him. It had taken rare strength of character to enforce her wishes, especially when Arscott was undermining her authority with subtle encouragement to the servants who usually took their orders from him.

Jakob suspected that, even now, Desire didn't fully realise it was the steward who had prompted the first cry to lynch him, a cry that had been enthusiastically taken up by almost every other man on the roof until Benjamin arrived.

He owed her his life. He respected the fierce integrity that had compelled her to save him. Most of all, he liked her directness and her honesty. There was nothing coy about Lady Desire. She'd wanted him to kiss her and she'd come very close to saying so. The memory of her gracious, though carefully unspecified, permission brought a smile to his lips. And she was as passionate as she was honest. The remembered feel of her in his arms, warm and responsive, stirred his blood anew. His smiled faded as he recalled what had happened next. She hadn't received a fair return for her lack of guile. He could hardly blame her for her anger at the way he'd just treated her.

He frowned at an ash-covered bed of lavender. One of the earliest decisions he'd made after discovering he would one day inherit his grandfather's title was that, since he would eventually end his days in England, he would wait and take an English wife. He'd seen how his Swedish-born mother dreaded moving to England when her husband inherited. In the end she'd been spared that upheaval by the unexpected death of James Balston in a quayside accident but, for more than a decade, the eventual move had been a continual source of background anxiety to her. With his mother's example before him, Jakob had never had any heart to set up a cosy family in Sweden, only to uproot it and transplant it to an unfamiliar land.

The decision had imposed little hardship on him—as a younger man he hadn't been ready for the restrictions of marriage—but it had made him cautious. For the whole of his adult life he had been careful never to let any flirtation become too serious, and never to allow any woman to harbour misplaced dreams of becoming his wife. Keeping a woman at a distance—while at the same time taking whatever uncommitted pleasure she was willing to give—had become a habit.

He'd instinctively fallen into the same pattern in his flirtation with Desire. The unusual circumstances of their initial meeting and continuing contact removed most of the restrictions that normally protected a gently bred young woman. It was easy and very pleasant to tease and kiss her. But Desire did not understand the rules of the game he usually played. If they continued as they had been, he risked hurting her even more badly than Kilverdale—not to mention destroying her reputation.

He stared into the darkness. His original decision had been to delay marriage because of the peculiar circumstances of his inheritance, not avoid it permanently. That thought led him back to Swiftbourne. Desire was just the kind of wealthy noblewoman that any sensible man would wish his heir to marry. Jakob was sure that Lord Swiftbourne had begun to calculate the advantages of the match from the moment he'd learnt of Jakob's involvement with Desire.

The thought set him on edge. He knew that, sooner or later, he would end up living permanently in England. He'd come now to acquaint himself with the Swiftbourne estates and dependents, but he still wasn't sure whether he wanted to stay here while he waited for Swiftbourne to die. The role of the dutiful—or impatient—heir did not appeal to him. He only meant to remain in England if he could find something to do that satisfied his need for independent, fulfilling action. He would have to be much more cautious in his dealings with Desire. He had no wish to play fast and lose with her feelings or expectations.

In the meantime, his most important task was to keep her safe. He stood up and followed her down into the house.

There were very few mirrors in Godwin House and most of those had been removed to save them from the fire. Desire had to search through several, seldom-used rooms before she found one. She held up a candle so she could see herself clearly. The scars were there, just as she remembered. Two jagged lines across her cheek. Perhaps they were a little less pronounced than they had been when she was a child. She had another scar on her leg that snaked over her thigh, but that didn't matter because no one else ever saw it. Only the scars on her face were important.

She traced her fingers along the ugly ridges. She could remember her life before she'd had them—but she couldn't remember what it was like not to be scarred. It seemed that all her life she had been turning her face aside to avoid curious glances from strangers.

She stroked her fingers back over the scars. It was a long time since she'd studied them in such close detail. They were not beautiful, but they were not—she did not think they were...repellent. Today she had met many strangers and none of them had acted as if they found her appearance repulsive. She'd seen curiosity in their eyes, but not revulsion.

Fear of rejection had haunted Desire ever since she'd overheard Kilverdale's cruel words six years ago. But perhaps she'd been afraid of it even before their betrothal had been discussed. She'd always known her fortune made her an attractive bride, yet she'd been twenty-four before her father had begun marriage negotiations on her behalf.

She stroked her hand once more over her cheek. Had it been her father's fear for his beloved only child that had delayed his marriage plans on her behalf—he'd always been more protec-

tive of her tender feelings than her practical-minded mother—
or the complications of the ever-changing political situation? Or
had he simply not wanted to lose her company?

One reason Lord Larksmere hadn't sought a husband for his
daughter earlier had been the death of Lady Larksmere. Desire's
mother had died, after being ill for nearly two years, when
Desire was twenty-one. Desire had nursed the Countess for most
of that time, always sure her valiant mother would get better,
never once giving any thought to a suitor for herself. Despite the
forewarning, the Countess's death had come as a shock to the
whole household. By the time Lord Larksmere had recovered
sufficiently from his personal grief to look outwards once more,
Cromwell was dead and the whole country once more teetered
in uncertainty. It wasn't until the return of Charles II, when
Desire was twenty-four, that her father had made a serious attempt to find her a husband.

With hindsight, Desire could see that the proposed marriage
between Kilverdale and herself would have been a mismatch in
more ways than one. The Royalist returned from exile and the
daughter of one of Cromwell's allies were from completely different worlds. Lord Larksmere had not supported the execution
of the King and had withdrawn from public life from that time
forward, but he had always remained on good terms with
Cromwell.

When Desire had first overheard Kilverdale's cruel comment
about her, she'd taken it as a personal rejection of her, but for
the first time she wondered if she'd been wrong. Was her appearance the real cause of the anger and bitterness she'd heard in his
voice that dreadful day? Or had he simply vented his anger and
grief at everything the Parliamentarians had cost him on the
nearest available target? Perhaps even regretted his cruelty later?

Because everyone she'd met today—Jakob, Athena, Lord
Swiftbourne, even Lord Halross—trusted without question that
Kilverdale would diligently protect the fortune she'd sent to
Kingston. There must be more to the man than casual unkind-

ness if he could inspire so much confidence in those who knew
him. If she'd been wrong about Arscott and wrong about
Kilverdale, how much else had she been wrong about?

A creaking board caught her attention. The big old house was
full of creaks and groans. Most of the time she hardly noticed,
but tonight she lifted her candle and glanced around the shadows of the seldom-used chamber. She could see nothing to alarm
her. The oldest parts of the house had been built more than a cen-
tury ago. Even the newest additions dated back eighty years to
the reign of Elizabeth. Desire's grandfather had had the new wing
built, Arscott's grandfather had been one of the masons who'd
worked on it.

Desire's grandfather had died before she was born. Her only
knowledge of him came from his portrait, which usually hung in
the great parlour, and the stories told by her father. He'd been a
staunch Roman Catholic who had never forgiven his son—Desire's
father—for becoming a Protestant. It was strange to think that, although Desire did not share the same form of worship as her grandfather, she had inherited so much else from him. Not only the house
in which she lived, but the links between her family and Arscott's,
which dated back at least three generations. She could still hardly
believe the steward was guilty of everything Jakob claimed.

Jakob.

She turned back to the mirror, finally allowing herself to remember what had happened on the roof. Her immediate reaction had been anger, hurt and a bitter sense of rejection. He was
as cruel as Kilverdale. Humiliated pride demanded that she ban-
ish him from her house and presence at the first opportunity.
Only the certainty that he wouldn't obey such a demand had prevented her from uttering it on the roof. It would be even more
humiliating when he ignored her order.

But now she was calmer, she was able to see that there was
a huge difference between what the two men had said—and
what they'd meant. Kilverdale had said he didn't want her under
any circumstances. Jakob had implied the absolute reverse.

Do that one more time and your skirts will be up around your waist and you'll be astride me.

Desire flushed with mortification at the image conjured by the crude words, but they weren't a rejection. Ungallant, unromantic and brutally direct—but not a rejection. They were a warning: she'd stirred his lust to danger point. He'd wanted her so much he'd been on the point of taking her right there on the roof.

She laid one hand against the wall beside the mirror. Even in the candlelight she could see the turbulent expression in her eyes. She couldn't doubt Jakob's physical readiness to make love to her. *Her* kisses had created that response in him. Until she'd met Jakob, she'd never imagined she could ever have such a potent effect upon a man. She was excited, scared and furious.

Part of her anger was directed at Jakob for playing games with her. It wasn't fair to tempt her to kiss him and then blame her when his male passion became too fierce. But she was also angry at herself because her lack of worldly experience made her so susceptible to him. A more sophisticated woman wouldn't have permitted him to toy with her so humiliatingly.

She'd played right into his hands. Wondering how to make him kiss her! He must be laughing himself sick at her innocence. The little pigeon so desperate for masculine approval she'd even given him permission to pluck her—or at least to kiss her. What had she been thinking? Jakob was an opportunist scoundrel who had kissed her at every available opportunity since she'd knelt before him in the rowing boat.

She whirled away from the mirror so fast the candle nearly blew out. He was beautiful and she was not. Did he think it was an act of charity to kiss her? He had taken advantage of her and she had let him because no other man had ever wanted her. But that wasn't good enough. She was not his plaything.

She strode out of the small chamber into the long gallery, which stretched the full length of the east wing. She started to pace up and down. The candle flame flickered wildly in the breeze she created. She set it down a safe distance away and continued to march up and down the shadowy gallery, working out her anger and frustration in the exercise. Her footsteps echoed on the floorboards. To the end and back. To the end and back. She'd walked miles in this gallery over the years. Hundreds of miles? Thousands of miles? And never gone anywhere.

She reached the end of the gallery and turned on her heel with an angry swish of her skirts. A fine cloud of ash blew up from her hem, reminding her of the destruction and lost chances beyond the safety of her walls. A single candle was inadequate to light the entire length of the gallery—most of it was in darkness. The shadows didn't scare her. She was familiar with them. The world beyond her gates was far more daunting. So was Jakob. The growing strength of her attraction to him and her suspicion that he was simply amusing himself at her expense both scared and angered her. She hated being at such a disadvantage.

But she also needed a husband. There were many good and practical reasons for marriage—she needed a strong man to protect her and give her children. But she also need a husband for her own personal contentment. A husband who would escort her into society, talk to her, ease her loneliness, tease her, kiss her...

Jakob had proved to be competent at all of those things—apart from a tendency to withhold essential information from her, though perhaps she could train him out of that error. But was he looking for a wife? That was a question of utmost importance.

The answer was immediately obvious. A man who would one day inherit an earldom must be eager to ensure the succession. Her father had reconciled himself to the will of God on the matter, but only after Lady Larksmere had endured several miscarriages and Desire's five older brothers and sisters had all died before their second birthday. Desire knew it had been a lingering sadness to her father to the end of his life that his title would die with him.

So Jakob needed a wife. No doubt he would prefer one who was young and unblemished, but in her favour was her fortune and the fact he apparently liked kissing and teasing her. That was a lot more than many marriages were founded upon.

She stopped dead in the middle of the gallery and drew in a deep, resolute breath. Jakob seemed a very good candidate to become her husband. But she needed to know more about him, and she definitely had to make sure he didn't play games at her expense. It was time to take over the direction of her own life. Tomorrow she would make a start.

Chapter Eleven

'Colonel Balston slept all night on a bench in the long gallery,' Lucy announced.

'What?' Desire twisted round to stare at her maid. 'Why?' She rubbed a hand to her temple. She was tired from lack of sleep and tightly wound at the prospect of putting her new plans into action. She couldn't immediately make sense of what Jakob was doing in the long gallery.

'Didn't anyone provide him with a bedchamber?' she asked. She was so unused to having guests she hadn't given any thought to where he would be housed. Benjamin had made the arrangements for Lord Halross's men. She'd just naturally assumed he'd do the same for Jakob. Apparently not.

Oh, dear. It was true she'd decided not to pander to Jakob's arrogant male whims, but it was hardly sophisticated to leave her potential...possible...well, maybe...suitor to fend for himself on an oak bench. Even if it did serve him right for being so insufferably pleased with himself.

'He was given a chamber on the second floor,' said Lucy, 'but he said he was guarding you.'

'Guarding me?'

'In case anyone tried to steal you in the night,' said Lucy, her eyes glowing with excitement. 'It is so romantic. Don't you think he's handsome, my lady? And such a gallant gentleman.'

'Um…yes,' said Desire, wondering exactly how gallant he'd been to her maid. Did he flirt with every female he encountered?

'Guarding me? In my own house?' The thought of Jakob sleeping outside her door to protect her caused a strange flutter behind her ribs. Of course he wasn't immediately outside her door. Her bedchamber was connected to the long gallery by a small, connecting parlour. There had been two solid oak doors between them all night. All the same, he must have been thinking about her last night, just as she'd been thinking about him. Though his thoughts had probably consisted of muttered curses about the draughtiness of the long gallery and the discomfort created by oak planks.

'That's what *I* said,' said Lucy. 'Surely her ladyship is safe in her own bedchamber, I said to the Colonel. But he says it's a big house and…not wanting to frighten you, my lady…but there's so many passages and rooms, it would be easy for a villain to creep in and hide somewhere and come out at night.'

'Nonsense,' said Desire. 'Well, possibly,' she acknowledged after a couple of seconds. Even under normal circumstances, when the house was fully staffed, there were many rooms never visited by Desire or the servants from one week to the next. It would be relatively straightforward for an intruder to remain undetected for days if he chose. She shivered at the notion.

'I'm sure Colonel Balston exaggerates the risk,' she said firmly.

'And then there are ghosts,' said Lucy, with what Desire considered to be unnecessary relish. 'I told you how I've heard them—slithering and creeping about the place.'

'Lucy, you know it was only a pigeon that flew in an open shutter and couldn't get out again!' Desire exclaimed.

'Yes, my lady.' Lucy didn't look convinced. 'You're not going gardening this morning, are you?'

'Why not?' As it happened, Desire had no intention of gardening, but she wondered why her maid sounded so disapproving of the notion.

'It's nasty and dirty on the roof and you can't wear the pretty blue gown,' said Lucy. 'You look so lovely in it. It would be just the thing to wear when you see Colonel Balston.'

'Thank you.' Desire was touched by Lucy's praise—and secretly relieved by the maid's blatant attempt at matchmaking. It seemed as if Lucy's romantic ambitions were on her mistress's behalf, not her own.

'No, I'm not going on the roof, but I don't think I should wear the blue gown,' she said, and saw Lucy's expression turn stubborn. 'What else have we got?' she asked. 'I know we didn't send most of my clothes away. When there was so much else to be saved, I didn't think they were worth worrying about. Haven't I still got the grey silk that was made up for me at the time of the Coronation?'

'I don't remember it,' said Lucy, but she went willingly to investigate Desire's limited store of clothes.

'I haven't worn it since you became my maid,' said Desire. Lucy had served her for barely a year. It had been a worrying time for Desire when her old maid had become too old to serve her, yet, now she thought of it, she realised the transition had been far less traumatic than she'd anticipated. Lucy was so cheerful and good natured.

'Is this the one you mean?' Lucy shook out the folds of sombre slate-grey silk.

'That's the one.'

'It's very finely made,' said Lucy dubiously, obviously not wishing to hurt her mistress's feelings. 'But it is not…'

'I know,' said Desire. 'It is nowhere near as beautiful as the blue. But it will do very well for what I have in mind.'

Jakob stood up as the door opened. It could have been the maid, but by some instinct he was sure it was Desire. Despite his resolution to be more formal with her from now on, he was glad to see her. The haughty tilt of her chin as she looked at him filled him with amused appreciation. It seemed the Earl's daughter had made some resolutions of her own overnight.

'Good morning, my lady,' he said politely. 'I trust you slept well.'

A hot spark of indignation flared in her eyes, but her expression remained serene.

'Good morning, Colonel Balston,' she replied coolly, ignoring the second part of his salutation.

Jakob's amusement grew. The lady clearly deemed it an impertinence for an upstart rascal such as he to enquire after her night's repose.

'If you lift your chin any higher, your nose will be touching the ceiling,' he said.

Her chin came down and the spark of indignation in her eyes blazed into fiery outrage.

'I did not ask you to sleep outside my door like a dog!' She glared at him. Are you afraid I might run away from my own home?'

'No, my lady. I am not here to keep you in, but to keep others out.'

She took a deep breath. Jakob was distracted by the press of her breasts against her bodice. She was dressed from throat to toes in sober grey silk. He was sure the gown was her own, not one she had borrowed from Athena, because it was somewhat old-fashioned in style and fitted her perfectly. Besides, it looked like the kind of dress a wealthy but puritanical man might expect his daughter to wear. It was definitely not intended to stir a man's lust—yet it stirred Jakob's. The gown showed off her trim waist, and he couldn't help imagining the pleasure of loosening the tightly laced bodice.

'Do you think there is a real risk that someone—Arscott— may try to take me from my own bedchamber?' Desire asked.

'Probably not,' he said, pushing aside a vision of his tongue tasting Desire's soft breast. 'But Arscott is as familiar with this house as you are. And we mustn't forget the house was only protected by a couple of porters for the past two days. I had no trouble slipping past them on Tuesday to take you from the roof. I'm sure it would have been just as easy for Arscott to gain secret access yesterday.'

He saw Desire give a small shiver.

'I don't think it is likely,' he said more gently. 'But it is better for us to be on our guard until he is found.'

'Yes, of course,' she said, but she looked a little bleak at the prospect.

For a moment she forgot to play the haughty lady intent on keeping him in his place. In the past few days the solid certainties of her life had disintegrated and her expression revealed her sense of loss and confusion. Jakob resisted the urge to put a comforting arm around her.

''Perhaps Arscott will prove to be innocent after all,' said Desire. 'In the meantime, I hope you do not find the bench *too* uncomfortable,' she continued, with determined brightness. 'Perhaps Lucy can find you some pillows or a bolster.'

'There's no need,' Jakob replied. 'I don't want to be *too* comfortable.'

'I suppose not.' She frowned. 'If you fall asleep, he might stick you with a sword!' she said suddenly. 'He needs me alive so he can marry me—but it would be far more convenient to him if you're dead!'

'That thought had occurred to me,' Jakob conceded, gratified by Desire's sudden anxiety on his behalf. In fact, he'd spent most of the night in the antechamber between Desire's room and the gallery. It was more comfortable than the gallery and he'd been able to sleep, secure in the knowledge that anyone trying to open the outer door would crash into the barricade he'd placed across it. He'd only returned to the discomfort of the gallery just before dawn, but he didn't feel any need to explain that to Desire.

'Oh, no.' She put both hands to her head and began to pace

around in circles. 'This is no good! If you fall asleep he'll stick you. But you can't stay awake all the time... You haven't planned properly, sir!' She spun around to face him, both hands propped on her waist. 'You must make up a proper schedule with Lord Halross's men. They can take it in turns to perform sentry duty here, in the long gallery, during the night.'

'I have posted men to guard all the staircases that lead to this floor,' Jakob replied, not at all offended by her suggestion. In fact, he appreciated her practical response to the problem. 'I am not the first, but the last, line of defence for you, my lady.'

Desire stared at him. 'Good,' she said at last. 'And this afternoon you must appoint two of Lord Halross's men to guard me so you can catch up on your sleep.'

'Why not this morning?' he asked curiously, noting but not commenting on her flattering assumption that it would require two men to replace him on guard duty.

Colour stole into Desire's cheeks. 'I have a task for you this morning,' she said, her attempt at boldness tinged with awkwardness.

'Really? What is it?'

'You may join me in the parlour for breakfast,' she said. 'I will tell you then.'

'Thank you.' Jakob rasped his hand across his chin. 'Perhaps, after I have seen you safely to the parlour, I might have a few minutes to myself before I join you for breakfast,' he said.

Desire's gaze focussed on his unshaven cheeks, then flickered to his mouth. Her blush deepened and she looked away. 'Yes, of course,' she said.

'This morning I am going shopping,' Desire announced to Jakob and Benjamin.

She ate a piece of cheese while she awaited their response and wondered if any of the servants Lord Halross had loaned her could cook. No fresh bread had been baked since Saturday. She was sure there was food in the house, but apparently no one knew how to prepare it.

'*Shopping?*' Benjamin looked first startled, then disapproving. 'My lady, this is hardly an appropriate time for such an activity. Besides, all the shops are burnt.'

'Not all of them.' Desire threw Jakob a quick glance, trying to gauge his reaction to her plans. 'Those in the New Exchange will not be damaged. It is not even very far away. I can easily visit it. Did Lord Halross send us a cook?'

'A cook?' Benjamin's face went blank.

'Surely the entire household—such as it is—is not living solely on cheese?' said Desire. 'There must be *something* else in the larder.'

'I'm sorry, my lady.' Benjamin flushed. 'I didn't think. The stables are my usual domain. You sent the housekeeper to Kingston. Arscott would usually—'

'I am not blaming you,' Desire reached out to lay a hand on his arm. 'I didn't mean you to take my words as a criticism.' She smiled at him and briefly tightened her grip before releasing him. 'How could I when you galloped to my rescue yesterday. Your loyalty means so much more to me than…' Her voice caught, so she stopped talking before she embarrassed them both by bursting into tears.

Benjamin cleared his throat. 'Nevertheless, I am sorry you have only cheese for breakfast,' he said gruffly. 'I will attend to the matter.'

'Thank you.' Desire managed a wobbly smile and washed down another piece of cheese with some weak ale.

'But I do not approve of your plan to go shopping,' Benjamin said. 'The city is full of rogues and looters. It wouldn't be safe for you on the streets.'

'I don't see that I will be any more at risk on the streets than I am at home,' Desire said. She looked at Jakob for support and discovered he was watching her closely. Flustered, she hurried on, 'As Colonel Balston has already pointed out, Arscott could have slipped back into the house before we returned yesterday. At this very moment he could be skulking in the shadows, waiting to leap out when our guard is down.'

'Skulking in the shadows?' Benjamin repeated sceptically. 'I don't think Arscott would do that. Besides, he didn't know you would be coming back here.'

'I doubt very much he is currently inside Godwin House,' Jakob said, entering the conversation for the first time. 'But until he is found it would be foolish to let down our guard. We do know Arscott left Kingston before you did yesterday, Benjamin, and certainly before Kilverdale arrived there. Apparently he came straight here and didn't find Lady Desire. We don't know where he went after that, but it's likely that he headed back to Kingston to see if she'd arrived while he was away. It's only when, or if, he arrives at Kingston and discovers Kilverdale guarding Lady Desire's movable wealth that he may realise he's under suspicion.'

'Then what?' said Desire, feeling a little sick as she thought of what the absent steward might do. She pushed her plate aside.

Jakob shrugged and reached across to pick up the piece of cheese she'd set aside. 'May I?' He raised an eyebrow in her direction.

She nodded. 'We'll get you something else to eat when we're out,' she said, briefly distracted by her hostessly duties. 'You are so large, I expect you require a lot of food.'

Jakob smiled. 'So my mother always complained. As to what Arscott will do next—you both know him better than I do. He could deny everything—come back and try to brazen it out. He could lose his nerve and run. Or he could make an attempt to capture either the heiress in London—' Jakob gestured towards Desire with the hand in which he held the cheese '—or the fortune in Kingston. Which he chooses might depend on whether he considers me or Kilverdale the most dangerous opponent.'

Having delivered his opinion, Jakob put the cheese in his mouth, apparently unconcerned by the possibility of another encounter with the steward.

'Oh, my God!' Desire murmured. The first thought that flashed through her mind was that Arscott would fear Kilverdale the most. But then she realised her opinion was distorted by her past experience with the black-haired, arrogant Duke. She didn't like Kilverdale, but she was sure he was a far less formidable opponent than Jakob. The battle-hardened Arscott was more likely to consider the Duke a pampered fop than a genuine threat. On the other hand, he might not even know Jakob was guarding her in London, though the burly porters in Halross's livery who now watched the gates of Godwin House might give him pause

'But even if Arscott succeeded in wedding me by force, I would repudiate the marriage,' she said slowly, continuing her assessment aloud. 'Now that I have you—' she looked at Jakob '—and Lord Halross and Lord Swiftbourne to stand my friends, Arscott would never get away with marrying me by force. Lord Rochester might not have been severely punished for trying to abduct an heiress, but my steward wouldn't get off so lightly would he?'

'No.' Jakob shook his head.

'So if he truly is guilty—greedy for wealth—it is much more likely that he will try to steal my money chest,' Desire decided. 'Coins are anonymous. They can't denounce him. Good.' She felt as if a huge weight had fallen from her shoulders. 'It would be silly for Arscott to try to take me when he could take the money instead. You must send a message to the Duke that he should be especially vigilant. And in the meantime there is absolutely no reason why I should not go shopping today.'

Benjamin still didn't like the idea. It was only after Desire agreed to be carried in her sedan chair that he was reconciled to the expedition. Fortunately the chair hadn't been sent away to Kingston. Benjamin hurried off to have it prepared, leaving Desire alone with Jakob.

She flicked a nervous glance at him. During breakfast she'd tried to push the memory of his kisses to the back of her mind. She didn't want him to realise how completely he occupied her thoughts, or how powerfully his physical presence effected her senses. She must appear calm, serene—

'What do you wish to buy?' he asked.

Nervous butterflies immediately started dancing in her stomach. She had absolutely no notion what she wanted to buy. The shopping trip was only an excuse for her to venture out into the world. To another woman it might not have seemed a particularly bold or daring adventure, but Desire was alternately excited and scared by her imminent visit to the New Exchange. She was finally taking control of her life and extending it *beyond* the walls of Godwin House.

'What I buy is not your concern,' she said loftily, unwilling to admit she wasn't even sure what was sold in the New Exchange shops.

'I dare say I shall shortly find out.' Jakob grinned at her over the top of a tankard of ale. 'Since I will be hovering attentively at your side while you fret over gloves and fans and other frivolities. Would you like me to carry your purse and bargain on your behalf?'

Desire looked away, unexpectedly hurt by his comment. How could he speak so disparagingly of her shopping for beautiful things when—?

'Yesterday you accused me of dressing like a washerwoman—and now you're making fun of me buying *frivolities*!' she burst out. 'As if pretty things are beneath your notice. How can you be so fickle? Unfair?'

'Are you going shopping to please me?' he exclaimed, lowering his tankard without drinking. He looked startled, and perhaps a little disconcerted, at the possibility.

'Of course not!' Her temper suddenly blazed. 'You assume too much. I wouldn't do anything to please you. You're a man without conscience or finer feeling!' Her anger covered underlying insecurity. She wanted to appear poised but, once again, he had made her feel foolishly inexperienced.

'Perhaps,' said Jakob, watching her with an unsettling gleam in his eyes. 'Or perhaps my finer feelings are wounded by your cold and brusque manner towards me this morning. Wherein lies my offence, my lady? And what can I do to make amends?'

Desire was first stunned, then infuriated by his shameless behaviour. She hadn't expected him to apologise for his behaviour on the roof the previous night, but nor had she anticipated a direct challenge.

'You are a brazen knave!' she began hotly. She saw him smile and her temper soared. She thrust to her feet and planted her hands on her hips, glaring down at him. 'You are a brazen knave,' she repeated. 'Your behaviour is outrageous! Insufferable! But I am not a saucy maid, and I will not be treated—'

'Are you not?' He laughed softly, such a wicked gleam in his eyes Desire wanted to box his ears.

She restrained herself just in time. The expression on his face warned her his response would be damaging to her dignity, if not her person. He'd thought nothing of tying her up and throwing her over his shoulder when he'd 'rescued' her on Tuesday.

'I am a *lady*,' she said, inwardly seething, but trying to sound cool and imperious. 'And I expect you to treat me as a gentleman.'

'You wish to be treated as a gentleman?' His gaze flickered up and down her body. 'It would be a pleasure to see you in doublet and breeches. Is that what you intend to buy today?'

'*No!* You are an impossible man.' Desire let her arms fall to her sides and started to pace around the parlour. 'Perhaps I ought to send you back to Lord Swiftbourne and request someone more suitable,' she muttered.

'More suitable for what?'

'Being respectful.'

'There is a difference between "being respectful" and respecting you,' said Jakob, an unexpectedly serious note in his voice.

Desire turned to look at him, then crossed her arms in front of her as she remembered Arscott's 'respectful' marriage proposal.

'It is not fair for you to tease me when you have so much more experience of the world than I do,' she said.

'But you are learning so quickly, *älskling*,' he replied, a lingering smile in his eyes. 'And you fire up so entrancingly.'

'That is no excuse for you to take liberties.' Her breath caught. *Entrancingly?* Did he think she was entrancing.

His smile broadened. 'If I don't take them now, I may not have another chance,' he said. 'In another day or two you'll be able to lay any man low with one searing glance from your fine eyes.'

'Don't make fun of me.' Desire teetered between flustered delight and a deep-rooted fear that he was laughing at her.

He looked at her. After a few seconds the humour vanished completely from his face. His gaze intensified until Desire could see nothing but his clear blue eyes. Her heart-rate increased. She felt dizzy but hardly realised she was holding her breath.

'The chair is ready,' said Benjamin.

Desire heard the Gentleman of the Horse speak, but his voice seemed to come from a long way off. She was snared by Jakob's potent gaze, unable to break the connection between them. It was only when Jakob glanced at Benjamin that she regained control of her thoughts and movements.

She took several shallow breaths. The brief, silent interchange between her and Jakob had been disturbing. Overwhelming. For a moment she wondered if some wizardry was at work, because now he'd withdrawn his gaze from her she felt as if her bones had turned to water. As if he'd drawn all her strength from her with that one, devastating look.

She squared her shoulders. She would *not* allow herself to fall victim to his handsome face and dangerous charm. She'd decided to assess his suitability to be her husband. A man who could reduce her brain to thistledown and turn her legs to water was definitely not suitable. He would have far too much power over her.

'Thank you, Benjamin,' said Jakob. 'If you will give me a few minutes, my lady, I'll arrange your escort.'

'I want you to escort me,' Desire said, still too unsettled to be anything less than direct.

'I will,' he replied. 'But we'll take a couple of Halross's footmen with us as well. Excuse me, my lady.'

Desire had five minutes to collect her composure before she climbed into the sedan chair. As soon as the door closed on her she felt a flurry of panic. She knew it made no sense. She was protected from the curious gaze of strangers in the chair, but she'd never liked travelling in it. She hated the sensation of being shut up in such a confined space, at the mercy of whoever was carrying her. She would much prefer to walk, but she knew it would upset Benjamin. He was hardly reconciled to the trip as it was.

She took several deep, shaking breaths. After a few seconds she decided that, if she still felt uncomfortable in the chair when they were out of sight of Godwin House, she *would* get out. Benjamin wasn't coming on the shopping trip, and what he didn't know couldn't worry him. Having made that important decision, she looked out of the window at Jakob.

'Let us go,' she said firmly, giving the order for her first voluntary departure from Godwin House since she'd watched the Coronation procession.

Jakob walked on one side of the sedan chair. It was carried by two of Desire's porters, but one of Lord Halross's liveried servants walked level with Jakob on the opposite side of the chair. He had placed a second Halross footman in front of the chair and a third behind it. Jakob had no idea what condition the streets were in and he was taking no chances with Desire's safety. As long as he saw nothing to alarm him, he'd let Desire's shopping trip go ahead, but if they encountered disorder the lady would find herself unceremoniously escorted back to Godwin House. He was pleased to see that, although Desire's porters were struggling a little with their unfamiliar and unwieldy burden, Halross's men were fully vigilant to their task.

Remaining alert to his surroundings was second nature to Jakob. Even as he took note of everyone who passed close to their small procession, Desire occupied a portion of his thoughts. Somehow his intentions towards her had gone awry. He'd meant to treat her with friendly but cool courtesy. Instead he'd teased and provoked her from the moment she'd emerged from her bedchamber. For all his self-discipline and good sense, he couldn't resist the temptation to bring a flush to her cheeks and fire to her eyes. He'd been on the verge of pulling her into his arms and kissing her when Benjamin interrupted them.

His stomach muscles clenched at the memory. That was no way to avoid a formal entanglement with the heiress. Much as he would enjoy an *informal* entanglement with her—an image of her legs wrapped around his hips flickered in his mind—he must be more careful in future.

'Stop!' Desire ordered sharply.

Instantly Jakob clapped his hand to his sword hilt, scanning the street for a threat. What danger had she seen from the chair that he had missed? The Strand was full of refugees from the fire, sitting or standing in small groups amidst their bundled-up possessions, but the only person within ten feet of Desire's small procession was an elderly woman who kicked up ash at every shuffling step.

In the meantime, the porters who'd been co-opted to act as chairmen for the day came to an untidy halt. The man in front stopped first and started to lower his end before the man behind had comprehended the unexpected command. The chair tilted forwards and Jakob heard Desire's startled exclamation, then a bump from inside, followed by some unladylike mutterings.

Having assured himself that they were not in immediate danger of attack, Jakob opened the door and peered into the shadowy interior of the chair. His gaze first fell on an untidy heap of grey silk from which Desire suddenly erupted, her brown eyes blazing with indignation. She grabbed his arm and used its support to lever herself out of the chair.

'I will not ride any further in this evil contraption!' she declared. 'It's like being stuck in an upright coffin.' She stood beside him, and shook out her skirts in a way which reminded him of a ruffled house-cat.

'Benjamin—' Jakob began, smiling at the picture she made.

'We won't tell him,' she replied. 'You can ride in it,' she added generously.

'No,' he said.

'I suppose not,' she said, after a moment. 'It wouldn't be very convenient if you have to draw your sword, or—'

'We'll bring it with us,' said Jakob, disinclined to linger unnecessarily in the debris-covered street. 'Shopping can be a very tiring activity. You may be grateful for the ride later.'

Desire looked at him suspiciously. 'Do you mean tiring—or tire*some*?' she asked.

'Tiring,' he said. 'My mother and sisters are always eager to go shopping—and then when they get home they complain about how exhausted they are.'

He gave a few quick orders to rearrange their cavalcade. Now one of Halross's men would to walk ahead of Desire and Jakob, the other two would be immediately behind with the now empty sedan chair bringing up the rear.

'We can put our purchases in it,' Desire said, when they were once more underway. 'Um…' She frowned and leant closer to Jakob. 'Did Benjamin give you any money for me to spend?' she whispered anxiously.

Jakob suppressed a sudden urge to laugh. 'Yes, my lady,' he lied.

'Oh, good.' She sounded relieved. 'I don't know why I didn't think of it before.'

Jakob smiled. 'I dare say you never have occasion to handle money,' he said.

'I do,' said Desire indignantly. 'Whenever income is received from my estates I count it and record it before I put it into the chest.'

'You do?' Jakob was mildly surprised.

'Father taught me how to keep accounts and that it was very important to oversee and approve all financial business,' said Desire. 'It is true that it is Arscott who gives the housekeeper and Benjamin the money they need to manage their parts of the household, and it is Arscott who deals directly with the goldsmith in Cheapside…'

'Goldsmith?'

'The income from the Larksmere estates in Devon is sent to me as a Bill of Exchange,' she explained. 'Arscott takes it to the goldsmith, who exchanges it for coin that we put in the chest, which is usually kept in my bedchamber. Now Kilverdale is guarding it in Kingston.'

'Would Arscott normally have unlimited access to the chest?' Jakob asked, intrigued by this insight into the management of Desire's fortune.

'Oh, no. There are two keys. He cannot open it if I am not present. Father always insisted on that precaution.' Desire laid a hand against the base of her throat.

'You wear it round your neck?' Jakob said, lowering his voice as he interpreted her gesture.

She glanced up at him and nodded. A second later she dropped her hand and looked around, as if afraid someone might have noticed her instinctive action.

'My lady, I am impressed,' said Jakob honestly. 'You have managed your affairs very well.'

A smile lit up her face at his compliment, but then she sighed. 'Not so very well,' she said. 'I've kept good accounts at Godwin House, but I've done nothing to improve the management of the estates outside London. Arscott used to visit them twice a year. He would be gone for days. But since Father died I have not been to Devon. And I've only visited Kingston two or three times. That must be amended when this is over.' She nodded her head, as if underlining her determination to make changes.

They walked in silence for a few minutes. Jakob considered

the implications of what Desire had just revealed. If Arscott stole the money chest, could he open it with a sharp axe, or would he need the key hanging around Desire's neck?

'I don't suppose Benjamin gave you much money for me to spend,' said Desire suddenly, whose thoughts had obviously been running in a different direction. 'I am not fully acquainted with the price of…of fans and gloves and such things. If it looks as if I am about to buy something I don't have enough money for, you must discreetly warn me. It would be very embarrassing if I couldn't afford it.'

Jakob grinned. 'Have no fear,' he said. 'I won't let you embarrass yourself.'

'Good.' Desire glanced around and he saw her smile fade as she noticed a family sitting in the shelter of house wall. They clearly weren't beggars. Their clothes were dirty, but of reasonable quality. Jakob guessed they were tradespeople, forced out of their home by the fire and now waiting to return to the City. Waiting to find out what they could salvage from the ruins.

'There will be a relief fund,' said Desire quietly. 'I know there will be. Last year there was a collection for the relief of plague sufferers. And in the past I have contributed to appeals for other towns that have had fires. I will ask Lord Halross about it at the first opportunity.'

Chapter Twelve

The New Exchange in the Strand was a two-storeyed building with long galleries containing rows of shops. It was Desire's first visit, and she looked around curiously. She knew it was not as fashionable as the Royal Exchange in Cornhill—but the Royal Exchange was now a burnt-out ruin. With so many shops in the heart of the City destroyed, perhaps the New Exchange would become more popular.

Many of the shop-fronts were shuttered, but others were open for business. Either their owners had trusted that the fire would not come so far west—or they'd hurried back with their goods as soon as it appeared safe. Business had to go on if the shop-keepers and their families were to eat, Desire realised, and felt a little less guilty at indulging in a frivolous activity in the midst of the catastrophe.

Several of the shops had women standing outside them. As Desire and her small party approached them, the nearest of the shop assistants began to call out their wares.

'Fine linen and lace, sir?'

'Madam, an Indian painted fan?'

'Gloves and ribbons here, my lady?'

Desire faltered. She had not expected their appearance to create such a stir. She had never shopped for herself before. Virtually all regular purchases were dealt with by Arscott or other appointed members of her household. In the past, even when she *had* bought new clothes for herself—for her planned betrothal to the Duke or mourning dress after her father's death—tradesmen and dressmakers had come to Godwin House to display their goods to her. And someone else had always negotiated the price. Today would be the first time she had ever spoken to a shopkeeper on their home ground. She swallowed and clutched Jakob's arm a little tighter. Without being asked, he guided her towards a silk mercer's booth.

'Sir? Madam? What is your pleasure?'

Desire noticed immediately that the girl who addressed them was very pretty and several years younger than she was. The girl threw a cursory glance in Desire's direction, then turned her attention to Jakob. She refrained from smiling too boldly at him, but there was an admiring, saucy light in her eye when she looked at him. Not quite an invitation, but nearly.

Desire had anticipated her scars might draw curious glances, but it hadn't occurred to her that she would be ignored while a shopgirl blatantly flirted with Jakob. Her temper rose at the discourtesy.

'I would like to see—' she began, but, when the girl turned to look at her, she was forced to break off. She had so little knowledge of fabrics and dressmaking that she had no idea what to ask for.

She saw the moment when the girl noticed her scars. The widening of her eyes, the sickening curiosity, then the disbelief in the girl's eyes as her gaze tracked back towards Jakob. Though the shop assistant never said a word, it was clear she didn't understand why such a handsome man was attending such an uncomely, dowdy female.

Desire's muscles tensed till she could barely draw breath into her lungs. The waterman's crude insults the previous day had not disturbed her one whit as much as the pretty young shop assistant's disparaging gaze.

'Her ladyship would like to see your finest silks, satins and brocades,' said Jakob. His deep voice was relaxed as if he hadn't noticed anything unusual—but there was a crisp note of authority in his tone. An indication he would not tolerate impertinence.

'Yes, sir.' The girl curtsied to them both and turned to rummage through her stock.

Desire carefully released a shaky breath, trying not to let Jakob hear it. She hated that it had been necessary for him to speak for her, yet she didn't know what she would have done if he hadn't. It occurred to her that, if she'd only had the good sense to visit a nursery garden for her first shopping trip, she would have known exactly what to ask for.

Jakob put his gloved hand over hers as it lay on his arm. His gesture first startled her, then made her feel unbearably vulnerable. She had meant this expedition to be her first step towards greater independence—instead she had revealed once more how ill equipped she was to deal with the world. She squared her shoulders, determined to prove she was equal to the unexpectedly complicated task of buying dress material.

The shop assistant produced several bales of fine fabric. Desire gasped as a cascade of silver tissue rippled over the counter. It was joined by a river of black moiré silk, then a fall of crimson satin and a length of rich flowered brocade.

She touched the silver tissue rather gingerly. She was afraid she might make it dirty. The furnishings of Godwin House had all been very fine and grand when they were new—but their original magnificence had faded over the years. Desire wasn't used to looking at such shimmering luxury.

Jakob, on the other hand, seemed to feel no inhibitions about either touching the fabrics or commenting on them. Shortly he and the shop assistant were engaged in a conversation in which words sounding like 'damassin', 'birdseye', 'figuretto' and 'alamode' were bandied about at every turn.

'Finest silk from Turkey,' the shop assistant said at one point, as she unrolled yet another bale.

'I fancy you mean Spitalfields,' Jakob corrected her cheerfully.

'You are very knowledgeable, sir.' Wary respect replaced the girl's initial admiration for him.

Jakob smiled and turned towards Desire.

Over the next few minutes he managed to draw her into the conversation in such a way that she was able to conceal her ignorance. As she might have expected, he had firm opinions of his own. He rejected the black moiré out of hand. He refused to consider an insipid pale blue Desire quite liked. He preferred the deep crimson silk. Finally, when they had settled on their purchases, he bargained with the shop assistant with a competence that made Desire blink. At last they were ready to stow their carefully wrapped packages in the sedan chair and move on to the next shop.

Now she knew how it was done, Desire began to grow in confidence. She still left the bargaining to Jakob because she had no idea what would be a reasonable price for any particular article, but she was no longer too shy to ask for what she wanted. She bought gloves, ribbons, a fan…stockings. She was mildly scandalised at buying stockings in Jakob's presence, much less allowing him to bargain over the price for her, but her liking for them overcame her modesty. At last they came across a used-clothes shop. To her surprise, she discovered Jakob wanted to make purchases for himself here.

'All my belongings were left at my lodgings,' he explained ruefully. 'By now everything will either be burnt or stolen.'

'You mean you don't own anything but the clothes you're standing in?' Desire stared at him. 'Surely your grandfather—'

'I'm not destitute,' Jakob interrupted impatiently. 'I simply have no clothes in London.'

'And even the clothes you're wearing—' Desire began, following her own line of thought.

'I am well aware of that,' Jakob cut across her musings once more. 'I won't delay you here any longer than necessary, my lady.'

'Oh, I don't mind delaying,' Desire assured him. 'I think it will be fun to buy clothes for you.'

'*I* am buying clothes for me,' said Jakob firmly.

'But I can help choose,' said Desire, undaunted. It was amazing how well a successful shopping expedition could boost one's confidence. 'You have helped choose things for me, now I will help choose things for you.'

The woman in the used-clothes shop was older than the silk mercer's assistant and, despite the tragedy that had befallen her city, much more cheerful. After describing her horror at the calamity, forcefully blaming it on the Dutch, and commiserating with Jakob about losing all his clothes, she entered into the task of providing him with a new wardrobe with a good will. Unfortunately, Jakob's unusual height meant there was very little that would fit him.

'Now, if only his Majesty had only seen fit to sell some of his clothes to me, you would be well suited,' said the shopkeeper after another coat had turned out to be too narrow across the shoulders. 'Two yards high he is said to be. You must be at least that.'

'A little more,' said Jakob ruefully. 'Let us see what you have in the way of shirts and cloaks.'

At last he was supplied with a basic wardrobe, but Desire was not satisfied.

'We must buy go back to the linen draper and the silk mercer for *you*,' she declared. 'And then summon the tailor to make up some clothes that will fit you.'

'Perhaps on another occasion,' said Jakob quickly. 'Is there anything here you would like to see, my lady?'

'Oh, no, I don't think…'

'I have a very fine dress, made for a lady of quality but never worn,' said the shopkeeper hopefully. 'A lady of the Court. When it was finished she couldn't pay for it. Gambling debts, so I heard.' The shopkeeper lowered her voice confidentially. 'But it's a beautiful, fashionable gown, my lady.'

'Perhaps I could just look at it,' said Desire, fascinated to know what kind of gown a fashionable—and probably scandalous—lady would wear. 'But I don't think I will… Ohhh,' she breathed, as the shopkeeper laid the costume upon the counter.

It was made of deep rose silk and trimmed with an abundance of cobweb-light gold lace—a combination that reminded her of the rich, mellow beauty of late summer. The bodice was heavily boned in the current fashion, with a deep point at the front. The separate skirt spilled over the counter in a prodigal display of luxury.

'Very good,' said Jakob approvingly. 'The colour becomes you. Take it.'

'I…could.' Desire touched it gently. 'It is very pretty.'

'It has never been worn,' the shopkeeper reminded them. 'Your husband is right, madam,' she added encouragingly. 'The dress would suit you so well it might have been made for you.'

'He's…oh.' Desire flushed and couldn't look at Jakob. 'I'll take it,' she said breathlessly, suddenly desperate to get out of the shop.

How could the woman have mistaken Jakob for her *husband*?

'At least she didn't mistake you for my mistress,' he murmured provocatively, a few minutes later when they were once more strolling along the upper gallery of the Exchange. 'Think how much more offended you would have been then.'

'I don't see why she should have made either assumption,' said Desire, somewhat huffily.

'When a woman comments on every purchase a man makes, even down to the quality of his handkerchiefs—'

'I was interested. I've never been shopping before,' Desire interrupted. 'And men's clothes are not the same as women's clothes—'

She broke off as she saw Jakob's grin.

'I'm glad I've provided you with so much amusement,' she said stiffly. 'We may now return to Godwin House.'

'Yes, my lady.'

They proceeded in a cool silence for several minutes, but Desire was too excited by her morning's work to be quiet for long.

'How come you to know so much about fine cloth?' she asked Jakob. 'That you could recognise the silk came from Spitalfields, not Turkey.'

'My father frequently traded to Turkey,' Jakob replied. 'Among other places.'

'Traded?' Desire was surprised. 'I thought he was a soldier.'

'No. Why would you think that?' It was Jakob's turn to be surprised. 'He was a merchant in Stockholm.'

'Because...I don't know,' she confessed. 'Weren't many English and Scotsmen recruited to fight in the Swedish armies during the long wars on the continent? I thought your father must have been one of them. And *you're* a soldier,' she said, almost accusingly. 'You said you were.'

'I was,' he said. 'I joined the Swedish army when I was seventeen years old.' He paused. 'The year Andrew died,' he added, as if there was a connection between the two events.

'Andrew?' Now Desire was completely bewildered. 'Who...?'

'My cousin Andrew.' Jakob frowned a little. 'The complications of my family can hardly be of interest to you,' he said curtly, as if he regretted having said so much.

'Cousin Andrew?' Desire tried to call to mind what little she knew of the Balston family tree. 'Ah, he was the son of Lord Swiftbourne's oldest son,' she recalled. 'The heir. So...when he died and your father became the direct heir, with you next in line...you joined the army?' She stared at Jakob. 'What on earth for?'

'It was an honourable employment,' he said coldly. 'I see no call for your surprise.'

'I didn't mean to suggest it wasn't,' she said hastily. 'But you made it sound as if you joined the army *because* your cousin died. I just wondered—'

'You wonder too much,' said Jakob. 'You would do better to curb your endless curiosity.'

Desire withdrew her hand from his arm. They walked on in a very chilly silence. She was shaken by his cold, almost angry, response to her simple enquiry.

At last he sighed, caught her hand, and pulled it back through his arm. She tensed, not liking his peremptory action and meaning to reclaim her hand, but then he started to speak, so she waited to hear what he would say.

'When Andrew died, my father knew that he and I would one day most likely have to come to England,' said Jakob. 'Of course, at that time, King Charles was still in exile and Swiftbourne had not yet been granted the earldom. But, even so...'

'You were still heirs to the viscountcy,' Desire said. 'And a large estate.'

'Yes.' Jakob's voice was flat. 'Father had already been training me in the ways of his business,' he continued after a few moments. 'Gustaf, my brother, is three years younger than me, so I was the first to be instructed. But when Andrew died, Father knew that one day I would have to come to England, so it was decided that Gustaf would be the principal heir to the business in Sweden. I became a soldier.'

'Your brother inherited your father's business?' said Desire. 'While you were excluded—'

'I was not excluded!' Jakob's voice cut across her words. 'I was not *forced* into the army. I *decided* to become a soldier. Father left me land in Sweden and a share in the business. I am simply not an active partner.'

'I'm sorry. I didn't mean to imply...' Desire floundered, seeking for a way to express her thoughts that wouldn't offend Jakob. Given that Lord Swiftbourne had already lost his eldest son to war, she found it hard to imagine that he'd been pleased to discover Jakob had deliberately put himself at risk, fighting in a foreign army.

'How did your father come to be a merchant in Stockholm?' she asked instead. 'Surely London would have offered as many, if not more, possibilities for trade?'

'Perhaps. But Swiftbourne—then Viscount Balston, of course—was the English ambassador to Sweden for five years in the early 1630s,' Jakob explained. 'He took his wife and youngest three children with him. When my grandfather left, my father stayed. As a younger son he—my father, I mean—knew he had to make his own way in the world.'

'Which, by your account, he did very successfully,' said Desire.

'Yes, he did. My father was not only a merchant,' he said, with obvious pride, 'he also owned a shipyard in Stockholm. I watched the ships being built... Now Gustaf makes very fine ships. He asked me, before I left Sweden, to go into full partnership with him.'

Desire began to understand why Jakob seemed less than enthusiastic about the title he would one day inherit from his grandfather. His English inheritance would come at a higher price that she'd realised.

'But if you did that—went into partnership with your brother—wouldn't you have to return to Sweden?' she asked, trying to keep her voice light.

'Perhaps. But in any case I only meant to make a short visit to England this time,' Jakob replied. 'I wanted to become acquainted with the Swiftbourne lands and tenants while my grandfather is still alive. But there's no pressing need for me to stay in England, twiddling my thumbs indefinitely. The old man may live another twenty years or more.'

Jakob's words completely deflated Desire's buoyant mood. She'd been enjoying her first ever shopping expedition, but now she was so depressed at the thought of Jakob going back to Sweden she had to force herself to continue the conversation. Even walking had suddenly become an effort instead of a pleasure. Maintaining a serene expression took all her resolution. Her cheeks felt stiff and she couldn't be sure her disappointment wasn't visible in her face She glanced around, pretending a completely false interest in her surroundings, so she didn't have to look at Jakob.

'And is there a pressing reason for you to return to Sweden?' she asked, trying to strike a bantering note, which sounded mortifyingly unconvincing to her own ears.

'You mean, is there a lovesick Swedish maiden pining for me?' he said.

Her heart lurched at the accuracy with which he'd interpreted her would-be casual question. Embarrassed that he'd apparently read her so accurately, she risked a quick glance at him and saw his eyebrow quirk in unspoken amusement at her question.

'No, *älskling*, he said. 'The only maiden pining for me will shortly be gowned in rose silk and gold lace.'

Mortified by his teasing, and his impertinent assumption about her, Desire withdrew her hand from his arm.

'You are unbelievably conceited,' she said coldly.

Jakob smiled but, before he had a chance to respond to her accusation, there was a commotion ahead of them.

They were walking a few yards behind the sedan chair, which now contained their purchases. Suddenly three men burst out of a side alley.

Desire saw one of the men lift a cudgel. She barely had chance to realise the chairmen were under attack before Jakob lunged forward, drawing his sword. At the same time, Lord Halross's footmen closed to form a protective shield around her.

The chair crashed onto the cobbles and the porters spun to face their attackers. Desire saw the chairman at the back dodge the cudgel blow just in time. It smashed against the corner of the chair. Wood splintered. Shouts filled the air.

Blood pounded in Desire's ears. She was too shocked to be frightened. One of Halross's footmen held her arm in a firm grip in complete disregard for protocol. She was so focussed on the dramatic scene in front of her she didn't notice. Later she realised it was so that he could hustle her to safety without delay if the need arose.

Two of the footpads attacked the chairmen, but the third wrenched open the door of the sedan chair. He thrust his head inside, then pulled back and spun around. The lower part of his face was concealed behind a scarf. Desire heard him shout something, but the cloth muffled his words and she didn't know what he said. At that moment one of the porters took a savage blow to his shoulder and he collapsed on to his knees.

'You have to help them!' Desire cast off her initial shock. 'I order you to help them!' she shouted, when the footmen protecting her didn't move from her side. She saw that they had all drawn weapons and were standing ready to fight for her.

'I'm sorry, my lady,' said the footman who held her arm. 'Our orders are to protect you first. This could be a diversion—' He broke off. Desire heard his sharp, satisfied intake of breath as Jakob caught one of the attacking footpads unawares and off balance. A second later it was the brute with the cudgel who lay on the cobbles, not Desire's porter.

She expected Jakob to turn his attention to the other two attackers, but he didn't. He ran in the direction the footpads had come from, towards the mouth of the alley.

A shot rang out. Jakob seemed to fly forwards until he lay full stretched upon the ground.

Desire uttered a strangled scream. She tried to rush forward, convinced Jakob was hurt, but her guards wouldn't let her move. She hardly noticed their restraint. All her attention was locked desperately on Jakob.

Still lying on the ground, he lifted his arm and fired his own pistol. Before Desire could gasp with relief, he catapulted back to his feet. He raced into the alley, disappearing from view behind the corner of a house.

Desire pressed her hands against her mouth, swallowing a cry of protest. Jakob was a soldier. He knew what he was doing.

Closer to hand, the uninjured chairman managed to overpower the footpad who'd attacked him. The third footpad who'd opened the door of the chair now fled in the opposite direction to which they'd all come. Suddenly, all the noise and action was over.

Desire stared at the scene before her. One of the footpads was unconscious on the ground, the other had been forced to his knees with one arm wrenched up behind his back by the victorious chairman. The other chairman leant against the side of the chair, clutching his injured shoulder. It occurred to Desire in a moment of complete irrelevance that they'd proved much better at guarding the chair then they had been at carrying it.

Where was Jakob? She couldn't see him?

Her heart hammered against her ribs. Her legs trembled so badly that, for a few seconds, she sagged against the footman standing next to her. She felt sick with shock and fear. But her need to know Jakob was unharmed overrode every other consideration. She tried to push past her guards, or drag them with her, to see where Jakob had gone. When they wouldn't let her move, she forgot about being respectable and ladylike.

'Jakob!' she shouted, on the verge of panic. 'Jakob! Where are you?'

'Let her come,' he called, his voice so calm the worst of her fear receded. He couldn't be hurt when he sounded so normal. 'But don't relax your guard, men.'

Desire walked towards the mouth of the alley within the protective escort of Lord Halross's footmen. She turned the corner and stopped short. Rationally she understood what she saw—perhaps she'd even expected it—but it was still hard to believe the evidence of her own eyes.

Arscott knelt on the ground, a knotted black scarf hanging around his neck. Jakob stood behind him. The point of his sword poised at the nape of Arscott's neck.

'What's happening?' a woman's voice shrieked from an upper window. 'Is it the French?'

'No,' said Jakob. 'This is an English-born scoundrel.'

'You're the villain!' Arscott claimed furiously. 'My lady, I was trying to rescue you.' He stared up at her, his eyes blazing with anger and frustration. 'I warned you of the danger of falling into a fortune-hunter's clutches,' he reminded her.

Desire stared at him. She had trusted him for so long that, for a moment, she thought he might be telling the truth. Then she remembered the porters who'd acted as chairmen had both been employed by her for several years. The footpads, under Arscott's orders, had clearly believed Desire was in the chair. But Arscott must have known the chair was being carried by Desire's own servants. If he'd really wanted to rescue her, he could have ordered them to carry her to safety while he focussed his attack on the strangers in her escort. Even if he'd had doubts about their loyalty, there had been no need for such a violent assault upon them.

'Yes, you warned me,' she said bleakly. She looked over his head at Jakob. 'He must be questioned,' she said.

'Yes. For now we'll take him back to Godwin House.' Jakob smiled grimly. 'The gaols are in no fit state to contain prisoners.'

Chapter Thirteen

A mine exploded at the base of the outer wall. The house shook. A woman screamed. Men shouted. Cannon thundered a response from within Larksmere House. In the parlour farthest from the fighting, Desire tried to attend to her stitching. Another explosion made her head jerk up. She jabbed the needle into her finger and cried out with pain.

She put the finger into her mouth to suck away the hurt and crept into the hall. She'd been told to stay where she was, but she was lonely and frightened. Where was her mother? She slipped through the besieged house, unnoticed by everyone as she tried to find Lady Larksmere.

She hesitated, shrinking against a wall when she saw two maids talking to each other, afraid they'd take her back to the safety and loneliness of the sewing parlour.

'She should surrender!' said one maid bitterly. 'If she surrenders now, they won't hurt us. But if they take us by force, it'll be rape and murder! We'll all pay for her pride.'

'Hold your tongue! I wouldn't surrender to those Royalist devils for anything. His lordship will be back soon—and then *they'll* be the ones who pay.'

Murder? Desire hugged her arms around herself. Would they all be killed if the Royalists won? It was hard for her to believe anyone could defeat her mother. But until four weeks ago she had not known that such fighting and violent death existed in the world.

Unseen by the maids, she flitted back along the corridor. The house was usually filled with the scent of fragrant herbs, but now it reeked with gunpowder, stale food and worse.

She found her mother in an upper chamber. Lady Larksmere was standing behind the shutters, peering out through a narrow crack at the besieging force.

'Mother?'

'Desire?' Lady Larksmere turned her head in sharp response. 'What are you doing here? Go back to the parlour at once.'

'Are we all going to be murdered?' Desire hugged herself very tightly as she stared up at her mother.

'Of course not.' Lady Larksmere walked around a table towards her.

A mortar shell hit the wall of the house, just beside the window. The shutters exploded inwards in a fusillade of jagged splinters of wood and twisted metal. Desire's world fractured into blinding confusion and vivid pain.

'*Desire!*'

She heard her mother scream, but Lady Larksmere's voice seemed to come from a vast distance. She tried to call out to her mother, but she couldn't move or speak. All she could feel was pain—and even that faded into suffocating darkness.

'*Såja, älskling. Det var bara en mardröm. Du är trygg här.*'

Desire woke to find herself wrapped in strong, comforting arms. Her upper body was pressed against a broad chest, her head rested on a masculine shoulder as he rocked her soothingly, in rhythm with his soft, incomprehensible reassurances.

She was confused, still caught up in the world of her nightmare where Jakob had no existence. For a moment she was still the child she'd been in her dream. She half-believed it was her father who held her and that her mother would soon walk through the door. Then she remembered that Lady Larksmere had been dead for years. For several seconds she felt the sting of loss as sharply as she had done on the day of her mother's death. Then time slowly unwound until she knew where she was and that it was Jakob who was sitting on the edge of her bed, holding her in his arms.

The room was dark. The light of the waning moon shining through the window did little more than reveal the shadowy outlines of the sparse furniture. Desire rested bonelessly against Jakob, too emotionally drained by the horrors her nightmare had recalled to pull away from him. He continued to rock her gently, murmuring all the while to her in a mixture of Swedish and English.

'Hush, *älskling*. It was only a bad dream. You're safe.'

His shoulder beneath her head was solid, warm and very real. And when he brushed his lips across her forehead his hair fell across her face in a protective veil of rough silk. Her fingers clutched the soft linen of his shirt. She could feel the firm muscles of his chest beneath her hand. She closed her eyes, surrendering to the seductive security of his embrace. He was still talking quietly to her. She didn't care what he said. The tone of his voice was everything. She could have stayed like that for the rest of the night. More comforted than she had been for years.

'*Älskling*, what frightened you?' he asked at last, his deep voice stroking all her senses.

She sighed, but she couldn't quite summon the energy to reply. After a moment he said, 'Was it the fire? Did you dream of the fire? Or Arscott?'

The steward was now under guard in a securely locked chamber in Godwin House, waiting to be brought before a magistrate. Desire shivered as she remembered her interview with Arscott. She had questioned him in Jakob's presence. It had been an unpleasant experience. Arscott had persisted in claiming his innocence. Desire wanted to be fair to Arscott, but the steward had asserted that Jakob was the true villain. It was the obvious counterclaim for the steward to make, but he hadn't helped his case by arrogantly suggesting she'd been blinded to reason by Jakob's handsome face.

The accusation offended Desire. She still had a few doubts about whether Arscott had really ordered the original attempt to abduct her—but she had no doubt that she no longer wanted to employ him. Even when he was her prisoner, he acted as if he believed he had a God-given right to control her decisions.

But Jakob had asked her about her nightmare, and it was not Arscott she had dreamed about. She shook her head against his shoulder.

'The siege,' she whispered.

'When you were wounded?'

She nodded, clinging tighter to his shirt. He rubbed his knuckles gently up and down her arm.

'It was a long time ago,' he said.

'It was so *loud*.' She released his shirt, instinctively lifting her hand to cover her ear. 'For days. Weeks. So loud it hurt.'

'The siege? They're apt to be,' he agreed gently.

'Do you know?' She lifted her head to look at him in the shadows.

'Yes, I know,' he replied, stroking one of her curls out of her eyes.

'From inside?'

'Yes.'

'I don't know why men think it is such a fine thing to go to war,' Desire said fiercely. 'It is ugly, wasteful—and it stinks.'

She sensed rather than saw Jakob smile. 'I would rather walk in your sweet-smelling garden than defend a siege,' he agreed.

She sighed, the momentary fire dying out of her. 'My garden is covered in ash,' she said sadly.

'But you'll make it right again,' he replied. 'Another couple of seasons and it will be as beautiful as before.'

She stirred jerkily in his arms, resisting his gentle encouragement. 'I think it was a folly,' she said bitterly. 'I laboured so hard—and what have I to show for it all except a heap of ash?'

'That's not true!' Jakob suddenly sounded angry. 'Your garden is still there. A little hard work and its beauty will be restored.'

'It *can't* be restored!' Desire said vehemently. 'It's gone.' She rubbed her hand against her cheek, feeling the ugly ridges of the scars. Suddenly she was back in the exploding room of her nightmare, just before her life had changed for ever.

She remembered a flash of brilliant light—perhaps it was when the shutters were destroyed and sunlight and destruction had burst into the room in equal measure—and then the haze of pain and darkness that had followed almost instantaneously.

'It's gone,' she said. Now she wasn't thinking about her lost beauty, but her stupidity in placing so much trust in a man who'd never had her best interests at heart. How could she ever have faith in her own judgement again when she'd allowed Arscott to deceive and manipulate her? He had encouraged her fears about the outside world entirely to serve his own interests.

'It's all a folly,' she said bitterly. 'And so am I. And all the pink silk and gold lace in the world won't change that. I was a fool to think things could be different. I'll never be—'

The next second the breath was almost knocked out of her as Jakob thrust her back on to the bed.

'What is it you'll never be?' he growled, his large body pinning her to the mattress. 'Beautiful? Desirable?'

Desire gasped, too stunned to respond.

'Do you know how insulting it is when you say that?' His breath was hot against her cheek.

'What?' She didn't understand what he meant. 'How is it insulting?' She twisted beneath him, tried to push him away, but he didn't move. 'I can say what I like about myself! *Get off me!*'

'Insulting to *me*,' Jakob said furiously. 'You know damn well how much I want you! Don't I count? Or are you only interested in the judgement of a callow Duke?'

'Callow Duke?' It was hard to think clearly when Jakob's

body covered hers, filling her senses with his virile energy. 'Oh, you mean Kilverdale?' she said breathlessly. 'You want me?'

Jakob growled wordlessly. His body seemed to vibrate with powerful, barely contained emotions. 'You enshrine his ridiculous words—and pay no heed to *me*!' he accused her.

'I didn't!' Desire protested, still preoccupied by his claim that he wanted her. 'I haven't. I would never enshrine anything he—'

'Stop talking!'

Desire opened her mouth to drag in an indignant breath. He had no business pinning her down and getting angry with her. She fully intended to order him off her bed and out of her bedchamber.

But that was before his mouth unerringly found hers. She was completely unprepared for the kiss. It wasn't gentle or reassuring. He ravished her mouth with his lips and tongue. Her confusion changed quickly to arousal. All her overwrought emotions of the past few days found outlet in the passion he unleashed between them. His mouth was hot and urgent upon hers. She clutched his shoulders and kissed him back with almost desperate eagerness.

Jakob moved over her until he could stretch full length beside her on the bed. The bedclothes were tangled around her waist, but she didn't know or care. He kissed her cheek and then her neck. His lips caressed her sensitive skin until she sighed with pleasure. When his hand slid up to cup her breast through the soft cambric of her shift she caught her breath, but had no thought of refusing him. Desire whimpered as his thumb rubbed across her nipple. Then he muttered impatiently and she heard the soft sound of ribbon sliding against fine linen as he dragged her neckline lower, freeing her breast to the cool night air.

He gave a deep hum of satisfaction and bent his head. His lips closed on her nipple and he began to suckle. Deep, wordless pleasure pulsed through Desire's body—together with thrilled amazement.

She was dazed with arousal. Her thoughts were fragmentary and easily overwhelmed by sensation, but she was no longer caught in the shock of initial surprise at Jakob's sensual assault. A small part of her took time to marvel at the knowledge that Jakob was really here in the dark with her, giving and taking pleasure, just as he had done in Putney. Sometimes she'd wondered if she'd only dreamed his passion, but now she could feel how real it was. And tonight he was touching her naked flesh. It felt glorious. His hair brushed across her sensitive skin. His tongue abraded her nipple, then his fingers replaced his mouth on her breast and he kissed her lips.

She kissed him back, opening herself to every erotic stroke of his tongue and lips, trying to reply to passion with passion. There were too many places she'd never seen, too many experiences she'd never had. Tomorrow was perpetually uncertain. She would not deny herself this pleasure tonight.

As he moved over her, the linen folds of his shirt brushed teasingly against her sensitive breasts. She moaned, both aroused and frustrated by the randomly sensuous contact of fabric with skin. She squirmed beneath him, dragging at his shirt until she could slip her hands inside and touch the ridged muscles of his chest.

He jerked as her hands stroked over his ribs, and momentarily lifted his head as she pushed his shirt up beneath his arms. When she'd exposed him to her satisfaction she put her arms around him, half-lifting herself and half-pulling him down until she could rub her breasts against his chest. She loved the way the tight curls on his chest teased her soft skin. He was so splendidly different from her.

He groaned, muttering words she didn't understand, and buried his face in her neck. He sucked, drawing heat to the surface. Her head fell backwards, exposing her throat to more hot kisses. She relaxed on to the bed and swept her hands across his broad back, delighting in the flex of taut muscles beneath her fingertips.

He lifted himself away from her and she uttered a soft, wordless sound of protest. But he only took the time to strip off his shirt and sweep aside the bedclothes tangled around her hips before he returned to her. She sighed with satisfaction as his weight settled upon her again. They shared another hot, wet kiss. Then he turned his attention once more to her breasts.

The only sounds that disturbed the velvet darkness was their quickened breathing, as he traced warm circles on her breast with his mouth. Then Desire moaned as he rapidly flickered his tongue over her exquisitely sensitive nipple.

She moved restlessly beneath him, her fingers digging urgently into the muscles of his arm. Her whole body was on fire and she was greedy for more of his touch. He laid his hand on her stomach and she felt the heat sear through her thin shift. Excitement and a portion of nervousness filled her as he began to pull the garment up. A few moments later he slipped his hand beneath it and touched her thigh. She could feel the roughness of his healing palm. It was a momentary reminder of what had brought them to this enchanted moment in the darkness, but then his fingertips stroked upwards and she forgot about everything except the anticipation building within her.

His hand cupped her hip and she held her breath, her heart beating fast with excitement as she waited for his next move. Nothing had prepared her for the combination of pleasure, delicious frustration and eagerness that consumed her. She *ached* with her need for Jakob.

His fingers stroked lightly across the pit of her stomach. She gasped, and her flesh retracted instinctively in response to his teasing touch. His hand dipped lower, brushing against her tight curls. Her legs trembled, her muscles tensing at the unprecedented invasion of her privacy. His fingertip pressed a little closer, delicately stroking the taut flesh that protected her inmost femininity. Provocatively he drew his hand back towards her stomach without pressing any deeper.

Desire whimpered and drew her knees up, aching for fulfilment of the need he had aroused in her.

Jakob's breath hissed beneath his teeth. Once more he slipped his hand between her legs, this time deliberately stroking deeper, touching soft feminine folds that were swollen and hot with arousal.

Desire cried out when he touched her there. Her body tensed with surprise. It was so intimate and so powerful. She almost pulled away. But when Jakob continued to stroke her a new, exciting pleasure began to build within her. When he abruptly took his hand away she made a small sound of protest. She slid her hand down his arm and realised he was fumbling with the front of his breeches.

Her heart fluttered in her throat as she understood the culminating moment had almost arrived. In a few moments she would finally know what it meant to join her body with a man's. To become one with Jakob.

His hand returned to her thigh. He stroked upwards and murmured something in Swedish when he found the moist flesh that ached for his fulfilment.

'Gently, *älskling*,' he murmured hoarsely, when she jerked beneath his touch. 'Easy, sweetheart.'

He put his hand on her hip, then let his outstretched fingers span her stomach before gliding softly over her other hip and down her other leg—and there he encountered her scar. And stopped. A few seconds later he began to explore the long-healed wound on her thigh.

At first Desire didn't know what he was doing. She was so used to being self-conscious about the scars on her face, she'd never thought about the ugly mark on her body.

Realisation came to her slowly. This was not a new, exciting caress. Jakob was investigating the extent to which her body had been marred by her old injuries. Before she had time to react to his discovery, he withdrew his hand and pulled the hem of her shift back over her legs. A moment later he fumbled at the neckline of her gown. She was too shocked to notice how his hands trembled as he drew gently on the ribbon until she was once more modestly covered.

He levered himself off the bed and she was aware of him fastening his breeches. In the darkness his harsh breathing sounded very loud.

Desire was numb with disbelief.

He didn't want her. At the last moment he had been so repulsed by her imperfections that he had not been able to join his body with hers.

For a few seconds the shock was so great she felt no pain—then the anguish of rejection blotted out all other sensations.

She had exposed herself to Jakob, offered herself to him without reservation, and he'd tossed the gift aside as if it meant less than nothing to him.

In a sudden flurry of movement she seized the bedclothes and dragged them up to her chin. Tears scalded her eyes. Bitter shame burned through her body.

'It's true then,' she jeered at him, her voice sharp with newly inflicted pain. 'All it takes is one touch of my scars, and even a randy knave cannot act the man for me. You *boasted* of your lust, but—'

Jakob swore, vicious words in Swedish that Desire didn't understand. She could sense his anger roiling around the shadowed room. She wanted to scream obscenities back at him. He had hurt her worse than Kilverdale. At least Kilverdale had never pretended he wanted her. There had never been any suggestion that her union with the Duke would be anything other than a marriage of convenience. But Jakob *had* claimed to want her. He'd tumbled her on to the bed beneath him and swept her away with his lovemaking—only to reject her the very moment before completion.

'I could act the man for you!' he snarled in English. 'Even now, I could play my part. And then where would we both be, my lady Desire?' His tone savagely mocked her name. 'You're only looking for someone to frighten away the ghosts that haunt you, and I—'

'And you what?' She was shaking beneath the bedclothes. Filled with hurt and humiliation and betrayal.

She heard him take a couple of deep, carefully controlled breaths. Suddenly she couldn't bear to hear whatever he had to say. His rejection or excuses, or even a forced apology through gritted teeth, would not make her feel better.

'*Get out!*'

'Desire—'

'Just get out! Now!' She stretched blindly towards the stand beside the bed. She seized the first object her hand found and hurled it at him.

The pewter cup clattered against the opposite wall.

The sudden silence that followed her action seemed very loud. A sob rose in her throat. Jakob couldn't see her in the shadows of the bed, so she stuffed the sheet into her mouth. She *wouldn't* reveal her misery by crying in front of him.

He didn't move for several long moments. She wanted to shout at him again, but she was afraid her voice would betray her.

'Goodnight, my lady,' he said at last, his manner stiff and formal. 'We will talk in the morning.'

She heard his footsteps as he walked across the room, and then the gentle opening and closing of the door. She flung herself back on the bed and drew the covers over her head.

She huddled there for a long time, struggling to subdue the sobs that would overwhelm her if she didn't use all her strength of will to hold them at bay. Even Kilverdale's rejection had not left her so desolate, so unable to control her misery. At last she pushed back the covers and forced herself to breathe slowly and carefully. She would not weep for Jakob. But waves of humiliation crashed over her again and again as she remembered what had just happened between them. In her distress she bit her lip until she tasted blood. She would send him away tomorrow. Now that Arscott had been caught, there was no need for Jakob to remain at Godwin House. His job was done. He could go back to Sweden for all she cared. She hoped he stayed there. She hoped he drowned on the way...

No, she didn't. She never could wish harm upon him. He was so wonderful. But he'd hurt her so badly. Destroyed her newly hatched hopes before they'd ever had a chance to take wings and fly. The urge to toss back and forth was overwhelming. At every new recollection of humiliation she jerked into another position. She closed her eyes, wishing she could erase every thought from her mind, every emotion from her heart. Just for the night. Just until she could gather her strength to face whatever came next in her life. She made herself lie still, seeking peace in the familiar, quiet darkness of her room.

A soft sound near the fireplace caught her attention. She stiffened as she realised there was a rat scampering behind the wooden panels. She hated vermin, but at least it was a distraction from her present misery. When everything was back to normal, she would order in the ratcatcher. Perhaps she ought to keep some cats. She didn't like to allow cats on her roof for they chased and sometimes killed the birds, but they could do no harm and perhaps some good inside the house.

The soft slithering noise repeated. Her heart quickened with irrational alarm. It sounded closer than before, but that was only an illusion. There were no rat holes in her room. Despite herself, she imagined a rat scuttling across the shadowy floor and running up the brocade hangings on to the bed.

Then she heard the rat breathing.

Fear paralysed her limbs. No rat could breath so loud. Was it real? Or was she trapped in another nightmare? One shadow, darker than the others, moved. She opened her mouth, sucking air into her terrified lungs. Before she could scream the shadow was upon her. A heavy weight pinned her to the mattress. A pillow pressed over her face.

She struggled. Fighting the tangled bedclothes. Fighting her assailant. But her arms were trapped beneath the sheet. Her heart pounded furiously. Her lungs burned. The pillow suffocated her.

'Scream and I'll shoot the first man through that door.'

Desire went still at the grim warning.

'The light will be behind him. You know I won't miss.'

Arscott.

Shock and fear jangled through Desire's body.

'I'm going to take the pillow away,' he said, in the same low voice. 'You know what will happen if you call out.'

An instant later the stifling weight was removed from her face.

'How...?' she croaked.

'You'll see. Get up.' He dragged back the bedclothes and seized her arm. 'This way and not a sound.'

Desire followed him across the dark room to the fireplace, her bare feet cold on the floor boards. Whatever he planned for her she had to resist. Her heart hammered so loudly she couldn't think clearly. But in her mind she cried over and over again: Jakob. Jakob...

At the wall Arscott stopped. 'Remember what I said,' he warned her softly. 'Not a sound.' He released her arm and started to bend down.

Without hesitation Desire flung herself away from him. He lunged after her. She fought desperately in the smothering darkness, never daring to make a sound. One flailing arm connected with Arscott's wrist.

He hissed with pain and his arm flew up. Desire felt something fly through the air, close to her head. She heard a soft thud as it landed among the bedclothes. She hoped it was his pistol, but she didn't dare count on it. He might have two. She whirled away from him.

His hand closed on her upper arm and he swung her about. Desire slammed suddenly against the panelled wall. The impact struck the breath from her body and she gasped for air.

Arscott closed behind her, one hand on either side of her body. He leant into her, trapping her against the wooden panel.

'That's enough.' His own breathing was laboured. 'If you fight, you'll get hurt.'

'Do you care?' she gasped.

'I can't marry a corpse.'

Marry?

A new fear surged through Desire, but it was tempered by relief that at least Arscott wasn't intending immediate revenge.

Apparently he still hoped to gain a husband's rights over her property. No doubt he believed that if he kept her close and they managed to elude pursuit for sufficient time he would get away with his scheme.

'We'll have to do this in the dark now,' he muttered. 'Dammit. Why do you always have to make things more difficult?'

'It is dark.' Desire didn't understand what he meant.

'I was trying to unshutter the lantern when you went wild.' He sounded irritated. 'When we're married I'll not tolerate your ill discipline any longer,' he said sourly.

He pushed himself away from her. Desire heard rather than saw the soft rasp of his hand over the panelling as he felt his way along the wall. With his other hand he nudged her in the same direction as his questing arm. They moved crabwise along the wall towards the fireplace. He was behind her, one arm stretched out beside her as he felt along the wall. Desire contemplated kicking him in the shins with her heels, but her feet were bare and he wore boots.

A cold draught suddenly curled around her ankles. Her hand touched empty space beside the fireplace where there should have been solid wall.

'In and up,' said Arscott against her ear. 'Remember I'm behind you. If you scream, I'll shoot the first man who comes running.'

'What is it?' In the darkness Desire couldn't make sense of where the wall had gone.

'A priesthole. Your Catholic grandfather riddled the house with them. Isn't it a pity your father turned Protestant? Your grandfather never forgave him for that—and never shared his secrets. But my grandfather told me. Now *up*!'

He pushed her through the narrow opening revealed by the

false panel. She found herself in a narrow, vertical tunnel, cut into the side of the chimney. It was barely wide enough for the breadth of her shoulders. She moved her hands a few inches and encountered a cold metal rung embedded in the brick.

'Up!' Arscott prodded her impatiently.

She tipped back her head. High above her in the darkness she saw a paler rectangle. Was that the sky? She reached up and by feel discovered another rung above her head.

'Hurry!'

She stubbed her toe against the chimney in her sudden haste, but finally found the rung she needed for her foot. With fear roiling in her stomach and trembling limbs, she began to climb upwards in the claustrophobic darkness. Her arms and shoulders continually scraped against the walls on either side. She banged her knees on the chimney and the metal rungs. The rungs hurt her feet and she curled her toes in an effort to cling tighter.

Every time Desire let go of a rung to reach upwards for the next her fear grew. What if the next rung wasn't there? What if she froze with fear in the darkness? What if she suddenly lost her grip? She'd crash down on to Arscott.

He started to climb below her. She heard the same slithering-gritty sound she'd heard earlier. In a moment of understanding she realised Arscott's shoulders were wider than hers. He was a slim, wiry man, but even he had a little difficulty in the confined space. Her thoughts skittered to Jakob. He'd never fit into the priesthole. If he tried he might stick.

Hysteria bubbled up inside her. She swallowed it before it could overwhelm her. She must find a way to save herself. If she could seize Arscott's pistol…

She looked up. The light above seemed closer. The familiar smell of smoke grew stronger. Parts of the city still burned.

Space suddenly opened up on her right side. Without thinking she waved her hand into emptiness. It must be another room on the floor above her bedchamber. Was this where Arscott had entered the priesthole to reach her room? In a few more rungs she'd be able to slip through the gap. If she could do so before Arscott realised what she intended…

His hand closed on her ankle.

'No tricks,' he growled. 'Keep climbing.'

She took a careful, calming breath, and continued upwards. Suddenly there were no more rungs above her. She had reached the top.

Arscott caught her ankle again. This time his unexpected touch was less shocking, but no less unpleasant.

'Climb out. But mind I'll not hesitate to hurt you if you defy me,' he warned.

Desire scrambled on to the roof leads. She crouched beside the chimney, trying to get her bearings in the darkness. There was a faint glimmer of light towards the east. It would soon be dawn.

She did not often come to this part of the roof. Her garden was on the roof of the south wing, but she knew there was not usually a gaping hole next to the chimney.

'I opened it before I fetched you,' said Arscott, answering her unspoken question. 'I was always good at reconnaissance.'

'Where are we going?'

'Down.'

Arscott clamped one hand around her arm, forcing her across the ash-covered leads. She stumbled, almost losing her footing. Her stomach lurched into her mouth. This part of the roof had not been designed for everyday access. If she tripped, it was a long way to fall.

'Step over.'

At Arscott's command Desire carefully negotiated the low parapet that separated the east from the south wing. She was back in her garden. When Arscott began to drag her in the direction of the doorway that led to the stairs, she realised he meant to leave the roof by the usual route. Probably he intended to head straight across the garden as Jakob had done and spirit her away on the river. By the time anyone discovered either of them were missing they would be long gone. She had to do something. But what? And when?

Perhaps when Arscott opened the river-gate she could run and hide in the garden. In the dark, among the rose bushes and formal maze she could evade him for some time.

She wondered again if he had more than one pistol. Where had he got them? She dismissed the question as irrelevant. Once he had discharged his weapon or weapons there would be a safe interval to capture him. Even Arscott could not reload instantaneously. Her mind focussed on that idea. If she could force him to fire harmlessly, it would warn the household and put Arscott at a disadvantage.

'Damn.' Arscott cursed suddenly, startling Desire with the crudeness of his language. He had always guarded his tongue in her presence.

The door to the stairs was locked from the inside. Desire was surprised. The door was never locked. The side door at ground level was kept bolted at night, but there was no need to bolt the door to the roof. She'd often come up to see the sunrise.

But Jakob was in charge of household security now, she recalled. He didn't leave such matters to chance.

Arscott slammed his shoulder against the door. The wood creaked, but the door didn't budge. 'Damn Baker, he should have opened it by now,' he swore.

Baker? Desire recognised the name of one of her footmen. Was he in league with Arscott? Were *any* of her household to be trusted? As Arscott made another attempt to break open the door, she backed up a few paces. It was already getting lighter. She'd spent so much time on the roof. There had to be somewhere she could hide.

'Stand still.' Before she had an opportunity to edge any further away, Arscott grabbed her arm once more. He looked around the roof. In the grey half-light Desire could see as well as sense his sudden desperation. His plans had suffered a dangerous setback. The new wildness in him intensified her own fear. What would he do now?

He started to tow her across the roof.

She dug her heels in.

'Where are you going?'

'Come on!' He jerked her arm.

Her bare feet skidded on the ashy gravel. She stumbled and almost lost her balance.

Ascott hauled on her arm again, giving her no chance to regain her footing. A moment later he stopped by the parapet overlooking the gardens. He leant over, looking down.

For a reckless moment Desire considered pushing him off. But his hand was clamped so tightly around her wrist he might take her with him. She couldn't risk it. Then it was too late. He turned to look at her and she gasped at the expression on his face. Yet she'd seen it before. There was the same reckless, overexcited blaze in his eyes she remembered from twenty-two years ago. He had looked like this during the siege of Larksmere just before he had accomplished some dangerous and deadly act for the defence of the house.

'We'll go down,' he said. 'If it was good enough for that blond devil, it's good enough for us.'

Chapter Fourteen

Jakob paced up and down the long gallery outside the antechamber to Desire's room. His raging emotions needed the outlet of action, but he was trapped at his post as surely as any sentry.

He suspected, though he hadn't shared his suspicions with Desire, that one of her household might be in league with Arscott. The attack on the sedan chair had been in the nature of an ambush planned, however hastily, in advance. No one could have predicted Desire's sudden urge to go shopping. The steward might have been watching the house and seen them leave, but Jakob had been alert to that possibility and kept a careful watch on their surroundings. He hadn't noticed anything untoward.

So there was a possibility that someone in Godwin House had warned Arscott he was under suspicion, and also informed him of Desire's plans. But if that was the case, who was it? And had he acted out of misplaced, but perhaps understandable, loyalty to the man who'd ruled the household for so long—or for more sinister motives? Jakob had spent the afternoon questioning all the staff, but he hadn't come to any certain conclusions. The only thing he knew for sure was that, while he still had doubts about the loyalty of her household, he wouldn't leave Desire unguarded.

But he wished to God he could undo what had just happened between them. He should have soothed her after her nightmare and then left immediately. He paced up and down, angry and frustrated. His body ached with need for the fulfilment he'd denied both of them. He was tormented by vivid sensations of her body pressed against his. He'd been half out of his mind with need for her but, at the last moment, he'd regained a shred of clarity and honour. He knew Desire had just woken from a nightmare, that she was deeply hurt by Arscott's betrayal and desperate for comfort and reassurance. It would have been dishonourable to take advantage of her vulnerability.

He paused in his pacing, honest enough to admit to himself there had been another reason for his withdrawal. If he'd made love to Desire, it would have been a commitment, a final irrevocable acceptance that his life now lay in England. There had been other women in his past, but none of them had expected more from him than a short-lived tryst. Desire needed a husband, not a lover. And if he wasn't willing to be the first, he could not mistreat her by becoming the second.

But he knew she'd misinterpreted his action. Knew he'd compounded the wound Kilverdale had inflicted upon her six years ago. That had been the last thing he'd intended. He swivelled on his heel and strode back along the gallery. He'd tried to explain earlier, and she'd thrown her cup at him. But at that point he'd barely had his own emotions under control. He was calmer now. Perhaps he shouldn't wait until morning to talk to her?

The smell of smoke had become so commonplace that at first he hardly noticed it. But as he continued to pace, the smell grew stronger. He frowned, wondering if the wind had picked up. Was the fire once more threatening Godwin House? He turned and walked to the end of the corridor, meaning to look out of the window, but the smell of smoke decreased with every stride. He turned on his heel and went back towards Desire's room. The scent of smoke grew stronger. He'd left the door to the antechamber open. When he went into it the smell of smoke was even stronger. Then he heard it. The deadly crackle of fire.

'Desire!' He crashed into her room.

Smoke billowed around him. Blinding him. Choking his lungs. He lifted his arm to protect his face. Tried to reach the flaming bed.

'Desire!' Terror for her drove him forward against the searing flames. If she was on the bed, she could not still be alive. But he had to be certain.

'Desire!' Surely she wasn't on the bed. He turned desperately, searching the room for her. Already the flames had started to lick at the wall panels.

Was she hiding in a corner? Half-blinded by smoke-induced tears, he searched for her on the edge of the room.

He almost missed the way the smoke curled against the wall beside the fireplace, disappearing into the black shadow. But the roiling smoke had not yet filled the entire room and the walls were livid with the light of the leaping flames.

There was an dark opening in the panels.

Without hesitation he pushed through the narrow gap. Far above he could see a patch of light. Smoke coiled around his legs and body, sucked up the narrow chimney-like vent.

He felt iron bars on the side of the chimney. But when he tried to climb he stuck. His shoulders were too wide. The gap too narrow. His coat snagged on unseen hazards, holding him fast.

He wrenched out of the gap, back into the room. The fire was already climbing the walls. Plaster fell crashing from the ceiling. He fought the need to cough, knowing it would only drag more smoke into his lungs.

He ripped off his coat and shirt and shoved his pistol into the back of his belt. He pushed back into the hole and stretched his arms above his head, compressing his shoulders and pressing his arms as tight to his ears as possible.

With no room to manoeuvre, he forced himself upwards. The narrow walls scraped skin from his sides and arms. He couldn't turn sideways. The gap between front and back was even narrower than side to side. The smoke grew thicker, suffocating in the confined space.

His mind seethed with questions. Was this the way Desire had come? How long ago? Who had started the fire? How long had it taken to gain such a hold on the bed?

He banged his chest against an iron rung. He reared away instinctively and grated his back on the rough brick behind him. He bit back a curse of frustration and anxiety. What if he stuck? He'd be of no use to Desire if he burned to death in this hellish false chimney.

Suddenly there was free space by his right elbow. He pushed and pulled himself a few more feet upwards and discovered another open panel, similar to the one in Desire's chamber. The floor was at chest height, but he couldn't lever himself through the gap because there was no room to turn around. He forced himself up another few feet. Then it was only a matter of stepping off one of the rungs into the room beyond.

He looked up at the hole at the top of the vent, now less than six feet away. He hesitated for barely a second. Even if he managed to squeeze his shoulders through the opening he would be a sitting target for several moments. He inserted himself through the narrow opening into the chamber. The room was already filled with choking smoke. He coughed. Stumbling over unseen hazards he reached the window by feel. He forced open the window and leant out, gulping in cleaner air. Then he heard muffled voices, coming from the roof.

Desire.

Relief filled him. She was still in a condition to talk and ask questions. He suppressed a betraying cough, and pushed further out of the window. He looked upwards, feeling for handholds. He'd climbed from decorative buttress to ivy and back again when he'd scaled the wall beneath Desire's garden. But there was no ivy here. He'd have to rely on finding handholds in the masonry to cover the small distance to the parapet. Moving silently, he stood on the windowsill and reached up as far as possible. He could just get his fingertips over the lower part of the crenellated parapet. With his foot he felt the surface of the wall beside the window until he discovered a tiny crevice.

He paused, balancing himself carefully. Ignoring the giddying drop below him, in one smooth movement he used the toehold to give him the leverage he needed to get one hand over the parapet. He hung for a moment by one hand and the toehold. His muscles screamed at the punishment. His instincts screamed with the need for haste to reach Desire before she suffered any hurt.

He got his other hand over the parapet and hauled the full weight of his body upwards on his arms so that he could see through the crenellations of the parapet.

There was no one on the part of the roof closest to him. He straightened his arms until his waist was level with the lowest part of the crenellations and shifted his grip on the rough stones so that he could lift one leg over. After that it was easy. He crouched by the wall for a moment, locating the direction of the voices. Then, keeping low among the chimney stacks and shadows, he went towards them.

'Down the wall?' Desire backed as far away from Arscott as the unrelenting grip on her arm allowed. 'You're mad!'

'No. He climbed up the wall. We'll climb down. The ivy and the wall will help us.'

'I can't!' But almost instantly Desire stamped down on her rising panic. If she had to, perhaps she could climb down the ivy. But once they were on the ground the chances of being discovered before they left the property rapidly diminished. She *had* to delay Arscott until Jakob found them.

'Why can't we go back the way we came?' she said. 'Into the second-floor chamber, the way you came? Why don't we go that way?' Don't you know any more priestholes that could get us out unseen?'

She never wanted to venture into another priesthole as long as she lived, but if she could only distract or confuse Arscott...

'Maybe.' Without warning he dragged her away from the south-facing wall towards the east wing. He didn't go far before he stopped, cursing.

In the grey light Desire saw thick smoke billowing from the hole beside the chimney. There was no going back that way. The smoke made no sense to her, but she had no time to think about it. A few moments later she was back by the south wall.

'You first. Put your leg over,' he ordered.

Her heart thudded in sheer terror. 'I cannot.'

'You can.' Arscott's face stretched into a demonic grin. 'If I'm not to wed you, no one else will. You'll be a bride or dead by the end of this day. *Go down!*'

Desire carefully swung one leg over the parapet. The rough stone scraped the bare skin of her thigh. There was no time to worry about the immodesty of her clothing, and her bare feet might make the descent a little safer.

She tested her foothold for firmness and tightened her grip on the parapet until her knuckles were white, her sinews cracking under the strain. She swung her other leg over the wall. For several, hideous, stomach-churning seconds her free foot wavered in the air, desperately seeking another foothold. Then she found a piece of jutting brickwork to support it.

'Keep going down,' said Arscott. With far less hesitation than Desire he climbed over the parapet until he was poised beside her.

Suddenly Desire saw a flicker of hope. If she could persuade him to keep going down faster than she did, perhaps she could scramble back over the wall to the relative safety of the roof. Whoever held the high ground had the advantage. That was one lesson never forgotten from the siege.

'I'm stuck,' she whispered, putting her plan into action. 'My arms and legs won't move.'

'Damn. I never thought you'd be so craven-hearted,' Arscott

snarled. 'You climbed up the chimney. Climb down the ivy the same way.'

'I…I cannot.' Her voice trembled, adding conviction to her words. Her toes already shrieked with pain. Her arms shook so badly she wasn't sure if she'd be able to haul herself back over the wall. Yes. She could. She had no choice.

Very gingerly she lifted one foot and pretended to search for another foothold. Immediately she gave a soft cry, closed her eyes, and huddled back against the wall, in a simulation of terror that was not so very far from her true feelings.

'I can't do it,' she sobbed. 'There's nowhere to put my feet. You go down. Show me where it's safe.'

Arscott cursed again, but nevertheless climbed downwards. She heard him give a soft grunt of pain. Was that from where she'd hit his wrist earlier? Or had he been hurt in some minor way when Jakob captured him yesterday? Even if he was only a little handicapped by injury, she might be able to take advantage of it.

His hand gripped her ankle. This time her shriek of alarm was absolutely real.

'Quiet. Relax your leg. I'll put your foot on the next safe place.'

Desire took a deep breath. It was now or never. She tightened her grip on the parapet.

A man leant over the wall. Her breath froze in her throat, stifling her appalled scream. Before she had time to recognise Jakob, he seized her arms in two strong hands.

'Let go,' he ordered, his voice hoarse.

It took a long, dangerous second for her to force her hands to relax their grip. Arscott pulled on her leg. Jakob held on grimly to her arms. For several sickening heartbeats she was suspended between the two men. For a moment it seemed as if she would be torn in half before either man relinquished his prize. But then Arscott's hand slipped from her foot and Jakob hauled her on to the roof. They fell in a heap behind the parapet. Nothing had ever been as good as the feel of Jakob's arms around her.

'Are you hurt?'

'No. No.' Desire tried to cling to him, but she sensed urgency, not comfort, in his hardening muscles. He put her aside and crouched behind the parapet.

'He has a pistol.' A wave of new fear flooded over her. She didn't want Jakob to take any more risks.

'So have I.'

He rose carefully and she saw the pistol in his hand.

The door to the stairs banged open, startling both of them.

Jakob half-turned towards it and Desire heard a shot. Jakob grunted, then staggered against the low wall. Desire lunged forward, grabbing his belt and pulling him down on top of her. His weight crushed the air out of her. Then he threw himself in front of her, facing the intruder.

Desire peered over his shoulder. It was her footman Baker. The man Arscott had claimed would open the door for him. Baker held two pistols. He'd already fired one, but he levelled the other pistol directly at Jakob.

'Mr Arscott says he'll make me rich if you marry him,' he said to Desire. 'So you'd best come with me, my lady. I'd just as soon not shoot you, Colonel. But if you don't get out of the way, I will. I haven't anything to lose. Not after finishing off the man who was guarding Mr Arscott.'

'Get out of the way!' Desire shouted at Jakob. She *couldn't* let him be shot. She shoved desperately at his rock-solid shoulder. When he wouldn't move, she tried to crawl out from behind him.

'Hurry up!' Baker started to get nervy.

'Anything to oblige,' said a voice from behind the renegade footman.

Desire saw a swordstick smash down on Baker's arm and the pistol fell out of his hand. An instant later he crumpled into a heap on the roof. She found herself staring at the Duke of Kilverdale instead.

He was magnificently dressed in his black periwig and

brocade coat. His right fist was still upraised from the blow he'd delivered to the base of the footman's skull. She could not immediately comprehend what had happened. Then she realised Kilverdale had come up behind the footman and pole-axed him.

Jakob swore softly in Swedish. Desire felt his rigid body relax as if he too had been pole-axed.

'For once in your ramshackle life you arrived in time,' he said to the Duke.

'I aim but to serve.' Kilverdale strode over to them. 'Are you badly hurt? My lady? Jakob? Your message said Arscott was safely under guard. What happened?'

'I'm not hurt. Jakob's hurt.' Desire struggled to articulate clearly. 'He's been shot.'

'I wasn't,' he contradicted her. 'He shot the pistol from my hand. But I think it was by accident.' Jakob pushed himself to his feet and looked over the wall. He cursed again, this time more violently. 'Arscott's getting away. Catch him, Jack!'

'Catch him? What the devil am I? The family bloodhound?' Kilverdale demanded in exasperation.

But Desire saw him follow the direction of Jakob's gaze and then he glanced back at Desire. Somehow she'd scrambled to her feet and he stared at her. In her overwrought condition she couldn't begin to interpret the expression in his dark eyes.

'Your house is on fire,' Kilverdale said abruptly. He shrugged out of his coat and handed it to her. Desire stared at it, not immediately understanding the reason for his action. Jakob took it.

'You'd best get off the roof,' said Kilverdale. 'I'll catch your murderous steward for you, my lady, since Jakob bungled the task. Call it recompense for past misdemeanours.'

He turned, lifted the unconscious footman over his shoulder, and disappeared down the stairs before either Jakob or Desire could respond.

'Here.' Jakob helped her into Kilverdale's coat. It was too large for her, but it covered her torn chemise quite adequately.

'Oh, my God,' she whispered. 'Oh.' Her lips trembled, but she was too shocked to cry.

Jakob enfolded her into his arms and she closed her eyes, savouring the familiar, comforting feel and smell of him. She couldn't stop shaking. Her legs weakened and only his arms around her prevented her from falling.

His hold on her tightened until it was almost painful, but she didn't notice. If she could have burrowed any further into his embrace she would.

'Du är trygg här, min älskade,' he murmured. 'You're safe. It's over. But we must go down.'

Before she could respond he lifted her in his arms.

'Put me down. You're hurt.'

'You haven't got any shoes on,' he replied, carrying her to the stairs. Smoke billowed over the rooftop.

For the first time Desire became aware of the sharp, stinging pain in her bare feet, rubbed raw by the gravel and ash covering the roof. A gust of smoke blew suddenly into their path. She coughed and her eyes watered.

'Fire!' She twisted in Jakob's arms towards the east wing. 'Is my house on fire?'

'Yes.' Jakob carried her down the stairs. 'Your bedchamber was ablaze when I left it.'

Desire had been battered by so many disasters that this last one seemed almost too much to bear.

'My house,' she whispered, clinging to Jakob.

He took her out into the garden. By now the rest of the household had discovered both the man who had been knocked unconscious by Baker when he freed Arscott, and the fire. Men ran to and fro, shouting urgently, but with little sense of purpose. When they saw her and Jakob they crowded around, shouting over the top of each in their excitement and need for direction.

'Fenton's got a thick skull... Arscott's escaped... Your room, my lady... Colonel...the house... Thank God you're safe, my lady! Colonel, what are we to do?'

Jakob set Desire down on a bench and immediately took charge. Two of Lord Halross's footmen were given strict instructions to remain with Desire at all times. Everyone else rushed to obey Jakob's orders.

He had put Desire down on a bench close to the west side of the south wing. After sitting quietly for a few minutes, she stood up and demanded to be taken to the injured man. To her relief, though he was unsteady on his feet, he didn't seem to be seriously hurt by his temporary loss of consciousness. She could only be thankful that Baker had not yet learnt to pursue his ambitions as ruthlessly as Arscott. Then, despite the protests of her guards, she hobbled around to the other side of the house. From her new vantage point she could see smoke pouring out of the windows along the whole length of the first floor. The fire had already moved up to the second floor. Roaring flames devoured the whole of the east side of the house. Desire folded her arms across her stomach and nearly doubled up with grief for the loss of her home, so all encompassing she felt it as a physical pain.

'My lady, come away,' said one of the footman. Between them her two guards half-walked, half-carried her away from her burning house.

Night had long since fallen by the time Jakob arrived at Swiftbourne's house. He was exhausted, his hair and clothes acrid with smoke—and he was sick at heart at the news he must bring Desire.

'Mrs Quenell is waiting for you,' said the porter.

'Mrs Quenell?' It was Desire Jakob wanted to see, but, before he could ask where she was, Athena emerged from a nearby door.

'I thought it was your voice,' she said. 'Where's Gabriel?'

'He'll be here soon. He's giving the final commands to the men who'll be on watch tonight.'

'Good.' A trace of anxiety eased from her eyes, to be replaced with concern. 'You look tired.'

'Don't fuss.' Jakob knew she spoke only from her affection for him, but he wasn't in the mood to deal with feminine exclamations of worry.

'Where's Desire?' He consciously made an effort to soften his voice. 'Is she with you?' He started into the parlour Athena had just left, then stopped abruptly when he discovered it was empty.

'Go in.' Athena put her hands on his shoulders and pushed.

He strode forward a couple of places and swung to face her. 'Where is she?' he demanded.

'In the west parlour—'

'On her own? Why aren't you with her?' His eyebrows drew together in a frown. 'She shouldn't be alone. First that villain tried to take her by force, now she's just lost her home—'

'Jakob.' Athena laid her hand on his arm. 'Before Lady Desire would agree to leave the gardens of Godwin House, she picked bundles of the plant needed for her salve. When she first arrived here, she insisted on making it for anyone who might get burned. She made pots of it.' Athena smiled, not in amusement, but in sympathy at Desire's desperate need to occupy herself, to feel as if she was doing something useful.

'She said that it had helped your hands so it was bound to help others. She only stopped when there was no more butter left. We'll be eating dry bread for days. And then I did sit with her. She tried very hard to be gracious.' A sheen of tears glimmered in Athena's eyes. 'She asked me about my life in Bruges and how I make my lace. She admires me for being so well travelled and asked me about Venice...' Athena paused.

'It was so hard for her, Jakob,' she said. 'I wanted to comfort her, but she was so determined to be strong and gracious. It was kinder to leave her alone.'

Jakob pulled Athena into his arms and hugged her, just as he would have hugged one of his sisters if they had looked at him with such sad, worried eyes.

'*För bövelen!* I stink of smoke!' he exclaimed and quickly released her. 'I can't go to her smelling like the death of her house. Does Halross have anything I can wear?'

'Now I know you think of him as one of the family,' said Athena, smiling despite the tears in her eyes. 'You and Kilverdale—you wouldn't make free with the clothes of a man you didn't like. Come on.'

Jakob briefly resisted her tug on his sleeve. 'He makes you happy,' he said. 'Anyone with eyes can see that. Of course he is part of the family. But God help him if he ever hurts you. Then he will have me to deal with. And Kilverdale.'

Athena threw her arms around him and squeezed tightly. 'You are my best cousins,' she said against his chest. 'I hope it does not take long for Kilverdale to find Arscott. I'm worried about him. Arscott is such a treacherous villain.'

Jakob laughed softly. 'But no match for Kilverdale,' he said, with absolute confidence in his cousin. 'Don't fret, he'll be back with us soon,' He patted her comfortingly on the shoulder and then gently disengaged himself. 'Clean clothes,' he reminded her.

With the smell of smoke hastily sluiced from his hair and in borrowed clothes, Jakob went to find Desire. He discovered her sitting on the window seat in the small west parlour. She'd drawn her feet up on to the seat and hugged her knees to her chest. Her head was buried between her arms and she didn't look up when the door opened.

Jakob closed it quietly behind him. His stomach clenched in pain and sympathy for all she had lost. He dreaded the task that lay ahead of him. Godwin House had been her home and her sanctuary for so long. Arscott's betrayal of her trust had cost her dearly.

Jakob's hands closed unconsciously into fists. He bitterly regretted Arscott's escape. Now that the fire at Godwin House was under control, his instinct was to follow Kilverdale in the hunt for the treacherous steward. He wanted the pleasure of bringing Arscott to justice himself. But Kilverdale had his own reasons for avenging the wrong done to Desire. Jakob recognised in his cousin the need to make amends for what she'd overheard him say. Desire's need was to have her friends close by her, to console and to protect her.

He walked across the room to stand a few feet away from her. She still didn't look up. Her hunched body was silent and withdrawn, so lost in her own thoughts she didn't know he was there. The strength of his reaction to her grief stunned him. He felt her pain like a physical wound within him. He reached towards her, compelled by the need to give and receive comfort.

Just in time he arrested the gesture. She didn't know he was there. The last thing he wanted to do was frighten her with an unexpected touch.

'Desire?' he said softly.

After a moment she lifted her head. The parlour was lit by the glowing embers of the hearth and a single candle, but even that was enough for Jakob to be shocked by her appearance. There were no tears in her eyes, and no indication she had been crying, but her face was pale and gaunt, with deep, dark hollows beneath her eyes.

As she looked at him, some of the strain seemed to ease out of her expression. She pulled in a breath as though it cost her some effort, and then carefully lowered her feet to the floor and smoothed out her skirts. She moved stiffly, as if her body ached. It probably did, Jakob remembered. It was less than twelve hours ago that Arscott had forced her to climb up the side of the chimney to the roof. And she'd had no more than a few hours sleep in the last two nights.

She folded her hands together in her lap.

'What is the news?' she asked politely, with no more emphasis than if she were asking a polite question about the weather.

Jakob sat down beside her. 'The fire is almost out,' he said. 'Halross is posting men to watch in case the flames rekindle overnight, but I don't think it is likely.'

'How…bad?' It seemed as if she had to force the question past stiff, reluctant lips.

Jakob hesitated. His muscles tensed as if to ward off a blow. He was not afraid of Desire's anger when he confirmed her worst fears, but it was hard to say words that he knew would cause her terrible sorrow.

'Most of the west wing has been saved,' he said. 'But the east wing and the south wing are—' He broke off. He'd been about to say the house had been gutted, but the word seemed too brutal. 'We couldn't save them,' he said instead. 'Parts of the walls are still standing, and the chimneys, but the roof has gone. Everything inside burned.'

Desire gave a sharp intake of breath, as if she'd received a physical blow. She closed her eyes for a few seconds, then opened them again, her brittle composure still firmly in place.

'That is what I expected,' she said. 'I do…thank you…for your efforts to save…it. I hope you did not take any risks. I did not want any lives risked for the sake of bricks and…and mortar.' Her lips trembled. She paused to regain her composure. 'I made salve,' she whispered. 'In case anyone—'

Jakob couldn't bear it any longer. He reached over and lifted her on to his lap. She went rigid, whether from surprise or rejection of his comfort he wasn't sure. It made no difference. He needed to hold her. He pulled her closer and stroked her hair.

'I am sorry, *min älskade*,' he murmured. 'I am so sorry.'

She didn't say anything, but, after a few seconds, the tension drained from her body. She turned her face into his neck and he heard a sob catch in her throat.

'*Ah, älskling.*' His heart ached for her. He couldn't reassure her that it was just a bad dream as he had done before. This time the nightmare of pain and loss was real and inescapable.

Another sob escaped her, then she began to cry in earnest, her body racked by desolate, gut-wrenching tears. Jakob gave her the handkerchief Athena had thrust into his hand just before he'd entered the parlour, and then just held her close, rocking her and murmuring meaninglessly in a mixture of English and Swedish.

He kept his voice soft and soothing, while all the time he raged silently at Arscott.

One of Desire's hands was locked in the front of his coat. She clung to him as if he was her only safe harbour. Even when her sobs eventually subsided she didn't pull away. She nestled against him, limp in his arms, the damp handkerchief clutched in her other hand.

'It could be worse,' she said, her voice choked and unsteady from weeping. 'I sent all the most important things to Kingston when we thought the house was in danger from the…the *real* fire…'

'That's good,' said Jakob, wary of making a cheerful comment about rebuilding that she might not yet be ready to hear. He knew a home was more than bricks and mortar.

'Yes. And…' She caught her breath and dabbed the handkerchief to her cheek. 'I don't feel the same about it now I know it had secret…secret passages.' She swallowed an unwary sob. 'It feels as if the house was never mine—but Ar-Arscott's. He knew its secrets.' She turned her face into Jakob's neck again. He felt the dampness of her tears against his skin.

'Never think that,' he said fiercely. 'It was—and is—your house. Arscott's grandfather had a hand in building it, that's all.'

'Family secrets I didn't know. I'll go to the house in Kingston,' she said, lifting her head. 'And drive Templeton mad,' she added, with an attempt at humour.

'Templeton?' Jakob queried.

'My head gardener.' Desire made a gallant attempt at a laugh. 'He doesn't like it when I interfere in his domain.'

'Another roof garden?'

'No, the house isn't suitable. I am sorry I wept all over you,' she added, and he sensed her growing awkwardness at their situation. She tried to slip off his lap, but he tightened his embrace and wouldn't let her.

'Rest a little longer,' he said.

'I am not in need of rest.' She made another, somewhat half-hearted, effort to climb off his knee.

'I am.'

'Are you hurt?' Desire sat upright and began to pat his shoulders in a distracted way. 'Do you have any more burns? I will get the salve and anoint you.'

'I don't need your salve, *älskling*. Holding you does far more good for my aching muscles.' As he spoke, Jakob realised it was true. From the moment he'd crashed into Desire's burning bedchamber until he brought her the bad news about the house he had been engaged in a desperate struggle, first to keep her safe, and then to preserve her home. Holding her in his arms was reassuring proof that he had at least succeeded at the first of his tasks. Keeping Desire safe had come to mean a lot more to him than the simple concern of an honourable man to protect a vulnerable woman.

'When I found you gone from your room, I was afraid I wouldn't find you in time,' he said, his arms involuntarily tightening as he relived the horror of the moment.

He felt her tremble, then she said. 'But you did. You saved me.'

'So now let us both rest.' He knew he ought to send her to her bedchamber, but he didn't say anything. For just a little while longer he indulged himself by keeping her warm body on his lap.

Gradually the rhythm of her breathing changed. Her grasp on his coat relaxed and her hand slid lower down his chest. Her body softened and settled into his. He realised she had fallen asleep. And realised too how much his expectations and ambitions had changed in the past day.

He had been falling ever since he met Desire, drawn towards her but resisting the attraction because of his reluctance to fully embrace his English destiny. He'd come to England determined not to allow his grandfather to interfere with his life, but now he realised he'd been carrying within him the resentment of the seventeen-year-old youth who'd suddenly had his future expectations turned upside down.

Once he'd realised he would never have a long-term role to

play in his father's merchant business, he had held himself aloof from it, afraid of investing too much of his heart in something that would never ultimately be his. But at the same time he'd stubbornly tried to preserve his independence from Lord Swiftbourne. Joining the army had been an assertion of his right to choose his own life and he did not regret the decision. But he was a man now, and he no longer needed to prove himself in such a way. In all other aspects of his life he had learned to make his decisions without undue concern for what others thought. It was time to make his decisions about his English future in exactly the same way. And if the decisions he made happened to be particularly pleasing to Swiftbourne, he could no doubt put up with the old man's satisfaction.

Chapter Fifteen

Desire walked around the blackened ruins of Godwin House. For days the acrid smell of smoke had saturated the air, but today it stung her throat with the bitterness of personal loss. She was only one of thousands whose homes had been destroyed. By comparison with most she was lucky. She was only a wherry ride along the Thames from her Kingston house. What would all those who had no such alternative do?

'Don't go any closer.' Jakob caught her arm as she moved towards the house. 'It's not safe.'

Desire accepted his warning with a nod. Her eyes still felt swollen and bleary from the tears she had wept the previous night. Her head felt as if it was stuffed with hay, her thoughts were slow and disjointed.

The scene before her was so strange she could hardly recognise it. The ground around the house was strewn with debris, including one or two unburned household items that must have been thrown to safety in advance of the flames. Desire saw a stool lying on its side, two legs parallel to the ground, one thrust jauntily into the air. She struggled to see something familiar about it, but it was just a stool, probably from the servants' quarters. Most likely she'd never seen it before. It held no memories for her.

She walked on, Jakob staying silently at her side. Parts of the building still smouldered. The east wing was the most completely destroyed. The western end of the south wing had partially survived. Most amazingly the west wing seemed almost undamaged. It was the oldest part of the house.

'I hardly went into it from one month to the next,' Desire murmured.

'You had no need,' said Jakob.

'No. But the east wing—I walked and walked in the long gallery.' She bit her lip, remembering the last time she'd done so. 'It's not there any more,' she whispered. She stared at the blind, empty windows that pierced the blackened eastern wall. There was no roof. The oak floor on which she'd paced was gone. This part of the house was an empty shell.

She pressed her fingers to her temple, trying to comprehend the loss. With her own eyes she could see the destruction. Her mind accepted the inevitable consequences of the devastating fire, but in her heart she couldn't believe in the finality of the dreadful transformation.

'If I close my eyes it's all still there,' she whispered. 'How can this have happened?'

Jakob didn't say anything. She didn't expect him to. She understood the sequence of events that had led to this. She just hadn't had time to adjust to them.

'They say you should be careful what you wish for,' she said after a moment. 'I used to wish I could walk through Cheapside and visit St Paul's. Now they're both gone for ever—'

'They'll be rebuilt,' said Jakob. 'London is full of merchants and tradesmen. They have to conduct their business or they'll starve. The shops and houses will go back up.'

'Yes,' said Desire. 'Perhaps…'

'Perhaps what?'

'Perhaps, when the last fires have stopped burning, I ought to go and see the ruins of London,' she said. 'And then visit again when the shops and houses are rebuilt.'

If she did that, at least she'd be able to say she'd been part of the new London from the start, even though she'd never been part of the old.

Before the fire, she'd also wished she could venture out from behind the safety of her walls. Now she had been forced out. However difficult life became, she could never retreat to the peaceful sanctuary of her roof garden.

'I must speak to Lord Halross.' She folded her arms across her body.

'Halross? Why?' There was an unusually sharp note in Jakob's voice, but she barely heard it.

'I need a new steward,' she replied, walking away from the house. At the gate she stopped and took one last look at her ruined home. 'Lord Halross may be able to recommend someone suitable.'

Jakob put his hand under her elbow as they headed back towards St Martin's Lane. They had an escort of three of Halross's footmen. With Arscott on the loose and with his guilt proven beyond doubt, Jakob wasn't taking any chances with Desire's safety. She was grateful for his caution.

An image of the horrifying experience of climbing the side of the chimney flashed into her mind. It was so overwhelming that for a moment she felt she was right back in the dark, claustrophobic space, with Arscott behind her, threatening and deadly. She shuddered and covered her face with her hands. She didn't realise she was standing stock-still in the middle of the street until she was suddenly swept off her feet.

She gasped, her heart thudding with alarm, then realised Jakob had picked her up.

'What are you doing?' she demanded.

'Taking you to safety.'

She had a limited view of his face, but his expression seemed uncharacteristically grim.

'I can walk,' she protested, but made no effort to extricate herself from his arms. It was embarrassing being carried through the streets as if she'd lost the use of her limbs—but it was also rather thrilling to lie in Jakob's arms while he strode purposefully forward. She realised anew how strong he was, how full of virile energy. He'd held her the previous night, even until she'd fallen asleep, but she'd been so grief-struck she'd taken only comfort from his embrace.

Today it was exciting to be in Jakob's arms, except...

Her muscles cramped with mortification as she remembered what had happened the last time she'd been excited in Jakob's embrace. That memory was just as real and, in its own way, just as devastating as Arscott's attempt to steal her by forced.

'We're nearly there, *älskling*,' Jakob said reassuringly, apparently misinterpreting the sudden tension in her body. 'You'll be safe in Swiftbourne House and you can rest.'

'I must go to Kingston,' she replied. It was suddenly unendurable that she was so entirely dependent upon the good will of others. She wanted to go to her own home, even if it was a home she'd only rarely visited in the past. 'I will speak to Lord Halross, if he has a convenient moment to talk to me—and then I'm going to Kingston.'

Even though he knew it was an irrational response, Jakob's jaw clenched with annoyance at Desire's plan to ask Halross for advice without, apparently, even considering Jakob in the role of adviser. Did she take him for nothing but a soldier, useful only for the quick power in his muscles? He had land of his own in Sweden. He could not lay claim to an inheritance equal to Desire's, but he was not ignorant of the responsibilities of a landowner. And his years in the army had given his vast experience both of ruling men, and judging their character.

He knew two or three men he could have recommended to replace Arscott, all of whom were honest and competent. Of course, they were all Swedish, and only one of them spoke any English. All the same, Desire *should* have asked for his opinion instead of assuming he was only good for the task of portering her back to St Martin's Lane. Despite his annoyance, he kept his tongue between his teeth and listened as she talked to Halross.

'I thought you might be able to recommend someone,' she said to the Marquis.

'One or two possibilities come to mind.' Halross frowned thoughtfully. 'Can you tell me a little more about the location and condition of your estates, my lady?'

'Of course,' she replied, and proceeded to give Halross a very full account.

Jakob listened, impressed, as he had been before, by the breadth of Desire's knowledge. She might have travelled no further than Kingston during the past six years, but she had clearly maintained a close watch on the income and expenditure of all her properties.

'That's very helpful,' said Halross, when she'd finished. 'I need to make a few enquiries, but I'll give you some recommendations as soon as possible.'

'Thank you.' Desire smiled at the Marquis.

It occurred to Jakob how much more at ease she had become in the company of others. He knew she was grieving for the loss of her house, but she did not seem unduly daunted by the challenges that lay ahead of her. It was almost as if she had been in hibernation for a few years, resting quietly until it was time to wake up and take on the world. When she'd fully recovered from the shocks of the past few days she would be a formidable lady indeed. The image was an enticing one. It pleased him so much he hardly noticed when Halross left the parlour.

'Now I must make arrangements to go to Kingston,' said Desire briskly. 'Benjamin said the roads are dreadful. I'd like to go riding again soon, but for now I'll send a message to have the Godwin barge brought back from Kingston. That seems best, don't you think?'

He looked at her, his mouth suddenly dry as he realised the moment to speak was upon him and he wasn't prepared. She glanced at him questioningly, obviously expecting an answer from him. What had she just said? Oh, something about travelling in the barge.

'Very likely,' he said, 'as long as you don't expect me to row.'

'Why should I expect that?' She stared at him in astonishment.

'No reason,' he replied gruffly, embarrassed by his ill-considered remark. Of course he wouldn't have to row the barge. No wonder she was looking at him as if he'd lost his wits.

He stood up and walked across the room to the window. After years of being completely sure of himself in feminine company he was suddenly, hideously, at a loss for words. Desire said something to him, but he didn't notice. He stared blindly out of the window. His whole body knotted with tension as he sought desperately for the words he needed, but his mind was completely blank. Sweat broke out on his forehead. At last, after a stomach-churning interval of confusion, a coherent sentence formed in his mind. His panic receded. He knew what to say. He turned to face Desire.

'Will you marry me?' he said. To his own ears his voice seemed over-loud and unpolished, but his usual, easy self-assurance had deserted him.

He watched Desire's face intently for some sign of her response. His heart thudded as if he was waiting to go into battle, but surely her answer would be favourable? How could it not be when she kissed him so willingly, and even trusted him sufficiently to fall asleep in his arms.

But she simply stared back at him, no discernible expression in her eyes, except perhaps mild bewilderment.

His stomach clenched with unfamiliar, sickening anxiety. He'd expected…what? Pleasure? He'd hoped for excited happiness, but surprise would be understandable. Even maidenly confusion would be acceptable. *Something* more than this coolly unemotional response.

'Didn't you hear me?' he demanded, the horrible uncertainty and fear roughening his voice and his temper. 'Or am I not even worthy of a reply?'

When she still didn't reply, a strong sense of injustice suddenly overwhelmed him. She said she'd tried to let Arscott down gently when she'd intended to refuse him. Presumably she had at least spoken to the steward when he'd proposed to her. So far she hadn't deigned to say a single word to Jakob.

Then, to his horror, she started to laugh!

'Do you think my proposal is funny?' he demanded, filled with furious, frustrated disbelief.

'Vill ni gifta er med mig?'

Desire gazed at Jakob, wondering what he'd said. Her mind was full of travel arrangements and he'd been staring silently out of the window for so long he'd taken her by surprise when he suddenly spoke.

He stared back at her, a disturbingly intense, expectant expression in his eyes. She tried to repeat in her mind whatever he'd just said to her so she could answer, and discovered only a collection of garbled, meaningless syllables in her memory.

His brows drew together over his penetrating gaze. Impatience and tension radiated from his large body.

'Hörde ni inte vad jag sade?'

It belatedly dawned on Desire that he was speaking in Swedish. He'd occasionally done so before, but never in the obvious expectation that she'd reply. She was just about to point out his slip when he said something else.

'Eller är jag inte ens värdig ett svar?' He sounded so unaccountably aggrieved with her she couldn't help laughing.

'Tycker ni att mitt frieri är lustigt?' he snarled, fury blazing in his eyes.

'I'm sorry, but if you want me to answer you'll have to speak English,' she said. His inexplicable display of temper disconcerted her, but she refused to be cowed by it. In the circumstances it was quite ridiculous of him to be vexed with her.

'Vad? För bövelen!' Before her fascinated gaze, Jakob's angry expression turned to one of deep chagrin. He half-turned

away from her as he muttered something inaudible under his breath.

'Did I just say *everything* in Swedish?' he asked, once more facing her.

'Yes.' Desire had never expected to see the usually self-assured Jakob flush with obvious embarrassment. There was something both comical—and endearing—about a handsome, virile man blushing like a nervous maiden. A smile tugged at her lips, but she did her best to keep a straight face. She didn't want to upset him again.

'Even my proposal?'

'What proposal?' She looked at him blankly, then remembered they'd been discussing travel arrangements. 'Have you decided it's not a good idea to send for the barge?'

'Barge?' He stared at her as if she'd gone mad. 'What barge? What are you talking about?'

'What am *I* talking about?' Desire exclaimed indignantly. '*You're* the one who started shouting at me in a foreign language. I'm just trying to make arrangements for going to Kingston. Could you instruct a messenger—?'

'Will you stop talking about barges!' Jakob exploded.

Desire was so startled by his sudden shout she took a step backwards.

Jakob glared at her, bristling with incomprehensible but unquestionable outrage. She swallowed, suddenly nervous. He'd spent hours yesterday struggling to contain the fire at Godwin House. Had the smoke somehow addled his brain? He'd never before behaved so bizarrely.

'Are you feeling quite well?' she enquired delicately. 'Perhaps you should sit down. I know an excellent remedy for agitation of the nerves—'

'My nerves are not agitated! I defy any man to remain even-tempered when he asks a woman to marry him and she laughs in his face!'

'I *didn't* laugh in your face. But it was funny when you bristled up like a frustrated hedgehog when—' Desire broke off as the meaning of Jakob's words finally sank in. 'You asked me to *marry* you?'

'That's what I just said,' he said belligerently.

'Oh.' She stared at him. It was so far from what she'd been expecting that, for a few seconds, she felt nothing but blank surprise. 'You want to marry me?' she repeated.

She saw Jakob's chest expand as he drew in a deep breath. He scowled at her, every line of his body radiating barely controlled masculine outrage. She received the distinct impression he considered her at fault in the exchange.

His anger triggered her memory of the last time he'd been angry with her. He'd felt the scar on her leg and climbed out of her bed—leaving her aroused, exposed and humiliated—and then he'd accused her of looking for someone to chase away her ghosts. She still had a vivid memory of his barely contained fury swirling around her bedchamber. He'd said they'd talk in the morning, but Godwin House had burned instead.

Arscott's terrifying assault on her, followed by the destruction of Godwin House had crowded the painful memory to the back of her mind. Jakob had rescued her from Arscott and tried to save her home. He had not, by word or deed, referred back to the moment of her utmost mortification, and she had tried to pretend it had never happened.

But it had. He had come to her bed. Kissed her, teased her and left her in disgust when he discovered the extent of her scars. She burned with shame as she remembered how she'd wept in his arms the previous night. How could she have been so lacking in self-respect that she allowed herself to fall asleep on his lap?

'Desire?' He reached towards her. His blue gaze was focussed on her with unnerving intensity. Was he hoping she'd say 'no'?

He must be asking her to marry him from pity or compassion. He'd soothed her grief as if she were a child, not a woman who aroused his passions. He had not kissed her once since he'd left her bed, and he'd kissed and teased her often before that. And he'd asked her to marry him in a language he knew she didn't understand. What greater evidence could there be of his reluctance to wed her?

'No,' she said, lifting her chin.

'No what?'

'No, I won't marry you,' she said.

'You're refusing me?' He sounded absolutely dumbfounded.

His surprise gave a spur to Desire's own temper. 'You are so vain!' she flung at him. 'Did you think you'd only have to issue an order and I'd come to heel? Grovel with pathetic gratitude at your feet?'

'Of course not.' His voice was laden with scorn and anger. 'I asked you to be my wife. Is that not an honourable position?'

'I'm sure women from London to Stockholm are vying for the honour. But I'm not one of them.'

'You've made that very clear, my lady.' Jakob's jaw clenched. 'Since my offer seems to be a source of both amusement and offence to you, I withdraw it.'

'Just like a man.' Inside Desire was crying, but she was too proud to reveal the depth of her misery. 'You would never want it known you'd suffered the humiliation of rejection. So much easier to pretend you never asked.'

A muscle in Jakob's cheek twitched, but he made no other response to Desire's accusation.

'I apologise for misjudging your feelings,' he said coldly. 'As soon as we are assured Kilverdale has captured Arscott, I will relieve you of my presence. Until then, I will continue to guard you from possible threats.'

'There is no need—' Desire began.

'Yes, there is,' he said flatly. 'It is a matter for my conscience that I fulfil the task I set out to do. Your opinion is of no relevance.' He turned and stalked out of the room.

Jakob was by turns numb with shock and incandescent with rage. After years of holding himself aloof, he had finally made a commitment to England and to the woman who had won his heart—and she had laughed at him!

He clenched his fists. Beneath his anger and mortification he was unbelievably hurt. How could she have so little regard for him that she rejected his proposal with no consideration for his feelings? Apparently he rated less highly than her murderous, treacherous steward. Or was this her revenge for his cousin's long-ago lack of kindness to her?

'Balston, have you had bad news?' Halross demanded, encountering Jakob in the hall.

'Bad news?' Jakob frowned at Halross. Such an unfeeling rejection of his proposal might be considered bad news, he supposed, but not news he intended to share with the Marquis. 'No,' he growled.

'I see.' A faint smile played on Halross's lips. 'You look so thunderous I thought you might have had word of another outrage by Arscott,' he said.

'No. Are you going out in the next few hours?' Jakob asked.

'I have no plans to. Why?'

'Then may I request you ensure Lady Desire's safety?' Jakob said through gritted teeth. 'And do not, on any account, allow her to go to Kingston without me.'

'I believe I can do that,' said Halross. 'When will you be back?'

'I cannot say,' said Jakob, frustrated by the need to supply an explanation to Halross, but constrained by common courtesy to say *something*. 'I am going for a walk.'

'Ah,' said Halross, a world of extremely exasperating understanding in his voice. 'Conversation with a lady can have that effect.'

Jakob scowled at the Marquis, unwilling to admit such a motivation.

Halross grinned. 'The important thing is to be back in time for the next conversation,' he said. His smile faded and his ex-

pression suddenly grew serious. 'Don't leave the intervals between conversations too long,' he said, 'or the chance may be
gone forever.'

Jakob acknowledged Halross's comment with a curt nod, but
it lingered in his mind as he went to see the smouldering ruins
of London.

Jakob had asked her to marry him. But he considered her
opinion of no relevance!

Desire strode around the room. A chair blocked her path and
she shoved it aside.

Her opinion was on no *relevance*!

She kicked a footstool out of her way. The corner of a table
caught the top of her leg and it hurt. She muttered angrily, rub-
bing her aching thigh. How on earth did Lord Swiftbourne put
up with such a cluttered parlour? She leant her weight against
the heavy oak, nudging the table aside to create an unimpeded
circuit of the room.

She marched around it, longing for the freedom to stride up
and down her own long gallery. But that was gone for ever. Her
stride faltered as a sudden wave of grief washed through her. Her
house was lost. If it hadn't been, Jakob would never have asked
her to marry him. He'd been prompted by pity, or...

She didn't know what 'or'. Why had he proposed in such an
abrupt manner, in a language she didn't understand? It was clear
he hadn't truly wanted her to say yes. He'd shouted at her!

Men did not shout when they proposed to the lady of their
choice. Desire did not know much about the world, but she was
sure that was so. Even Arscott had taken her hand and pretended
to be solicitous of her feelings. Jakob stood two yards away and
shouted and bristled. Desire bristled herself at the memory.

But her anger was rooted in confusion and agitation rather
than genuine fury. Her pace around the room slowed as sad bewilderment gradually overwhelmed her other, more immediate,
responses to Jakob's proposal.

He had asked her to marry him. It was only a day or two ago she'd paced the long gallery of Godwin House, wondering if he would be a suitable husband. In this very room he had taken her hand on the day of their return from Putney and she'd anticipated a marriage proposal. Instead he'd revealed Arscott's treachery. Perhaps that was why she didn't believe in this proposal today.

After they'd spent the night together at Putney, Jakob might have felt some compulsion to protect her reputation with an offer of marriage. She wouldn't have been surprised, because she would have known Jakob was motivated by his sense of honour, not by personal attraction to her.

But how was she to interpret this proposal? He didn't truly want her. He had proved that the night he left her bed. One touch of his hand on the scar that marred her leg and he'd pulled away from her. A tiny sob escaped her lips. She'd always thought the scar on her body didn't matter, but now it seemed it mattered more than the scars on her face. She laid her hand on her thigh where the ugly, snaking scar was hidden by her clothes.

Why had Jakob proposed? She wished she'd asked him. She wished she hadn't been anxious and preoccupied with travel arrangements when he asked her to marry him. She wished she'd been politely ladylike and hadn't laughed when he shouted at her so incomprehensibly. She should have indicated to him delicately that he was speaking the wrong language. How could she ever find out why he'd proposed now? He'd withdrawn his offer. It was as if it had never been. *Could* never be again. For how could they ever overcome the awkwardness of their last encounter?

Her hands flew to her cheeks as she imagined the embarrassment of their next meeting. And then she realised the true reason Jakob wanted to marry her. Not for her money—or not exactly. She didn't believe he was a cold-hearted fortune hunter. But Lord Swiftbourne would favour the union of his heir with the Godwin name and estates. She remembered how much interest Jakob had taken in her descriptions of her estates and their income when she was talking to Lord Halross. At the time she'd felt flattered by what she'd believed to be his admiration for her understanding and good management. Now she realised it had been her lands he'd been admiring. What a naïve fool she was.

She sank on to the nearest chair. Now her sense of loss was far more acute. She'd only just learned to hope for romance, but now, before she'd ever truly believed such magic could be hers, her hopes had been destroyed. There was no romance, only a practical assessment of land and rents. Tears pricked her eyes. She rubbed her temple, determined not to cry. She had many important decisions to make. She tried to give her attention to the future of Godwin House, the need to appoint a new steward, the travel arrangements to Kingston—but all she could think about was Jakob.

She thought about him laughing with her, teasing her, comforting her, kissing her. Her fragile hope that maybe he was the man she hadn't known she was looking for…

She heard the door open and leapt up, swirling about in the certain expectation it would be Jakob.

'I hope I'm not disturbing you,' said Athena.

'Oh. No.' Desire's shoulders slumped in disappointment. 'No, of course not.' She forced a welcoming note into her voice and a smile to her lips. 'I am just making my plans for going to Kingston,' she said.

'Would you mind very much delaying your journey?' Athena asked.

'Delaying it?' Desire was confused. 'Is there some reason why I should?'

'Not a reason, exactly. I would like you to come to my wedding.' Athena's eyes glowed with happiness as she mentioned her forthcoming marriage. 'If you would like to,' she added, a little more hesitantly, as if she suspected Desire would have something more important to do.

'Of course I would like to.' Desire took the hand Athena offered. 'I would very much like to see you get married,' she said.

Chapter Sixteen

Athena and Lord Halross were married in the village church, two miles from Halross's Oxfordshire estate. As the bridal couple passed Desire on their way back down the aisle, she was overwhelmed by the expressions of love and joy she saw on their faces. She felt tears blur her vision. She was so happy for them, but it hurt too, because she couldn't help wondering if she would ever know such love.

'My lady, it is our turn to leave,' said Jakob, in the formal tone he used now whenever he spoke to her. Desire hated it. It made him sound so cold and distant, quite unlike the man she'd first met.

For the past two weeks they had been guests at Lord Halross's country house. Before that they had been Lord Swiftbourne's guests in St Martin's Lane. Because they'd been living under the same roof, either in London or in Oxfordshire, they'd had no choice except to go on seeing and talking to each other. But their first encounter after Desire had rejected Jakob's proposal had been in the presence of others. Desire had felt tense and uncomfortable, and very conscious that their conversation was being overheard. She'd taken refuge in cool politeness, so had Jakob, and to her dismay that had become the pattern for all their subsequent meetings.

'Yes, of course. I'm sorry.' She allowed him to escort her from the pew. Once they were in the aisle, he offered her his arm. She hesitated fractionally, then laid her hand on his sleeve. She was awkward about touching him now—even in this most formal of contexts. He never touched her at all, except on those rare occasions when he'd helped her into or out of a carriage. And once when they'd gone for a walk with Athena and Lord Halross and he'd assisted her over a stile. For hours after the walk was over she'd recalled the warm clasp of his hand on hers—and spent even more time trying to decide exactly what the firm pressure of his fingers signified.

It was a month since the fire. It had been one of the most emotionally exhausting periods of Desire's life. She was always on edge, her mood swinging between hope when Jakob unexpectedly smiled at her, to despair when his manner was particularly cold or distant. When she was in his presence she was wound to such a pitch of nervous agitation she could hardly think straight. She wanted to behave towards him in a way that was friendly but did not seem overly anxious to impress. She wanted to give the impression that, if Jakob felt like talking to her, she wouldn't rebuff him—but that she could live quite happily without his attention.

It was a difficult balance to strike, and she was usually exhausted by the end of the day. Unfortunately, instead of sleeping, she had a demoralising tendency to lay awake, remembering every stray thing he'd said to her and examining his words for every possible nuance of meaning. And the next morning she'd feel tired, highly strung and even more self-conscious in his company. On a couple of occasions she'd seen him in the distance and darted away before he saw her, simply because she was so agitated she didn't think she'd even be able to say 'hello' without betraying her feelings.

She was in love with Jakob. She knew that without a doubt, and she couldn't imagine anything more miserable or ridiculous than her current situation. What woman with a particle of sense or refinement would set out to win a husband—and then laugh at the man's marriage proposal!

But Jakob hadn't asked her because he loved her. At least, she didn't think he had. He'd never said anything about love. He'd enjoyed kissing her, and then he'd pulled away from her when he'd felt the scar on her leg. But she didn't think there was any obligation for a husband to look at his wife's legs when they were in bed together—or even touch them if he didn't want to, so that really wasn't a good reason not to marry her. And he'd kissed her as if he wanted her...

Her thoughts kept going round and round, like a dog chasing its own tail, until she thought she'd go crazy with confusion and frustration. If only they could go back to the way it had been before Jakob had proposed, when most of the time he'd been relaxed and good humoured. Surely there must be some way to overcome the awkwardness between them. At the very least she wished they could be friends again, at ease in each other's company.

'Halross seems to be well liked by the local people,' Jakob observed.

'What? Oh, yes.' His words recalled Desire to a sense of her surroundings.

Even from inside the church she could hear the roar of welcome from the waiting villagers as Lord Halross emerged with his bride. A few moments later she walked beside Jakob into the autumn sunlight and the cheering crowd. The route of the bridal procession was strewn with rosemary and other scented herbs. Halross had brought musicians from London and they played with skill and verve. Young men and women from the village, dressed in their finest clothes, danced for the entertainment of the bride and groom. Lord Halross distributed alms freely to everyone who had congregated to see him wed. The wedding procession was a noisy, energetic celebration of the marriage in which all the local people could participate.

Desire tried not to feel self-conscious at being a part of the bridal train. She was growing more used to meeting strangers and, with the beautiful bride to claim their attention, no one was likely to spare her more than a passing glance. Lord Halross was laughing and bantering with the crowd. Most of them were his tenants. Everyone seemed in good spirits today. He had arranged for a feast to be laid on and free wine and ale provided at the village inn. Everyone present anticipated celebrating the wedding in grand fashion, even if they were not among those who dined with Halross and his new lady in the great hall.

It had been planned that the bridal couple would travel most of the two miles from the village to the house in Halross's carriage. Several of the other honoured guests were also going to travel in a similar style, though many of the gentlemen and some of the local ladies had opted to ride. As they strolled towards the waiting carriages, Desire felt a surge of reluctance to climb into a coach. She didn't want to sit in a confined space and make small talk to virtual strangers. She wanted an end to the unbearable awkwardness between her and Jakob.

'It's such a beautiful day, perhaps we could walk,' she said impulsively. As soon as the words were out of her mouth she was afraid he wouldn't like the idea. She held her breath as she awaited his reaction. When he didn't immediately reply, she hurried into speech.

'Of course, sir, if you'd rather ride in the coach I'll be happy—' She was desperate to avert a flat rejection to her suggestion.

'No. If you wish to walk, by all means let us do so,' he said.

It was an acceptance, and he didn't *sound* put out by her request. She risked a glance at him. His expression was impassive. 'A walk will certainly sharpen my appetite for the feast ahead,' he added.

That was not the response for which Desire had hoped. She wondered if she'd made a mistake, then she stiffened her resolution. They had managed together in perfect harmony—well, perfectly satisfactory disagreement and teasing—until the moment of the marriage proposal. Surely they could at least recover that earlier good will. But Jakob looked dauntingly remote and didn't seem at all inclined to initiate a conversation. She swallowed past the nervous pulse beating in her throat.

'Since your appetite will be so keen, it is lucky the feast will consist of more than cheese,' she said, making her first bantering comment to him in weeks.

The wedding celebrations were in full swing. The air was heavy with the scent of good food and wine, and hot wax from the many candles. Music and laughter rang in the great hall.

Desire sampled a marchpane tartlet while she watched her fellow guests. She was so used to being alone that at first her senses had been overwhelmed by the lively clamour and movement all around her. Like a skittish animal she'd been unable to eat the feast because she'd been too busy looking this way and that at her fellow feasters. The boom of unexpected laughter, the clatter of a knife on the floor, all had prompted an immediate, head-turning response from her. Now she felt more settled, lulled rather than agitated by the ceaseless roar of conversation all around her. Both her neighbours at the table were currently more interested in talking to the guest on their other side than to her, and she was quite content with that. It gave her time to reflect on her conversation with Jakob—though her thoughts gave her no pleasure at all.

There had been no conversation. Jakob had hardly said a thing to her on the walk back to the house. She had been on tenterhooks all the way, full of nerve-tingling anxiety, uncertainty and hope. But during the entire walk he had only made three spontaneous remarks. She'd tried to initiate a conversation several times, but in the end her ideas and her courage had both dried up. They'd finished the walk in stony silence, and separated as soon as decently possible when they arrived at their destination.

He wasn't seated next to Desire, which meant she didn't have to struggle for something to say to him while they ate. On the one hand that was a relief, but it did mean she had to endure the sight of him smiling and laughing with the daughter of one of the local gentleman. Miss Ludlow was much younger than Desire, pretty and pert, and Jakob didn't seem to have any difficulty thinking of things to say to her. It hurt to watch them together, so Desire tried not to look in that direction, but her gaze kept drifting back towards him. On one occasion he glanced around and caught her looking at him. For a long moment their gazes locked. Then Miss Ludlow spoke to him and he turned away.

Desire released a shaky breath. A hot flush washed over her body. She was embarrassed he'd noticed her staring at him. What did that look he'd given her mean? Was he annoyed with her for acting like a love-sick fool? Or telling her without words that he'd found someone new to entertain him? She decided not to risk looking at him again. She'd given him the perfect opportunity to talk to her if he'd wanted it, and he hadn't taken it. So now she would forget about him and enjoy the party.

While she was fiercely assuring herself she didn't care who Jakob flirted with, the celebrations moved on. The tables were set to the sides of the large chamber and Halross called for dance music. He and Athena danced the first measure alone. They were such a handsome couple, and so clearly aware only of each other as they moved gracefully through the steps.

'May I have the honour, my lady?' Jakob appeared suddenly before her.

Desire's heart began to beat double-time. Why did he want to dance with her when there were many other ladies available? Especially since he'd had nothing to say to her earlier. Perhaps he believed it was a courtesy he owed to Athena and Lord Halross.

She let him lead her into the dance, holding her head high and doing her best to appear serenely indifferent to her surroundings. She knew Jakob naturally drew the attention of others. When she danced with him she would not be able to avoid curious, and probably jealous, glances. She would be mortified if she stumbled or forgot the steps in front of an audience. She concentrated very hard on getting everything right, and neither she nor Jakob said a word through out the dance.

When it was over, Athena's younger brother gallantly claimed Desire for the next dance. She parted from Jakob with her emotions in a state of tumultuous regret and unhappiness. The situation between them was stretching her nerves to breaking point.

Later, Lord Halross came over to speak to her.

'Athena would like you to join her,' he said. 'It is time for the bride and groom to retire.'

'Oh.' Desire's attention was distracted by the sight of Jakob laughing aloud at something Miss Ludlow had just said to him. It was horrible to watch him flirting in full public view.

'Oh, I'm sorry, my lord!' she exclaimed, giving her full attention to Halross and embarrassed that he might have seen the direction of her gaze. She was determined not to let anyone think she was *pining* for Jakob. 'Thank you for telling me, I'll go to her at once.'

She took her leave of the Marquis and hurried over to Athena. On the way she noticed that Jakob was bending down to hear something Miss Ludlow said to him, his head close to hers. And he had allowed the brazen wench to lay her hand on his arm!

Desire gritted her teeth. This is what it would have been like if she'd married him. He was too beautiful and too used to women's fawning attentions. Unless he married a woman as beautiful and assured as he was himself, his wife would be doomed to endless disappointment and humiliation. It was unquestionably a good thing she'd laughed when he proposed. He thoroughly deserved to receive such a setback.

Jakob heard only one word in ten his companion said to him. He fixed an attentive expression on his face, and laughed and nodded at what seemed to be appropriate intervals while he watched Desire from the corner of his eye. He was proud of the way she'd conducted herself today. No one watching her dance in her new burgundy silk gown would ever guess this was her first large party. She held her head up. There was no sign of the woman who'd hidden her face from him at their first meeting on her roof, and only occasionally did she show a shy reticence, which was entirely acceptable among so many strangers.

Not that he had any right or business to be proud of her. He hadn't seen the faintest hint she regretted rejecting him. Except on rare occasions, her manner to him over the past few weeks had been as warm and welcoming as the first frosts of autumn.

'You must tell me more about Sweden, Colonel,' said his companion, leaning forward to artfully reveal a little more of her bosom. 'It must be very beautiful.'

'Yes, it is,' he said, recalling with frustrated pleasure the first time he'd seen Desire in a similarly low-cut bodice.

Her new burgundy gown suited her even better than the blue one she'd borrowed from Athena. Unfortunately, the fashionably styled gown revealed her charms not just to him but to all the other male guests present. It had taken all Jakob's self-control not to stride across the room and plant a fist in the face of one of Halross's middle-aged neighbours when he had leered at Desire's chest for the entire time they were supposedly dancing.

Jakob gritted his teeth, suppressing a growl of pure frustration. He didn't know if he was more infuriated with Desire for being so stubbornly blind to her own best interests, or with himself for having allowed the situation to get so disastrously out of hand. Even as a youth he'd never lacked social address, but suddenly all his usual easy confidence had disserted him. Two miles he'd walked beside Desire—and he'd been unable to discuss anything more scintillating than the state of the local roads. Each time he'd tried to make a more personal remark he'd remembered how he'd bungled his proposal and writhed inside with embarrassment. With every step, his discomfort had grown until the fear of making a fool of himself again had prevented him from saying anything at all. No wonder Desire had parted from him with such cool disdain when they'd finally arrived at the house.

He would have done better to throw her over his shoulder and carry her off to some secluded spot to sort out their differences. She wouldn't have been cool then! He remembered the hot-tempered way she'd railed at him when he'd taken her off her roof. With her hands and legs tied up she hadn't hesitated to call him a scurvy, double-dealing numskull. But it was weeks since she'd called him anything except 'sir' or 'Colonel'. He hated it when she called him 'sir' in that chilly manner.

För bövelen! He *was* a numskull! He'd always considered himself adept with words at least until the dreadful moment of his proposal—but Desire had never been particularly impressed by any of the things he'd said to her. She'd doubted his explanation for abducting her, been suspicious of his connection to Kilverdale, questioned the truth of his accusation against Arscott...

But she *had* been impressed by *him*. He remembered that with renewed confidence. She had been impressed by his *actions*! She'd never once rejected him when he'd kissed her or held her. Obviously the way to win her was not through pretty speeches but by more active courtship. His rising excitement suffered a momentary setback when he remembered, with some chagrin, that he hadn't always performed very well in that respect either. His honourable attempt to do the right thing the night of her nightmare might well have sewn the seeds for her subsequent rejection of him. But he could make amends for his apparent lack of ardour. In fact, he was eager to make amends!

Newfound purpose surged through him. He looked around the great hall, intent on locating Desire. He was determined to put his new plan into action at once. He couldn't see her, but he did catch the eye of Lord Halross who made a silent, easily interpreted gesture.

Jakob's companion cleared her throat impatiently. He'd completely forgotten her presence. Now all he wanted to do was get away from her and find Desire, but first the bride and groom must be bedded.

'Forgive me, Miss—' What the devil was her name? Halross

had introduced them, but damned if he could recall who she was. 'Gracious lady,' he substituted, with only a minor internal wince at sounding like a florid courtier, 'I regret I will have to tell you about Sweden another day. It is time for me to attend the bridegroom.'

The stately bedchamber was bright with candles and cosy from the fire flickering in the hearth. The air was lightly scented with the herbs and flowers scattered over the bed. Because of the season most of the flowers were dried, but they smelled no less sweet for that.

The women laughed and joked as they removed the exquisite cloth-of-gold dress in which Athena had been married. Desire watched as Athena's sister, Tabitha, unlaced the bodice.

'Hurry, the men will be here soon,' said one girl, her eyes bright with excitement and mock anxiety.

'Where is the brush?' Tabitha snatched it up from the dressing table.

Athena stood quietly, dressed only in her shift as Tabitha began to brush out her hair until it cascaded around her shoulders like pale, shining silk.

'You are very beautiful,' said Desire, captivated by the image Athena presented, and momentarily forgetting to be on her guard among so many strangers.

Athena met her gaze and smiled. 'As long as Gabriel thinks so,' she said softly. 'I have learned that it is what he sees that counts.' She held Desire's gaze for a second longer. Desire's stomach gave a tiny flip. Was Athena trying to tell her something in that silent exchange of glances?

'Since you have been married before, I do not suppose you need any advice from me,' said Lord Halross's sister-in-law.

Athena's eyes danced with sudden merriment, but she responded with appropriate courtesy to the woman who had been wife to the previous Marquis of Halross.

'Than you, my lady, but on this occasion I don't think I need advice,' she said. 'Though I will gladly learn more from you on the management of the household.'

There was a pause for a moment as former mistress of the house and the new mistress regarded each other.

'What a cheerful fire,' one of the other women observed, a little too brightly.

'She'll not care about that. His lordship will keep her warm!' another replied, provoking a gale of knowing laughter that eased the momentary tension.

Desire felt herself blush on Athena's behalf. She could not imagine the awkwardness of appearing in front of others dressed only in her shift. At least, not when she'd had forewarning of what to expect, she amended, remembering how scantily she had been clad when Arscott tried to take her from Godwin House. At the time she'd been too afraid to care about how she was dressed.

Athena seemed to be bearing up very well under the scrutiny of her companions, though Desire did notice the new Lady Halross had a tendency to cross her arms over her chest as if she wasn't entirely at ease being the centre of the women's teasing attention.

'I can hear them coming!' one of the women suddenly gasped. 'Quick, my lady, get into bed.'

They pushed and pulled Athena across the room. She climbed up the steps and scrambled under the covers, just as the door opened.

All the women laughed and clapped as Lord Halross entered, dressed only in a nightshirt that revealed his muscular calves and strong bare feet. He was accompanied by the male guests who, as Desire immediately noticed, included Jakob.

'Your bride awaits you, my lord!' the women cried.

Halross grinned. 'I'll not try her patience any longer,' he replied. Without any further ado he strode across the room and climbed straight into bed beside Athena.

His enthusiasm prompted good-natured, though somewhat

bawdy jests from the men and shrieks of laughter and mock disapproval from the women.

The room was suddenly full of wedding guests, all crowding around the bed for a view of the bridal couple. The air was alive with expectation and disturbingly potent emotions.

Desire was jostled by her companions, then something was thrust into her hands.

'Here, my lady, try your luck at throwing his lordship's stocking!'

'Oh, no,' she instinctively demurred, but her protests were ignored. Later she realised she'd been among those selected to take part in the traditional ritual because, with the exception of the newly married Marchioness and Lord Halross's widowed sister-in-law, she was the highest-ranking lady present.

She was pushed to the end of the huge bed and turned so her back was towards the couple sitting in the middle of it.

'Throw the stocking!'

'Aim for his lordship's nose!'

Desire took a deep breath, closed her eyes for luck, and tossed the stocking over her shoulder. She was rewarded with cheers and laughter.

'A hit! An undeniable hit!'

Desire turned round to find the stocking lying draped across Halross's head, half-obscuring one eye. He smiled wryly at her. She had the feeling he was patiently tolerating, rather than enjoying, the antics of his guests.

''Tis a sure sign you'll be wed soon!' exclaimed one of the older men. 'Which one of us will you take, lass? I've a lusty arm—'

'It's not your *arm* that's lusty, Arthur Endicott,' one of the women scolded. 'Hush now, it's time for the posset.'

The smell of warm wine and fragrant spices filled the air. Everyone watched as the finely wrought goblet was presented to the couple in the bed. Desire knew it contained a rich mixture of milk, wine, egg yolks, sugar and spices.

Athena took only a few sips, but Lord Halross lifted it in a salute to her.

'To my beloved wife!' he declared, and drained it with gusto to the acclaim of everyone present.

'Now we've furnished you with so much entertainment, leave us to ours,' Halross commanded. 'Or I'll get up and *chase* you out!' he roared suddenly, provoking another burst of laughter from the guests.

Desire edged towards the door. The highly charged mood in the bridal chamber unsettled her. Unnoticed by the others, she slipped from the room. Jakob was in there. A man, just like all the other men, joking with the bridegroom. He'd seen her throw the stocking and heard the cry that she would soon be married. It meant nothing. It was only a traditional game. But did he think…what did he think?

She felt confused and jumpy. Unsure what to do or where to go. Music and laughter still echoed up from the great hall, and the guests who'd escorted the bride and groom to bed would soon be returning there. The party would continue until the early hours of the morning, even without the presence of the host and hostess.

Desire had a sudden, overwhelming need to be alone, for silence and solitude and a chance to regain her composure. She hurried down the hall and up a flight of stairs, anxious to reach the refuge of her bedchamber before the rest of the wedding guests spilled out of the bridal chamber.

Her room was dark except for the moonlight that shone in through the window. No welcoming candles or cosy fire had been lit here. No one had anticipated she would leave the party so soon.

The moon was almost full. There had been a full moon the night she lay beside Jakob in Kilverdale's house at Putney. A whole month had passed since then. She moved restlessly about the room. She had come here for sanctuary, but being alone gave her no respite from her confused emotions. The events in the bridal chamber had left her feeling excited and edgy. Desire wandered over to the dressing table to examine the gloves Halross had presented her with that morning, one of the traditional gifts from the bridal couple to their wedding guests.

The exquisite gold-work embroidery glimmered softly in the moonlight. Halross had spared no expense on his wedding. Gold was often considered an appropriate colour for a widow to wear and Athena had been glorious in a shimmering cloth of gold. By marrying a widow with no fortune of her own in such pomp and grandeur, the Marquis had sent a powerful message to his friends, family and neighbours. The new Lady Halross was to be treated with all the respect and courtesy due to her. She was in every way his chosen bride.

Melancholy crept over Desire. She wondered if she would ever be the recipient of such public devotion. She laid the gloves aside. She didn't know what to do next. She thought she could still hear music and laughter echoing faintly in the distance, but perhaps she could only hear it in her imagination because she knew the party still continued. This part of the house was very quiet—disconcertingly quiet, in fact. The rustle of her skirts when she moved seemed unnaturally loud. She stood uncertainly by the dressing table. She didn't want to rejoin the celebrations, but she wasn't calm enough to sleep. Indeed, she couldn't go to bed until her maid unlaced her. She couldn't put on or take off her new gown without assistance.

The silence was broken by muffled footsteps approaching her door. She tensed, her heart jumping in alarm. Was this a reveller who'd lost his way in the large house? Surely he'd pass by without disturbing her. If a male guest in his cups discovered her alone, the situation might prove awkward. A sudden image of Arscott flickered in her mind. Kilverdale was still in pursuit of the treacherous steward. She glanced around and snatched up the first movable object that came to hand.

The door opened. Her heart leapt sickeningly into her throat. She lifted her makeshift weapon in an instinctively defensive gesture.

Chapter Seventeen

A man paused on the threshold. His face was in shadows, but she recognised him immediately. Her fear of genuine danger subsided, but now her racing heart was stimulated by a different kind of nervousness.

'I've never known a woman so eager to groom me,' said Jakob, unmistakable amusement in his voice. 'Would you like to me to sit down to save the strain on your arms?'

'What?' Desire saw she was holding her brush aloft in the full beam of moonlight. No!' She threw it down on the dressing table in disgust.

'What are you doing here?'

'Why did you leave the party?' They spoke together, their words cutting across each other.

'Why did you leave the party?' Jakob repeated.

'Did you follow me?' Excited butterflies danced in Desire's stomach. Following her was good, wasn't it? It gave her hope he might still feel something for her.

'Of course.' He stepped into the room and closed the door. 'You are under my protection,' he said easily. 'You cannot believe I would let you wander the corridors alone.'

'I'm sure I'm not in danger from Arscott here.' Disappointment flooded her. He'd only followed her to ensure her physical safety, not because he wanted to talk to her.

'Very unlikely. But I don't know most of the guests in the house. A woman should not wander far from the safety of the main party.'

'You're protecting me from the other wedding guests?'

'I'll protect you from the whole damn world if I have to,' Jakob said grimly.

'I don't need your protection!' she flung back, offended by his tone. The way he spoke made it sound as if guarding her was the most irksome of chores, but then she noticed the actual words he'd used. He'd said he'd protect her from the whole world if he had to. That sounded…not entirely unhopeful…

'What are you doing here?' he demanded.

'I came…' Desire was still caught up in trying to interpret the difference between what he'd said and the way he'd said it, and didn't have a ready answer to his question. 'I came to fetch my new fan,' she said, fixing on the first excuse that came to mind.

'Are you feeling overheated?' He strolled closer. 'Where is it? I'll fan you before we go back to the great chamber.'

'I'm not going anywhere with you.' She'd made a mistake about his motive for following her. He was obviously impatient to get back to the party, to the pretty girl he'd been flirting with all evening.

'You can go back to Miss Ludlow right now,' she said furiously. 'Since you're so worried about my safety, I'll barricade the door after you've gone.'

He made a disparaging noise at her suggestion. 'There's no barricade would keep *me* out if I wanted to come in,' he declared. 'Who the devil is Miss Ludlow?' he added.

'Who is—?' Absolutely incensed, and forgetting all her good intentions to keep her distance, Desire seized his sleeve and tried to drag him to the door. 'You insensitive buffoon! You couldn't take your eyes off her earlier. You don't want to come in—so just *go*!'

He let her pull him across the room, but when she reached to open the door he set his broad shoulders against the oak panels and folded his arms across his chest.

'An insensitive buffoon, am I?' he mused. She thought she saw him grin in the moonlight. 'Why are you so anxious for me to leave? Are you waiting for a lover?'

'A *lover*?' Desire exclaimed scornfully. 'Who would that be? The man in the moon?'

'You're not expecting a lover? Then you came up here to dream about a lover in the moonlight.' Jakob's voice dropped to a deep, coaxing murmur. 'Who is he, *älskling*? Whose touch do you dream of in the dark of the night?'

'You are an arrogant, insensitive oaf!'

Jakob laughed softly and pushed away from the door. At his advance Desire backed up, then tried to dart around him. He seized her before she could make good her escape.

'Let me go!' she blustered.

'Do you really want me to?' His hands circled her upper arms in a firm, but not painful grasp.

'I am not your plaything!' she flung at him. 'I will not be placated with a few soft words when I've just watched you spend the evening trying to crawl inside another woman's bodice!'

'You saw me *what*?' His grip tightened. '*För bövelen!* You're the most exasperating woman I've ever met!' he declared. 'The only bodice I'm interested in is yours. And lately you're so cold I'd freeze if I ventured anywhere near it.'

'You're interested in my bodice?' she exclaimed.

'Not the bodice, what's inside it.' Jakob released her and half-turned away, running a hand through his hair.

'You are interested in what's inside my bodice?' Desire repeated, fascinated by his sudden loss of composure. She was suddenly feeling a lot happier than she had done for weeks. Arguing with Jakob had that effect upon her. 'It has a very fine silk lining—and bones,' she added as an afterthought, because she was currently very conscious of how the tight lacing compressed her ribs and breasts.

Jakob muttered something in Swedish. 'That is *not* what I meant to say,' he continued in English.

'Oh?' Desire put her hands on her hips. 'You mean you are not interested in—'

'Will you be quiet!' His voice rose. 'It's not surprising a man can't keep a straight thought in his head when you're around.'

'Do I muddle your thoughts?' Desire was amazed—and then thrilled. Muddling his thoughts was a good thing, wasn't it? Jakob had been muddling *her* thoughts from the moment they'd first met, and it wasn't because she didn't like him. She held her breath, waiting for his response.

It was too dark to see his expression, but she felt the weight of his gaze upon her.

'Why did you refuse me?' he asked.

The butterflies in Desire's stomach flew straight up into her throat. She swallowed. 'Why did you ask me?' she parried.

They stared at each other in the moonlight, neither speaking, each one striving to see the answer to their question in the other's shadowed face. At last, with a muffled oath, Jakob caught her arm and pulled her to stand directly in the swathe of moonlight. His put his hand beneath her chin and gently pushed her head up until he could look into her face.

She saw the gleam of moonlight in his eyes, felt the solid warmth of his body only inches from hers. The only physical contact between them was his hand on her chin, but he had not touched her so intimately since he'd comforted her after the destruction of Godwin House. Excitement tingled through her. She leant towards him, as if he radiated some magnetic power she could not resist. For a few moments she completely forgot to breathe.

Jakob lowered his head an inch or two and she felt the warmth of his breath against her skin. Anticipation surged through her veins, dizzying as fine wine. The tension stretched between them, sweet and frustrating.

Unable to resist the temptation, Desire put her hands on his chest. Beneath the supple velvet of his coat she could feel the hard, virile heat of his body. His fingers brushed lightly over her cheek, and he gently caressed her mouth with the side of his thumb. A soft sound escaped her lips. Her fingers clenched in his coat…

The next second his arms were locked around her as his mouth found hers. Passion flared instantly between them, fierce and hot. Jakob held her tight against his body. He devoured her mouth with his lips and tongue until she was dizzy with arousal. She closed her eyes and clung to him. When he finally let her go, her legs were weak, her lips swollen, and there was a yearning ache low in her belly.

It belatedly occurred to her that the last thing she should be doing was allowing Jakob to kiss her. And she certainly shouldn't be kissing him back. Not when she'd just watched him flirt with another woman and he'd not given her a single explanation for why he was now kissing her. But he wasn't showing any signs of letting her go, and she lacked the resolution to pull herself out of his arms.

'Why…why did you do that?' she whispered.

'Why do you think?' he rested his forehead against hers.

'You are a rogue and a philanderer. An hour ago you were flirting with Miss Ludlow.'

'Miss *who*?' He lifted his head. He still denied knowing the young woman's name. 'I haven't flirted with any one but you since the day I met you.'

'Ludlow!' Desire exclaimed, trying to push him away. 'In the great hall. She had her hand on your arm and you were trying to climb into her bodice.'

'Is that her name?' he said lightly. 'I couldn't remember. She wanted to know about Sweden—at least, I think that's what we were talking about. I wasn't really listening.'

'She made you laugh.' Unsure whether to be mollified or suspicious, Desire allowed him to pull her closer. 'What was she saying to you?'

'No, she didn't. I was thinking about you.'

'And the thought of me made you laugh?' Desire pushed him away again.

'I was laughing to be polite. I think she meant to be amusing. The thought of you was driving me out of my mind with frustration, not good humour.' He locked his arms around her so that she couldn't escape.

'Oh.' She braced her forearms on his chest. 'Why?'

'I asked you to marry me,' he reminded her.

'Only for my land.' She was too overwhelmed with sensations and conflicting emotions to guard her words.

She felt Jakob go rigid.

'What?' he growled. He was holding her so close it seemed as if his outrage vibrated through every particle of her body. 'You think I want you for your *fortune*?' Now it was his turn to push her away.

'Not my fortune, my lands.' She stumbled a little without his support and righted herself.

'*Heliga guds moder!* What have I ever done to make you believe me a fortune hunter?' he demanded.

'Not a fortune hunter.' His anger shook her, but didn't scare her. Instead it fed her growing hopefulness. 'You asked so many questions about my estates,' she said. 'You seemed impressed, and then—'

'And then I proposed. *För bövelen!*'

'Well, yes.' Desire stood still and watched as Jakob revealed his agitation by pacing about the room. She was beginning to feel a rather heady sensation of optimism. He seemed to be just as insulted as a man with strong feelings for a woman *ought* to be if someone accused him of marrying her for her fortune.

'Mind the stool,' she said helpfully, when he strayed too close to the dressing table.

'Is that why you refused me?' He swung to face her. 'Because you thought I only wanted your land?'

'Well, yes...' She stretched out the word uncertainly. She

couldn't bring herself to admit it was also because he'd made it so clear he didn't want *her*. At least not in the way a husband was meant to want his wife. Besides, she wasn't so sure of that any more. The way he'd just kissed her gave her hope that he might have overcome his initial feelings of revulsion when he'd discovered the scar on her leg. After all, he hadn't been expecting it. It must have come as an unpleasant surprise to him. Perhaps she should have warned him.

'What else?' He came back to her, putting his hands on her shoulders.

'You spoke to me in Swedish. You knew I couldn't understand. I think...I thought it was a sign that though your mind knew it would be a sensible union, your heart did not want me to accept,' she said resolutely, proud that her voice was only a little unsteady.

He was silent for several long moments after she'd spoken. She suddenly dipped her head and tried to pull out of his grasp. He wouldn't let her go.

'So if you had believed I asked you to marry me with a whole heart—what would you have answered?' he said at last. There was emotion in his voice she could not fully interpret, but she felt it resonate deep inside her.

'Did you—?' She stopped.

She heard him draw in his breath, then he pressed a light kiss against her forehead. "Swedish is the language of my heart, *min älskade*,' he murmured, his lips caressing her skin. 'I did not even realise how much until the day I proposed. *Jag älskar dig. Vill ni gifta er med mig?*' Then he translated it for her. 'I love you. Will you marry me?'

She stood very still for a moment, then she slipped her arms around his waist and leant against him, letting his words wash through her. She had been so sure for so long that she would never be loved in this way. It took a little while for her to absorb the full meaning of what he'd just said. For her heart to unfurl with deep, profound joy that she loved and was truly loved in return.

He stroked her hair and kissed her temple.

'Does this…softness…mean yes?' he asked against her cheek. 'Hmm, *min älskade*?'

She smiled as she lifted her head. She thought that from his tone and the way he was holding her he already knew that it did.

'Perhaps…' She lifted a hand to stroke his cheek, then began to trace his eyebrow with one finger.

'What bothers you now?' His arms tightened compellingly around her. 'Desire?' he prompted her, when she still hesitated.

'Do you think…?' It was so hard to speak openly of this, but she couldn't bear to experience another rejection. 'Do you think that, in time, you will overcome your…?'

'Overcome what?' He sounded baffled, and something else— wary? Uncertain, a little belligerent. Not emotions she associated with him. 'What is it about me you do not like?'

'About you?' she said, confused.

'Some habit, some characteristic in me you do not care for,' he said, an edge in his voice. 'The reason you held me aloof for so long. What is it?'

'Not in *you*!' she exclaimed. 'Well, perhaps a little,' she acknowledged, after giving it a moment's thought. 'But you grew accustomed to my face so quickly I never anticipated—'

'What are you trying to tell me?' he interrupted impatiently.

'I never even thought of the scar on my leg until it caused you such…such revulsion,' she whispered, clinging tightly to his coat, half-fearing he would pull away from her now she had drawn her disfigurement to the forefront of his mind.

'Revulsion?' he said blankly. 'What revulsion?'

Desire's face burned with mortification. And some degree of annoyance. How dare he claim ignorance after the hurt he'd caused her. She pulled out of his arms.

'You *know* what revulsion,' she said. 'I felt it in you. Don't insult me by pretending otherwise.'

Jakob put his hands on his hips and stared at the ceiling. He gazed upwards for so long Desire looked up too, in case he'd seen something remarkable.

'I am looking for patience,' he said in a long-suffering voice.

'Patience?'

'Desire, there is nothing about you that causes me revulsion.'

'You pulled away! At the very moment… You felt my scar, and you pulled away!' She crossed her arms over her chest, the pain of his rejection still uncomfortably raw within her.

'No.' He sighed regretfully. 'I'm sorry,' he said. 'I'm very sorry. I never meant to hurt you, or for you to think that's why I pulled away. I remembered who you are. It wasn't revulsion. Fear, perhaps. I wanted you, but I wasn't ready for what must inevitably follow if I had you.'

'You don't really want a wife?' Desire watched him painfully. 'You don't really want *me* as your wife?'

'I want you. I have just said so, haven't I?' he said with a flash of temper. 'I wasn't sure if I wanted to remain in England.' His voice softened. 'I never meant you to think it was because of your scar I pulled away. It didn't occur to me you might think that.'

'It didn't?' she whispered, still feeling a little doubtful.

'No.' He cupped the side of her face with his hand, stroking his thumb over the scars on her cheek. 'I told you a long time ago I don't see your scars,' he reminded her.

'Yes.' She bit her lower lip to stop it trembling, but tears of gladness welled up in her eyes as she took his reassurance to heart.

'You should have remembered, *min älskade*,' he scolded her gently. 'How can I be expected to guess what you *think* I'm thinking—when such a thought has never occurred to me?'

'I suppose you can't.' She clung to the front of his coat, smiling at him through her tears as she allowed herself to believe him.

'Of course I can't.' Jakob teased his thumb lightly over her bottom lip, then bent his head to kiss her. There was so much tender conviction in his kiss it didn't leave room for a single shred of doubt. Relief and joy suddenly expanded to fill Desire's whole being. He didn't care about her scars. He truly didn't. She put her arms around his neck and kissed him with growing passion until they were both breathless.

'So have you decided to stay in England?' she asked a few minutes later, her head resting on his shoulder. 'Or are we to go to Sweden?'

'We're staying in England. Would you come to Sweden if I asked?' He sounded surprised at her question.

'Of course. If I am your wife, I will go where you go. Are you staying here to please your grandfather?' She looked up at him.

'Not if, *when* you're my wife,' he corrected her. 'No, he's irrelevant.'

'Lord Swiftbourne is irrelevant?' The idea startled Desire.

'I realised that the day Godwin House burned,' said Jakob. 'For years I'd felt as if my life was lived in the shadow of my future inheritance. I made every important decision with reference to it. Not with the intention of pleasing Swiftbourne, mark you—'

'But to prove you are your own man despite him,' said Desire.

'Something like that. But when Arscott seized you—when your house burned, I realised everything had changed. I had...' he paused '...I had something more important in my life,' he said.

'Now tell *me*!' he said, suddenly fierce. 'I have bared my soul to you. Now tell *me*!'

'I love you,' she said, tears trembling in her eyes.

She heard him draw in a deep breath and then release a long, emotion-filled sigh. She closed her eyes and clung to him, savouring his strength, his warmth and his love. After several long moments he eased slightly away from her and put his hands on her shoulders. She felt his lips caress her forehead.

'Then let me show you how much I love you, *min älskade*.' He kissed her temple, his breath warm against her skin. 'And then there won't be any more room for doubt.'

'Show me?' she whispered, lost in the emotions and sensations his tenderness aroused in her.

'Is that a question or a request?' he said, an undercurrent of urgency in his soft voice.

'A request…? Oh.' She opened her eyes and looked up at him in the moonlight. 'You want to make love to me *now*?'

'I always want to make love to you. From the moment I first saw you—'

'You did not!' Despite her newfound confidence Desire didn't believe *that*. 'You just wanted to abduct me.'

'Protect you,' he corrected, stroking the nape of her neck.

'Protecting me was just an excuse for you to have an adventure and avoid your grandfather,' she said, although his featherlight caresses were already weakening her resistance. Who could have guessed her neck would be so sensitive?

'You wanted me on the boat, maybe, when I…I threw myself into your arms.' She caught her breath as he kissed her below her ear. How was she supposed to think straight when he was doing such delightful things to her? 'But *not* on the roof.'

'On the roof,' he said firmly, though his words were muffled against her skin. She adored the sensations the little vibrations created inside her. 'Even when you had your back turned I wanted you. You have a very seductive neck.'

'I do? My *neck*?' Desire belatedly caught up with what he was saying. 'You think I'm more seductive with my back turned?' That wasn't what she wanted to hear. She stiffened in his arms and started to pull away.

'You are completely seductive from all directions,' he said, holding her tighter. The next instant she felt his lips against her cheek as he kissed her scars. It was the first time he had ever done so.

'They don't matter,' he murmured. 'I don't see them when I look at you. They don't matter, *min älskade*. Don't ever think they do.'

Desire's eyes filled with tears. She had waited so long for someone to say that to her. But she had to be completely sure.

'Not even…not even the one on my leg?' she whispered.

'No. Never. I am sorry you were injured. I wish you'd been spared that pain. But every part of you is desirable to me.'

Tears spilled onto Desire's cheeks. She felt Jakob's tongue against her skin as he gently tasted her tears. He kissed her just below the corner of her eye, his tongue stroking and soothing her.

'Don't cry, *älskling*. Let me show you.'

'Yes…'

He went quite still for several seconds. Then he let her go and stepped away from her. For a moment she didn't understand why. She stared in bewilderment, then realised he meant to light some candles.

'Oh, why…? Surely we don't need…?' she said uncertainly.

The shadowy moonlight was illumination enough for her. The idea of disrobing before Jakob in brighter light was disconcerting—and a little intimidating. She already knew how well formed he was, but she was not so perfect.

'I want to see you,' he said, his voice a deep caress. 'And I want you to see that looking at you gives me pleasure.' As he spoke he went to the window, closing the shutters on the cool moonlight so that the room was bathed only in the warm glow of the candles.

Then he came to stand before her. He was so tall and splendid in the blue-and-silver lace suit he wore—but she could only think of the lean, hard-muscled body beneath the finery. He touched her shoulders lightly, almost hesitantly. Tension coiled inside her. He bent his head and kissed her forehead.

Desire closed her eyes and her breath caught in her throat. Only his lips had touched her, but already the virile promise of his large body filled all her senses.

Jakob lifted his head. She opened her eyes and saw that he was looking at the swell of her breasts pushed upwards by her fashionable bodice. With one finger he traced just inside her neckline in a tantalising caress.

'The first time I saw you in such a gown in nearly drove me out of my mind,' he said hoarsely.

'When…?' Desire quivered beneath his touch. Her legs felt weak. She could barely form a coherent thought.

'When you were presented to Swiftbourne. I couldn't take my eyes off you. I nearly undressed you right there and then.'

'I didn't realise.' She gasped, then bit back a moan, as his fingertip began to trace tiny, feathery circles on the exposed part of her breast.

'Am I tormenting you, *älskling*?' he asked, his voice roughened with arousal.

'Ah…' She clutched his coat for support. Her body ached with unfulfilled arousal and she longed to feel the palm of his hand against her breast. She swallowed. Tried to find the words to answer his question. 'I think so.'

'Good. Because you have tormented me from the first time I saw you!'

'I didn't mean to.' Her legs trembled. She gripped his coat even tighter.

'You can't help yourself, he said hoarsely. 'And nor can I.'

He turned her around and began to unlace her bodice. He fumbled a little with the points. Desire didn't associate Jakob with clumsiness. His hesitation confused her, but then she heard his uneven breathing and realised he fully shared her excitement…and perhaps even a little of her nervousness.

She had never before had a lover—but this was the first time Jakob had made love to the woman he was going to marry. He touched her so carefully, as if he was afraid to hurt her. As if she was most precious to him. It was a heavenly idea. Desire closed her eyes, overwhelmed by emotions so warm and profound she had no name for them.

Jakob opened her bodice. He slipped his hands inside, sliding them gently around her body until he could cup her breasts through her shift. When she looked down she couldn't see his hands beneath her bodice, yet she could feel his fingers toying with her arousal-hardened nipples. It was a secret intimacy that seemed almost scandalously erotic. A sigh escaped her lips and she lent back against his broad chest. He lowered his head and kissed her temple. She let her head fall to one side, and felt his lips stroke her cheek, then close warmly upon her earlobe.

Desire quivered and moaned.

She felt his quick intake of breath and a sudden tension seized his body. He lifted his head. For a few moments he remained motionless except for the rise and fall of his chest against her back. Then he eased her away from him and carefully removed her bodice. He kept one hand pressed against her ribs, just below her breasts, as he tossed the garment aside. His possessive touch was incredibly exciting. He moved closer, pulling her back against his chest, and lifted his hands to hold her breasts in his palms. This time when Desire looked down she could see her erect nipples pushing against the thin cambric. She gasped, both shocked and stimulated when Jakob began to circle them with his fingers.

'Shouldn't...?' She caught her breath, tried to control her voice. 'Shouldn't we...do this...in the dark?' she whispered, even as she couldn't help arching her body, eagerly lifting her breasts for his continued attention.

'No.' His voice was raw against her ear. 'I like to see you.'

Desire watched, her breathing quick and shallow, as he untied the thin ribbon that gathered the neckline of her shift. A moment later he spread it wide. Then she saw his large hands caress her naked breasts. Her vision hazed at the exquisite pleasure he gave her. Her head lolled sideways as she instinctively undulated against him.

He groaned, uttered a soft, rasping curse, and turned her to face him. His blazing blue eyes filled her vision, then his mouth covered hers in an urgent kiss.

She felt his hum of masculine satisfaction deep in his chest. One of his hands swept lower, pressing her supple body hard against him. Desire's fingers clutched convulsively at a silver button. She was as hungry for him as he was for her. She kissed him back as hotly as he kissed her. His tongue pressed demandingly past her lips. She sucked upon it and he groaned and jerked against her. She felt the fierce tremors that shook his powerful body as he fought for self-control. She was a little frightened by the depth of his passion—but far more excited. Her own body was on fire with hot, demanding need.

When he lifted his head they were both panting. She stared hazily into his face and saw his pupils were so dilated his eyes seemed almost black. She tugged impatiently at his coat, trying to push it off his shoulders, then pulled up his fine cambric shirt.

With no further bidding he tore off his clothes until his upper body was naked. Desire instantly reached to touch his chest. He gave her no opportunity to indulge her curiosity because he hauled her back into her arms, kissing her until she had no strength left in her legs. She hardly noticed when he lifted her off her feet and carried her to the side of the bed. He set her down and searched impatiently for the fastenings of her skirt and petticoats. When she realised what he was doing she helped him. With a grunt of satisfaction he pushed the unwieldy mass of material down over her hips and lifted her out of it. Then he hauled up her shift, bunching it in his hands to pull it over her head.

Desire was so caught up in their mutual feverish urgency that, for a moment, she didn't fully register that she was now almost completely naked. Then she looked at Jakob and saw how his hot gaze devoured her. She flushed, belatedly self-conscious, and moved in an involuntary gesture to shield herself.

Jakob pulled her closer. His naked chest brushed against her bare breasts. It was a very stimulating distraction from her embarrassment. Excited, Desire arched her back and deliberated stroked her breasts against him. He groaned softly, gave her a fierce kiss—then picked her up and tossed her on to the bed. She gasped at his peremptory action. Rolled over with a half-formed intention to protest...

And watched instead, a nervous pulse beating in her throat, as Jakob stripped off the rest of his clothes. She was glad now of the candlelight, for it gave her the chance to enjoy him as he had declared he wanted to enjoy her. The flickering flames bathed his powerful body in a warm glow that reminded her of the first time she'd seen him, golden in the sunset. His muscles bunched and flexed as he moved. She was fascinated by the play of light and shadow on his broad chest, and the ridged hardness of his stomach. Her fingers tingled with the urge to touch him.

Then, for the first time, she saw all of him. Her fingers clutched convulsively at the sheet as she explored his lower body with her eyes. His legs were so long—lean and strong. But it was the unequivocal evidence of his passion that held her slightly apprehensive attention. She stared at his erection. It excited her— but she was also a little afraid. Jakob was so strong, and sometimes he could be so fierce. Would he hurt her in the throes of his passion?

He climbed onto the bed and propped himself up on one elbow beside her.

'*Älskling*, don't look at me like that,' he said huskily.

'How?' She licked her lower lip worriedly.

'Scared.' He smiled a little ruefully as he stroked a strand of hair back from her face.

'I'm not scared,' she protested uncertainly. 'Of course I'm not scared.' She boldly put her hand on his chest to prove it.

'My brave Desire.' He cupped her cheek with his palm and kissed her lips with achingly sweet tenderness. Then he moved lower, kissing and caressing her breasts until her body throbbed with unfulfilled passion. His hand stroked across her stomach and came to rest on her hip. His hair teased her sensitive skin and she felt his warm breath as he kissed her low on her belly. She moaned and moved restlessly beneath him, her legs instinctively moving apart. She remembered and ached to feel the exquisite caresses he had given her once before, but he laid his hand on her thigh instead. And then, with a shock of profound wonder, she realised he was kissing her scar. His lips tracked the full length of her old injury, as tenderly and passionately as he had kissed her breasts.

Tears filled her eyes. She'd yearned for such total acceptance. She put her hands on his shoulders.

'Jakob…' Her heart was so full she had no words to express her emotions.

'You are beautiful to me, *min älskade*,' he said hoarsely.

'And you are beautiful to me,' she whispered.

'Because I look like an angel?' He lifted himself over her.

'No.' She rubbed her hands over the taut muscles of his arms. 'Because you are kind and loyal and noble and clever…'

'Kind?'

'And you tease me,' she added breathlessly 'I hated it when you stopped teasing me.'

'I will make it my goal to infuriate you at least once every day from now on,' he promised, his breathing noticeably ragged.

He rubbed his muscular thigh over her legs. His erection pressed compellingly against her hip. Potent evidence of his urgent masculine arousal. The pressure excited her. All her other thoughts unravelled as she moved instinctively against him, though she did feel a small tingle of renewed nervousness. His body was hot and hard, his muscles tense with barely controlled passion. He was so much more powerful than her.

She couldn't help her momentary hesitation. Jakob sensed it. For a second he held his body quite still. Desire tried to speak. She wanted to tell him to pay no heed to her foolishness. It was only that she…

He bent his head and closed his mouth around her nipple. He teased and stroked with his tongue, intensifying her pleasure until she writhed and moaned beneath him. He hummed against her breast, a sound of deep masculine satisfaction that she was learning to associate with extreme arousal. She felt it in the inmost core of her body, and the ache between her legs grew more insistent.

He slid lower and kissed her belly and his hair tickled her sensitive skin most erotically. She felt his large hand on her hip. There was a place she needed his touch more urgently. Her thighs parted in a silent, instinctive invitation. Immediately he slipped his hand between her legs and began to stroke her swollen femininity.

When he lightly flickered his finger across her most exquisitely sensitive flesh, Desire cried out and clutched at the sheets. She drew up her knees, unconsciously demanding more and in an instant his body covered hers. She opened her eyes and saw his face, taut with arousal, poised above her. Small shudders shook his powerful frame as he fought for self-control. She lifted her hands to touch his waist and he jerked in response.

His chest expanded as he drew in a deep, steadying breath. Then he reached down between them so he could align his body carefully with hers. Desire caught her breath, her heart hammering with anticipation as she felt his hard tip against her hot, sensitive flesh.

He looked into her eyes, his own eyes blazing with urgent passion. His gaze still locked with hers, he deliberately stroked himself back and forth along her moist cleft. She moaned as her body responded with small, uncontrollable shudders of need.

He jerked and swore softly as tension shook his muscular frame. Beneath Desire's clutching fingers his shoulders were damp with perspiration.

'I know you don't want to hurt me,' she cried in sudden frustration at his continued delay. 'But will you hurry up and *do* it! This is like being under siege and not knowing when the cannon-fire will start!'

Jakob's eyes widened in momentary shock.

She struggled for self-control and managed to smile at him. 'I love you, Jakob,' she said, her voice so thick with need she barely recognised it. 'Please let us be one.'

'*Min älskade…*' he started to speak in Swedish, then stopped and switched to English. 'I love you, Desire,' he said hoarsely. 'My lady Desire.'

He positioned himself quickly and thrust deep.

She cried out, more in surprise than pain. His breath rasped in her ears as he fought to control the ardent demands of his body.

'*Älskling?*' he muttered desperately.

'I'm…' She dragged in a shaky breath of her own. 'Kiss me,' she demanded, wrapping her arms tightly around him.

'*Ja.*' His voice was guttural with passion. His mouth covered hers in a blatantly carnal kiss. The urgent thrust of his tongue past her lips was an erotic imitation of that other joining of their bodies.

Desire lifted her knees higher as her body adjusted to his intimate invasion. He was hard and hot inside her, and she could feel her own womanly places throbbing and aching with an urgent need for more… more…*more*…

She was possessed by such wild yearning that she lost all conscious awareness of what she did. She moaned and turned her head away from Jakob's kisses as she lifted her hips against him. He responded by pulling out of her, then pushing back in. At first his movements were carefully controlled. Desire put her arms around him, frantically trying to touch every part of his body she could.

She was on the brink, desperately seeking…

The rhythm of Jakob's thrusts became faster, more urgent. Desire moaned in time with every stroke as the excitement built within her. Until at last her body clenched with exquisite, pulsing ecstasy. Waves of pleasure surged through her, blotting out all other awareness. She gasped and shuddered, panting beneath Jakob, surrendering to the overwhelming sensations. He drove into her one more time and she felt his release of hot passion. He groaned and swore, his body jerking spasmodically with sensual fulfilment, and then his movements gradually slowed until he relaxed upon her sated body. After a few seconds he lifted himself carefully away from her to lay by her side, his arm still possessively draped over her waist.

As her heart-rate slowed and her breathing returned to normal, Desire glowed with contentment from the inside out. She could still feel lingering sensations of the physical ecstasy she had experienced deep within her body—tiny ripples of continuing fulfilment. More important, and far more profound, Jakob had told her and shown her that he loved her. All of her.

'We must be married soon,' said Jakob, with all his usual, familiar arrogance.

'Mmm?' For the first time in weeks Desire was on the verge of quiet, peaceful sleep. 'Oh, yes, as soon as possible,' she said drowsily. 'You will be a very good husband.'

She felt him shake with silent laughter. 'I will do my best, *min älskade*,' he promised. 'From now on I will consider it my sacred duty to provoke you every day to call me an insensitive buffoon…or numskull…or…'

Desire woke up enough to lift her head and put her hand over his mouth. He looked at her, his expression a mixture of profound love and irrepressible good humour. She sighed with deep contentment and snuggled her head down on his shoulder. 'Yes, that will be very satisfactory,' she said, and fell asleep.

Epilogue

Kingston-upon-Thames, late November 1666

Desire was in the garden, looking at the rosebushes, when she saw a lone horseman ride up to the entrance of the house. Even from a distance she thought she recognised him. The Duke of Kilverdale was a memorable figure. She began to stroll towards him.

They'd received a letter from him a week ago to say that he'd finally caught up with Arscott at Harwich. The steward had led Kilverdale on a tortuous journey all the way to Plymouth in Devon and back to Harwich on the Essex coast with many diversions in between. Harwich was the usual route to Holland and they'd speculated that Arscott might have been intending to throw in his lot with the Dutch. There was at least one regiment of die-hard English republicans in Holland who hoped to overturn the restored Stuart monarchy. Arscott might well have had friends among them. But he'd never left England. Kilverdale had chased him on to a ship bound for Flanders and, rather than be taken, Arscott had jumped over the side. He'd tried to swim to shore, but his body had been found a couple of days later. So it was over.

Kilverdale had seen Desire and was walking towards her.

She stopped and waited for him. She was still not entirely at ease at the prospect of talking to him, and a letter that Jakob had recently received from the Duke's mother had rekindled some of her doubts about Kilverdale. But she no longer feared him and she was very grateful for all his efforts on her behalf.

'My lady.' He bowed before her. 'I hope you got my letter telling you Arscott is dead.'

'Yes, I did. Thank you.' Desire took a steadying breath. 'Thank you very much for all you have done for me,' she said.

'It was not very much.' He hesitated, glancing away across the garden as if to give himself time to collect his thoughts, then he looked back at her. 'I'd met Arscott before,' he said, 'though at that time I didn't know his name.'

'When?' Desire was puzzled. Unlike Benjamin, the steward hadn't been among those who'd accompanied her and her father to Kilverdale's Sussex house.

'When I followed you and Lord Larksmere back to London,' said the Duke. 'But when I went to Godwin House he told me—Arscott told me—your father had given orders I should be horse-whipped if I ever went near you again.'

'What?' Desire didn't know if she was more shocked to discover Kilverdale had followed her or by what Arscott had told him. 'Father never gave such an order! I'm sure of it.'

'I believed it,' said Kilverdale. 'I could hardly blame him if he had.'

'Why did you follow me?' Desire asked curiously.

'I was—am—sorry for what I said, for what you overheard me say,' said the Duke. He spoke stiffly, though she sensed his reserved tone owed more to the inherent difficulty of apologising, rather than a haughty belief in his own superiority.

'I was angry with Heyworth for arranging the marriage,' he continued. 'I wasn't angry with you. You were just…there—where I didn't want you to be. If you'd had fair hair, I'd have declared I only liked black-haired maids. What I said meant no more than that.' He looked at her, his dark eyes steadily meeting her gaze. 'I do not make excuses. I should not have said what I did. I am sorry.'

'I see.' Desire took a moment to compose herself. 'Is that what you would have said to me six years ago if Arscott hadn't denied you admittance?'

He smiled faintly. 'More or less,' he said. 'I'm afraid it might have emerged a little more belligerently six years ago, but in my own defence I will say I followed you of my own free will. The apology would have been genuinely and freely offered.'

'Even though the marriage proposal wasn't,' Desire murmured. 'Yes, I understand. Thank you. I'm sorry Arscott denied you.'

'You didn't know.' He held out his hand to her. 'I hope we may now be friends,' he said.

She smiled at Jakob as he joined them, then took the hand Kilverdale offered. 'Since we are now cousins—at least by marriage—I hope so too,' she replied.

'Marriage?' His eyes widened, then he broke into a delighted grin. 'You have married Jakob already? *Diable!* Two marriages I have missed! Couldn't you have waited another few weeks, coz? I would have celebrated your wedding with a good will.'

'You are hardly in a position to complain,' Jakob countered, putting his arms around Desire.

She leant back against him. It was still a new and wonderful pleasure to be close to him.

'You didn't invite us to your wedding,' Jakob said to the Duke.

Kilverdale was momentarily baffled. 'When I am married you will both be honoured guests—' he began, and then broke off as Desire and Jakob exchanged glances. 'What is it?' he demanded.

'We had a letter from your mother yesterday,' said Jakob. 'She thought you'd probably come here first when everything with Arscott was settled—'

'Is she ill? Has something happened to Toby? What's wrong?'

'They are both in good health,' said Desire quickly, seeing the sudden anxiety in his eyes. However questionable some of the Duke's morals appeared to be, there was no questioning his love for his family.

'It's your health that's in question,' said Jakob.

'My health?' Kilverdale looked blank. 'I've never felt fitter. What are you talking about?'

'The young woman who recently arrived at Kilverdale Hall claiming to be your widow,' said Jakob.

'My…what?'

'Or rather, Jack Bow's widow,' Jakob continued. 'Your mother says the girl has your ring, and she claims you were married two days before the fire broke out. Apparently she went to find you at your favourite coffee house—asking for Jack Bow. She was told you were deceased, so she has gone to Sussex to claim her widow's rights.' Jakob grinned at his cousin's dumbfounded expression. 'Jack, what were you doing when you weren't at home to receive that message I sent you from Newgate?'

* * * * *

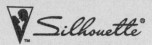

Silhouette®

ROMANTIC SUSPENSE

Excitement, danger and passion guaranteed!

Same great authors and riveting editorial
you've come to know and love.

Look for our new name next month
as Silhouette Intimate Moments® becomes
Silhouette™ Romantic Suspense.

Bestselling author
Marie Ferrarella
is back with a hot
new miniseries—
The Doctors Pulaski:
Medicine just got
more interesting....

Check out her
first title,
HER LAWMAN
ON CALL,
next month.

Look for it wherever
you buy books!

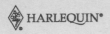

HARLEQUIN®

EVERLASTING LOVE™

Every great love has a story to tell™

The love story of a century...

**Dancing on
Sunday Afternoons**
by **Linda Cardillo**
ON SALE IN FEBRUARY

She was born in an Italian village and then immigrated to a rough-and-tumble New York. Over the years, Giulia has remained the very heart and soul of her family. As a young woman she experienced the kind of love that shaped her whole life, and through letters and memories, shares the story with her granddaughter Cara.

> *Find out how
> a great love
> is a legacy
> to be treasured!*

Also available this month:

Fall from Grace by Kristi Gold

A deeply emotional love story
about what marriage really means.

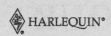

REQUEST YOUR FREE BOOKS!

Harlequin® Historical
Historical Romantic Adventure!

2 FREE NOVELS PLUS 2 FREE GIFTS!

YES! Please send me 2 FREE Harlequin® Historical novels and my 2 FREE gifts. After receiving them, if I don't wish to receive any more books, I can return the shipping statement marked "cancel." If I don't cancel, I will receive 6 brand-new novels every month and be billed just $4.69 per book in the U.S., or $5.24 per book in Canada, plus 25¢ shipping and handling per book and applicable taxes, if any*. That's a savings of close to 15% off the cover price! I understand that accepting the 2 free books and gifts places me under no obligation to buy anything. I can always return a shipment and cancel at any time. Even if I never buy another book from Harlequin, the two free books and gifts are mine to keep forever.

246 HDN EEWW 349 HDN EEW9

Name	(PLEASE PRINT)
Address	Apt. #
City	State/Prov. Zip/Postal Code

Signature (if under 18, a parent or guardian must sign)

Mail to the **Harlequin Reader Service®**:
IN U.S.A.: P.O. Box 1867, Buffalo, NY 14240-1867
IN CANADA: P.O. Box 609, Fort Erie, Ontario L2A 5X3

Not valid to current Harlequin Historical subscribers.

Want to try two free books from another line?
Call 1-800-873-8635 or visit www.morefreebooks.com.

* Terms and prices subject to change without notice. NY residents add applicable sales tax. Canadian residents will be charged applicable provincial taxes and GST. This offer is limited to one order per household. All orders subject to approval. Credit or debit balances in a customer's account(s) may be offset by any other outstanding balance owed by or to the customer. Please allow 4 to 6 weeks for delivery.

Your Privacy: Harlequin is committed to protecting your privacy. Our Privacy Policy is available online at www.eHarlequin.com or upon request from the Reader Service. From time to time we make our lists of customers available to reputable firms who may have a product or service of interest to you. If you would prefer we not share your name and address, please check here. ☐

HH07

This February...

Catch NASCAR Superstar **Carl Edwards** *in*

SPEED DATING!

Kendall assesses risk for a living—
so she's the last person you'd
expect to see on the arm of a
race-car driver who thrives on the
unpredictable. But when a bizarre
turn of events—and NASCAR
hotshot Dylan Hargreave—inspire
her to trade in her ever-so-structured
existence for "life in the fast lane"
she starts to feel she might be
on to something!

COMING NEXT MONTH FROM

HARLEQUIN®
HISTORICAL

- **THE LAWMAN'S BRIDE**
by **Cheryl St.John**
(Western)
The last thing Sophie Hollis wants in her life is a lawman—with a
past like hers, it can only lead to trouble. But Clay Connor won't
take no for an answer.

- **A SCANDALOUS MISTRESS**
by **Juliet Landon**
(Regency)
Scandal followed Lady Amelie Chester. Especially when she
falsely confessed to an intimate relationship with Nicholas,
Lord Elyot! Enchanted and intrigued, Nicholas was quick to
take *every* advantage of the situation....

- **WARRIOR OR WIFE**
by **Lyn Randal**
(Roman)
Deserted by her lover, high-born Lelia becomes Leda—the
gladiator! When her soldier returns to claim her, Lelia must choose
between the danger of the arena and the more frightening prospect
of giving her heart.

- **ASHBLANE'S LADY**
by **Sophia James**
(Medieval)
Alexander Ullyot, Laird of Ashblane, should have had no
compunction about using the beautiful Madeleine for his own
ends—but he desired her. Was Alex in danger of falling for the
woman who was his means of revenge...?